Tara!
Welcome to
the series!
Now your on
of the
[signature]

GETAWAY *GIRLZ*

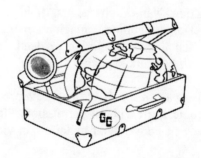

Joan Rylen

[signatures]

ISBN 13: 978-0-9856736-0-4

Library of Congress Control Number: 2012905109

To Dad, here it is finally. The Book.
Love, Robbyn

To Danielle, Sadie, Cayce and Cameron – Love, Mommy

Prologue

Six weeks ago

"WHO IS WITH THE KIDS? And who the hell is that?"

Vivian Taylor stared in disbelief at the woman stepping out of the pool, bikini riding up her ass. The woman looked at Vivian with a nonchalant expression before calmly reaching for her towel.

The look on Vivian's husband's face, however, was one of disbelief.

"Vivian, leave her out of this."

Daggers shot from Vivian's eyes. "You better move that car, bitch, or I'm running it over."

Rick Taylor followed the woman out of the pool and walked toward Vivian, his palms to the ground indicating she should calm down.

She didn't.

Vivian swung a right hook at Rick's head, which connected, and the cell phone she'd been holding shattered into pieces. She chunked her left wooden sandal at him. It smacked his shoulder, bounced into the bushes and disappeared. Her right knee jerked up, landing squarely in his groin.

He doubled over, gasping for breath. Vivian grabbed his shoulders and shoved him backward, into the pool.

"I hope you drown in there, asshole." His head popped out of the water and she kicked her other sandal at him, but it missed and flew across the pool.

Barefoot, Vivian went into his apartment and gently retrieved her four sleeping children from their third-story bedroom. She loaded the kids into the minivan and tried as calmly as she could to drive them home.

It took everything in her not to fall to pieces, like that phone.

———

Vivian didn't get a wink of sleep. The next morning she took the kids to

5

the sitter, called in sick to work, and started cleaning house like a mad-woman. She had caught up on two years' worth of ironing and though she tried to stop thinking about the pool, the scene kept playing like a bad B-movie.

Vivian hadn't told anyone, not friends, not family, that Rick had moved out. Prior to last night, she was convinced he would realize what a mistake he'd made and come back.

Obviously the man is thinking with the wrong head, she sighed to herself. Even if he wanted to come back now, she didn't think she would take him. *Once a cheater, always a cheater, right?*

Finally, she found the courage to pick up the phone and made her first call. Lucy.

Tears streamed down her face before Lucy even picked up. Vivian half hoped she wouldn't.

Two rings, three rings. Vivian exhaled and pulled the phone away just as Lucy's perky voice exclaimed, "Viv! What's up, lady?"

Vivian couldn't speak.

"Are you there, Vivian? Hello?"

"Here," Vivian choked, and started sobbing. Uncontrollable, animal-like sobs.

"Oh my god, who died? Are you okay? Did you fall down the stairs again? Hang up and call 911!"

Vivian's ears were hot and her face burned. She glanced at the cordless phone and wondered if it could electrocute her due to the conductivity of water.

"Rick" is all Vivian could say.

"Rick is dead? Oh no, Viv! What happened?"

"No, he's not dead."

He should be, but he's not.

"He left," Vivian blubbered.

"What do you mean he left? Left to where?"

"He LEFT me, Lucy. Gone! Moved out! AND he filed for divorce!"

"Shut UP. No way. When did this happen?"

"He left two months ago. Said he just couldn't cope."

"What? Where are the kids?"

"They're at the sitter."

"I don't believe it."

Vivian closed her eyes. *That makes two of us.*

Lucy had a barrage of questions, which Vivian attempted to answer. Most of her responses were head shakes, but Lucy saw them.

Vivian was still in shock. She thought Rick would figure out he left the best thing that ever happened to him. She gave him four beautiful children and great sex. What else could a man ask for?

How about fake boobs, a nose job and bad highlights. He thought the grass was greener with her, but he was campin' out on artificial turf!

Lucy assured Vivian she would be fine. She was strong, beautiful, smart and fabulous.

Vivian looked at herself in her way-outdated 1970s wet-bar mirror. Her naturally curly blonde hair had become unruly and stuck out everywhere. Her green eyes were almost swollen shut, and her face was red and splotchy. Though her twin-pregnancy double chin was now just a chin, her double D's remained.

Screw fabulous, Vivian thought. *I'm a wreck. I will be 30 and divorced with four kids in less than two months. How did this happen?*

Lucy's voice brought Vivian back. "I'll come down for your birthday. No, better yet, I'll figure something out and we'll get you out of town for your birthday. Do you think your mom can keep the kids? You really need to get away, girl. Leave it to me."

Thank god for my dear, dear friend, Vivian thought, but "okay" was all she could muster.

"Listen, Viv, you WILL be fine. Of all of us, you are the one who can handle this. I'll call you back with birthday details. Love you, Viv. Hang in there."

Click.

Vivian put down the waterlogged phone and walked closer to the wet-bar mirror, getting a better look at herself through the tacky, two-tone squiggles. She hated that mirror, so she flipped it off.

1

Day 1- Bienvenidos a México

True to her word, Lucy did call back after talking to their mutual best friends, Kate and Wendy. The three had picked a destination, booked flights and a hotel. Fast forward a month and a half later and Vivian found herself on a plane headed to Playa Del Carmen, Mexico where it was sunshiny and a warm 82 degrees.

Vivian's seat was toward the front in coach, but a middle seat.

Whatever, she thought, *I'm just happy to be getting out of town for a few days*.

The 50-something guy in the window seat wore a business suit, glasses and sported a bad comb-over. Why do men do that? Grow one long wisp of hair and wrap it around their head as many times as it will go?

Not good guys...not good.

The lady in the aisle seat was a bit of a chubster but had a friendly face. She smiled and moved to let Vivian in, gathering up her long flowery sundress, which practically needed its own seat, and informed Vivian she was headed to Cancun for her brother's wedding.

Vivian didn't feel like talking, but raised with southern manners, she forced herself to be nice. She responded with the usual "sounds fun, blah blah" niceties and reached for her seatbelt. She clicked it and pulled the strap tight, let out a sigh (mostly because she couldn't breathe) and shut her eyes, feeling mixed emotions about the trip.

She closed her eyes and thought about it. On the one hand, she deserved a break. The divorce had been dragging out a bit more than either of them wanted, but the end was definitely near. Her mom came up for the week to keep the kids, but Rick would still get them on his scheduled days. On the other hand, she wondered why she was leaving the four most precious things in the world to her at such a tumultuous time.

Maybe I should unclick this seatbelt and go home? She thought.

Vivian heard a thud and opened her eyes. The airplane door was sealed. That settled that, she was going.

Vivian noticed the book in Seat Buddy's lap, one of her favorite authors, Janet Evanovich. They chatted while the flight attendant instructed on what to do in an emergency. Vivian had seen the blow-up-the-seat-cushion/life jacket thing, so she decided to get her own book, which was properly stowed under the seat in front of her. She moved her body in an unnatural position, twisted and scrunched, and reached for her bag. Vivian's chin was practically in Swirly Heads' lap. Yuck.

Vivian dug around in the bag, and pulled out her latest read, a good one by DeMille. She straightened herself up and flipped it open. She couldn't concentrate though.

Bump! Vivian felt the plane move. She craned her neck to look out the window and saw the runway zooming past. She decided to close her eyes and lean forward, resting her forehead in her hands, and started perspiring.

No fiery death yet. This is good.

She hated the feeling of being pressed into her seat. She heard the landing gear retract and listened for any abnormal sounds (like she'd know them if she heard them). She took a deep breath, and flowery seat buddy asked if she was all right. "You look a little pale," she said.

"I'll be fine. Thanks," Vivian answered. Her ears popped.

Seat Buddy dug in her seat-back pocket and found the barf bag.

"Here you go, just in case."

Vivian took it, opened it, and kept leaning.

She wished she would have arrived at the airport earlier and had a drink *or three* before boarding the plane. Vivian detested flying. She tried to distract herself from images of doom and thought about her friends who put their lives on hold for a week just for her. They were all still close, although they lived in different cities. Vivian moved to Fort Worth after college, Kate Troutman stayed in Austin, Lucy McGuire landed in Boulder and Wendy Schreiber stuck it out in the Get Down.

The four of them grew up in Pasa"Get Down"dena, a suburb southeast of Houston. The Get Down was famous, or was it infamous, for the honky-tonk Gilley's. "Looking for Love" popped into her head, and she knew it'd be stuck there the whole way to Cancun International. Pasadena also had a propensity for refinery explosions. While the refineries had put the Get Down on the map, one day they could also wipe it out completely.

Vivian had known Wendy the longest, since first grade. They lived six streets apart, and their parents had carpooled them to Brownies, dance class, you name it, they were always together. In their neighborhood it took hell (divorce) or high water (usually combined with a hurricane) to dislodge you. Vivian's parents and Wendy's mom still lived in the same houses. Because of the tendency to stay put, they had gone all the way through 12th grade together, adding friends along the way. That's where Kate and Lucy came in.

In junior high Wendy and Vivian joined the band. Yep, band dorks. Vivian played clarinet, and Wendy played flute. Their band director had a Fonzarelli fixation, and tried to look the part. This was inhibited by his wattle that flapped to the beat of the music as he swung his arms around conducting them. Vivian would never be able to hear Chicago's "25 or 6 to 4" and not think of his perfectly puffy hair. He had an earring hole, too, which was far out to the sixth-graders in Pasadena, Texas.

Vivian and Wendy met Lucy in sixth grade. Another band dork, she was in the drum line, which was a fraternity all its own, except she was a girl, and the only girl at that. The guys refused to call her by her first name, so they created a new one for her: Wonkita. No one knows how it came to be, but it stuck like Galveston beach tar to her heel. She was smart, fun and got great grades in science (which helped Vivian in high school!).

Kate turned the trio into a quartet in ninth grade. You know it, in band. A classic overachiever, she dominated first-chair flute, was president of everything and eventually led the band as drum major. She was a total brainiac, but the girls loved her anyway.

That band glue held them together through high school, and then Kate, Lucy and Vivian went off to Austin and the University of Texas. Wendy stayed in the Get Down and attended the community college affectionately known as "Harvard on the Highway," then moved on to the University of Houston to finish her degree.

After what felt like forever, the plane flattened out and the PA system ding-donged. The pilot went into a spiel about how many gazillions of feet they were above the Earth, what time they should land, etc. He then said they could move about the cabin (which Vivian wouldn't do) and drinks would be served (which she would do). She sat up and fanned herself with the barf bag.

Might as well use it for something.

2

While she waited for her first frosty beverage, Vivian thought about college. Life was so much simpler. No kids, no soon-to-be ex-husband, no mortgage payment. Her biggest worry had been making it to her 9:00 class in semi-clean clothes.

Lucy and she had been roommates in Austin, which worked out great for Vivian since Lucy was an OCD neat freak; and she, a creative mess. Their apartment was always pristine except for Lucy's cat, Fredericka, who never grasped the litter box concept. Her spastic tail would undo the entire purpose of using the litter box, and she'd sling shit everywhere.

Fred was Vivian's first and last cat.

Though she was still in Houston, Wendy would occasionally get a wild hair and head out for Austin on the spur of the moment. She would call when she was 30 minutes away to make sure Vivian and Lucy were home. If not, she let herself in with the key they left for such occasions.

Kate lived in a dorm her first couple of years at UT, and then took an apartment close to campus. Vivian and Kate's educational paths rarely crossed, Kate being an architecture major and Vivian journalism. Though studious, Kate did occasionally embrace the party scene. Their junior year they went to a Halloween party together involving the "devil's cauldron" conveniently full of mushroom tea. Kate adamantly refused to drink the magical brew; Vivian however, was a bit of a wild child and partook freely. The rest of that evening had been in Technicolor and the thunderstorm two hours later felt like a Pink Floyd concert on steroids.

Vivian signaled the flight attendant for a second rum and Coke and adjusted the air vents so all three blew on her. Swirly Head and Seat Buddy either didn't notice or didn't care. Vivian was not a good flier. Was it the lack of control over her destiny? Was it the plane crash that nearly took out Lucy's house in high school? Whatever it was, Vivian couldn't get on a plane without having a physical response that was quite unpleasant. Maybe

11

she should try hypnosis? For the duration of the flight, alcohol would have to be her personal cure.

The flight attendant arrived with a mini-bottle of rum, a fresh Coke and more ice. She also handed Vivian three snack packets. Vivian ignored the hint and pushed them into the seat pocket and happily cracked open the little bottle.

These are so cute, she thought. She fought an incredible urge to sneak into the galley and steal a bunch. She wouldn't let the flight attendant collect her empties. She liked to line them up on her tray table.

The last time the girls had been together was at Kate's wedding, when Vivian was about ready to pop and she and Rick were doing fine, or so she thought. Lucy and Steve were fine, or so he thought. And Wendy was dating a guy named Jake who had definite potential.

Nine months later, Vivian had doubled her kid count and was on the brink of divorce. Lucy and Steve had separated, with her moving into an apartment. Wendy and Jake had gotten more serious, and Kate and Shaun were still in the lovey-dovey, honeymoon phase.

With the second drink going down Vivian began to ease up. Her knuckles were no longer white, the sweat circles on her blouse were drying, and she could unclench her jaw. She began to look forward to the next week, lying on the beach, relaxing by the pool and drinking her worries away, or at least trying to.

Vivian never expected to be divorced. Did anyone? She certainly didn't think it after four kids. Rick was an attorney. A criminal defense attorney, but still, he should have known better.

Vivian swirled her ice around, poured in the rest of the rum and added the bottle to her lineup. She let out a big sigh. *My poor kids. Will they be screwed up from this? Fuckin' Rick. What kind of man does this? The twins aren't even a year old. Will I have a nervous breakdown? Isn't that normal after something like this?*

Her mother's side of the family was prone to the dramatic collapse.

Nah, I'm not the breakdown type, she thought. *But I am definitely pissed.*

Two hours later and shortly after drink three arrived, the descent into Cancun began. An announcement was made about tray tables and whatnot, so she sucked down her drink while the flight attendant stared at her, holding the bag of trash. Vivian gave her the 'just a sec' index finger, kicked around her bag and twisted down to dig out her camera. She snapped a quick picture of her bottle collection before it hit the trash.

Vivian leaned forward and glanced out the window. Not a good idea. She needed to stick to staring at the seat back in front of her.

Damn, a landing plane makes a lot of noise, she thought.

Death could be near, so she did her usual silent goodbyes and added a new one. Something about various parts of Rick's anatomy shriveling up and falling off. She then braced for the impact that never was as bad as she anticipated.

"*Bienvenidos a México*," the flight attendant announced just as the wheels touched down. Welcome to Mexico. *Amen to that!*

The taxi to the gate was nothing, and before Vivian knew it everyone stood and began grabbing their belongings. Swirly head seemed eager to leave so she unbuckled and prepared to get up. Her Mexican vacation had officially begun.

I need to relax and enjoy this, she thought, as she grabbed her bag from under the seat and pushed it up on her shoulder. She glanced down at her blouse. Vacation or not, the sweat circles were back.

Damn.

Vivian wished seat buddy well at the wedding, *which had a 50 percent chance of failure*, and made her way off the plane. Finally free of the tin death trap, she followed the crowd toward baggage claim and more importantly, *el baño*, which was her first priority. There was a line, of course, and her three-drink bladder was not happy.

She suffered through, washed up and looked at herself in the mirror. She fluffed her hair and noticed that her dent was ultra-shiny so she rifled through her purse for her powder compact.

Vivian's "dent" was a circular indentation in her forehead. Her friends had affectionately dubbed it her "dent." It was not really noticeable in person, but in pictures it looked like there was a giant sunshine right in the middle of her forehead. Especially when there was a flash involved. At her wedding, Lucy smacked her dent with powder before each and every picture.

Vivian popped open the compact and bits of broken make-up fell into the sink.

"Dammit," she said out loud to no one in particular. "I just bought this thing."

She was about to close it when she noticed that not only was the powder broken into pieces, but the mirror was cracked too.

Thank god Kate's not here, Vivian thought. *She'd be freakin' out, going on about seven years of bad luck. No way I'm telling her about this.*

Kate, though smart as a whip, was mega superstitious. Her Taiwanese background lent itself to all sorts of weird good luck/bad luck scenarios and she often confused cultures. It made for an interesting belief system, that was for sure.

Vivian closed the compact and tossed it into the trash. *So much for that $18 bucks*, she thought, and walked out.

She reached the conveyor belt just as a buzzer sounded and bags came out of the shoot. Her super-sized suitcase was the last to emerge. It was mega-sized and a festive UT burnt orange. Hook 'em! She practically needed a forklift, it was so heavy and she decided the alcohol was playing a role in this. She did tend to over pack though, especially shoes.

Next stop, Immigration. They scanned Vivian's bag, gave her a stern look and moved her on to Customs. Vivian answered their questions appropriately. She was a U.S. citizen there on vacation. She pressed a button which highlighted a green guy walking with his luggage. Lucky break. The red light would mean an authority figure rifling through her bag looking for no-no's. She didn't have any of those, but she was glad to get green.

Vivian had been told on numerous occasions by her father that she had a problem with authority. Didn't need to test that theory in a foreign country.

Ready to roll, Vivian exited the sliding glass doors and saw Wendy, Kate and Lucy standing just beyond them. Each girl had a free arm (she needed both of hers for the ginormous suitcase), and they all stretched to give her a hug.

Immediately, Vivian's indestructible walls crumbled and the tears she had been holding back for months spilled over. Her friends circled and squeezed.

Vivian had become an all-or-nothing crier these days. She didn't cry for a long time and then, when she did, look out! She was a sobbing machine.

This wasn't always the case. A month ago at a co-worker's mom's funeral, the organ music turned on a fountain in her eyeballs. She couldn't control herself. People turned around in the pews to look at her.

Vivian's co-workers, who were across the church, said they could hear some poor woman bawling and wondered why she wasn't sitting with the family. It was Vivian. And she had never met her co-worker's mother.

In the airport, this manifestation of Vivian's emotions worked in their favor. It kept the unruly tourist advisors (actually locals trying to get you a cab, book scuba diving, get you to visit a timeshare property where you have to listen to their sales pitch bullshit and get free whatever), at bay.

Wendy reached into her purse and handed Vivian some tissues. The girls shuffled her to the rental car counter amid a barrage of comments.

"We're here for you." "He's a fool." "There's no excuse."

The rental car lady seemed eager to get them on their way. Sobbing customers were bad for business.

Lucy had reserved a piece-of-crap economy-sized four-door, and by the time they clamored in Vivian had almost recovered. She had her best friends with her and sunshiny days lie straight ahead. They turned the a/c on high (which did no good), tried for tunes on the radio (didn't work), and pointed the car toward the wild turquoise yonder.

3

Wendy, always large and in charge, got behind the wheel. Don't be fooled by the large part. At 5-7 she was slim and a gem, with long, brown hair to match her expressive eyes. "Brown-eyed Girl" was a common opening line for men who crossed her path. She was a hottie, and had mastered the class of "Assertive Not Aggressive." Usually, though there was that one time... The girls would sometimes tease her, calling her "captain safety" because she had a knack for always being prepared. The contents of her purse never failed to amaze in an emergency.

Vivian got in the back seat with Kate, who was a hugger, and put an arm around Vivian's shoulders. Vivian dabbed at her eyes with a tissue and her mouth felt as dry as a summer day in West Texas. Beer could fix that.

Vivian called up to Wendy, "*Cerveza*. I need *cerveza*. Can we find a gas station or something and pick up a 12-pack? *Pronto.*"

Lucy and Kate seconded the motion. Wendy pulled into a station just ahead, and quicker than jackalopes Lucy and Kate hopped out. Wendy manually rolled down the window and yelled for them to buy bottled water, too. Lucy gave the okay sign.

In no time the troops were back with beer, ice, four waters and four "life's a beach" koozies that would be put to good use. Being the conscientious drinkers that they were, only three koozies would be used while driving. Plus, they had all seen the show *Locked Up Abroad*, and these four broads had no intention of getting locked up abroad.

They cracked open three cans and a water, slipped on the koozies, and Kate offered a toast.

"To the first girl's getaway. May there be many, many more."

Their koozies squished together, and Wendy put the car in reverse.

Kate patted Vivian's leg. "First of all, happy birthday, Viv. Second, what the hell? We had no idea y'all were having problems. What's wrong with that man?"

Vivian took her first sip. "Who knows? I was…no, am…just as shocked. I thought things were okay."

"Were there any signs, you think?" Kate asked.

"I don't know, maybe. He was grouchy, played golf a lot, whatever. Then right before he left in early June he just went overboard. He was rude to me and the kids, yelling at them for no reason. I asked what was going on, and he would just grunt at me. Then one night when we were in bed I asked him what was wrong because I was tired of him acting like a complete and total ass."

Vivian looked down at her hands as she fidgeted with her beer can. "That's when he started in with the whole 'I feel trapped' bullshit."

"He did not!" Wendy exclaimed.

"He did," she sighed and started again. "At first I just said things like, 'We have four kids under 4. It's natural to feel overwhelmed.' Then I started asking more questions, like is there someone else. He said no, and I believed him. He said he loved me, he loved the kids, but that just didn't matter enough to him anymore. He thought we should try a separation, so I agreed, only because I didn't know what the hell else to do. He rented a small apartment on the other side of town. We have been living like that since June, and had just started with the visitation schedule when *it* happened."

"I can't believe he would do this," Lucy said. "It just doesn't sound like him."

Wendy looked at Vivian in the rear-view mirror. "Viv, why didn't you tell us when he first left? We would have come and tried to help or something."

"I don't know, I guess I thought it would pass. Or maybe I was in a daze or something."

Lucy turned around to face Vivian. "Whatever it was you could have and should have called us sooner. I don't know what we would have done, but we would have done something. Maybe hired a hit man."

Vivian couldn't help but grin. "I know, and I'm sorry. I've been a bit of a recluse."

Kate, still patting her leg, said, "Well, we're here now. How did you find out he was cheating?"

Vivian's face got hot and her heart beat hard as the scene replayed in her head. It was as vivid as if she still stood by the pool holding her cell phone, ready to put another smack down on that idiot stick.

"It was his first night to have the kids per our separation agreement, and I was worried. He rarely would take care of Audrey and Lauren alone, much less all four. Plus the twins were getting over a cold, and I wanted to just check in.

"I called and called, at least four or five times, and no answer. I had been out to dinner with some work friends and his apartment was down the road from where I was, so I decided to stop by. Make sure everything was okay. We had to swap cars because of the car seats so I was in his truck and he had my minivan.

"His apartment is three stories — bottom level a garage, second level living space, third level two bedrooms. The garage door was up, my minivan was in it and there was another car right behind it. I thought that was rude, but it is an apartment complex and neighbors can suck. I could have gone up through the garage but I didn't feel right, since it's not my apartment. I walked around to the courtyard, and there he was in the pool, making out with *her*."

Wendy almost drove off the road. "What the fuck, Viv? What an asshole! Where were the kids?"

"Asleep on the third story of the apartment in a bedroom. Alone."

"Candidate for parent of the year? I think not!" Kate said.

"How could he be so irresponsible?" Lucy asked.

"Needless to say, I went ballistic. Seriously, it was something out of Jerry Springer. I broke my cell phone over his head, threw my sandals, kicked, hit, screamed a lot…"

"Holy crap," Kate said, who was not much of a cusser. "He totally deserved it, that dip wad."

Lucy and Wendy just shook their heads. Everyone was quiet for a minute. Then Wendy glanced back at Vivian.

"You broke your cell phone over his head?"

Vivian smiled. "Yep, smashed it right into the side of his head. It broke into about 100 pieces. After I put the kids in the van and as I was driving off — I threw his only set of truck keys in the bushes!"

"Good for you!" Wendy gave her a high-five from the front seat.

"And you want to hear something funny? He found my sandals the next day and eventually gave them back to me. Dumb-ass."

Vivian finished her beer and pushed another into her koozie.

"My divorce should be final in a week or so. I'm just glad I found out about the SPS —swimming pool slut. It helps explain things. I missed a lot of signs."

"So do you think you could forgive him and maybe y'all work things out?" Kate asked (obviously just married).

"He did call in the middle of the night a few weeks after he left and before the pool incident and asked, 'What's wrong with me?' I told him he had five people at home who loved him very much, but that was pretty much the only time he made any effort to reach out. He's gone."

"How are the kids taking this? Have they met the SPS?" Wendy asked reluctantly.

Vivian's tears started up again.

"They're so young. They really don't understand, but no, I don't think they've met her. I've already called a child therapist, but she can't see Audrey for two months. She just turned 4 so she asks questions, but she's the only one, and she just wants to know why daddy isn't home anymore. I can't even use the word 'divorce' around her yet. The twins are too little to have any idea, and Lauren doesn't get it, either. One day they will. I'll just cross that bridge when I get there."

"I can't believe you're getting divorced," Kate said.

"Well, they say that 50 percent of marriages go south. When I took my vows I meant them. Sure, the FedEx guy at my office was tempting. I mean, he's there twice a week, and he always seems to brush his fingertips across more than my hand when he gives me that little pretend pen, but come on. I wasn't straying. Who has the time? Or energy?"

"Apparently, he did," Lucy muttered. Then she turned to Vivian. "Sorry."

"It's okay."

"What about his family? What are they saying?" Kate asked.

"They're devastated. His parents couldn't believe it when I told them the swimming pool debacle. The only person who wasn't surprised was my lawyer. She knows Rick and she had a sneakin' suspicion something was going on. She even called the day after I found out about the SPS to check on me."

"Do you think she knew?" Wendy asked.

"I think she knew something, but not everything. She asked if I wanted to change any of the divorce terms. I told her hell yes. I want it *all*. Before I was okay splitting some of the assets. Not anymore."

"Is Rick pissed?" Lucy asked.

"Yeah, but he's not fighting. I'm getting pretty much everything. Only thing Rick gets is a broken DVD player, an old microwave and a $500 piece-of-nothing property in the middle of nowhere."

"I can't believe he would agree to that," Kate said.

"Well, with news of his affair spreading like wildfire across the courthouse, I guess he thought better of it. So now it's almost done. Not exactly where I was expecting to be on my 30th birthday. Money will be tight, but things could be worse. For now, I just want to have a great trip, and I'll probably need lots of liquid encouragement along the way." Vivian tilted her beer up.

The rest of the drive they spent catching up — relatives, jobs. All of the families and extended families were good. Wendy's 18-month-old niece, Lizzie, was responding well to cancer treatment from Dr. Burzynski in Houston. She had been diagnosed at 6 months old with a rare form of adrenal cancer and given only four months to live by other cancer centers. Though her tumors were shrinking, every day for her was a miracle.

Lucy started Handel's "Hallelujah Chorus," and they all chimed in. They were in band, not choir, and it was a good thing nobody else could hear them. Lucy had a great voice, but the rest of them…not so much.

The drive to their hotel, La Vida de Playa, went by quicker than a drunken afternoon on the Guadalupe River. The hotel was on the main drag, but parking eluded them and the front door appeared to face the beach.

"I can handle a beachfront entrance to my hotel in paradise," Vivian said as they circled the block.

Parking proved to be bumper to bumper on both sides of the road with no open spaces. Wendy double parked in front of a different hotel and Lucy jumped out and disappeared around the corner to inquire about parking.

While they waited, Vivian checked out the tourists and wondered where they should go later.

Wendy started singing "I Love the Nightlife" to pass the time.

"I love that song. Who sings it?" Vivian asked, but before Kate or Wendy could answer, Vivian saw a shadow to her right and heard a knock on her window.

Just like in high school Wendy blurted out, "Beers down!"

At Vivian's eye level was a gun and an assortment of other bring 'em down doodads. Her gaze traveled up to the badge.

Shit. Welcome to paradise.

4

Mr. Po-Po was in full police uniform and looked hot, as in temperature hot.

Vivian put her fear aside, rolled down the window, batted her eyes and put on the biggest smile she could muster.

"No parking *aqui*," he said, pointing at the car.

Vivian gave him a wave and in her sexy Texas drawl said, "Hola, mister policia. We're staying at La Vida de Playa. Do you know where we can park?"

He responded with an accent, but otherwise good English. "Ah, Americans. La Vida de Playa has no parking. You have to find a spot on the street. You cannot park here."

Wendy leaned toward the back window, pushed her boobs out and gave an innocent smile. "You're cute. What's your name? Umm...*como te llamo?*" (her two years of high school Spanish kicking in).

He put his hand on the roof of the car and leaned down. "Arturo. This is your first time in Playa?"

Vivian smiled at him, checking him out. He had rosy red cheeks, which added to his charm, and didn't look a day over 25.

"Yes, and it's so beautiful!" Wendy said. "We're from Texas."

About this time Lucy popped out from around the corner and walked up with a look of 'oh crap' on her face. She recovered, flashed a wide smile and said confidently, "You girls causing trouble already? Y'all are just a menace to society!"

Mr. Policia got one look at her green eyes, auburn hair and curvy figure and said, "Special today for Texas girls. Reserved parking."

He moved a barricade that previously blocked their entry into a lot owned by another hotel. They pulled in, blew kisses, spilling out their thanks and their cleavage.

"Did we luck out or what?" Vivian said. "Hopefully this kind of service will be available the whole trip."

They piled out of the car, popped the trunk and grabbed their stuff while Lucy introduced herself to their new favorite policeman.

"Well, aren't you too cute for boots," Lucy laughed. "Thanks for the great spot. I'll be seeing you later, Mr. Policia Arturo," pointing her finger at him, Marilyn Monroe-like.

They waved as they walked away. Arturo couldn't take his eyes off Lucy.

"I think he's in love," Vivian snorted and gave Lucy a bump with her hip. Then she let go of her luggage long enough to make a heart with her index fingers and thumbs.

"I'd say so!" Kate chimed in.

"Love, lust, whatever. It's always good to make friends with local law enforcement," Wendy said. "Especially in a foreign country."

"Right!" Vivian turned her finger-heart into two guns. "Pow, pow! Never know when that will come in handy."

"Hell, got us a free parking spot. Rock and roll," Lucy said, pushing Vivian's guns away. "Holster those bad boys and move your ass."

Next stop, front desk. They lugged their bags through the sand, but Vivian had no complaints. *I'm on vacation, and it's my birthday!*

The hotel lobby sported a beach theme with an abundance of tropical plants. Vivian almost expected to see monkeys swinging around or tropical birds perched above. The floor was squeaky clean, like somebody with a mop followed behind everyone who walked in off the beach. Neat-freak Lucy looked pleased. Overall, the lobby made a first-rate initial impression.

Check-in was a breeze. The gracious staffer (who spoke great English) told the girls where they could find the business center, restaurant, etc. She pointed to the stairs, which would take them to their room on the second floor.

"Who the hell uses the business center," Kate mumbled as they walked away.

"Losers," Lucy answered.

At their room, Vivian inserted the key card in the door and it hummed open. Beautiful turquoise water gleamed from beyond the balcony. Nice touch, very dramatic.

The room was simple and clean, with more beach theme.

"This is heaven!" Kate threw herself on the bed and kicked her feet in the air.

"It's pretty damn perfect," Wendy said as she walked toward the view. "Not too fancy. Just right."

Lucy gave the room the evil eye, thoroughly working it over. She couldn't find much wrong. "No TV, but who cares." Unable to help herself after her room inspection, she made a beeline for the temperature gauge and set it to 65.

Freak, Vivian thought and had to smirk. In her old life with Rick, he would have been having a conniption fit about now. He couldn't have made it without ESPN. The girls, of course, could care less. Vivian had a feeling they wouldn't be spending much time in the room anyway. The spacious, ocean-facing balcony was by far the rockin'-est place to be, and she planned to spend a few solitary minutes out there each morning.

After taking in the room and view, they unpacked the essentials and decided to do the obvious, hit the beach. Time for standard Playa attire: bikinis. Well, except for Vivian. Her body was still in bounce-back mode from the twins, who were born full term, 7 pounds 12 ounces and 6 pounds 5 ounces. Monster babies, she called them.

Towards the end of her pregnancy she looked like a freak of nature (her doctor actually told her this). Vivian's pelvic bones felt like they were going to crumble into little shards and fall into her legs, and she looked like she had a submarine around her middle.

Since their birth the "twin skin" had yet to elasticize back into place completely, and she wasn't sure it ever would. She opted for a tankini. Her arms and legs were normal size, thank goodness. With her tummy tucked behind a tropical swirl of color, Lucy in a black and gold bikini, Wendy in a metallic red bikini, and Kate in a hot pink string bikini they were ready to hit the sand. They grabbed hats, towels, sunscreen, sunglasses and the ever-important koozies and headed out the door.

Kate stopped Vivian as the door closed behind them. "Wait. Viv, don't you want to take off your watch?"

"Yeah, like we care what time it is," Lucy said. "We're on vacation!"

"I wear it all the time, I don't even think about it. It's waterproof so no worries."

"Then let's boogie." Wendy danced over to the stairs. "I'm ready to hit the beach!"

They woo-hoo'ed and danced down the stairs and through the lobby to the gorgeous Playa del Carmen beach.

A young Hispanic man, wearing a royal blue shirt, khaki shorts and mirrored wraparound sunglasses, approached them as their toes hit the sand. His name tag read: Manuel.

"Hola Señoritas. Bueñas tardes. Something to drink? Eat?"

His wavy brown hair fell into his eyes and he brushed it back with his fingertips. He smiled at them. "Beach chairs, umbrella, food, anything. I here for you."

Vivian realized through his broken English that he had said food and clasped her hands in a begging motion.

"Food! I need food." She had been running late for the airport this morning and skipped breakfast. Then, thanks to her nerves, she had drunk her lunch on the plane.

"Four chairs and an umbrella would be great too," Wendy added.

Manuel nodded. *"No problema, señoritas,"* he said, and headed off toward a cabana. He was good to look at from the back, and they all took a moment to admire the view.

"Mmm, mmm. That man is a beautiful brown stud." Lucy fanned herself with her big-brimmed sun hat, looking at Manuel, her sunglasses pushed down on her nose.

Vivian put her hand to her heart and gave Lucy her "I'm shocked" look.

"What?" Lucy pushed her sunglasses back up. "I'm married, not blind."

"I realize this," Vivian said. "I'm just not sure I've ever heard you say anything like that."

"I have!" Kate said. "Remember that time at the daiquiri bar in Houston? The one with the muscled-up bartender. What was his name? Larry?"

"Oh, that's right. I do remember him. Lucy thought he was hot-to-trot," Vivian teased. "He had long, silky hair. She kept ordering drink after drink just to get him to come near her."

Lucy did a throat clear. "First of all, his name was Lars, not Larry. Secondly, he was extremely talented behind the bar. He could have been cast in *Cocktail* alongside Tom Cruise."

"Are you insane? Everything came out of frozen daiquiri machines," Vivian said. "Lucy, that doesn't take any talent."

"Yeah, but that man could work those handles. He had some truly gifted hands, and he would shake his ass to the music as deliciousness filled the plastic cups." She looked off into space with a satisfied smile on her face.

"You're a sick woman," Wendy said.

Lucy raised an eyebrow and her smile turned devious.

"More importantly," Vivian recalled, "do you remember getting sick as a dog on the way home after all those ass-shakin' daiquiris?"

"I just knew you were going to bring that up," Lucy said. "I had gotten my flu shot earlier that day!"

"Flu shot my ass!" Vivian laughed.

"Oh Lucy, that was horrible." Kate patted Lucy's arm in confirmation.

"Yes, it was," Vivian said. "Blue spew all over the passenger window and door. It was disgusting."

"Okay, enough," Wendy said. "Let's not talk about anyone getting sick. Bad vibes."

"Ma'am, yes ma'am," Vivian gave Wendy a salute. "No barf banter. Gotcha."

They laughed as they eyed the water, and picked a spot a little ways down the beach. Manuel had four beach chairs, an umbrella and most importantly, a menu. He carried everything with ease. He slipped Vivian the menu and put out the beach chairs according to Lucy's instructions.

Vivian settled into hers and stretched her legs, enjoying the feel of the sun on her skin. Kate plopped down on Vivian's left and Wendy on the right. Lucy wiped off her chair, giving it a thorough inspection before she took a seat next to Kate.

How does she live like this, being a germ-a-phobe? I'd go nuts, Vivian thought.

Manuel used a shovel and dug the umbrella hole. He then got the umbrella adjusted to Lucy's specifications. She had pasty white skin and wanted to keep it that way. When finished, Lucy smoothly passed him a $20 bill.

Vivian looked at her and raised an eyebrow. "Quite the tip there, huh Lucy?"

Lucy pretended not to hear Vivian and flipped open a magazine.

Unexpectedly, a young lady bearing tequila shots materialized, Tiempo Loco, she called it, and passed one out to each of them, compliments of the hotel.

God bless Mexico! Vivian thought, though she was not a huge tequila fan. She passed the menu to Kate and grabbed for her shot.

Wendy raised her shot glass high. "To Viv! May this birthday be a new beginning."

"To Viv, *aye ya yai ya yai*," they all chanted.

I love my friends, Vivian thought.

Vivian licked, slammed, and sucked the tequila back. She smiled over at the girls and just couldn't resist…

"At least the tequila's not blue. Right Lucy?"

5

Kate ordered chips and salsa, quesadillas and ceviche from Manuel, who rapidly proved to be a do-it-all kind of guy. Vivian, ready for more drinks, ordered her favorite, Dos Equis lager, and the other girls put in drink orders too. Lucy wanted another tequila with a beer back which made Vivian shudder. Kate ordered a fruity drink complete with paper umbrella and Wendy a margarita.

The girls caught up some more, remembering old times. They laughed about the Greek Goddess costumes they made for Halloween in Austin on 6th Street when they were 20. They didn't have much money, so they bought a lot of cheap white fabric, cut it to size and wrapped it around themselves like togas. They bought greenery for their heads at the dollar store and did themselves up in body glitter.

"For less than $5 each, we looked pretty damn good," Vivian declared.

They even won second place in a costume contest at a bar. They lost to an Elvis impersonator who made them wonder if the King was still alive and walking around Austin.

Manuel arrived with the drinks and must have heard them talking about Elvis because he launched into his own impersonation. He turned his back to the girls, moved his hips a little and turned his head to the side. Then he looked down at the sand and slowly, dramatically, brought his head up and held a pretend microphone in his right hand.

He sang "Love me Tender" in its entirety. On the last verse he knelt next to Kate and finished with a dramatic kiss of her hand.

He stood up as they cheered his portrayal.

"Bravo! Bravo!" Vivian said as she clapped. "Encore!"

"Thank you, thank you very much," he said with an Elvis smirk.

He looked back, raised one side of his lip and pointed to the girls as his accolades rolled on.

"Never thought I'd see that in Mexico!" Wendy said.

Others beachgoer's heard Manuel, so he got little applauses here and there. One lady gave him a tip. "Maybe he should do that more often," Kate laughed, who saw him get the tip.

The girls settled back in their chairs and talked about who was doing what with whom from high school. Who married their sweethearts. Who then divorced them...

"Speaking of high school, whatever happened to your old car, the La Bamba, Lucy?" Kate asked. "When we got into our rental today, it reminded me of it."

"That car still lives, believe it or not. My cousin has it now."

Lucy had a total junker in high school they called the La Bamba.

"That car was a tank," Wendy said.

The La Bamba was a 1980 Pontiac Grand LeMans. It was a dull brown, with a hint of rust, so the dirt blended in. The power steering was bad, which gave Lucy ripped upper arms from turning the wheel. In the back seat the headliner hung down so far that it blocked Vivian's and everyone else's vision. Eventually it got pulled off, leaving behind a nasty, gummy residue, and the ceiling became a place for sticky notes, napkins, gum wrappers, even hall passes. "La Bamba" was sung a lot in that car. "Low Rider" also fit and was a crowd favorite.

The sun smiled down on Vivian, Wendy and Kate, and Lucy hogged the umbrella shade. Lucy didn't want to go up even one notch on the pale scale. She liked to stay between one and three and was convinced the rest of them would die of skin cancer. Vivian and Wendy were a six and hoped to leave Playa an eight, minimum. Kate was around a five and wouldn't mind being a seven.

From Vivian's perspective, a zero on the pale scale was a glow in the dark, never seen the sun, bright light reflected off your body could sear retinas, paleness. A ten was a sun-drenched Hawaiian Tropic tan. Dermatologists frowned on sunworshipers like Vivian, but at least she didn't do fake-n-bake. She needed real sunshine, not a coffin-like contraption that could, for real, fry her eyeballs.

Manuel stopped by to check on them. "Food *en uno momento. Mas* drinks?"

"Absolutely," Lucy said. "Another shot for me."

"No more tequila for me. How about a bucket of Dos Equis?" Vivian looked back and forth between Wendy and Kate. "Sound good?"

"Yep," they both said without moving.

Manuel quickly arrived with their beverages. Vivian loved the sight of their bucket of beer. Six *cervezas* crowned with cup of lime. Very picturesque.

She reached for one and disrupted the symmetry. Wendy and Kate grabbed one, too, and the beautiful bucket suddenly looked empty again.

Lucy licked, slammed and sucked her shot quickly. "Mmmm, zat wah good," she mumbled, the lime peel smiling out from between her teeth.

She discarded her lime and hopped off her beach chair. "I've got to wash my hands before I eat. I'll be back in *uno momento*."

Vivian pushed down her sunglasses so she could look at Lucy tint-free. "Girl, you better slow down on those shots. It's not blue, but you could still spew."

"Nahhhh, I'm good. I'm on vacation," she said, then pushed her feet into her flip-flops.

"Yeah, okay, but you're drinkin' like a deformed Houston ship channel fish."

"Silly Viv," Lucy laughed, and put her hand on Vivian's shoulder. It could have been for effect or so she wouldn't fall over, Vivian couldn't tell. "You know fish can't survive in the ship channel," and she ambled off toward the ladies room.

With Lucy out of earshot, Kate said, "You know the saying 'one tequila, two tequila, three tequila, floor'?" she pointed towards Lucy. "Well she's on three."

Vivian watched Lucy grab for the restroom door handle and miss. Got it on the second try though. *Maybe she's seeing double*, Vivian thought.

"I can't remember her slamming back so many drinks so quickly," Wendy said, pushing her bottle into her koozie. "Not even in college."

"She always liked tequila, but she was never a big drinker. Not like *moi*!" Vivian said. "She's usually our designated driver."

"I wonder if there's more to the Steve story than she's telling us," Kate said with concern. "She has to be stressed out about something to be suckin' 'em down like this."

The three of them groaned, contemplating the thought of tequila and the Steve trouble. Vivian's groan was for Steve-trouble. They had all been there, done that, some of them more recently than others.

"We'll talk to her this week, she'll probably open up," Wendy said. "The time away will do her good. Distance making the heart grow fonder, and all that."

"They've had some ups and downs. She may reach a different conclusion," Vivian said. "Either way, she needs to lighten up on her tequila intake or she's going to regret it in the morning."

"Hell, she may be in the restroom regretting it now," Wendy said.

Once the limes were thoroughly squeezed and in their beers, Wendy proposed a toast.

"Here's to a vacation of no regrets." They clinked their green bottles together and drank to that.

6

Lucy, walking a little straighter Vivian noticed, returned from *el baño* just as Manuel delivered the food, four settings of silverware, napkins and salt and pepper.

"Thanks Manuel," Wendy said, and made Lucy a plate. She put quesadillas on one side and started to put ceviche on the other. Lucy shook her head.

"No way," she said, wagging her finger. "That fish is raw."

"It is not!" Wendy continued to put it on her plate. "I was a skeptic, too, until I saw the lemon and lime juice cook the fish in front of me. It's really good, Lucy, low fat too. Just try a small bite. Please?"

"Un-uh, no way. The tequila won't make me sick but that will," Lucy said, gesturing at the fish. "Just give me an extra quesadilla."

Wendy handed Lucy the plate, but as she did her arm knocked over the salt shaker and granules formed a pile on the table.

"Oopsie," Wendy said, not thinking twice about it, but Kate gasped.

"Hurry, throw some over your shoulder," she said.

"Kate, I don't believe in that stuff."

Vivian couldn't help but wait to hear Kate's response.

"Well, do it anyway, for me."

"Fine," Wendy said taking a pinch. "Which shoulder?"

Kate's mouth twitched from to the side as she thought about it.

"I can't remember. You aren't supposed to look over your right shoulder at a new moon, or is it your left? And then the salt goes over the other one."

"Geez," Wendy said, and tossed some over both. "There. I'm covered."

Kate sat back, satisfied.

Wendy scooped up a big bite of the ceviche and stuffed the whole thing into her mouth, just to gross out Lucy. "Mmmm, yum yum!"

Lucy ate her quesadilla slowly. Too slowly in Vivian's opinion. *That girl is hammered.*

Manuel came by and offered more beverages. "Bottled water for that one," Wendy said, pointing to Lucy.

"Manuel, *no mas* for Lucy!" Vivian said. "She's cut off. She's got to make it out with us tonight."

Manuel gave them a grin and a wink. "*Señorita es muy loco!* Crazy!"

"Manuel, Lucy's tolerance for alcohol is about the same as her tolerance for the sun. Zero, zilch, *nada*," Vivian said. "Please, *no mas* for now."

He gave her a thumbs up.

Wendy looked over at Lucy and shook her head. Then she noticed Lucy's arm had turned a not-so-subtle shade of scarlet.

"Lucy, your elbow looks like it's been in the sun too long. You're moving up the pale scale!"

Lucy giggled and didn't bother to move her arm or the umbrella, probably because she couldn't. Wendy got up and tilted the umbrella, knowing the importance of pastiness to her.

Kate made herself a small plate of food and gracefully took her chair back to resume her sun soaking. Vivian thought she looked like a movie star with her huge sunglasses and her hot-pink bikini perfect body.

"So how's married life? You and Shaun still livin' in honeymoon mania?" Vivian asked her.

Kate gave a thoughtful grin. "We dated for so long before we were married that I thought our relationship would be the same, but it's not. It's better! We are closer than ever. In fact, we're looking at property, and I've started working on the plans for a house." She took a chip, scooped on salsa and crunched down.

Kate was a mongo-talented architect and had worked for the same firm since graduating from UT. Her mom was from Taiwan, and her dad had been an American sailor. The combo produced a stunning, slim, runwayesque femme with light brown hair, hazel eyes and a natural allure that men found irresistible. Inner beauty completed the package: brains, looks, kindness. Kate had it all.

"And will this house have a nursery?" Vivian had to ask.

"Oh, we both want kids but not until the house is finished. In the meantime, we're considering a dog."

Wendy was a dog fanatic, and her ears perked up. "What kind? Boxers are great! My two are protective when they need to be but otherwise so sweet."

"We were thinking standard poodle," Kate said. "That or go and pick out the ugliest dog from a shelter who is doomed to die. We'll see."

"Go with the shelter then," Wendy said. "My good ol' girl, Radar, came from the SPCA. I'm so glad I adopted her."

Obviously all was well with Kate, so Vivian turned to Wendy. "What's up with you and Jake? Y'all still hot and heavy?"

Wendy, never one to bed and blab, rubbed her sandy feet together. "I have to admit, it's going well. Believe it or not, I'm starting to think he may be the one."

Kate and Vivian looked at each other, eyes wide. Lucy finished her quesadilla and stayed silent in her shade.

"Wow, the one." Vivian said. "I'm shocked!"

"I know, me too," she said. "I can really see us together long term. One thing though, Jake never wanted to stay in Houston permanently. In fact, he had an interview last week with a company in his hometown."

Vivian didn't realize he wasn't from Houston. They met there so she assumed he was from the area.

"Where's that?" she asked.

"Winston-Salem, North Carolina. They say it's pretty there."

Who are "they?" Vivian wondered and tensed up a little. North Carolina was far. Boulder was far, but everyone wants to visit Boulder. She tried to keep her voice calm. "You planning on moving if he goes?"

Lucy picked her head up off the chair. "Girl, don't move until there's a ring on your finger."

A moment of clarity for the inebriated, Vivian thought.

Wendy laughed. "We'll see what happens. We're not quite there yet."

Kate and Vivian looked at each other again and in unison gave a big "Hmmm…"

Lucy suddenly swung her legs out of the shade and stood up, rather gracefully, considering.

"I'm hot. Hand me the bucket of beer, will ya, Viv?"

Vivian looked at it and then back at Lucy. Two beers remained, but she and Wendy were almost done with theirs.

"You want a beer?"

"No, no. No beer. I need the bucket."

A bit unsure, Vivian removed the two beers and handed it to Lucy.

Lucy dumped the cold water in the sand and put the bucket on her head. It fit perfectly.

"Ahhh, that's better."

The handle hugged her chin like a helmet strap and the bucket came down to just above her eyes. She started dancing around which was odd behavior, especially since there was no music, only crashing waves.

"I guess we need to make some music for this wild woman!" Vivian laughed and stood up to dance with her. The words to "Safety Dance" popped into her head.

Vivian sang with gusto, though when it came time to sing "safety," she replaced it with "bucket," given Lucy's head gear.

Wendy and Kate hopped up, joining in the goofiness. They received strange looks from other beach-goers.

Manuel walked past and Lucy snatched his arm and swung him around in a do-si-do move. He tossed his cocktail tray on the nearest lounger and round he went.

Vivian decided the moment needed to be captured forever, so she paused to get out her camera and snapped a few.

They kept singing but couldn't remember all the words. Eventually, Lucy, still wearing the bucket, released Manuel's arm and plopped back down into her chair, not so gracefully this time.

"Thanks, Manuel. You rocked the bucket dance," she said, then laid back and let the bucket slide down over her eyes.

"Guess we won't be seeing Lucy for a while," Vivian said. "I'm burnin' up. Let's go down to the water. Manuel, get us another, will ya, *por favor*?" She tapped the bucket on Lucy's head.

"*Si*, bucket babes. *No problema*," he said, and did the bucket dance all the way back to the bar.

7

Wendy, Kate and Vivian left Lucy dozing on the beach and headed for the crystal clear ocean.

The water was cool enough to enjoy but warm enough it didn't freeze them out. The waves rolled gently and they picked a spot that was constantly being refreshed. Vivian laughed about feeling very Bo Derek in *10*, minus the braids.

Manuel arrived with the b-o-b just in time to get hit by a knee-high wave. The hazards of working at the beach.

Vivian decided to build a sandcastle in honor of her kiddos. She was no architect, and Kate shook her head as Vivian mounded sand into a few lumps here and there. The waves kept encroaching which called for a moat. Vivian lacked good moat-building tools, so she improvised with her feet, digging her heels deep.

"This is probably good for my calluses," she said.

Wendy and Kate picked out a few seashells and decorated Vivian's tee-pee shaped mounds of sand.

They were on the finishing touches when two jet skis roared up, creating a tidal wave that annihilated Vivian's creation.

Kate laughed and said it was probably for the best, but Wendy glared at the two guys who caused the destruction. Seeing the anger flash in her eyes, one of the men hopped off the jet ski and apologized.

"I'm so sorry, ladies. We're still learning how to handle these things. Did we interrupt something-ola?"

"I'd say so!" Wendy harrumphed and pointed to the mound of wet sand that used to be a work of art. She tended to be protective of her friends, even in situations as minor as the demolition of a crappy sandcastle.

The guy pulled the jet ski up to balance on the beach and crouched down next to Vivian.

Sweaty or not, he smelled good. A mix of musky and salty. Downright lickalicious. She could feel his body heat, which got her a little flushed, and couldn't help but stare at his mouth.

He was about 6-2, dark hair, brown eyes, but zero tan. He was the definition of pasty. He'd score a three on the pale scale (and that was giving him a point for being so cute). He wore a knee-length black and white tropical print swimsuit, no shirt underneath a life jacket. His teeth were dazzlingly white, and his lips were the most beautiful deep red Vivian had ever seen. *Mmm mmmm good.*

The other jet skier had more of a bodybuilder physique but was just as pale. With his shaved head, he was handsome in the same fashion as Mr. Clean. His swimsuit was a little shorter, and crimson red, which was a stark contrast to his skin.

"It was completely unintentional," lips said and flashed a spectacular, boyish grin. "I'm really sorry."

"It's fine," Vivian said. "It wasn't any good anyway."

"I'm sure it was pure genius." He pushed the sand back into some sort of pile. "I feel terrible. We needed another layer of sunscreen, and our stuff is here. I really am sorry-ola. Can I make it up to you somehow?"

"No, no. It's no biggie. " Vivian shrugged, and started to stand up.

He stood and reached for her hand, helping her up.

"I insist," he said. "We have 30 minutes left on our rental. Tell you what, we can take turns taking the three of you out, and afterwards I'll help you make another sand masterpiece. It might even turn out better than what you had."

Vivian looked over at Kate and Wendy. They nodded in approval with goofy smiles on their faces. "Okay, sounds fun." Vivian splashed water on her legs to wash sand off. "I've never been on a jet ski before."

"It's fun-ola!" He stuck out his hand again. "I'm Jon. This is Pierre."

Vivian took his hand and shook it. He had a strong grip, but didn't squeeze her to death, and smooth skin, yet a little rough. *Nice combination.*

"Our sunscreen is right over there." He pointed up the beach toward the hotel. "Just give us a sec and we'll be ready to go. I can feel the sun frying me as I speak," he said then turned around and jogged up toward their beach chairs. Pierre followed. Vivian watched.

Wendy and Kate came up on either side of her, then went around in front to block her view.

"Oh my god Viv, he's sooo totally flirting with you!" Wendy squealed and playfully swatted Vivian's arm.

"Nah, he's just feeling bad because of the sandcastle," Vivian said.

"That had nothing to do with any sandcastle," Kate said. "I swear I've never known anyone with pheromones like you! You've had them since puberty. Guys practically lie at your feet wherever we go."

Vivian and Kate have had this discussion before. Kate was convinced Vivian exuded lust inducers.

"Whatever. I stink! I've been sweating in the sun."

"Maybe that makes them stronger," Kate teased. "I'm jealous."

"Yeah, and I'm jealous of your perfect ass, so we're even."

Kate turned around and smacked it.

Wendy interrupted. "He's not lying down at your feet, but he's totally hot for you, you lucky dog. He's gorgeous. Jesus! Did you see that mouth!"

"Yeah, I saw it," And with that they turned and watched him slather on the sunscreen. It made him even whiter and look kinda goofy.

He caught them looking and waved. Wendy and Kate turned back to Vivian, their eyebrows sky high.

"Okay, he may be flirting a little," Vivian said. "I haven't been flirted with in forever! What should I do?"

She couldn't help but be flattered. It had been 10 years since she could "for real" reciprocate flirting.

"Jump on that horse and ride him like he's never been ridden before." Wendy did a little gallop around Kate and Vivian, waving a pretend lasso in the air.

"*What?* I just met him and I'm not divorced yet. I can't do that."

"Viv, Rick has this comin', that prick," Kate said. "The whole 'do unto others' logic applies here. Besides, he'll never know. I guarantee ya we're not tellin'."

Vivian gawked at her. "I can't believe you of all people just said that."

Kate shrugged.

Vivian didn't have time to respond because Jon walked up. Pierre was still by their beach chairs, putting on sunscreen.

"You didn't tell me your name-olas," he said, looking at Vivian.

"I'm Vivian. This is Kate." She gave a small wave. "And this is Wendy." Another wave.

Vivian looked up at Jon. "Before I do this, I have to ask: What's with the 'ola'?"

"Oh," he smiled. "I can't speak Spanish, so it's my version-ola! The tourists don't seem to mind. The locals, however, think I'm crazy-ola!"

They all laughed.

"Are you ready for your ride?" he asked and flashed those pearly whites.

"Actually, Jon, there are four of us fabulous femmes. One of us is similar in skin tone to yourself and won't leave her umbrella," Vivian said, then pointed to passed-out Lucy.

Pierre walked up. "What's this I hear about an umbrella?"

"Their friend is up on the beach refusing to leave the safety of her umbrella."

Jon hooked a thumb toward Lucy. "They don't feel they can leave her."

Pierre rubbed his bald head, which was a shade or two pinker than the rest of him. "An umbrella is sounding pretty good right now. How about the four of you go? I'll go introduce myself to your friend and put my sunburned head under the shade. What your friend's name?"

"Her name is Lucy," Wendy replied, "but she's taking a nap, compliments of Tiempo Loco tequila. She may not respond."

Pierre laughed. "No worries. I'll just borrow the shade."

"Cool! She's the one with the bucket on her head," Vivian said.

He cocked his head to the side and looked at Vivian like she was crazy. "I'll need to hear that story later," he said, and handed Wendy his life jacket and the jet ski key. "You'll find me and Lucy in the shade. I'll be the one *sans* bucket."

"Gracias."

He walked over to the girl's spot, and quietly sat down on the lounger next to Lucy. He looked at Vivian and gave a thumbs up. She waved back.

"Well, there you have it. The two shade seekers. Let's do this!" Jon unbuckled his life jacket. "Have either of you ridden on a jet ski?"

"I rode one once many moons ago," Wendy said. "It's like riding a bike, but Jon, is someone besides you and Pierre allowed to operate this? Aren't there rules and waivers and stuff?"

"Nahhhh! This is Mexico-ola!"

Wendy conceded and took the key.

Jon held out his life jacket as if it were a coat and offered it to Vivian. She stuck her arms in, a little nervous about getting on a jet ski with a stranger, and such a good-looking one at that. She clasped from the bottom but ran into a little (big) problem once she hit the DDs.

"The strap release will give you more room," Jon said, grinning and pointing to it.

"Gotcha," Vivian said and tugged for more strap, then got clicked in.

Wendy gave Pierre's life jacket to Kate. "Since I'm doin' the driving, you're more likely to fall off." Kate put it on without comment, though she had the opposite problem as Vivian when she clasped the top.

Jon helped Wendy and Kate get on the jet ski then pushed them into deeper water. Wendy revved up the machine and took off, giving a "yeeeehawwww" as she pulled away.

Jon got on the other jet ski and helped Vivian on behind him. She wasn't quite sure where to put her hands.

He sensed her hesitation and turned to face her. "Put your arms around my waist." He pushed the jet ski back form the beach. "And hang on tight. I'm pushing this baby full throttle-ola!"

8

Jon gunned the engine which raised the nose of the jet ski and he slid back into Vivian. She held on for dear life. Eventually they leveled out and her nerves began to settle. She unclenched her fists, opened her hands and felt his stomach. His muscles tightened when they were about to hit a wave, and she hoped it wasn't obvious she was enjoying it so much.

They flew along the coast, jumping waves and careening side to side. Jon let off the gas a bit and pointed out the hot spots in Playa.

"The hotel over there is the Yellow Dragonfly," he looked back over his shoulder and said. "It's super-trendy. The place to be seen on the Playa scene. The bar next door is the Purple Peacock, one of the best in Playa. You totally have to go there."

God, he feels good. Vivian tried to concentrate on what he was saying, but it wasn't easy. Her hands hadn't touched another man since Rick, who was a little doughy around the middle. His idea of a workout was punching the buttons on a remote control. She was glad she started anew with Jon. Rather than drinkin' a six pack, he sported one. Plus, he had soft skin and not a lot of hair. Rick was no Sasquatch, but Jon was different from what she was accustomed to.

Wendy and Kate pulled up next to them, then zoomed off. Kate looked terrified as Wendy cranked the engine and sought waves to propel into.

Jon glanced at a timer attached to the jet ski, turned his head to Vivian and said they better head back. He waved to Wendy to follow and flipped a 180.

Vivian took a moment to look out into the turquoise water. A sailboat dotted the horizon, but not much else. The jet ski noise seemed to fade into the background, and she felt overwhelmed by the emptiness of the ocean. Jon softly touched her hand that was still around his waist.

They pulled into a section of beach with half a dozen jet skis lined up, waiting for takers. A guy ran into the water to meet them. Jon hopped off and took Vivian's hand while she swung her leg over the seat and got off. Her legs shook as she stood up. *Is it from the vibration of the jet ski or my nerves?*

Jon also helped Wendy and Kate. *How polite is he?* She lived 10 years with someone lacking chivalry; which had dimmed her expectations.

Wendy and Kate walked over to Vivian with giant smiles on their faces. Jon shook hands with the vendor guy and said, "*gracias-ola.*" The guy gave him a weird look. Jon turned and walked over to the girls.

He reached towards Vivian's breasts and unbuckled the top clasp of her life jacket, startling her.

"As fashionable as this makes you look, we have to give it back."

"Oh, of course!" she laughed, and quickly unbuckled the other clasps. He helped her shrug out of the life jacket and gave it to the guy. Kate handed the other to him, too.

Jon smiled at the three of them. "Ladies, we'll have to walk to La Vida de Playa from here. It's not far, though."

"Thanks for sharing the jet ski," Kate said. "That was fun!"

"I dunno," Vivian said. "When I looked at you, you looked petrified."

"I had to get used to it," Kate said. "Usually I psyche myself up for stuff like that. We just jumped on and went! Plus, we all know Wendy drives like a bat out of hell. Who knew what she'd do with a jet ski!"

"Yeah, yeah," Wendy grinned. "I love speed, what can I say? You liked it, though."

"And what about you, Vivian, did you enjoy yourself-ola?" Jon asked, grinning as he touched her elbow.

She realized she needed to speak but felt breathless. *Who knew an elbow had so many nerve endings?* She managed to nod her head.

I've got to pull myself together.

As they walked down the beach there was a bit of an awkward silence. Wendy broke it.

"So where are y'all from?" she asked him.

"Well we know where *y'all* are from, don't we?" Jon said jokingly. "Tell me, seriously though," he paused dramatically. "Who shot J.R.?"

"Ha ha, funny man," Vivian said. "I could tell ya, but I'd have to kill ya!"

"Yep, it's an ancient Texas secret," Wendy said.

"Ah, yes, the Lone Star State! Not surprised. Texas has *the* most beautiful women. Where's that big Texas hair I hear about, though?"

Kate did an exaggerated fluff of her hair. "We only pull that out for special occasions," she joked.

"I see. Pierre and I are from Montreal. He is actually from Edmonton but moved to my neighborhood in high school."

Vivian sucked at geography, so though she did know where Canada was, she didn't know where to find either of those cities on a map. They were both above the Red River, so she thought of them as 'up there' somewhere.

"So how long have y'all been in Playa?" Wendy asked. "You don't have a tan yet, so not very long, huh?"

"Let me think," Jon said. "We've been here about a month-ola now."

"Wow, really? I'd have thought you'd have a deep, golden tropical tan by now. Or at least be sunburned."

"I can't afford to get burned. I'm an actor. Have to keep my look consistent, you know?"

"Wow! Have you been in anything we might have seen?" Kate asked.

"Not yet. I've done some commercial work in the U.S., and I just finished a soap opera, but it only aired in Canada."

Vivian was finally able to speak without choking on her words. "What do you mean, finished? I thought those things went on forever."

Jon suddenly pulled Vivian toward him and she gasped. He pointed to a piece of broken glass in her way. "Look out there."

He stopped to pick it up, then continued. "I just finished up a five year contract and was written off the show."

"Oh, man, I'm sorry. That sucks," Vivian said.

He waved off the comment. "No, it's good. They wanted me to stay on, but I've been wanting to branch out. Maybe try to get into film."

"I've seen people written back into soap operas who you thought were long gone," Kate said. "They can bring you back any time. Even years later!"

"How'd they get rid of you?" Vivian asked. "Did you get blown to smithereens or something?"

"In fact, yes, I was!" he said. "I was in a horrible explosion that wiped out a city block, including my house. My wife and baby lived, though. Guess it's bad to kill off kids," he joked. "My agent already has something new in the works."

"Oh, you need to get a movie part so you can be on Ellen!" Wendy said, who watched The Ellen DeGeneres Show every day.

"Wendy is addicted to Ellen," Vivian said with a laugh. "And hey, if you aren't upset about the soap giving you the boot, then neither are we."

"I'm not," he said with a wide smile. His brown eyes held Vivian's gaze while they walked. "If I hadn't been written off I wouldn't have been able to take this much-needed vacation, and look what I would have missed."

Her heart pounded and her mouth felt dry. She glanced down at the waves licking her toes to break the moment.

"I feel like we're in a soap opera right now," Kate whispered to Vivian.

They were near the hotel and saw Manuel digging an umbrella hole for some new arrivals.

"There's Lucy, still safely tucked under the umbrella," Wendy said.

"Yep," Jon said. "And Pierre is trying hard to share the shade. Is he wearing a bucket on his head?"

They all looked harder.

Pierre saw them and gave a wave.

"Looks like he hijacked her headwear, all right," Wendy said. "Nice look."

"I'm parched," Vivian said. "I'll go get us a round. We've gotta toast to new and improved opportunities for Jon."

"I second that," he said and reached his arm around her back and led her toward the bar. "Vivian and I will be back in a jiffy."

The touch of his hand on the small of her back sent tingles to great places south of the border.

She took a deep breath.

I may be in trouble...-ola.

9

Jon and Vivian went to the bar while Wendy and Kate went back to their spot on the beach. He ordered a round of shots for all and bottles of water. The bartender told them he would have them delivered. Jon said to put it on his room and they walked back toward the others.

"So you have a soap opera wife, huh," Vivian said, "but no real one?"

"Nope, never been married-ola. That's another thing I want to change. I feel like I haven't done a good job of balancing my social life with my work life. I've had girlfriends, but things just haven't worked out. The feelings always died off."

"Relationships can be tough," Vivian said with a sigh.

They got back to their spot and Jon excused himself. Lucy had eventually woken up so Pierre introduced himself and let her know about the impromptu jet ski excursion. She offered him her bucket since his head had turned a bright shade of pink.

"Sounds like y'all had fun," Lucy said. "I'm sorry I missed it. However, I'm thinking a bunch of alcohol splashing around in my stomach may have had some bad consequences."

Vivian agreed with her logic.

Lucy looked to her left at Pierre. "Scoot over here, Pierre. I want to look at your other arm. Did I see a tattoo?"

"Yes you did." He swung his legs off the lounger and showed her his left arm. "I've had it for about six years, I guess."

Lucy sat up and moved her legs next to his. She ran her fingertips over his arm, a little flirtatiously, Vivian thought.

"I've never seen anything quite like that. What is it?" she asked.

"It's Celtic in origin," Pierre explained. "I had it drawn up in Canada. Took several sessions to get it all finished."

"I love it. It's so vivid and unusual."

The center was a deep forest green with three black, curved prongs that jutted out and wrapped around themselves. The outside edges were blue, which made the prongs look like branches, but also kinda like wings. *Groovy*, Vivian thought.

Kate weighed in. "I didn't know you liked tattoos, Lucy."

"Sure. My dad had one," Lucy said. "It's no big deal."

None of the girls had ink.

Their shots arrived at the same time Jon reappeared. He carried a towel and wore a parrot blue and green tropical shirt with hula girls dancing all over it. *Festive.*

"You don't mind if I crash your spot, too, do you?"

"Nope," Vivian said. "The more, the merrier!"

They grabbed the shots and held them up.

"To new friends and new opportunities," Vivian offered.

Jon looked at her and clinked his shot glass to hers.

"To new friends," he repeated, and slammed back his shot and sucked on the lime.

"Whew!" He yelled and grabbed a bottle of water. "Now, about that sandcastle I so rudely destroyed…"

"Oh, I had forgotten! Yes, I guess you do owe me big-time for annihilating my masterpiece," Vivian teased. "It was going to be featured in *Architectural Digest* for its masterful design and modern features."

Kate gawked at that.

"Well, I'm not sure I can top that, but I'll lend some sandcastle-building expertise that I developed as a child," he said and reached for Vivian's hand to help her to her feet.

She tried hard to feel light as a feather as he pulled her up off the lounger.

They walked down to the water, leaving the others behind. Vivian felt the girls' eyes on her.

They picked a spot not in jeopardy of too much wave splashage but close enough to fill the moat.

Jon crouched down and pushed sand into the pile. "I have to warn you, it's been a good 20-plus years since I built a sandcastle."

"What? Just a few moments ago you were touting your expertise."

"I may have been exaggerating a little, you know, to impress your friends."

"I have more recent experience, so no worries." Vivian got down on her knees, and tried to suck in her tummy as she helped with construction. Her hair fell into her eyes in total curly chaotic mess. The jet skiing had taken its toll. She tried to push it out of her face, which just added sand to the curls. *Great. This looking good business is hard work.*

"So you know a little about me and my love life, or lack thereof. What about you?" He asked.

Vivian prepared for his immediate departure after she disclosed her screwed-up situation. She had to do it, though. Honesty being the best policy and all that crap.

"The truth is, Jon, I'm going to be adding to the divorce statistic in about a week or so. It's one of the reasons we're on this trip."

"Wow, sorry to hear that. How long were you married?"

"Almost five years."

"Geez… That sucks-ola. Are you okay?"

"It's still pretty fresh. I certainly didn't see it coming. My friends and family are super supportive, so that helps. In fact, the instant Lucy, Wendy and Kate found out about it they booked this trip. Look at me now!"

Jon moved over and gave her a shoulder-to-shoulder sandy hug. "Look at you now, indeed! I have a feeling you're going to make a full recovery."

He let go and got back to sandcastling. "You said that's one of the reasons you're on this trip. What are the others?"

"Well, for us girls to get together, of course."

She packed sand into a mountainous shape. *So much for architectural wonders.*

"And," she hesitated. "It's my birthday."

"Your birthday! Is today your actual birthday?"

"Yep. Today's the big day," Vivian said unenthusiastically.

"This is colossal! Happy birthday, Vivian!" He gave her another sandy shoulder hug but happier this time.

"This calls for a celebration! You cowgirls must meet Pierre and me tonight at the Purple Peacock. Do you remember me showing it to you when we were on the jet ski? You'll love it! And I'm sure your birthday will cause quite the stir. What do you say?"

Jon looked at Vivian with eyes that took her breath away. She tried to control her excitement when she responded.

"I'll talk to the girls, but I don't see why not. Sounds like…fun!"

Vivian dug a tunnel through the mountain. Jon scooted around to the other side and started a tunnel over there.

"Ouch!" Vivian felt a sharp pain in her hand. She looked down and pulled a broken piece of shell out of her palm. Blood trickled out slowly and slid around the sand on her hand.

"What happened," Jon asked, looking at her.

"Just got a little cut. It's fine."

"I'll be right back," he said, and in an instant jogged off toward the hotel.

A wave crept close enough for her to rinse off the blood. The cut stung

43

from the salt water. She took a closer look at the shells on the beach. Many of them were larger than the size of her hand and looked sharp as daggers. *Someone could get seriously hurt with one of these*, she thought. *I'll have to remind the girls to be careful walking in the water.*

A couple of minutes passed before Jon came back with an antiseptic wipe and a Band-Aid.

"Let's get you fixed up."

His hands were sand-free, so he must have washed them inside. He opened the antiseptic wipe and placed it on her palm. "This may hurt a bit."

Vivian flinched as the antiseptic did its job.

He wiped it a little more, then removed it and lifted her hand towards his mouth. He blew on it gently.

"You seem like you've done this before." Vivian felt a tingling sensation that started at her palm and extended to other areas.

"Well, I'm not a doctor, but I've played one on TV," he joked.

He opened the Band-Aid and placed it on her palm, tenderly ensuring the edges were down and sealed.

"I think you're going to survive, ma'am."

"Why thank you, doctor."

He stood and put the wrappings in his pocket and sat back down on his side of the sand mountain.

"This is something," Jon said and smiled at her from across the sandcastle. "Maybe this trip will be the start of new opportunities for both of us. I've got a good feeling."

"I have to admit, I'm kinda glad you obliterated my first sandcastle," Vivian confessed as she resumed digging with her unbandaged hand.

Their fingers touched as they reach each other within the formation. He interlocked his fingers with hers.

I may be in heaven.

"We have connected-ola!" he shouted. "The tunnel is complete!"

As soon as he said this, the whole structure crashed down on their forearms.

"Uh oh. We may not get into *Architectural Digest* after all," he said and tried to pull his arm out.

"I have a feeling Kate would hog my opportunity to make *Architectural Digest* anyway." Vivian laughed as she tried to free her arm.

They both tugged free and fell back, covered in sand. Wendy walked up and snapped a picture of them recovering from the collapse of the tunnel-free sandcastle.

"This was fun, Vivian. I should build sandcastles more often." He reached over and attempted to wipe sand off her face, but only added more.

"You just be sure to let me help if you do."

"I wouldn't dream of building one without you."

That totally sounds like a line from a soap opera, but honestly, I don't freakin' care!

10

J on and Vivian rinsed their sandy selves off in the surf, then walked back up the beach where their friends were having a good time. Lucy giggled at something Pierre said.

Uh oh, she's drunk and flirting, Vivian thought.

Jon looked at Pierre and pointed to his legs. "You're starting to resemble a lobster. You ready to call it an afternoon?"

"I'm done with the sun for today, but I am glad to have met you ladies," Pierre looked directly at Lucy as he said this. "I hope we see you soon."

They grabbed their stuff and turned to leave. "*Adiós*-ola," Jon called as he walked away. "And don't forget the Purple Peacock." He gave a final wave before they disappeared into the hotel.

Lucy pounced on Vivian's lounger. "Holy fuckbuckets, Viv! That guy is awesome! He's a total hottie, and Kate told me about the glass! How sweet!"

"What glass?"

"The glass he saved your poor little tootsies from on the beach, and then picked up and threw away! How dreamy," she said, then clutched her hands together under her chin and batted her eyes dramatically.

Vivian gave her a gentle push. "Oh, I had forgotten. Yeah, that was nice."

"And the sandcastle," Lucy said. "He helped you build one to replace the one he destroyed. Very nice."

"Not sure we could call it an official sandcastle, but it was fun building it. Our hands intermingled in the middle."

"Freakin' awesome!" Lucy exclaimed. "And he's my color."

"He is *definitely* on the lower end of the pale scale, but I can accept it," Vivian said. "Like I accept you."

Lucy gave Vivian's shoulder a push and got back on her lounger.

Wendy seemed impressed with Jon as well. "He practically swept you off your feet to get you to the jet ski and he was totally ogling your boobs when he helped you take off your life jacket. He's love-struck baby!"

Vivian's connection with Austin made her sing "Love Struck Baby" by Stevie Ray Vaughn. *Damn that's an awesome song.*

"Holy crap, she's love-struck too!" Kate shouted.

"I am not! She just made me think of that song." Vivian flipped over on her lounger so they couldn't see her face.

"You are a *liar* Vivian Taylor," Wendy said. "L-I-A-R."

"What's this about a peacock?" Lucy asked.

"Oh, he invited us to a place down the beach called the Purple Peacock, to help celebrate my smurfday."

"I bet he wants to lay a big birthday kiss on you!" Kate said.

Vivian ignored her, settled in and pulled the towel up over her eyes. "I told him we'd stop by after dinner."

"Yeah, for dessert." Lucy teased.

They were all quiet for a while. The waves rolled hypnotically. Vivian sighed and eventually made it to a semi-conscious, la-la-land place, but then heard a voice.

"*Hola.* Look, look."

Vivian blinked, getting use to the sunlight and saw an older local lady had walked up with a large wrap slung over her shoulder. The wrap the small woman carried was so full of stuff it looked like it weighed more than she did. She plopped it down in front of them and began to show off the contents — an array of Mexican jewelry, shells and hand-stitched Mayan calendars.

Vivian could tell by the sparkle in Wendy's eyes that she absolutely loved the calendars. She picked up one. "How much?"

Let the haggling begin!

After going back and forth a few times, Wendy pulled some money out of her bag. The rest of the girls said no thanks, but then the woman offered to braid their hair.

"I make you beautiful," she said.

If there was anything white girls shouldn't do, it was braid their hair into little rows. A sunburn on the scalp will eventually peel and look like dandruff. *No bueño!*

They politely declined the hair braiding and the lady moved on down the beach, attempting to sell her wares to the other tourists.

Vivian looked at her watch and asked the girls if they were ready to roll, which they were. The sun sat low over the water, and they needed something besides tequila, beer and a snack. They gathered up their stuff and traipsed through the sand toward the lobby.

They ran into Manuel coming out of the lobby and not knowing where to go for an authentic Mexican dinner, they asked him. He suggested a restaurant down from the hotel called Rico's Cantina. As he walked off in the direction of the beach, he turned back and said to them, "Stay in tourist place only. *Muchos banditos.*" With that he continued on his way.

"That was ominous," Wendy said under her breath.

"I don't want to meet any bandits," Lucy said.

"We'll stick to the main parts of town and we'll be fine," Vivian said, brushing off the warning.

"Hmmm," was Kate's only comment.

Back in their room, Vivian got de-sanded and showered pretty quickly, a skill she had acquired since having four children and needing to savor every moment of sleep she could get. While she waited for the girls, she stepped out on the balcony to air-dry her blonde curls and read. The ocean breeze felt fantastic, and the setting sun reflected off the water in pinks and oranges. She took a deep breath and smiled inside and out. *Looks like a freakin' postcard!*

Vivian deposited herself into a chair and put her feet up on the railing. She opened her book and took in a few chapters while she waited. The sliding glass door opened and the girls stepped out, each of them bearing gifts.

"Happy birthday, Viv!" they chimed.

They surprised her. "Y'all are crazy."

Lucy handed Vivian a small box wrapped in white paper with sexy, crimson high-heeled shoes all over it.

She opened the box to reveal a beautiful red rosebud and a membership to a flower of the month club from a Fort Worth florist. *How cool!*

"You go in once a month with this card and they'll give you their flower-of-the-month bouquet," Lucy said. "I thought you could either take to the office to spruce up your desk, or take 'em home and enjoy with the kiddos."

"You're the best, Lucy!"

Wendy handed Vivian a small, hot-pink bag containing a gift card to her all-time favorite happy hour spot, The Keg.

"I can taste the orange slices now!"

Next, Kate put a beautiful, red-velvet jewelry box in Vivian's hand.

"I half expect you to be on bended knee!"

"Ha ha…just open it up."

Inside the box were the most beautiful turquoise earrings Vivian had ever seen, beads of turquoise interspersed with silver, hanging in swirls.

"I love them, Kate! Thank you all so much! Y'all are the best friends ever!" Vivian stood up to give them a group hug but they stopped her.

"Hold your horses there, Viv, we have one more thing to give you," Wendy said and handed Vivian an envelope. "It's from all of us."

Vivian popped the glue on the envelope, and inside found a fake airline boarding pass. *What the heck?*

"It's for our next trip, Viv. Wherever we go on our next girlfriend getaway, we're buying your plane ticket."

"No way. Y'all have already done more than enough."

"We know," Lucy said, winking. "We just want to do this one more thing for you. Our trip is going to be amazing, and we're already gearing up for the next one. These girlfriend getaways are going to become an annual event. Maybe even semi-annual!"

"Y'all are too much! Thank you!"

They all embraced in a great, big group hug. *I love my friends!* Vivian thought.

Lucy broke from the hug first. "Now let's go get this birthday bash buzzin'!"

"Amen to that," Vivian said. "Wild Texas women on the town tonight. Watch out!"

11

The girls headed out the door for Rico's looking fabulous. Vivian wore a turquoise and green sundress, very flowy and strappy. Throw in her new earrings from Kate and it was what she dubbed "perfectly Playa."

Lucy wore a sexy strapless number, tight tight tight up top that flared out around the waist and was extremely flattering.

Kate, who looked great in anything, had on a black and white paisley dress with a goddess-style empire waist. It accented her boobs and her slim waist, yet was still elegant and classy. Classic Kate.

Wendy wore an orangey-pink dress, not cut too low, but not too reserved, that showed off her curves and ended just above her knee.

They completed their look with cute sandals, except for Lucy, who prided herself on her strappy FMPs. The girls warned her she would regret wearing those at some point that night.

"Hey, I brought eight pairs of sexy shoes, and I plan on wearing all of them on this trip," she said.

They got directions to Rico's from the front desk and made their way there. Vivian didn't think it looked like much from the outside.

"I don't know about this place," Lucy said. "I don't want food poisoning."

"Manuel recommended it. I'm sure it's fine," Wendy said. "Lots of good places look like dives. Let's go in and see what it's like."

The beach front restaurant had steel and glass garage doors that lined three sides of the long narrow room and opened to the view. The floor was covered in sand so that the line between the interior and exterior blurred. It could have been a converted car repair garage, but it perfectly transformed for dining al fresco. The mid-seventies temperature and breeze ensured open doors.

The restaurant had maybe 20 tables. Most of them were full, which was a good sign about the food. The décor was right on with bright blue-green walls that displayed ceramic suns, iguanas and turtles. Mexican blankets hung in the windows as drapes, and multicolored lights hung from the ceiling.

Vivian pointed out the lights to the girls as they waited for their table. "I love those little lights. I think I'll get some and hang them around the freshly painted deck back home. Recreate a mini-Playa."

"Freshly painted deck?" Kate asked.

"Oh yeah," Vivian answered. "Since I realized Rick wasn't coming back I've been a painting and project fool. I've done all the little things, and some big ones, that have needed attention for years. I've painted the living room, kitchen, hall, my bedroom and the deck. I have also planted shrubs and flowers, cut tree limbs and hung new lighting."

"Wow!" Wendy exclaimed. "You go girl."

"Rick never did squat around the house," Vivian explained. "I take that back, he did rebuild the fence he drove through four years ago. Instead a of do-it-yourselfer, he was a don't-do-it-at-all kind of guy. Plus, he never helped around the house unless I begged him, and even then he'd screw it up. Like, if he loaded the dishwasher, something came out warped, melted, broken, or otherwise unusable."

"His way of getting out of chores?" Wendy asked.

"You got it! And let me tell ya about my bedroom, it's *bright* red now. My therapist called it an 'angry red.' Ya think?"

As she painted her red room she did freak out a little. She had one full wall painted and was about to lay the roller on wall two when she had to call Lucy. Vivian would never forget what she said.

"Girl, the day of the accent wall is over. Keep painting."

So she did. She decided she loved it, but it was a dramatic change, and a little bit shocking the first few mornings.

The hostess seated the girls at a nice spot near the beach-front patio railing. Their waitress, Lizbeth, who looked all of 16 to Vivian, greeted them warmly and asked what they'd like to drink.

Lucy giggled and said, "Round of tequila shots!" She only sobered up a tad during the hour it took them to get ready.

"No way," Wendy said. "None of us needs another one of those. How about bottles of water for everyone and a pitcher of margaritas?"

Lizbeth suggested margaritas with Tiempo Loco tequila, they agreed.

"Lucy, what's with all the tequila shots?" Vivian asked as Lizbeth walked off. "I've never seen you drink like this, except for the one time with the blue spew, and that was only because you wanted to do the nasty with Larry."

"Lars!"

"Whatever!"

51

Lucy shook her head. "I know, I know. I just feel like I need to get a little crazy! Let loose a little, you know," she said. "Things with Steve have been tough, and although he's been very patient with me I don't know if I — if we — are gonna make it."

"What do you mean, 'make it'?" Kate asked.

"Yeah, I thought the counseling was helping," Vivian said.

"It is, I guess. I just think Steve has put the ball in my court now, and honestly, I'm just not sure I want to play anymore."

"I know, Lucy, but Steve *loves* you," Vivian said. "He would do anything for you. Do you still love him? I think that's the question."

"You know I do."

"Well, what is it then? Bad sex? That would definitely be a problem. I have high sexpectations!"

"At least bad sex would be sex."

"What are you talking about?"

"There is *no* sex. Hasn't been for years."

Lucy's words made Vivian hurt inside and she almost fell out of her chair.

Lizbeth arrived with a pitcher, put down four glasses and unloaded chips and salsa from a tray. Wendy filled them each a glass and passed them out. They waited for Lizbeth to leave before continuing their conversation.

Vivian repositioned herself in her seat to face Lucy. "Okay, I'm not sure I understand you. What do you mean there is *no* sex?"

"We haven't had sex in probably four years." Lucy looked down at the table, then took a gulp of her margarita. "It's been a rocky, rocky road. Some real highs but some real lows. I'm just not sure I can recover from the lows." Another big gulp.

"Okay, but everybody goes through bad times, Lucy. But no sex for years? Do y'all, uhhmmm, do other things for each other?"

"Negative. Nada," she said. "No intimacy. It's horrible."

"I can't believe you've never told us," Kate said.

"I know, but it's embarrassing and hard to talk about."

"You can talk to us about anything though," Vivian said.

"I know that, but we've been living a lie. Everyone thinks our marriage is perfect. It's so not."

"I can't believe this," Wendy said. "You look fantastic! Better than you have in years! How could he not want to jump your bones?"

Lucy had dropped nearly half of her body weight in the past two years and had become a workout fanatic. She had the body to prove it.

"I dunno, but he doesn't," Lucy said, as she finished her first cocktail and reached for the pitcher. "I've worked really hard for my new body, and I'm getting attention from men that I haven't had in a long time. It makes me think he doesn't appreciate all the work I've done. I mean, I've worked my ass off, literally, to look like this," she said as she ran her hands down either side of her.

"I know you have, Wonkita," Vivian said. "You look freakin' fantastic. Not to mention, you put all of us to shame in terms of physical fitness."

Nods all around.

"But you need to make the decision that will make you happiest," Kate said.

"Obviously we support any decision you make," Wendy added. "And we're totally here for you, whatever you need. For the moment, though, we need you to be able to walk tonight." She pulled Lucy's drink back two inches. "Also, drink some water and take some aspirin before bed or tomorrow is going to be really rough."

"At this point I'm not sure what I'm going to do. Thanks though. Talking helped."

At least we know a little more about why she's behaving this way.

Rico's turned out to be just what they all needed. Delicious guacamole, sizzling shrimp fajitas, spicy salsa, and the homemade tortillas — *holy cow*, Vivian thought. They were better than the Don'Key in the Get Down, and those were *good*.

The service was on "Playa time." They weren't in a rush, but it took some getting used to. If they wanted something in 10 minutes, they better have asked for it 10 minutes ago.

They finished dinner and walked out onto the streets of Playa, heading toward the Purple Peacock to meet Jon and Pierre. Lucy walked a little straighter having sobered up a bit.

Is it due to her tough revelation about her lacking relationship or our lack of shots at dinner? Vivian didn't know.

12

The streets of Playa hustled and bustled with vendors haggling and selling all kinds of stuff — jewelry, blankets, trinkets and t-shirts. A few men offered the girls "free massages." *Gross*, Vivian thought.

They browsed the shops but made no purchases. Plenty of time for that later. They reached the Purple Peacock after a few short blocks.

"How are your feet, Lucy?" Kate asked opening the door.

"So far, so good."

The bar was open on three sides, and, like at Rico's, garage doors could be pulled down if the weather sucked. Picnic tables on the beach surrounded a small stage and looked inviting. Neon signs obliterated one wall, and a large cast-iron peacock sat in a place of honor on a table by the front door.

All this peacock stuff reminded Vivian of a guy they went to school with, Marty Mills. His nickname was The Bird Man. He was way into birds of all kinds, and he even kinda looked like a bird. He was tall, thin with a small head, long neck and pointy nose. Plus, he could do spot-on bird calls, which he would occasionally demonstrate in class. Always a good distraction, though he got in trouble for it. In junior high he had a pair of peacocks in his back yard. Not your average house pet. Vivian heard he was a gazillionaire now. *Good for him.*

The huge, square bar in the middle of the club was the main attraction in the Purple Peacock. The wooden bar top matched the wooden seats on the swings. That's right, they didn't have stools at the counter, they had swings, as in playground swings. Some of the swings were double seats. Vivian was afraid the swing situation wouldn't help Lucy's equilibrium. However, it looked fun and they couldn't resist.

They looked around for Jon and Pierre but didn't see them, so they found four spots of singles together and had a seat. Actually, a swing.

The bartender hustled over, took their drink order and suggested Tiempo Loco tequila to their margarita request.

What's with this tequila? Sure it's good, but why does everyone keep recommending it?

"He is hunkalicious," Lucy said. "I may need to find myself a Latin lover!"

"Lucy! You wouldn't!" Kate exclaimed.

"No comment," Lucy said with a sly smile, but then continued. "Don't forget, I haven't had sex in four years."

None of them said anything to that.

Their drinks arrived and they toasted to their first night in Playa.

"It's gonna kick ass!" Wendy proclaimed.

They chatted about what happened with Jon during the sandcastle building.

"Oh my god, Viv, he so totally digs you!" Lucy said. "Even after you told him you're still technically married."

"Did you tell him about the kids?" Wendy asked.

"No, it didn't come up. I probably should have, but it doesn't matter. The man lives in Canada. It's not like he's thinking long term here."

"You should tell him, just in case this is a 'love at first sight' kind of thing," Kate said. "You never know."

"Yeah, well, he may choose to look again," Vivian said.

"I think he'll keep lookin' at you, Viv. Definitely," Wendy said.

"Bathroom break for me. Anyone else need to go?" Lucy asked.

"I do," Wendy replied and twisted her swing to get up.

Off they went.

Vivian sipped on her margarita as she swung in the swing. It took talent to stay on the swing with an arm wrapped around the rope and sip a drink at the same time. Vivian had that talent and managed without any mishaps.

"Wonder where Jon and Pierre are?" Kate asked and looked around.

"Dunno. I'm sure they'll show up soon. He was right, though, this place is rockin'."

"Pretty original with the swings. I've never seen anything like it," Kate said, as she used her feet to push herself back from the bar.

"We better keep an eye on Lucy in here," Vivian said. "These could bring out her less graceful side."

"Yeah, she's such a klutz," Kate said. "Remember the time she tripped over the concrete parking block in seventh grade?"

Vivian laughed as she thought about it. "The first of many Lucy moments." She could still see the scene as if they were 13 years old and it just happened. "I realize she was pushing the xylophone across the school parking lot and her view was impeded, I just don't know how she missed the bright yellow, six foot concrete block."

"Thank goodness for the guy wearing the snare drum who saved the xylophone from death and destruction. Mr. Quinn would have had a conniption." Kate paused a second. "What was that guy's name?"

"Hmmm…Brad, no. Patrick, no. Michael…" They still pondered the long-ago drummer's name when Wendy and Lucy rejoined them.

"Guess who we just saw?" Wendy teased as she slipped back into her swing.

"Jon?" Vivian asked.

"He's outside with Pierre and a really short Hispanic dude with a hot temper and two hot mamas," Wendy said.

"What? Who?" Vivian asked.

"Some guy walked by their table and glanced at the short guy's ladies. Shorty pointed his fingers at the guy, like they were a gun," Lucy explained. "And he pulled the trigger."

"That's odd" Kate said.

"Yeah, I guess he's a little over-protective," Lucy said, then continued, "and when Kate said the guy is short, she means short. He's the same height standing as Jon sitting. And I can say that because I'm short!"

"His height and his temper must not be affecting his lady action, because he's got a girl for each arm," Wendy said.

"Did Jon see you?" Vivian asked.

"Yeah, he did," Lucy said. "He waved to us and gave us the 'I'll be in in a minute' finger."

Vivian giggled.

"What?" Lucy asked.

"He gave y'all the finger."

The girls chatted as they swung to the beat of Selena's "Dreaming of You." They were in band, after all. Their high school band director, Mr. Cullen, would be proud.

Jon and Pierre looked extra-illuminated once they came inside, and Vivian wondered if they planned to spend more time on the beach getting sun, even though Jon wasn't supposed to because of his career.

Jon saw Vivian immediately and, being a friendly Texas girl, she gave him a wave and a wink.

He came over and hugged her. "You look beautiful birthday girl."

She blushed and smiled.

Pierre walked over to Lucy and pointed to the empty swing next to her. "Is this swing spoken for?"

"Swing away," she said.

Jon ordered the six of them a round of margaritas and Lucy announced to the bartender, and everyone within earshot, that it was Vivian's birthday. She got congratulations and "woo hoos" from the crowd in the bar. The bartender leaned over the bar and said, "I have something special planned for you later."

Double woo hoo, Vivian thought.

Jon sat down next to Vivian.

"So what do you think of the Peacock-ola?" he asked.

"Pretty cool," Vivian said and took a well-timed sip of her margarita as she swung forward. "The swings are a fun touch."

"Yeah, but they could be dicey if you sit here too long and take too many shots," he said.

"Oh, do you know this from experience?"

"Well, not my own, but I did see someone take a swinging spill about three nights ago. The benefit of having the alcohol, though, is you won't feel it 'til morning!"

"I hear ya!"

The bartender set down six shots of tequila, Tiempo Loco he said, and handed Vivian the limes.

"I didn't order these." Vivian said.

"Oh, I did it on the sly," Jon said. "You've gotta do a birthday shot. It's a law in Mexico."

"Oh really…" Vivian said reluctantly. She liked tequila in drinks but not necessarily by itself with salt and lime. "I'm not sure how many of these I can take today. I've already had a couple."

"Well, if you don't want the whole thing, just pass it over to me. I'm not afraid of your germs," he replied with a smile. He picked up his shot glass and held it out for a toast.

He stood up and said loudly, "To the beautiful birthday girl, Vivian, on her 30th birthday-ola. May this next year bring you trust, lust and an opportunity for me to get a better view of your bust."

That got a big laugh from everyone, who all had a hard time shooting their shot. Jon couldn't even take his because he was too busy saying, "I'm just kidding, I'm just kidding. There were only so many things that rhymed with trust."

Still grinning at Vivian, he licked the salt, shot the tequila and sucked on the lime. Vivian took a deep breath, decided to go for it, and took the whole shot. She didn't want to look like a wuss. She crinkled her nose afterward and felt the burn of the tequila go down her throat.

"What brings y'all to Playa?" Lucy asked Pierre.

"Jon needed a relaxing holiday. A month or so in Mexico fit the bill," Pierre said.

"I wish Americans would adopt the same vacation policy," Vivian butted in, wanting them to know she was listening. She had just realized Lucy was not wearing her wedding ring.

Lucy ignored Vivian. "A month? I'm jealous! My clients are so high maintenance, a delay in their upholstery order is considered an emergency of epic proportions."

Lucy was an interior designer in Denver and worked with extremely wealthy (a.k.a. spoiled), clients. They were very demanding. Her OCD made the challenge of accommodating such people almost a game to her. She got paid well to deal with them, though, and she enjoyed her work. Lucy had an amazing eye for detail and a fantastic sense of style, and Vivian thought one day she would be featured on some home designing magazine or show.

"Yeah, you Americans work too much," Pierre said. "You've got to take a break here and there."

"Speaking of breaks, I need a restroom break," Kate said. "Be back in a few." She slid gracefully off her swing and disappeared around the corner.

Pierre continued, looking at Lucy. "You've got to learn to relax more. Maybe you'd like a nice massage?" He rubbed his hands together, like he was warming 'em up and ready to provide her a great service.

Vivian popped up off her swing. "Lucy's got a cush job. She's not stressed. If anyone deserves a massage it's me."

Lucy looked perturbed. Vivian could tell because a little wrinkle appeared between her eyes.

Pierre turned his swing towards Vivian. "Really, Viv? Are you stressed out?"

"Heck, yeah! Didn't Jon tell you I'm getting a divorce?"

Vivian felt a hand wrap around her waist.

"No, I did not tell him. It didn't seem important-ola," Jon said, looking down at her sincerely.

Suddenly a woman rushed up to Jon and cut the two of them off.

"Dominik! You're alive!"

13

I've been so upset thinking you were dead!" The lady said to Jon. "Where's Celeste and the baby? Are they here with you?" Her lip trembled and her eyes filled with tears.

Jon turned toward her. "Of course I'm alive, and my name is Jon, not Dominik."

Pierre groaned. "Thousands of miles from Canada and we run into a fan. Never fails."

Vivian, Lucy, Wendy and Pierre watched in bewilderment as Jon politely led the strange lady a few feet away. She had a small waist and a "Baby Got Back" booty. Her dark olive skin complimented her long, straight and shiny black hair. At first glance Vivian thought she was wearing green contacts. It was hard to tell for sure through the torrent of tears.

"What's your name?" Jon asked.

She stammered, "St St Stella. The explosion looked so horrible, how did you survive? I, I, I thought you were killed, but you don't look like you were hurt. I've been praying you would live." She grasped him in a tight hug.

Jon tried to pry her loose. "The explosion didn't happen in real-life. It was part of the script on the soap-opera."

Lucy gave Pierre a bewildered look. He looked at Vivian.

"I think we forgot to tell Lucy he's an actor."

Pierre explained. "Jon was on the most popular Canadian soap opera and his character was just killed off. Celeste was his TV wife, and they had just had a baby. In fact," Pierre changed his voice to sound like a TV announcer, "they narrowly escaped the clutches of death."

Lucy, Wendy and Vivian laughed.

Vivian asked Pierre, "Does this happen often, crazy fans coming up like this?"

"No, thank goodness," he said. "This one seems to be quite the nut-job. Clearly this lady doesn't know fact from fiction."

Vivian couldn't help but notice that Nutty's short-cropped shirt and low-cut shorts revealed a big, black spider tattoo on the small of her back. *Interesting choice.*

Jon walked back over and gave Pierre a look. "I'm so sorry, Vivian, but we're going to have to go. This one is just a bit much for me."

"It's okay. I understand," Vivian said, trying to sound upbeat, but she was disappointed.

Lucy put her arm around Vivian's shoulder. "No worries, we'll give her a birthday to remember."

Wendy seconded that.

"Maybe we'll see y'all tomorrow," Lucy said, flipping her hair flirtatiously. "We won't be around until later, but let's try to get together."

Pierre smiled.

"Yes, tomorrow," Jon said hesitantly and glanced sideways at the crazy woman who was only a few feet away.

Jon smiled at Vivian and slid 10,000 pesos across the bar to the bartender. "No change, but please get these ladies another drink." He kissed Vivian softly on the cheek, letting his lips linger. "Happy birthday, Vivian," he whispered into her ear.

He and Pierre then walked off toward the beach. He turned once more and waved. *"Adiós-ola!"*

The three girls waved and watched as Jon and Pierre went off in the direction of the hotel.

Vivian saw Jon glance at a short guy and give him a nod. *Must have been the guy Lucy and Wendy were talking about earlier.*

––––––––

Kate was washing her hands in the restroom when a lady came in in meltdown mode.

"Oh my gosh, are you okay?" Kate asked the woman. "Let me get you some tissue."

She went into one of the stalls, got some toilet paper and handed it to the lady.

"Are you okay?" Kate asked again. She looked at the woman whose mascara was smudged beyond repair. Her long, black hair stuck to her face compliments of the tears.

The lady blew her nose, then finally responded. "I can't believe it. I just saw a friend of mine," she paused and bursts into tears again.

"Well, that seems like a good thing," Kate said, wondering what the problem was.

"Yeah, but this person is supposed to be dead," she wailed.

"Wait, I'm confused," Kate said.

"He faked his death." The lady wiped her smudged mascara onto the toilet paper.

"Oh my gosh," Kate said, shocked. "Why would he do that?"

"I don't know. Maybe he was feeling overwhelmed because of the baby?"

"Oh my gosh, he has a baby?" Kate asked. "Well you've got to tell someone. That poor baby!"

"And a wife," the woman said with a scowl. "And here he is hanging all over that floozy."

"A floozy?" Kate asked. "What a jerk! You've got to tell his wife he's alive! And maybe even the police. I think what he's doing is illegal."

The lady immediately clammed up. "Not sure I can tell her."

"Why not?" Kate asked. "She needs to know her husband isn't dead and that he's hangin' all over floozies in Mexico!"

The woman pulled herself together and took a deep breath. "Yeah, I just may have to do that," she said and swiped under her eye one last time with the toilet paper. She threw the tissue in the trash and started out the door, then turned to Kate once more. "If I see him with that hussy again, I'm... I'm...I'm just gonna lose it!" She turned and stormed out.

"Well, good luck," Kate called after her.

Kate looked at herself in the mirror and shook her head. She fixed a few stray strands of hair, then returned to the girls who informed her that Jon had been accosted by a crazy fan and had to leave.

"Oh, that's too bad."

"Yes, but he gave Vivian a nice long peck on the cheek before he left," Wendy teased. "And got us another round."

That was deserving of a cheers so they clinked glasses together.

Kate decided a peck on the cheek would not suffice for Vivian's birthday. She conspired with Wendy and they decided what she needed was a full-on birthday smooch from the hottest guy in the bar. "To cheer her up since Jon left," was their excuse.

They had an interesting search through the bar.

Behind door number one they found a group of college guys who obviously had been there awhile. Though cute, they were too young and too drunk and were immediately ruled out.

Door number two opened to a lone guy who sat at a corner table and didn't look like he was there to have a good time. He had a ponytail, dark clothes and a scar on the left side of his face. He had a definite creep factor. Slam that door quick!

Door number three revealed two older hippies. They'd seen too much sun, too much weed and probably too many loose women. Slam that door too.

Door number four was a big relief. A nice-looking, clean-cut guy with great teeth and a dark tan. Definitely an eight on the pale scale. His name was Pasqual and he was visiting from Sweden. They knew Vivian would think he was quite the birthday present. He was the winner.

Wendy and Kate were proud of their find and introduced the birthday girl. By way of his introduction, Pasqual swooped Vivian off her swing, into his arms, and within milliseconds his lips were pressed to hers.

He is hot hot hot, Vivian thought as she kissed him back. *He's one of Sweden's finest.* Granted, she had never been to Sweden, but she thought he represented the country well. Tall, dark and handsome didn't begin to describe him. A few more kisses like this, and she could have herself a happy, happy birthday.

After what felt like an eternity (a freakin' fantastic eternity), Pasqual looked over at Wendy and Kate and asked, "Was that what you had in mind?"

Before they could respond, Lucy, who must have been in shock from witnessing the dynamic display, fell out of her swing, taking her margarita with her, and hit the floor. Her swing popped back and smacked her in the head.

Vivian, still dizzy, had started to breathe again when she realized Pasqual had already put her back into her swing and helped Lucy up. Wendy and Kate pointed and laughed at Lucy, clearly unable to assist. Vivian grabbed the camera and snapped a quick picture, yet another for her photo album. The caption would read "Don't Drink and Swing."

Just as they got re-situated and put Pasqual on a swing in the middle of them, the bartender sauntered up and offered Vivian his hand. She didn't know where she was going but grabbed it anyway and found herself pulled up onto the bar. She worried a little about flashing the patrons since her sundress was pretty short.

What the heck, she decided. *I'll never see these people again.*

The bartender joined her on the bar and handed her a flaming drink layered in the colors of the Mexican flag. The music suddenly stopped and he began to sing. Sounded like a version of "La Cucaracha," but she couldn't interpret and Wendy was too busy laughing to help her out.

Vivian just stood there and danced a little while he sang. Mostly she couldn't help but wonder if she had done a good job shaving the back of her knees since they were at eye level and not far from Pasqual. She always missed spots there.

Vivian's serenade ended and she sipped the Mexican flag shot through a straw, flame and all, while the bartender slammed his tequila. As the crowd cheered, he skillfully jumped down and left her on the bar. Vivian glanced around and wondered how the heck she would get down without anyone getting a peep show. Pasqual graciously offered her his services.

The bar music started back up and the swinging and drinking continued for a bit, until finally the girls decided they needed to see more of Playa's nightlife.

They asked the bartender where to go for dancing. He told them it was disco night at Jungle Fever. They could get their "Jive Talkin'" on, so they said goodnight to Pasqual, though Vivian did casually mention where they were staying. They slipped off their swings and headed out to shake their groove things.

14

Vivian, Lucy and Wendy filled in Kate about Jon's encounter with the upset fan on the walk over to Jungle Fever after leaving the Purple Peacock.

"She is nuts! I couldn't believe she honestly thought Jon was his soap opera character," Vivian finished.

"Yeah, and you should have seen her eyes and her tattoo," Lucy said. "I think she wears fake contacts, her eyes looked a little funny. And what woman in her right mind would have a tattoo of a spider on her back?"

"It wasn't just any spider," Vivian said. "I think it was a black widow."

"I wonder how many of her mates are still alive?" Wendy speculated.

The thought of Stella eating her mates sent them into hysterics.

"You know what, from the way you're describing this lady, I'm pretty sure I met her in the restroom a little while ago," Kate said.

"Did she think you were on a soap opera too?" Wendy teased.

"No, but she told me about how she just found out someone she thought was dead was actually alive, and cheating on his wife with…" She stopped and turned to Vivian, pointing. "You're the floozy!"

"Excuse me?" Vivian said.

"She said he was hanging all over a floozy. I think she called you a hussy too."

"Great! I'm in Mexico six hours and I'm already a floozy and a hussy."

"Oh, that's not that big of a shocker, is it?" Lucy laughed and bumped Vivian's hip with her own.

"True," Vivian winked. "But it's been a while since I've been a 'real' hussy."

"Well, whatever you are, you aren't liked by her," Kate said. "She seemed pretty mad."

"Geez, and I haven't even done anything!" Vivian said.

"Yet." Wendy added.

"I wonder how many guys she's been involved with who noticed her tramp stamp during an intimate moment and worried about their fate?" Kate teased.

This, too, got a good round of laughs.

They walked up to Jungle Fever and heard the Bee Gee's "Stayin' Alive" playing inside. Vivian opened the door and a cloud of smoke billowed out.

"Great," Lucy said. "I'm gonna get cancer."

"Chillax. It's smoke machine smoke," Vivian said.

A huge disco ball hung down in the middle of the dance floor and Vivian fully expected to see John Travola in a white suit striking a pose, just like on the cover of the "Saturday Night Fever" album.

The walls of the club and the bar stools were covered in a leopard pattern. In fact, it was just about everywhere that wasn't painted metallic silver or accented in chrome.

Who was the interior designer? Tarzan? Vivian thought. *He could use Lucy's help. And who designed the waitresses outfits? Jane?* They looked like a leopard clad Wilma Flintstone but sassier and shorter.

Vivian waived off one of the Wilma's as the girls had decided they'd drunk enough alcohol for one night. They went straight to the crowded dance floor and made room.

Rose Royce's "Car Wash" boomed through the smoke so Lucy broke out with her version of a car wash, waving her hands back and forth, dangling her fingers like the thingamabobbers in a car wash. Vivian couldn't help but laugh at her.

The girls pulled out their old school dance moves, the water hose, the sprinkler, the lawn mower and the rake, to name a few. They got a few funny looks, but across the dance floor a bachelorette party was doing the same thing. *It's catching!*

The girls danced, song after song after song. Vivian felt good to lose herself in the music. They danced to a lot of their favs like "Dancing Queen," "Billy Jean" (is that really disco?), "Le Freak" and "Got to Be Real."

Vivian started to get tired and could tell the girls were, too, but she made it one more song. "I Will Survive" came on. Oh, yeah, Vivian could dance to that song. Hell, lately it had become her life's mantra.

They called it a night at the end of the song. On their way out they stopped by the bar and got a round of bottled water. Lucy took her shoes off.

"I'm impressed they made it this long," Kate said, and carried them for her.

Once on the street Vivian sang "I Will Survive" and the girls chimed in. They danced their way back to the hotel, even barefoot Lucy, not caring how silly they looked.

Great ending to my 30th birthday and our first day of vacation!

15

Day 2

The next morning the girls awakened to the sound of Lucy groaning. "Why did you let me drink so much?"

Kate sweetly responded, "We tried to warn you, and we even slowed you down at one point, to no avail."

"I told you so!" Vivian shouted.

Wendy, a.k.a. the walking pharmacy, knew Lucy needed hangover remedies. She gave her Tylenol, Pepto and a bottle of water. Wendy assured her she would be fine and announced they had to get going in order to catch their fishing boat, to which Lucy groaned even louder. The girls knew Vivian loved to fish and had made plans to go on a deep sea excursion.

With no one to impress but the fish, they threw on trashy clothes and left the hotel. Wendy jumped in the driver's seat and sang Robert Earl Keen's "Five Pound Bass" as she drove. Though bass could not be caught today, she sang with enthusiasm.

They arrived at the marina and made their way down the dock, toward the fishing boat *Mucho Grande*. Stepping on board, they met Captain Juan, and the first mate, Pedro, who introduced the girls to the other people charting the boat; newlyweds from Alabama and a guy from New Jersey with long, yellow toenails. *Gross.*

Captain Juan went through the spiel about equipment, safety, bathrooms and the beer cooler. *"Comprende?"* He asked when done.

"Si," everyone answered.

Wendy glanced at Lucy, who looked green around the gills, and realized she needed Dramamine. Lucy had a history of motion sickness and a hangover made it worse. She had seen a small store at the marina, which was more like a shack, and asked Captain Juan, "Do I have a few minutes? I need to make a run to the store."

He told her she had about 10 minutes.

Wendy glanced at the noisy bell above the door as she entered the small store. The aisle to her immediate right had medicine and such, so she grabbed the Dramamine, then checked her purse to see how many ibuprofen she had left. Not many, so she grabbed a bottle of that too.

As the clerk rang her up, she glanced past the clerk, out the large window that overlooked the parking lot. She noticed an SUV with the windows down, parked so that it faced the docks. The guy in the driver's seat held something up to his eyes. *Binoculars maybe?* She thought.

The clerk cleared her throat. "14,000 pesos por favor."

Wendy pulled out a twenty. "Is American money okay?"

The clerk took it and gave her Pesos in change, then put the items into a bag.

Wendy looked out at the guy again and saw the faint outline of a ponytail. He turned slightly in her direction and she saw that what he held was not binoculars, but a camera. One with a long zoom lens. Pointed in the direction of their fishing boat.

"*Gracias,*" Wendy said as she took the bag from the clerk, still looking out the window. The customer behind her reached around to place his beer on the counter, so she moved out of the way and went outside. She heard a car engine start and glanced back towards the parking lot just in time to see the "photographer" drive off.

That's a little weird, she thought. *Maybe he's taking pictures of the boats or something.* She walked back to the *Mucho Grande*, hoping she and her friends weren't in any of the weirdo's pictures.

As she climbed aboard, Lucy wobbled over and held out her hand. "Dramamine?"

Wendy opened the package and handed the bottle to Lucy. She grabbed a bottle of water and handed that to Lucy, too.

"Give it a few minutes. You'll feel better soon."

Captain Juan started the engine and pulled away from the dock. As they motored out of the marina Wendy pointed to another boat. "Look, is that Jon and Pierre?"

On another boat, also leaving the marina, were two guys wearing brightly colored tropical shirts, two girls, and a Hispanic guy at the helm. He looked like the guy Jon and Pierre acknowledged last night as they left the Purple Peacock.

"Hmmm, they're kinda far away," Vivian said. "It's hard to tell if it's them exactly, but it does look like their style of shirts. I wonder who the other guy is?"

"I don't know," Kate said. "But that is a nice boat."

Wendy couldn't see the details of the stripes going down the side of the boat, but the deep V-hull and sound of the engines impressed her. "Yeah. That's one helluva boat. It looks fancy, but the sound of those engines, wow. It turns on the speed freak inside of me."

"There is something wrong with you," Kate said, to which Wendy just grinned.

As soon as they left the wake-free zone Captain Juan gunned the engine and pointed the boat toward open water. They arrived at the fishing spot in about 30 minutes, and the crew got the equipment set up for them to take turns with the rod.

First up in the fighting chair was nasty New Jersey toenail guy. He maxed out at one on the pale scale. He practically knocked them down getting to the chair and insisted on fishing first. So much for chivalry.

"Where's Lucy?" Vivian asked.

Pedro pointed to the bow of the boat, grinned and said "feeding fish." Everyone laughed and Wendy grabbed another bottle of water and went to check on her, carrying her portable pharmacy along.

Toenail caught a Spanish mackerel shortly into his turn. After a bit longer and no more success, Pedro pointed for Kate to take the chair.

Kate, who had never fished before, started to say no but Pedro cast the line out and handed her the rod before she could finish. She turned and gave Wendy and Vivian a look of bewilderment and asked, "How do I work this?"

Before anyone could say anything they heard the *zzzzz zzzzz zzzzz* of the reel. Pedro jumped and pointed, "Big fish! Big fish!" then went to help Kate.

The rest of the passengers on the boat looked to where Pedro pointed and SPLASH! An amberjack leapt from the water with a blue marlin hot on its tail, chasing it — just like something from National Geographic. Seriously, Wendy heard the theme song in her head and started humming it.

Kate hooked the amberjack, which had been running for its life. Well, it lost. The blue marlin took the bait and got hooked too.

The fight was on. Vivian and Wendy took turns helping Kate bring in her catch. Lucy still camped out in the bow, unable to keep from heaving. Finally, after about an hour, Kate brought in her catch.

As the others fished, Kate, Wendy and Vivian enjoyed a few *cervezas*. The cold beer went down easy with the sun shining on them.

Lucy finally joined them, saying she felt better. They placed bets on whether New Jersey would catch anything good. Only Kate bet he would; the rest of them thought his toenails would scare off the fish while he sat in the chair.

Kate, Wendy and Vivian each took another turn in the fighting chair. They only caught a few throwbacks, but still had fun.

As Vivian finished her turn Lucy decided she'd like a turn. Pedro helped her up into the fighting chair and explained how to work the rod and reel. She no sooner got his instructions than there was a sharp tug on the line. Thirty minutes later, Lucy reeled in her catch, a four-foot long hammerhead.

The fishing expedition over, Pedro scurried around cleaning things while Captain Juan navigated back to shore. Once on the dock they took several pictures with Pedro holding their catch (they weren't going to touch it). Pedro cleaned the fish and prepped it for the chef at their hotel, who would cook it up for them for dinner. *Yummo!*

Wendy drove back to the hotel. On the way out of the marina she pointed out, "The boat Jon and Pierre were out on today was back at the marina. I noticed the name of it is *Belize It!,* and it's registered in Ambergris Caye. I wonder how long it would take to get here from there by sea?"

"I don't even know where that is," Vivian confessed.

"You and geography, Viv. *No bueño!*" Wendy said. "It's south of here, in Central America. I want to go there some day. Heard it's beautiful."

"Well, wherever it is, they are short one boat," Kate laughed. "Get it!"

The girls laughed at Kate's "short" joke.

"That Shorty," Lucy said, still laughing, "he kinda has a criminal look about him."

"He's short," Wendy said. "That's criminal, but not a crime!"

"If Jon and Pierre are hanging out with him he probably isn't too bad," Vivian said, then concluded with, "though he's way too short for my liking."

Wendy pulled up to the barricade for their "VIP" parking spot and brought that conversation to a close.

As Arturo let them into the lot Vivian rolled down her window. "*Hola!* We want to go salsa dancing tonight. Know any good clubs?"

"Salsa dancing?" Arturo replied. "You must go to Club Caliente. It's the best salsa club in Playa."

The four of them chimed in with "*Aye ya yai ya yai!*"

Arturo grinned then asked, "*Que hora?* What time are you going?"

Vivian answered, laughing, "Later, after dinner. Maybe we'll see you there?"

"*Bien. Adiós*, Texas girls," he said.

"Thanks for the spot." Lucy waved goodbye and smiled at him.

They ran by the restaurant in the hotel to drop off the fish. The chef came out to meet them and asked how they'd like their fish prepared. He also gave them options for the rest of dinner. They made their selections for appetizers and sides — shrimp cocktail, scalloped potatoes and sautéed spinach in white wine and garlic. *Mmm, mmm good*, Wendy thought.

They were salty and fishy so it was time to hit the showers.

16

The girls rested a bit and got cleaned up from their deep sea fishing excursion. Vivian made a final brush with mascara as Lucy said, "Hey, let's go down to the poolside bar and have a frosty beverage before dinner."

Vivian glanced at Lucy in the mirror. Yep, she looked 100 percent.

"Are you really up for that?" Kate put on a dab of perfume. "After all the tequila yesterday and being out on the boat today?"

"Yep, all the toxins have been heaved from my body and I'm ready for round two."

Vivian checked herself in the full length mirror before walking out the door, satisfied with her progress on the pale scale. Kate walked up behind her and draped an arm around her shoulders. "You look cute, love that dress. You look happy and relaxed, too. I'm so glad to see that."

"Yeah, for the first time in I don't know when. This vacation is just what I needed."

Lucy turned around in the doorway. "Come on you two. Let's get this party started!"

God help us, Vivian thought as they walked out the door.

They arrived at the bar and grabbed four stools together. "Round of margaritas *por favor*," Lucy said to the bartender when he approached.

"Look." Wendy pointed to the shelves of liquor bottles. "The only tequila up there is that Tiempo Loco stuff everyone keeps selling us."

"I wonder if the whole town has ownership in it or something and that's why they keep pushing it," Vivian said.

As they waited for the bartender to serve their drinks they couldn't help but notice and overhear the couple next to them talking, mostly because the couple was loud, but also because the woman was very animated, and sparkly.

They were quite the pair. He wore a shimmery, expensive-looking blue shirt, strategically buttoned to emphasize his gold chain and a thick tuft of salt-and-pepper chest hair. She was petite and younger by at least 20 years, and busted out of her hot pink, rhinestone-studded top. Her platinum-blonde hair had been mega-teased and must have been sprayed with industrial strength hair spray. It hardly moved in the ocean breeze, and when it did, it moved as one unit. The humidity held no challenge for that hair. Her lips and nails were the same shade of hot pink, and she was dripping in jewels — diamonds for every accessory: earrings, necklace, bracelet, rings.

Vivian couldn't stop staring and figured she might as well make small talk with them when they paused for a breath.

"Hey! How are y'all tonight? Isn't this hotel wonderful?"

"Oh yes, we love it here," the woman answered.

Vivian then introduced herself and the girls.

The man spoke up, "How you ladies doin'? I'm Al Russo and this is my wife, Adrienne." He started to keep going, but his phone buzzed. He glanced down at it, gave a smirk and said, "Gotta take this."

"Nice to meet you," the girls called after him.

"Y'all sound like you're from Chicago, maybe?" Vivian said.

"Al's third generation in Chicago, but I'm from New Orleans originally," Adrienne said.

"I thought I heard a hint of Louisiana in your accent," Vivian said.

"Give me a few more of these," she said and held up her daiquiri, "and I'll sound like I just stepped out of a cup of filé gumbo."

"Oh, that'll really throw the locals off." Vivian laughed and then continued, "It's so beautiful here, don't you just want to live here?"

"Oh my god, Playa is fabulous!" Adrienne said. "I could live here permanently. Are you girls staying out of trouble down here?"

"Never! We bring trouble wherever we go!" Wendy said. "We practically swung ourselves into the oblivion at the Purple Peacock last night. Right, Lucy? Then we went to Jungle Fever and discoed the night away. We are having a blast."

They proceeded to tell her about Lucy's swing incident the night before, Vivian's birthday serenade, the ever-so-gorgeous Pasqual and of course, soap-stud Jon.

"I think I've seen him, actually, now that you've described him. I didn't know he was an actor. Al and I are down here taking a break from the family and the business," Adrienne told them, "although Al can't seem to tear himself away from his phone." She used her hands as she spoke and the glare cast off her wedding ring blinded Vivian a few times.

"Damn, girl, that is quite the rock you've got there," Vivian couldn't help but say. She decided to be safe and put on her sunglasses.

Kate raised her eyebrows and said, "Which one? The earrings, necklace or wedding ring?"

"The ring," Vivian answered.

"Oh honey, this is nothing," Adrienne said. "I don't like to be too flashy on vacation."

Nothing? Her bling is blinding! Vivian thought.

Al returned with his phone in his shirt pocket, which made it droop and expose even more chest hair. He said to the girls, "What are you ladies up to?"

They didn't get a chance to respond because Adrienne replied, "They're fabulous, and so much fun! They've been catching rays and catching men, all while catching a buzz."

Al stepped back and ran his hand through his hair. "Oh, really?"

"We went deep sea fishing today, and I caught the big one," Kate said. "It was huge and took me forever to get him in the boat."

"Yeah, I've heard stories like that before," Al said then raised his right arm as if to measure the length of a fish. "I caught one this big…"

"No, really, the chef is cooking the fish for us tonight and there will be plenty," Kate said. "It really was a big fish. Y'all should join us."

"Appetizer and sides included," Wendy said. "It's gonna be delicious."

Adrienne looked at Al with a smile.

"Whatever you want, baby." His shirt buzzed and he walked away to answer it. "Excuse me again, ladies."

Adrienne rolled her eyes. She must have heard that a lot on this trip. "We'd love to join you for dinner," she said to the girls. "Thanks for the invite. I could use some girl talk."

They clinked glasses to that, finished off their drinks, and walked over to the hotel restaurant. It, too, was filled with tropical plants, but it wasn't quite the jungle the lobby was. The walls were painted a light terra cotta, which reminded Vivian of Santa Fe. Very soothing.

The hostess seated them at a table on the patio overlooking the beach. The evening sun cast hues of pink and orange on the water. Vivian excused herself to stand up and take a picture. She only wished she had this view from her dining room. As it was, she had a great view of her driveway. Sunsets just weren't as spectacular.

The waiter arrived shortly with a bottle of champagne. He popped the cork and said, "Compliments of the man in the blue shirt." Excellent way to start a friendship!

The waiter asked Adrienne how she and Al would like their fished prepared, then walked off without taking any other orders. No need as they knew what they were having.

The five girls raised their glasses to toast to new friends.

A few minutes later Al returned, and Vivian asked him, "How long are y'all here?"

"As long as it takes to relax."

"Must be nice to have an open-ended vacation," Wendy said. "I'm a mortgage loan originator and there's no time for lunch some days, much less a vacation. This is the longest vacation I've had in four years."

"What do you do for a living Al?" Kate helped herself to the just delivered shrimp cocktail.

"I own an Italian restaurant in Chicago's Little Italy neighborhood," he said. "Family business. My Poppi opened it in the '40s."

"Best cannoli this side of the Atlantic." Adrienne raised her glass to toast Al.

"So are y'all in the mob?" Lucy asked.

Kate nudged her. Lucy had seen too many episodes of *The Sopranos*.

Adrienne sucked in her breath but Al shook his head and said, "Nah, I try not to get involved in anything like that. I'm just a guy who owns a little Italian restaurant and goes to mass on Sunday."

Adrienne coughed lightly, and it looked like she was trying not to laugh.

Vivian didn't quite believe Al's story. Mass or not, he looked like he had a devilish side. To break the tension, she gestured with a shrimp, "Wow, this cocktail sauce is excellent."

Al flagged down the waiter and ordered a bottle of Vouvray, Vivian's all-time favorite white wine.

"So are you Cubs fans or White Sox fans," Wendy asked, "and why does Chicago have two teams?"

"Sox fans all the way." Adrienne held up her champagne glass as a toast. "There is no other team."

Al's face turned red at the mention of the Cubs. Okay, that discussion was closed.

Al's phone rang, and he was off to answer it. Three rings in less than an hour.

What's with that?

"Al works really hard at the restaurant," Adrienne said. "He came down here to relax but he's been on the phone non-stop. That damn thing might as well be duct-taped to his face. I feel like chunking it in the ocean."

"I understand how hard it can be to leave work behind and totally relax." Wendy rolled her shoulders. "It must be hard for him to leave the restaurant in the hands of others while he's away. Maybe you should try a couple's massage?"

"He's got his cousin running the restaurant and shouldn't be worried about it," Adrienne replied. "I already tried the couples massage, and he refused to turn his phone off. It rang twice and ruined my massage. Pisses me off."

"The longer it takes him to relax the longer you get to stay in paradise," Vivian reminded her.

"Cheers to that!" Adrienne held up her glass again.

Wendy excused herself, needing to powder her nose. As she left the restroom, she stopped to dig a pebble out of her sandal and overheard Al talking on the phone in the men's room, in Spanish. *"Atendere su fiesta la noche del Viernes."*

Wonder whose party he's going to Friday night? Wendy thought as she walked back to the table.

"So Al can speak Spanish?" Wendy asked Adrienne as she sat down.

"No. He can barely manage *'hola'*," Adrienne said.

Huh, Wendy thought. *I thought that was Al's Chicago accent mixed with Spanish, but maybe it was someone else I overheard?*

Al returned to the table just as the waiter arrived with the Vouvray.

He tasted the wine, nodded his approval then asked, "What are you ladies up to tonight?"

"A friend of ours suggested Club Caliente." Vivian drained her champagne glass. "We wanted to go salsa dancing, and it's supposed to be the best place in town. Y'all should join us."

Al started to shake his head, but Adrienne said, "We'd love to. I don't know how to salsa dance, but it sounds like fun!"

Al gave her a look so she put on her puppy dog face.

"Sounds like a plan then," he said, giving in.

Vivian suggested a toast with the wine: "To salsa dancing *aye aye aye!*" Clink!

A swarm of servers removed their appetizer plates and delivered dinner. Everyone was quiet while they dug in. The fish was perfectly grilled, and the sides complimented it well. Vivian loved it in combination with the Vouvray. *This is hands down the best dinner I've had since I don't know when. It's not like Rick ever took me out for something like this.*

After they finished dinner the waiter offered soufflés for dessert. They couldn't eat another bite so they politely declined.

As the group left for Club Caliente, Wendy saw a scowl cross Al's face. She glanced over at the poolside bar and saw the creepy guy with the ponytail. He had a clear view of their table from where he sat. Wendy glanced at Al, their eyes locked for a moment but then he looked away.

17

The girls, Al and Adrienne strolled down the sandy streets of Playa del Carmen, making their way to Club Caliente. Children still played in the street, though it was well after dark. A few other tourists were out, in search of libations.

"So how did y'all meet?" Vivian asked Al and Adrienne.

"I was a Luvabull," Adrienne began the story.

"A whattabull?"

"A Luvabull," Adrienne said. "It was 15 years ago. I was a cheerleader for the Chicago Bulls, they're called Luvabulls. Al is a huge Bulls fan so he hosted a charity event at his restaurant. The Luvabulls were the grand finale auction item. He bought me in the auction and we went on a date. I knew the first night he was *the one*."

"He bought you in an auction?" Vivian asked.

"The single girls agreed to be auctioned off to the highest bidder for a date. All of the money went to charity so I agreed to be in it. It was the best decision of my life — I met my sweetheart." She took his hand as they walked.

"I bet you cost him a pretty penny. What'd you go for?" Vivian asked.

"Viv!" Kate yelled at her. "That's not nice."

"It's okay," Adrienne said. "He bought me for $5,000, and I'm totally worth it!"

Al brought her hand to his lips and kissed her palm. "It was for a good cause, and yes, you are worth it, baby," then he let her hand go and smacked her ass.

"Trust me; he's paid for a lot more over the years." Adrienne not-so-subtlety adjusted her boobs.

They all laughed.

A few minutes later they arrived at Club Caliente and Vivian thought it was aptly named. It was just that, *hot*. The a/c was broken, non-existent, or they didn't turn it on. *Geez!* The thick humidity turned Vivian's hair into a frizz-ball and kicked her sweat glands into overdrive. No sweat circles, though, cuz she was spaghetti strappin' it.

Vivian thought all of the people in the club looked like they belonged on the cover of a magazine. Young, sexy, beautiful. *They must stay in shape walking up the gazillion stairs to get in here.*

Though hot and humid inside, the music invigorated Vivian and made her want to dance, even though she had never been salsa dancing and wouldn't know what she was doing.

Al grabbed a great table close to the dance floor and ordered a bottle of champagne. The girls didn't notice its arrival because they were mesmerized by the dancers, who looked like professionals. Vivian heard the pop of the cork and suddenly someone landed in her lap screaming, "Get down! Get down!"

Momentarily startled but quickly recovered, Vivian found Arturo's grinning face between her boobs.

"What, did it sound like a gunshot?" Vivian asked sarcastically.

He looked at her sheepishly and said, "False alarm."

False alarm, my ass.

Arturo looked pretty damn fantastic out of uniform. His jeans fit just right and his Guayabera showed off bulging biceps. His arms reminded Vivian of a boyfriend in college. Good memories came flooding in.

She cracked a smile and was brought back to the present when Lucy introduced Arturo to Al and Adrienne. "I see you've got good instincts," Al said to Arturo with a smirk. He looked at Vivian and said, "I think he just wanted to get a closer look at your ladies."

Arturo grinned. "You can never be too careful."

"You speak pretty good English compared to a lot of people I've met since we've been here," Al added.

"I lived with my aunt in San Diego for four years when I was a kid," Arturo answered. "Besides, it helps me get to know lovely Texas ladies who vacation here."

Lucy glanced toward the bar and smiled. "Well, well, looky who else is here."

Vivian turned to see Jon and Pierre. *Speaking of a nice body!*

"Those Canadians are totally stalking us," Lucy said with a smile.

"I think I've seen them at the hotel," Al said. "They make some interesting clothing choices."

Jon and Pierre had on tropical shirts again with bold, bright colors.

"I've seen them around town hanging out," Arturo noted. "They've been in Playa for a month or so."

"So you keep tabs on all the tourist?" Vivian asked.

"As Al mentioned, they stand out more than others because of their loud shirts," he laughed.

Adrienne sucked down her champagne. "Come on, Al. I'm ready to dance."

Al reached for his shirt pocket and checked his phone.

He's so trying to get out of this.

"I might miss a call."

Lame-o.

"Please, baby…for me." Adrienne batted her long eyelashes.

Al got up reluctantly. "Okay, just one song, but if anyone slings sweat on me it's over."

Off they went, Adrienne smiling as she drug Al to the dance floor.

Vivian decided to go say hello to Jon and Pierre and walked over to the bar. "Hello, boys. Are you stalking us or what?"

Jon smiled. "No, of course not, though I am glad we ran into you."

"I'm glad, too."

"You ready to salsa?" Jon asked.

"I don't know how."

"We were here a few nights ago and a *señorita* taught me some moves. I bet I can lead you through it."

Jon grabbed her hand and pulled her toward the dance floor. She gave in. "The girls are over there, go say hi," Vivian said to Pierre. She had a quick thought of 'turn around,' but then decided to try and fake it. She was semi-coordinated. How hard could it be?

Their first song was thankfully slower than the one just played. Jon did seem to know what he was doing, and for a guy with such pasty skin he could sure move his hips. *Who was this señorita who taught him to salsa? Did the lessons go beyond the dance floor?*

Though she hadn't been dancing long, she could tell that it got the hormones raging. Lots of pelvic action. She couldn't help it, she wanted to know more. "There's no way you learned all of this in one night."

"You're right, I'm busted," Jon admitted. "I loved the movie *Dirty Dancing* when I was a kid and wanted to dance like Patrick Swayze. I convinced my mom to let me take dancing lessons when I was a teenager. To this day, my dad doesn't know. He would have flipped. He was very much a man's man, you know."

"Really? Lessons?"

He looked around, as if anyone was listening. "Nobody knows I did that. I've never admitted it to anyone, especially my friends. I was embarrassed."

"Well, let me be the first to tell you that your lessons paid off. And your closet dancing secret is safe with me."

He suddenly stopped dancing, wrapped his arms around her, leaned down and kissed her. The moment felt a little strange to Vivian, because they were in the middle of a dance floor surrounded by at least 30 people, yet it felt oddly intimate. He pulled back and grinned, and got back to dancing.

———

Wendy, Kate and Arturo were the only ones left at the table. Pierre had whisked Lucy off to dance, despite her protests. They watched as Adrienne danced and Al attempted to.

Wendy saw the kiss between Vivian and Jon and nudged Kate. "Check them out."

"Ooooouuuu," Kate replied. "Things are getting even hotter in here."

Arturo didn't comment on the kiss, just polished off his glass of champagne.

"Good for Viv, she needs a little fun," Wendy said. "And damn it's hot in here. I need some fresh air."

"There's a bar outside on the balcony." Arturo poured himself another glass. "You and Kate go. I'll stay here and watch your stuff."

"Thanks," Kate said.

They made their way to the balcony and picked a pair of cushy-looking stools at the bar.

The bartender came over and laid out two beverage napkins. "*Hola, señoritas.* May I help you?"

"Dos margaritas, *por favor*," Wendy said, throwin' out that high school Spanish again.

He mixed 'em up with flair, tossed in two limes and served them with a smile, saying "Tiempo Loco tequila, the best."

Wendy took a sip. *Vacation rocks and so does my margarita!* she thought.

As they sipped, they scoped out the balcony action. They decided the bartender wasn't hard on the eyes, and some younger guys at the end of the bar weren't too shabby either.

Wendy recognized a guy sitting in the corner of the balcony. She leaned over and whispered to Kate, "That's the same pony-tailed guy we saw at the Purple Peacock last night, today at the dock and just now at our hotel."

"Where?"

Wendy gestured with her head. "Over there."

Kate glanced at him then back at Wendy. "What do you mean he was just at our hotel?"

"After dinner. I saw him at the poolside bar and Al saw him, too. Al looked like he recognized him and was pissed, but tried to play it off when he caught me looking at him."

"That's weird."

Both girls turned their heads to look at him again and saw he was watching them. They quickly faced the bar, then Wendy turned her head the other direction, trying to look nonchalant. "I don't believe this. Look, there's the short guy and the two girls we saw Jon and Pierre with last night and again today on the boat."

"What the heck?" Kate replied. "He's not the most attractive guy. What does he have going for him to keep the arm candy hanging around?"

"There's no telling. Maybe he has some assets we're not aware of."

"Yuck!" Kate replied. "I don't want to think about Shorty's assets."

"Ha! Me, either. What's with seeing the ponytail guy, the short guy and those two ladies everywhere we go?"

"It's weird. I realize Playa isn't that big of a place, but come on!"

"Let's go back inside and see how our salsa dancers are doing. I want to get away from the creepy Ponytail guy."

18

Inside the hot and steamy Club Caliente, Lucy and Pierre had given up on dancing and were back at the table, as were Jon and Vivian, but Al and Adrienne were still movin' and shakin'.

Arturo asked Kate, "You ready to learn from a pro?"

Kate laughed and said, "I'll give it one song."

The group at the table watched as Kate and Arturo danced. "Kate's doing pretty good," Vivian commented.

"She's more talented than I am," Lucy said.

"So, how did you do with the salsa?" Wendy asked her.

Lucy looked at Pierre and dabbed at her brow with a napkin.

Pierre laughed and answered for her. "I'm afraid she didn't have the best partner. The good dancers make this look easy, but it's harder than you think."

Lucy smiled. "It was fun, but the dance floor is too crowded. Grosses me out, all those sweaty people."

Kate and Arturo returned, having danced just the one song. Kate's sundress stuck to her legs and Vivian noticed Arturo glancing at her ass when she sat down. *Men.*

"This place needs to invest in a/c. I'm burnin' up," Kate said, fanning herself with her hand.

She titled up her champagne glass and drank every last drop. Arturo pulled the bottle from the ice bucket and refilled everyone's glass with a bit more bubbly.

"Have fun?" Vivian asked Kate.

"Oh yeah," Kate answered. "I'd love to come back here with Shaun someday. Maybe a second honeymoon."

Arturo cleared his throat.

"You're a great dancer, Arturo. Thanks for the spin."

He grinned at her. "Anytime."

Lucy gave Vivian a sly smile and a nudge. "Looks like *you're* having a good time."

Vivian ignored her sarcasm. "Yeah, Jon seems to know his way around the dance floor."

Wendy knew Vivian would appreciate a conversation diversion, so she said to Jon and Pierre, "Hey, y'alls friend, the short dude, is outside with his female bookends."

Jon looked surprised. "Didn't know they'd be here tonight. I'll go check in with *hombre*. Pierre?"

"No, you go ahead. I'll catch him later."

As Jon walked away, Kate asked Pierre, "How does the short guy keep two girlfriends around? He's not that cute. And, well, he's pretty darn short."

Arturo snorted back a laugh.

"Don't know," Pierre said. "We met him when we first got here. We've hung out with him a few times, mostly on his boat, which is bad ass. He's probably pretty successful." He paused and then added, "I think the girls are related somehow."

"Gross! That's disgusting!" Lucy yelled. "They aren't his sisters, are they?"

Pierre laughed. "Not related to him, to each other. I think they are cousins or something. Must like to keep things in the family?"

They all laughed at that, even though it was disgusting.

Arturo informed them, "I know who you're talking about. I think the girls are second cousins, even though they look like sisters."

After a few minutes, Jon walked back inside, looking perturbed. He sat down next to Pierre and shook his head.

"What's wrong?" Pierre asked.

"I'm not sure what the hell just happened outside," Jon replied, sounding pissed. "Julio sure has a short fuse. He wasn't at the table with Eva and Josephina when I first went out there so I sat down for a few minutes, you know, to wait for him to come back. We were laughing when he walked up and I guess maybe he thought I was hitting on them. He was furious, started shouting at me to get up, and when I did, he shoved me."

"Julio Zapata?" Arturo asked.

"Yeah. Is this typical of him?"

"*Más o menos*," Arturo said, gesturing with his hand.

The girls looked at Wendy for translation. "More or less."

"Maybe he's drunk?" Pierre asked. "What would have changed since this afternoon?"

"Beats me."

Just as Jon finished speaking, Shorty and The Ladies came in from the balcony and walked straight to the exit. Shorty hustled through the club and didn't even look their way. One of the girls gave a quick sideways glance toward Jon.

"Oh well, Viv, you ready to get back on the dance floor?"

She sucked down the bit of champagne that was left in her glass. "I'm in!"

This time on the dance floor things were gettin' steamy, and it wasn't just from the heat. One minute they were dancing and the next they were kissing. Funny how alcohol, music and the heat will do that to a girl. *I'll have to thank Al again for the champagne.*

The girls "woo hoo-ed" them so Vivian gave a little wave and keep shakin' her moneymaker.

Jon's a hottie, Vivian thought. He had good rhythm and could shake his hips with the best of them. He was pasty, but he made white guys look good, contrary to the old cliché.

They danced for a while, then Vivian needed another break and gave Jon the I-need-a-drink signal. Holding her hand, he led her off the dance floor.

Al and Adrienne were back at the table, looking like they needed to cool off. Al was red faced and his shirt was soaked through. Even his chest hairs were flat. Adrienne, though a little sweaty, looked happy, probably because Al hadn't been on the phone in a while.

Al signaled the waiter. "Order what you like on me."

The girls gave another round of "woo-hoos" and placed their orders.

Drinks arrived, and it was time to cheers again.

This time Vivian gave the toast to "Life, love and the pursuit of hot men on vacation," to which Al rolled his eyes but clinked with them anyway.

Jon put his arm around Vivian just as a waitress walked up with a martini in her hand.

"Are you Dominik?"

Jon looked at the martini, then looked at the waitress. "Yeah, that's me," he resigned.

She set the martini on the table in front of him. "Stella said this is your favorite."

Vivian looked around for Stella, but didn't see her.

"Great, thanks-ola," he said without enthusiasm.

"Who is Stella?" Adrienne asked.

The girls gave her, Al and Arturo the rundown of the woman from the Purple Peacock the night before. Including the floozy story.

"I don't think I've seen anyone fitting that description around Playa," Arturo said.

"What's up with her sending you a drink?" Adrienne asked. "Do you really like martinis?"

"I've honestly never had one," Jon replied. "I'm more of a beer man, can't have too many though." He rubbed his stomach. "Gotta keep up the physique."

Vivian smiled to herself. She had felt those abs and they were divine.

He continued. "On the set the 'martini' was just water, not the real stuff." He took a sip and made a face. "How do people drink these things? This is horrible. Eh!"

Regardless, in the next sip he sucked it down, the whole thing.

"Horrible, huh?" Vivian asked.

"Well, I don't want to be rude to a fan." He winked at her. "Even if she is cuckoo."

Vivian sipped her drink and watched the dancers, content just to be with her friends, new and old, especially Jon. She truly enjoyed his company, okay, and his lips. And she liked that she didn't feel any pressure from him. No, "wanna come back to my place?" Or, "why don't you come visit me in Montreal sometime?" Just being in the moment was good enough for both of them. Of course, they had just met, but in Vivian's experience she found some guys were ready to settle down by the second date. *Ugh!*

Al turned to Adrienne. "You about ready to go back?"

"Sure, honey," she said and stood up, polishing off her drink.

"It's been fun," Al said to the rest of them. "You kids stay outta trouble."

"Never!" Vivian said.

After they left, Jon offered, "How about another drink? On me this time."

Vivian gave her stamp of approval but Wendy said, "One more and that's it for me. I'm beat."

Lucy and Kate also agreed with her as it was already after 1 o'clock in the morning.

As the drinks arrived, the music turned funky and the lights dimmed. Two women and one man, dressed all in black, took the stage and lit batons on fire.

The guy was dressed in tight pants and a sleeveless shirt, showing off his nicely cut arms. The women wore short shorts and halter tops. Not much more than the essentials were covered. Their outfits wouldn't be complete without patent leather knee-length boots.

"Snazzy." Wendy commented.

"What's this?" Kate asked Arturo.

"Ancient Aztec dance," he responded.

"Somehow I don't think the Aztecs wore these outfits back in the day," Vivian said.

Jon laughed.

The trio started with one baton each, lit on both ends. They lit several more, tossed them to each other, around each other, on top of one another, etc. They threw those suckers around like they didn't have a care in the world for their hair. Nerve-racking, but impressive. At the table, Vivian felt the heat from the batons, though it was only marginally hotter than the air in the club.

The fire batons and the dancer's stunts were entertaining, but the girls, Arturo, Jon and Pierre gave the performance a nine out of ten because of the crappy music, which was techno'd out and repetitive.

"That was amazing," Kate said. "I want to be a fire thrower!"

"Not tonight, I hope," Lucy countered. "I'm done. You guys ready?"

Wendy took the last sip of her drink and grabbed her purse. "Yep. Ready."

Pierre stood up. "I'll walk you ladies back to the hotel."

Arturo also got up. "I'm going home too. *Bueñas noches.*"

"Nobody wants to stay?" Vivian asked.

"I'll stay," Jon said.

I was hoping he would say that.

"I'll probably be there in about an hour or so," Vivian told the girls. "Don't wait up!"

Lucy hugged Vivian's neck. "Okay, we'll see you in the morning. Don't have too much fun now."

"Moi?"

Kate smacked Vivian's butt and told her to be good.

"No, ma'am. Oh, I mean yes, ma'am."

Jon stood and gave them hugs. *"Adiós-*ola," he called after them.

Jon and Vivian hit the dance floor for a few more songs and then returned to the table. He sat close and put his arm around her. She felt butterflies in her stomach. She had a zillion thoughts going through her head. Most of them were pushing her in the direction of doing something she shouldn't. *He is pretty cute and has a nice bod, even if he has bad taste in shirts and is way too pale. Who knew the Canadians could be so sexy! Keanu Reeves is sexy, and I think he's Canadian, but I am still technically a married woman. Shit!*

"Okay, I'm officially hot," Jon said after a few minutes, then suggested, "Why don't we walk over to the hotel and have a drink outside at the bar?"

"Sounds good, let's blow this joint-ola."

He grabbed Vivian's hand and gave her a wink. "See, now you get it – ola!"

19

The streets were fairly empty and shops were closed as Jon and Vivian left Club Caliente for their hotel. Even the panhandlers had closed up for the night. Only a few people were out, all of whom seemed to be stumbling about a bit.

They walked through the sand to the poolside bar, which was deserted. The bartender was shutting down but agreed to serve them one more margarita.

Jon offered a toast "to beautiful Texas women."

Is he workin' it or what?

"Let's go for a walk on the beach," Jon said. "Just a short walk to end our night."

How can I resist?

Jon and Vivian said goodnight to the bartender and sauntered down to the beach. Vivian kicked off her shoes to walk in the surf. The water felt amazing, cool and refreshing after the sultry salsa club.

Jon held Vivian's hand. The gesture somehow seemed more intimate than the kissing and dancing they'd been doing.

"So tell me more about yourself," he said. "What do you do back in Texas?"

She smirked. "I'm a mega-multitasker."

"Multitasker. Excellent. I've never heard of that profession."

"Yeah, well I have a couple of jobs. I work at a hospital, but more importantly, I'm a mom."

"Wow," he took a step back and looked her up and down. "You don't look like a mom."

Good reply.

"I am," Vivian sucked in a deep breath. "In fact, I actually have four kids."

She waited for his response, be it him sprinting off down the beach away from her or a giant gasp. He did neither.

"They're all very young — Audrey is 4, Lauren is 2, and the twins, Olivia and Ben are only 8 months old." She hesitated, still listening for some sign of his reaction. "So you can see how the divorce was a bit of a surprise."

He stopped walking and turned her towards him.

"Vivian, sounds like you have a beautiful family. You've really got your hands full."

She looked up at him and shrugged. "Better full than empty."

"A single mom with four kids. Young kids…babies. That ex of yours must be a real jerk-ola."

"Yeah, pretty much."

"Wow, Vivian, that's heavy. Most people in your shoes would be falling apart."

"Well, I'm not a fall-apart kind of gal. I figure it's not going to do anybody any good, so why do it?"

"Good point, but still…"

Vivian turned away from him, stared out at the water and took a deep breath.

"I'm more of a pull-yourself-up-by-your-bootstraps kind of girl. He's a dick. He knows it. He's giving me everything in the divorce so I'm okay financially. Do I wish this were different? Of course. Am I nervous about what comes next? Absolutely."

With a little ferocity, she added, "No sense in becoming a depressed do-nothing damsel in distress. I wasn't one before; I'm not going to be one now."

"Damn, girl! I feel like I need to find a pedestal or something for you to step up on with your boots and bootstraps. You know, your message could really help a lot of people."

"There's no message. Just me."

He turned her back towards him again, cradled her face in his hands and leaned down. "I think you're amazing."

With that he gave her a long, slow, deep, toes-curl-in-the-sand, kiss.
Oh…my…god.

He pulled back and rested his forehead against hers. Her heart raced and the lyrics of Josh Weathers' "Mind, Body & Soul" ran through her mind. *"I love you…mind…body…and soul."*

She didn't love Jon's soul yet, but there was some definite lust going on. She did love his body and his mind, in that order.

Her legs felt heavy, *or are they weak?*, and she could tell she was going to regret some of the dance moves she made earlier in the night.

Vivian didn't want to regret any more, so she pulled back and took a deep breath. "I better go up."

87

Before turning around, he stopped to pick up something in the surf and handed it to Vivian. "Here, I want you to have this. Unbroken conch shells bring good luck."

As they walked back towards the hotel, Vivian touched the sharp point of the shell and ran her hands along the rough exterior spines, then the smooth interior. Though she was on the ocean, she held the large shell up to her ear to hear the ocean in it.

"Thank you very much. That's sweet and I can use all the good luck I can get." After pausing a moment she asked, "So what are you going to do now that you were written off the soap opera?"

"Actually I'm expecting a phone call from my agent any minute now," he said. "He went out tonight with a big-time producer in Canada. He's trying to get me the starring role in a movie."

"Wow! Sounds big time. I hope you get it."

"Thanks. It's been a long time coming."

They were back at the beach entrance of the hotel. "I've had a great time tonight," Vivian said.

He leaned down and gave her another passionate kiss. "I had a great time, too, Vivian. I know that things are going to turn out great for you. I can feel it."

She rested her head on his shoulder and he squeezed her tight to him. She melted perfectly into his form.

After a little bit she pulled back. "Are you not going up?"

"No, I'm going to wait a little while longer and see if my agent calls. See you tomorrow, though." He leaned down for one more kiss.

"Tomorrow," Vivian said, flashing her sexiest smile, then she turned and walked toward the lobby. She did hope to see him tomorrow. Though not ready for any kind of relationship, especially a long-distance one, she was not opposed to continuing her fun on vacation in Mexico.

She reached the lobby entrance and turned around. He was on his phone down by the water. He looked up at her, smiled and waved. *Maybe he got the part?* She waved back and went inside.

20

Day 3

Bang! Bang! Bang!

"Who the hell is banging on our door?" Vivian groaned from the couch.

Lucy, who had fallen asleep naked on the bed, made a mad dash for the bathroom.

Vivian kicked off her covers but Kate beat her to the door. Arturo, in uniform, stood on their stoop, along with another guy they didn't recognize.

Kate talked to them for a second then let them in. She shouted to Lucy that they had visitors, to which Lucy shouted back that she needed clothes. Wendy hopped out of bed, grabbed random items of clothing out of Lucy's bag and shoved them through the bathroom door.

Vivian sat up on the couch, pulled the covers back up to her chin and wondered why the hell Kate let them in. No one was dressed for visitors.

Arturo introduced the other man as Detective Vega and casually pointed to Vivian on the couch.

Detective Vega looked her dead in the eye. "Ms. Taylor, we need you to come with us to the station to answer a few questions."

Why does he know my name? Alarm bells went off in Vivian's head.

Her grip on the covers tightened. "The station? Why?"

After a moment of awkward silence Arturo answered, "Jon was found on the beach."

Vivian looked at Arturo, then at Detective Vega. "What do you mean 'found'?"

Vega took two steps toward her, tapping the gun on his hip. "Found dead."

Vivian's head started to spin and she saw a dark tunnel form around her. Little stars appeared and streaked toward her. She heard Kate calling her name in the distance but she could only hear one thing. Her voice saying:

"Holy crap. Jon is dead-ola."

21

The girls were shocked at the news of Jon's death. Wendy and Kate stared, mouths agape, at a stunned Vivian. Lucy gasped behind the bathroom door and said "Holy Mary Mother of God."

"Dead? You mean, as in not breathing?" Vivian asked in a minute, after the threat of passing out was gone.

"He is definitely not breathing," Vega said.

Vivian shook her head, not wanting to take this in. "How did he die?"

Vega squinted his eyes at her. "The coroner is looking into that now."

"Why do you need me?"

"The hotel bartender said you two were together late last night. He saw you walk to the beach."

"Well yes, we were together, but…"

He cut her off. "Save it for the station."

She furrowed her brow and thought: *Rude!* Then it clicked with her what he just said. "The station."

Wendy stepped between them and said, "She's not going anywhere without us. You're just going to have to wait a few minutes while we get dressed. She goes, we go."

"I had planned on extending the invitation to all of you," Vega said. "You have 10 minutes." Vivian felt a chill down her spine at the tone of his voice.

As Arturo and Vega went through the door, Vega turned and added, "Bring your passports," then slammed the door.

"I can't believe he's dead," Vivian said, tears welling in her eyes. "I just can't believe it."

Wendy looked at her. "What in the world did y'all do last night?"

"Nothing! We came back here, had a drink at the bar, went for a walk on the beach and," Vivian had to choke out the last few words, "that was it."

"Did you go back to his room?" she asked more gently.

Vivian wiped her eyes, trying to stave off the coming flood. "No. He didn't even walk me up. I left him on the beach."

Lucy cracked the bathroom door, her shoulders still bare. "Did they say Jon is dead?"

Vivian nodded in response.

Lucy opened the door fully and came out wrapped in a towel. "Our Jon is dead? As in the guy you were makin' out with last night Jon? I don't believe it."

"Yeah," Vivian whispered.

"When did you come in? I never heard you," Wendy asked.

"Me, neither," Kate said.

"I was quiet," Vivian said, sniffled, then continued, "and y'all were totally out. Of course you didn't hear me." As the first tear leaked out, she pointed to Lucy and continued, "and you were naked on the bed so I slept on the couch. I was probably in here by 2:30."

"I didn't hear you come in either, but I'll never admit that, Viv. I'll say whatever you need me to say." Lucy turned and went back into the bathroom and closed the door.

Kate sat down next to Vivian. "Do you think they think you did it?"

"No, I doubt it," Wendy said, trying to sound calm. She sat down on the other side of Vivian. "They probably just need a timeline or something. They couldn't honestly think you…" her voice trailed off.

That did it. Vivian doubled over, her head in her lap, as sobs wracked her body. Her world, which she had barely started to put back together, had been shaken to the core yet again. Rick's betrayal and the divorce had been awful, but the death of a friend, even a newly found friend, in the prime of his life, was more than she could handle at the moment.

Kate couldn't hold back her emotions and reached over in a half hug which was completed by a tearful Wendy. Lucy, fully dressed, knelt in front of Vivian and joined the group hug, also crying.

Finally, after several long minutes, Vivian sat up, took a deep breath and attempted to regain her composure. "It has to be an accident or something."

"Maybe he went for a swim and drown?" Lucy said. "Y'all did drink quite a bit."

"Well, for drowning, Detective Vega sure seems pissed off." Wendy handed out tissues and wiped her eyes.

"You'll be okay, Viv." Kate tried to reassure her, then glanced at the clock. "We better get ready to go."

Vivian went through the motions and before she knew it, their 10 minutes was up.

Detective Vega banged on the door. *"Vamanos!"*

The girls grabbed their purses, passports included, and left the room.

In the lobby, they passed Al and Adrienne, who looked like they were going to breakfast. They stopped to talk, but Vega was behind the girls and wouldn't let them slow down.

"They're taking Vivian to jail!" Lucy said.

"Oh my god! What happened?" Adrienne shouted.

"No, they aren't," Vivian said, hoping she was right. "They just need me to answer some questions."

"About what?" Al asked.

"Jon died last night," Wendy said.

Al dug in his pocket, Vivian assumed for his phone. "You girls call me if there's something screwy goin' on." He reached out to shake Vivian's hand and slipped her his business card.

The girls headed through the sand on the way to the street. Two uniformed men passed them carrying an empty stretcher toward a flurry of activity about 50 yards down the beach. On it lay a black, flattened body bag.

Vivian stopped and began to see stars again. Lucy and Wendy pulled up on either side of her and grabbed an arm, holding her steady but forcing her to press forward. As they turned the corner Vivian noticed several police cars parked around the hotel.

Arturo directed them toward two police cruisers. "I need to search your purses before you get in. Procedure."

He hadn't made eye contact with them, and Vivian felt like she had let him down. He went through their bags then motioned Vivian into a cruiser by herself, and Lucy, Kate and Wendy into the other. Wendy protested the separation to no avail.

Tears streaked down Vivian's face. She cringed as she peered through the metal cage that separated the front and back seats. *Please let this be a short ride*, she prayed.

Once Lucy, Wendy and Kate were settled into the back seat, Lucy, recalling her mobster shows, asked in a hushed whisper, "Do we need to get our story straight?"

"What story? We have no story!" Wendy whispered back, still a little teary-eyed.

"Oh, I know. I just thought we might need to figure out what we're going to say."

"We'll just answer whatever they ask us honestly," Kate whispered. "It was probably just an accident and this is just a formality."

"Maybe," Lucy said. "But they're taking Viv down to the station in a separate car."

"Shit, true," Wendy said.

Kate closed her eyes, tight, and shook her head, as if that would block out Lucy's words.

The ride to the station only took a few minutes and Lucy, Wendy and Kate were let out of the car at the base of the steps, where Vivian and Vega waited for them. He ushered them up the stairs and inside, where they saw Pierre sitting on a bench.

Pierre jumped up when he saw them. "What the fuck, Vivian, what happened last night? What did you do?"

Vivian was so shocked by this, she couldn't even answer him.

Vega looked at Pierre. "Sit down, Mr. Laroche," then ushered Vivian down a hall and into an interrogation room, where a police officer waited inside.

Vivian took in the whole one-way mirror, two chairs and a table thing. Before sitting down, she looked at herself in the mirror. Her face was splotchy and red, which made her green eyes look like they could glow in the dark. Her hair, with curls leftover from sauna salsa dancing, was a complete joke. She hadn't had time to even throw it in a ponytail. She took a second to try to smooth it, but it was pointless. She glanced over at the police officer who was standing by the door staring at her, eyebrows raised, and felt like she was on the set of *Law and Order*. She looked again at the mirror and wondered who was watching her.

Vivian was kept waiting for what felt like forever. *Is this some kind of police trick? Make me nervous so I'll look like I've done something wrong?* she thought.

Vivian was sweating just sitting still.

Surely they won't try to blame me for Jon's death?

22

Detective Vega, accompanied by another police officer, interviewed Lucy, Wendy and Kate individually before interviewing Vivian. He started with Lucy because she seemed the most nervous.

She did her interview standing up, arms crossed, not wanting to sit in the chair she thought of as a butt-sized Petri dish of germs. Her nerves were on edge, causing her right foot to tap uncontrollably. This was Lucy's personal cure, her way of dealing with stress.

Vega glanced at her foot, annoyed, and pushed the "record" button on a recorder. He started with the questions.

"State your full name and address for the record," he said with a thick accent, but otherwise proper English.

She did, then added, "And by the way, I'm a U.S. Citizen."

Vega ignored the last part. "What is your business in Mexico?"

"No business. Vacation."

"How do you know the deceased, Jon Tournay?"

"I met him here in Playa. He is staying, oh, *was* staying, at our hotel."

"And how do you know Ms. Taylor?"

"Let's see…Viv and I have been friends since junior high."

"Why did you choose Playa del Carmen?" He glanced again at Lucy's foot, getting more annoyed by her tapping.

"Well, Viv is getting divorced in a week and her 30th birthday was two days ago, so we all pitched in and bought her a trip to Playa. This is not exactly what we imagined for our vacation," she said, glancing around.

Lucy knew she was rambling but couldn't help it. Detective Vega's gaze was intimidating and words just kept tumbling out of her mouth. "Your police station needs a good cleaning. Don't y'all have janitors?" *Shit! I shouldn't have said that. Don't they throw people in jail down here for no reason?*

Ignoring her last comment Vega asked, "What have you and your friends been doing since you have been here?"

Lucy gave him a quick rundown of the past two days, ending with, "We went to Club Caliente last night and ran into Jon and Pierre."

"Tell me about last night," Vega said.

"We got there, and it was freakin' hot. I mean, like Brazilian jungle hot. Club Caliente really needs to upgrade their a/c or something because it felt like it was 110 degrees in there. Aren't there city ordinances against stuff like that?" *There I go again, dammit. Don't put me in jail, don't put me in jail...*

He rolled his eyes. "Focus on the events of last night, Ms. McGuire, not the temperature."

"Oh, okay. Sorry."

"Tell me what happened at the club."

"We went there with Al and Adrienne, whom we had met earlier at the hotel."

"Who are Al and Adrienne?"

"This fun couple from Chicago who are also staying at our hotel. They're a hoot! He might be in the mob, though. And let me tell ya, Adrienne was head-to-toe decked out. Al is beyond arrogant. He's always on the phone and it ticks her off. They're really loud, too." *Should I have said "mob?" What if he thinks I'm associated with the mob? Crap!*

"Again, focus. What happened when you got to the club?"

"I'm sorry, can you repeat the question please?" The more nervous Lucy got, the more difficult Vega's accent was to understand.

He repeated the question and she continued, "Al bought us some champagne. Some of us danced, some of us went outside to the balcony, we were all drinking. In fact, Arturo was even there. He did a dive into Viv's boobs when the champagne bottle was uncorked. He thought it was a gun shot."

Detective Vega sighed, shook his head and glanced again at Lucy's ever-tapping foot.

"You know, speaking of Arturo, have you talked to him about last night?"

"I am the one asking the questions, Ms. McGuire."

"Sorry. But he was there."

"What was Ms. Taylor doing?"

"She and Jon were tearin' it up on the dance floor!"

"And by tearing it up you mean...?"

"They were dirty dancing and kissing, you know...muggin' down."

"And what about Mr. Laroche. Where was he?"

"What? Who?"

"Pierre Laroche."

"Oh, I didn't know his last name. Sorry. He took me for a spin on the dance floor, but I was too hot and gave up. Besides, I was trying to behave, 'trying' the key word in that sentence, but Al kept ordering us drinks and I'm not one to be rude. I'm a social drinker. Basically, if you buy it, I'll drink it. Plus I'm on vacation!" *Sweet Baby Jesus, I've got to get out of here. The walls are closing in. Deep breath, focus.*

Vega stared at her for a moment before continuing, "Did anything out of the ordinary happen? Did you see anyone who did not belong?"

"Not really. I'm in another country. How would I know who belongs and what's out of the ordinary?"

"You seem extremely nervous, Ms. McGuire. Do you have something to hide?"

Oh no, here it comes, slammer time. "No, I don't have anything to hide. And what do you mean I seem nervous? Why wouldn't I be? I'm in a police station being interviewed about a man's death!" Lucy's hands shook and her foot tapped even faster, trying to keep tempo with her racing heart.

Detective Vega shook his head again. "What time did you leave the club and with whom?"

Lucy took a deep breath. "We all left, except Viv and Jon. Well, actually, Al and Adrienne had already left. Pierre walked me, Kate and Wendy back to the hotel. Arturo walked out with us but went his own way outside. It was probably around 1 a.m. or so. I don't remember exactly, I was a bit snockered." *Am I making Viv look guilty? But what if I would have lied? Oh my god.*

"Seems odd you would leave your friend with a stranger in another country."

"The hotel is just down the street and I think Viv and Jon wanted some alone time, if you know what I mean." *Oh crap.* "Wait! By alone time, I meant for making out some more, not...not for any...uh, not for anything bad." *I can barely hold it together. I've got to shut up before I get us all thrown in jail.*

Detective Vega stared her down for a full minute before continuing. He hit the stop button on the recorder. "How much is your freedom worth to you?"

Frazzled as she was, Lucy understood his meaning and reached into her purse. "About fifty bucks. This is all the cash I have on me." *Fuckin' A. Dirty rat bastard.* Lucy hoped her thoughts didn't show on her face. She really wanted out of that police station.

He stood and grabbed the cash, pushing it into his pants pocket. He kicked back his chair and stared her down.

She froze, unable to move, not even her foot.

He turned and showed her the door.

23

Detective Vega sat down across from Vivian while the other policeman stayed by the door. Both men were of medium height and lean build, much like their ancient Mayan ancestors, but Detective Vega had a harder look about him. His black, steely eyes and deadpan expression made her stomach, which was on the verge of turning to goo, do a flip.

Vega turned on a tape recorder and went through formalities such as name, address, date and time. Vivian didn't have as much trouble as Lucy in understanding his accented English.

"What is your relationship with the deceased, Jon Tournay?"

Vivian opened and closed the clasp of her watch before she managed to answer in a calm manner. "No relationship really. I just met him a few days ago."

"Where were you last night?"

"I went to Club Caliente with my friends." Vivian continued to snap her watch clasp absentmindedly.

"Please state exactly who you went with."

Vivian listed off the girls, Al and Adrienne. "And Arturo met us there too."

"What about Mr. Tournay? Did you have plans to meet at the club?"

"No, he and Pierre were just there."

"Witnesses tell us the two of you looked quite intimate last night."

"We were just dancing." Snap.

"I don't know many dances that involve kissing."

Vivian crossed her arms, then uncrossed them and put her hands in her lap. Sitting across from Vega in the interview room made her feel guilty of something, even though she had done nothing wrong and she wasn't sure how he would interpret her body language.

She answered after a moment's hesitation. "Okay, perhaps we added some unconventional dance moves, thanks to the heat, alcohol and hormones, but I still didn't have a relationship with him."

"You have been crying for a man you did not have a relationship with?" Vega shook his head.

"Of course I have been crying! Jon is dead! No, I hadn't known him for very long but he seemed like a genuinely nice person." Vivian wiped the smudged mascara from underneath her eyes in an attempt to look more presentable. She felt hung-over and knew she looked it and didn't think that bought her any brownie points with Vega.

"What time did you leave Club Caliente?"

"I don't really know. It was close to 2:00, I think. I didn't look at my watch." Snap.

"What kind of watch do you have?"

Vivian set her arms on the table. "Bulova."

"Who did you leave the club with?"

"It was just me and Jon." Snap.

"Where were your friends?"

"They left a little while before we did and went back to the hotel. They said they were tired. Pierre walked them back." Vivian tucked her hair behind her left ear, trying to look calmer on the outside than she felt on the inside.

"Why did they leave you in a strange town with a stranger?"

"I can take care of myself and Jon wasn't a stranger. We were having a good time and just not ready to leave yet." Snap.

The detective's eyes narrowed. "After you left the club what happened?"

Her stomach did another flip. "We went to the bar at our hotel and got a drink. Jon asked me if I wanted to go on a walk down the beach, and I said yes, so we did."

"Why did you agree to a walk on the beach?"

"It seemed harmless enough, and we didn't even go very far." Snap. Vivian placed her right hand over her watch to make herself stop fiddling with it.

"What happened on the beach?"

Vivian's face got hot. "We just walked in the water a bit, talked, kissed, and that was it. I went up to my room."

"How far out in the water did you go?"

"We only got our feet wet. Did he drown? Maybe he went swimming when I went up to my room?" *Oh god, that would be awful.*

Vega didn't respond to the question, only asked another. "Why did he stay on the beach?"

"He said he was expecting a call from his agent about a part in a movie."

"Did he say why the call would be so late?"

"He said his agent was out with the movie producer. They went to dinner or something."

Vivian was starting to get the feeling Jon's death was not from drowning or natural causes. "What's going on here? I thought you were just trying to get a timeline or something from me?"

Detective Vega opened a folder and shoved a picture in front of her.

Blood. All Vivian saw at first was blood.

She closed her eyes for a moment, then opened them again. Jon had a nasty gash in his neck and his handsome face was smeared red. Blood soaked his shirt and spattered and pooled in the sand around him. Vivian covered her mouth and turned her head. Tears spilled down her cheeks but she willed herself not to have a full blown meltdown in front of Vega. It took all her strength not to.

"Oh my god! That's horrible," Vivian choked. She pushed the photo away. "How did this happen?"

Vega had been gauging her reaction. "Let me see your hands," was all he said after a minute.

Still shaken at seeing Jon's picture, Vivian held out her trembling hands, palms up.

"Remove the Band-Aid." Vega pointed to her right hand.

Vivian hesitated. "Now," Vega said, so she complied.

"Did you cut yourself killing Jon last night?"

"What? No! I cut myself building a sandcastle two days ago," Vivian said, then continued, "Ask J…," she finished, suddenly realizing that Jon was not around to corroborate her story. She had to blink back more tears and hold in a scream.

"A sandcastle? How old are you?"

Vivian brushed her cheeks with the back of her hands. "I built a sandcastle in honor of my kids. Jon and Pierre drove their jet skis up on the beach and demolished it. That's how we met."

"Are you right or left handed?"

"Right. Why?"

He tapped the picture. "So you have no idea how this happened?"

"Of course not! He didn't even walk me to my room." *This is so not good.* "Why do you think I was involved?"

"You were the last one to be seen with him."

"Yeah, but I didn't do this," Vivian shook her head and gestured to the picture. "Do you have any suspects?"

"Do not ask any more questions, Ms. Taylor. Or should I say, Mrs. Taylor? You are married, correct?"

I need air. How does he know this?

"Uhh. Yes. But..."

He cut her off. "You are, in fact, going through a nasty divorce right now, are you not, Mrs. Taylor?"

"Divorce, yes. I don't know about the nasty part. My husband is a cheating asshole."

"Are you angry with men? Perhaps vengeance would be nice?

"No way! I don't need vengeance, not toward Jon at least." *This guy is crazy.* She tried to snap her watch clasp again but her fingers fumbled and she couldn't get it.

At this point Detective Vega picked up the picture between them and put it back into a folder. He gave her a long, hard stare.

Vivian slid off her watch and set it on the table. "Is there anyone that saw me go up to my room last night? Saw Jon still on the beach on the phone? The front desk clerk, maybe?" *Please let there be someone.*

"I am still investigating the case."

He pushed back his chair and stood, swiping the Bulova in the process. "Stay close to Playa until I tell you otherwise."

Vivian took this as a signal to stand up but it wasn't easy to do on shaky knees. Vega reached for the doorknob and hesitated. He turned back to her.

"One last thing *Mrs.* Taylor, hand over your passport."

24

Vivian couldn't believe this was happening. She had enough troubles at home and sure didn't need more in a foreign country.

Arturo ushered Vivian toward the exit and she looked around for the girls. The three of them were on the steps, looking dejected.

They had already compared notes about their interviews and gave her the details. Each had been questioned by a fiery Detective Vega who assumed Vivian was a man-hater. Their passports had also been confiscated. This pissed Vivian off. They had flights to catch in a few days and they couldn't get back home without their passports. It was one thing to have an extended vacation, but this wasn't what any of them had in mind.

"He mostly just asked us how you knew Jon, what time we left the club last night, when you came in, etc." Kate sat on the top step with her knees to her chin.

Lucy stood on the bottom step, looking ready to go. "I was paranoid my nervous rambling would get me thrown in jail. I might have smarted off a couple of times," she paused, "on accident."

"Not good." Vivian walked past Wendy and Kate and stood next to Lucy.

"No, I admit, it wasn't. And we had to pay him off in order for him to let us out of the interview room. I only had fifty bucks on me and didn't know if that would be enough to buy my freedom."

"I only had forty dollars in my purse." Wendy sat on the step beside Kate. "I don't like to carry too much cash around down here, ya know?"

"I only had thirty and I was really nervous he wouldn't let me go for that," Kate said, "but I guess it was enough."

"What a bunch of crap, having to bribe the freaking police down here so we don't get thrown in jail for something we didn't do," Wendy said. "Makes me appreciate America."

Vivian rubbed her left wrist. "Well, he took my watch."

"What?" Lucy asked. "Wasn't that a gift from Rick?"

"Yeah, his wedding present. But the box he gave it to me in wasn't a Bulova box so I figured he bought it at a pawn shop. Cheap bastard."

"At least it kept you from going to jail today," Kate said.

"True that."

"We have got to get out of here right now," Lucy said, who was obviously still totally freaked out. "I need a shower to get the grit and germs off of me."

"Yeah, I feel pretty freakin' nasty myself." Vivian looked around the parking lot. "How are we getting back to the hotel?"

"Arturo has two police cruisers waiting for us." Kate pointed to a couple of cop cars. "I don't think this is the usual service, so let's go."

The girls made their way to the cars and reluctantly got in the back. This time Lucy rode with Vivian so she wouldn't feel like such a criminal by herself.

The police dropped them off a block from the hotel and as they walked past the "special parking" they noticed their rent car's door was ajar. They went over to it and saw the glove box open and the console between the front seats was not shut all the way. The P.O.S. had been searched.

"At least there's nothing in here to steal." Lucy slammed the door closed.

"Fuck it," Vivian decided, so they walked to the hotel, where several police cars still lined the street.

In front of the hotel, a reporter was talking to a police officer, jotting down notes in a small notebook, and a photographer was taking a picture of the hotel sign.

"Let's try to avoid them." Wendy nodded toward the activity.

"But we have to go right by them to get to the hotel," Lucy said.

"It's fine. Just try to look touristy." Wendy forced a smile.

They walked by as nonchalantly as possible but Vivian could feel the reporter eyeing them. She glanced back after they were a good 20 feet away and saw the policeman turn and point to them.

"Crap, I think he just blew our cover!"

The reporter and Vivian made eye contact. The reporter flipped her notebook closed and yelled for the photographer.

"This is not good." Kate walked a little faster. "We need to make ourselves scarce before we end up on the front page of some Mexican newspaper."

The girls picked up the pace, walked around to the beach side of La Vida de Playa and looked up. The police were on a third-floor balcony that must have been Jon and Pierre's.

"I saw Pierre leave the station," Lucy said. "I wonder if he's in his room with the police?"

Vivian looked up at the balcony, determined. "I'm going up there, I want to talk to him."

Kate grabbed Vivian's arm. "You heard what he said at the station. Are you sure you should be talking to him?"

"Yes, absolutely. I *need* to talk to him. I'm going up."

The girls followed Vivian on her mission. They quickly went through the lobby and hit the stairwell. They were trying to be quiet but their flip-flops were flippity flopping as they plodded up to the third story, where they were met by a young policeman. He wore the same uniform they'd seen Arturo in.

"*Hola, señoritas.* Is your room on this floor?"

"No, we're on the second floor but we've come up here to talk to Pierre." Vivian pointed to Pierre's door. "Is he here? It's important."

The policeman looked at them individually, pondered, then held up a finger. "*Uno momento, por favor.*"

He walked over to an older man in plain clothes who looked like he was in charge. The detective opened the door and shouted, "Pierre, *cuatro señoritas estas aqui.*"

"I don't have anything to say to them," Pierre shouted back. "Tell them to go away."

The uniformed policeman looked at the girls and shrugged. "Sorry, *señoritas.*"

Feeling defeated, a little freaked out, embarrassed and certainly paranoid, they went down to their room.

Upon entering their room, OCD Lucy could tell immediately it had been searched. Things just weren't how they left them.

"Look! This is not where I left my suitcase. It was on the stand and not on the floor."

Wendy walked into their bathroom. "My toiletries have all been moved around, too."

"Don't they need permission to search our room?" Kate asked.

"We're in Mexico — who the hell knows?" Vivian sat down on the bed. "We don't have anything to hide, so I'm not too worried about it."

"Not worried about it! Viv, this is our stuff!" Lucy stood in front of her, hands on hips. "They probably didn't even wear gloves! God knows what sorts of bacterial bugs they left behind."

"Lucy, it's going to be okay. We'll buy some Lysol or something."

Lucy gave Vivian a sideways glance and a huff.

Kate opened the room safe. "Looks like our cash is still here."

"Thank goodness," Vivian said.

"Yeah." Wendy sat down on the other bed. "We might need that for more bribes."

"We need to regroup." Kate eased down next to Vivian. "Figure out what we should do."

"What we should do?" Vivian held her hands up in frustration. "What can we do?"

"Viv, you could be in serious trouble here," Kate said. "We need to talk about it."

"I told Detective Vega that I didn't have anything to do with, with ..." she stammered. It was difficult for her to bring herself to say it. "With his death."

"Do you think they'll charge Vivian with murder?" Lucy asked Kate.

"This is Mexico and from stories I've heard, they pin crimes on Americans without doing a thorough investigation just because."

"I agree, we need to discuss this situation," Wendy said. "We have to keep Vivian out of Mexican jail."

"Let's go to the pool for this discussion." Lucy tapped her foot in nervousness. "I don't really want to be in the room right now."

"I'll run downstairs real quick to see if the reporter and photographer are still here," Wendy said. She returned in a minute, "Coast is clear. There are still a few policemen, but I think we've faced the worst of those already."

Lucy took a quick shower to wash off the "grit, grime and funk" from the station, then they threw on their swimsuits, grabbed the sunscreen, and were outta there.

"I know it's early, but I could use a drink right now," Vivian said as they exited the lobby. "I thought divorce was stressful but this is way worse."

The girls walked to the poolside bar and ordered Tiempo Loco tequila shots.

Vivian raised her glass, "To Jon-ola." Tears welled in her eyes and her voice broke on the "ola."

The other girls chimed in, "To Jon-ola."

Vivian reached for a napkin before the water works began again. She had a feeling this would be the first of several drinks this afternoon to help numb the pain.

They ordered a bucket-o-beer, found four poolside lounge chairs and settled in.

Kate got right to the situation. "Viv, maybe we should find you a local attorney. You might need some legal help to get out of this and out of the country."

The welling of tears spilled out. *How could this have happened?* Vivian thought.

"I wouldn't know what attorney to call or who to trust," Vivian said in a shaky voice. "How will I know they would truly help me and not just take my money?"

"What about calling Rick?" Lucy adjusted the umbrella for better coverage. "You are still technically married to him, and he is a criminal defense attorney after all."

The thought of calling Rick for help put an end to Vivian's crying. "There's no way in hell I'm calling him for help. I'm clearly not his priority, and, who knows, he could use this against me. Besides, there's only one head he's thinking with right now, and it's not the one containing his brain. Let's see how today pans out. Maybe Detective Vega was just trying to scare us."

"Sorry for bringing up dickwad's name, but I think we need to look into all our options," Lucy said.

The girls kept plodding forward. "Maybe we should buy some calling cards," Kate said.

"And give me Rick's number."

"And your parents," Lucy said.

"I still have their number memorized." Wendy finished rubbing in the SPF 15 and handed the bottle to Kate.

"Maybe we should contact the closest U.S. Embassy or something?" Kate squeezed a bit of sunscreen into her hand.

Vivian pushed her sunglasses over her swollen eyes and ignored their worst case scenario planning. She thought again about *Locked Up Abroad*, and she definitely did not want to be locked up abroad.

Surely not, there's no way, not jail...Right?

25

Instructed not to go far and not knowing where to go or what else to do, Vivian sat by the pool, drank a beer, and listened to the girls spin ideas on how to get out of Mexico, legally.

After beer two, a shadow was cast over her and she looked up to see Big Al.

"Hey, man-eater."

A horrified Adrienne hit him on the shoulder. "Al, don't say that."

"Oh, I'm just kidding. She knows I'm kidding."

"Still."

"It's okay, Adrienne," Vivian waved her off. "I know I didn't do it."

"Heard any good rumors about who could have?" Wendy asked, sitting up in her lounger.

"Not really, but the police have been all over the hotel and the beach," Adrienne said.

"Yeah, they searched our room while we were at the police station." Lucy pushed her sunglasses onto her head.

"Really?" Al's eyebrows shot up in surprise. "Then you definitely need to do a room sweep and look for bugs."

"Oh, there aren't any bugs," Lucy shook her head. "I wouldn't stay here if there were."

"He's not talking about bug bugs, Lucy." Kate took a sip of beer. "He's talking about listening devices; you know, spy stuff."

"Oh. Well, I'm not up on those invasion of privacy gadgets!"

Al shook his head and sat down on the empty lounger next to Vivian. "Listen, sweetheart, I have a cousin, Salvatore, a.k.a 'Slinky Sal,' who's an attorney in Jersey. I don't mind putting in a call for you."

"Is he real limber and bendy?" Lucy asked. "I used to love my slinky."

"No, not really."

"Then why do they call him Slinky Sal?"

Al suppressed a grin. "It's rumored he's been known to send things end over end down stairs."

"What do you mean?" Lucy asked.

"Oh, you know, like the occasional witness."

Obviously, Slinky Sal was not a man to be toyed with.

Adrienne punched Al playfully in the arm. "You shouldn't be talking like that, Al."

He shrugged.

Vivian couldn't help but smirk at their exchange. "Thanks Al, but hopefully it won't come to anything like that."

Adrienne sat on the end of Vivian's lounge chair. "So what the heck happened after we left last night? Last I saw you looked like you were on your way to salami-ville."

"There was no salami-ville but, as you saw at the club, there was a lot of kissing."

With that, Vivian raised her beer and gave another toast to Jon. "To the best Canadian salsa dancing kisser in all of Mexico."

Clink.

Vivian then continued, "We left the club around 1:45 or 2, I guess, came back here, stopped by the bar and then went for a walk on the beach. That was it. He stayed down on the beach when I went back to the room. He was waiting on a call from his agent about a movie part."

"I just thought of something." Kate pointed to Vivian with her beer. "Did you tell Detective Vega we keep seeing creepy ponytail guy everywhere we've been and that Jon and Pierre were there, too? Maybe he was following them."

"No, I didn't even think about that. Did anyone else mention it?"

Wendy shook her head. "Nope."

Lucy: "Me, neither."

"It didn't seem like a big deal at the time," Kate continued, "but now that Jon is toast it makes me wonder if there's a connection."

"We've got to get hold of Detective Vega or Arturo and tell them this." Vivian looked around to see if Arturo was in sight. "This could be important. I can't believe I didn't think of this sooner."

"I agree." Kate sat up and swung both feet on the ground. "Jon, Pierre and Ponytail were there the first night at the Purple Peacock, then yesterday morning at the marina, *and* at Club Caliente last night."

That did raise the suspicion up a notch, or ten, in Vivian's mind. *It has to be Ponytail. He's the killer.*

"We've been to the Purple Peacock. Al didn't like the swings. Said they didn't feel stable." Adrienne looked at Al and tickled his robust stomach with her fingers. "Sweetie, isn't there something you can do to help find out who this ponytail guy is?"

"I know who you're talking about." Al reached for his phone, which was in his shirt pocket again, making it droop and show off too much chest hair. "Let me make a few phone calls and see what I can find out. Maybe some of my connections have connections down here."

Al walked off, phone in hand, and Adrienne patted Vivian's hand. "It's going to be okay. Al knows a lot of people."

Kate hopped up. "I'm going to the parking lot, see if I can find Arturo. He can help us. I know it."

She slipped on her flip-flops and trotted off down the sand.

Wendy turned to Lucy. "Lucy, go with her please. We're implementing the buddy system from here on out. No more going off anywhere alone."

Lucy put on her shoes and raced off to catch Kate. She could run the fastest of the girls, even after a tequila shot and a beer.

She turned around, jogging backwards and yelled out, "Good idea!"

Little too late for that rule to kick in. Dammit.

"So who are Al's contacts?" Wendy asked Adrienne.

She tried to make the question sound innocent, but Vivian knew better. Wendy was an avid reader and Vivian figured she was having a book moment, fancying herself as Nancy Drew or some such.

"Oh honey, Al has connections everywhere," Adrienne answered. "He's really into the local politics in Chicago and he's pretty good at trading a nice meal for information, too."

"The ol' wine and dine trick, huh?" Wendy put her hair up in a ponytail. "Bet he learns a lot that way. Loose lips and all."

"As long as his connections help me out, I don't care who, what or how," Vivian said.

Kate and Lucy came running back.

"We found Arturo in front of the hotel," Kate stood beside the lounger Vivian shared with Adrienne. "He called Detective Vega and he's on his way."

"Okay, let's be rational here," Wendy said. "Just because we've seen Ponytail a lot doesn't automatically make him a killer. He looks like a killer, what with dressing all in black and that huge scar on the side of his face, but we need to be careful. Playa is not a huge place and we don't want to make any more enemies."

Book moment over or she would have pinned it on Ponytail.

"Well, it is odd you have seen him so much." Adrienne slipped her sandals off and on. Vivian noticed they were Cole Haan.

Lucy got back underneath her umbrella. "He looks like he's been in a knife fight. I bet it's him."

"Ponytail's not the only person we've seen a lot of," Wendy said, book moment evidently not over.

"Who else?" Adrienne asked.

Vivian's mind flashed on an image of the short guy pointing his finger gun at a passerby. "There are Shorty and The Ladies."

"Oh, that's right." Lucy snapped her fingers.

Vivian continued, "They were at the Purple Peacock, and we think Jon and Pierre were on his boat yesterday. They were also at Club Caliente last night."

"Who's that?" Adrienne said, wiggling her toes and inspecting her pedicure.

"Some machismo-lookin' mini-guy Jon and Pierre were hanging out with. He had a girl on each arm, but I'm telling you, he doesn't look like a ladies' man."

"Mini-guy?" Adrienne asked.

"He seriously *might* be 5-feet tall." Vivian held her thumb and index finger an inch apart. "Mini."

"Shorty freaked out on Jon last night, remember?" Lucy noted.

"Oh yeah, I forgot. We were so flustered at the station this morning, I guess none of us thought of it."

"And don't forget the crazy lady." Wendy said, moving her finger in circles by her temple, the international sign for cuckoo. "We didn't see her last night but Jon got a drink from her, remember?"

"No…Jon didn't, Dominik did," Kate said, dipping her right foot in the pool.

"That's right, his soap opera persona. She's a good candidate, can't rule out the crazies," Adrienne said. "What did she look like?"

Vivian raised her arms above her head to stretch and ran her hands through her hair. "She's normal looking, I guess. Hispanic, about my height, with long, black straight hair. She wears green contacts, but I think her eyes are really brown."

Kate touched the small of her back. "And she has a spider tramp stamp. It looks like a black widow spider, actually."

"That's a bit strange." Adrienne said, cleaning her sunglasses with her form-fitting tank top.

When she lifted it Vivian noticed she had a belly button piercing. *She's blingin' everywhere!*

"What's her name again?" Adrienne continued.

Lucy stood up and yelled out, *Streetcar* style, "Stellaaaaaa!"

Adrienne and Vivian looked at each other and laughed. At least they could still find a little humor in things.

"See, so we need to be careful," Wendy said. "There are at least three strange people in this town…"

Vivian cut her off. "You can say that again!"

"Who could and should be considered 'persons of interest,'" Wendy finished, all that reading paying off with her amateur sleuthness.

26

Vivian looked up to see Pierre walk out of the lobby, heading straight for them, a scowl still on his face. She was relieved, however, that he was not carrying any objects that could impale them or be described as weapons.

He walked right over to her and sat down on the lounge chair Al vacated earlier.

"Vivian. Listen, I'm sorry about earlier at the station. Surely you can understand I'm upset, and having the police all in my business isn't helping. I'm sorry they brought you in, I feel bad about that. I don't think for a minute you did this."

Whew.

Vivian sat down next to him and gave him a long hug. "Thank you, Pierre." After a moment she asked, "Do you know what happened to Jon? Did the police tell you anything?"

Pierre leaned over and put his thumb and finger over his eyes. He had to clear his throat before speaking. "The evidence indicates his neck was sliced open with some sort of jagged edged weapon, severing his jugular. He was dead within minutes."

Vivian was too upset to speak. She leaned into Pierre and sobbed into his chest. He cried silently as he held her and the other girls were upset, too.

After a while the tears subsided and the group let out a collective sigh. Wendy then asked, "Did they find the weapon?"

He shook his head. "No. Vega didn't give me a lot of details. He started off interrogating me, though I don't think I ever really was a suspect. He said it went fast, that Jon took a few steps and collapsed."

Everyone was silent.

"It just doesn't make any sense." He cleared his throat again. "I can't imagine who would want to hurt Jon. Vega kept asking me that in the interview this morning, and I can't think of anyone. I've known him for years, and he's never had any enemies."

"I didn't know him for long." Vivian was sad thinking about Jon lying on the beach bleeding to death. "But I can't see anyone wanting to hurt him."

"Did he have any stalkers?" Lucy touched Pierre lightly on the arm as she asked this.

"No, not that I know of anyway."

Wendy asked, "Did Jon have a blog, Twitter account, Facebook page, something?"

"He has a Facebook fan page."

"Have you checked it since last night? See if there are any strange comments on his wall?"

"I didn't even think to."

"Can you check his Facebook on your phone?" Vivian asked.

"Battery is dead," he said with a sigh. "I left it in the room charging."

Kate, who had been pacing, stopped and asked, "Where's Jon's phone?"

"The police must have it."

"I'll go grab my laptop," Wendy said and dashed off.

Wendy was a loan officer for a mortgage company. She brought her computer on vacation "just to keep tabs on a couple of files."

Adrienne sat on the lounger, legs crossed, right foot shaking back and forth. "Did Jon ever do drugs? Could he have been into something you didn't know about, maybe money laundering or sleeping with married women? Those things can get a guy killed."

"No," Pierre answered. "Absolutely not. Compared to most people in show business, Jon led a clean, honest life."

Arturo walked up and announced, "Vega will be here in a few minutes."

Kate gave Arturo a nervous grin. "Can you tell us if the police were able to find the weapon that was used to kill Jon?"

He shifted from foot to foot and watched as Wendy arrived with her computer bag and sat back down. "I'm sorry, I can't say. You need to talk to Vega."

Vivian pushed her sunglasses on top of her head and looked directly at Arturo. "Do you know who this guy is with the scar on his face and the long ponytail? Have you seen him?"

Before Arturo could answer, Pierre interrupted, "What are you talking about?"

Vivian touched his hand and said, "Hold on a sec, Pierre," then continued, "he was at the Purple Peacock, at the marina *and* at Club Caliente. We think he's the killer."

"Whoa, Viv," Wendy interjected. "There's more than just him. You need to tell Arturo everything."

Pierre moved his hand away from Vivian's. "What guy? Do you think he was following us? What do you mean there's more than just him?"

"There's also Shorty short short and Crazy Stella," Wendy said.

"Who is Shorty? I have no idea what you are talking about." Pierre put his head in his hands and slowly shook his head back and forth.

Arturo, too, shook his head. "Sorry, you really need to tell Detective Vega. I shouldn't make any comments."

Al returned from calling his connections to find the group silent and somber. "What the hell happened? Did somebody die?"

Everyone looked at him with shocked expressions.

He clapped Pierre on the shoulder. "Oh, yeah. Sorry, man."

Adrienne asked Al if he had any luck. He reported that he spoke to someone who owed him a favor and he should be getting a call back shortly.

Wendy had the laptop fired up and handed it over to Pierre.

He went to Jon's Facebook page. "Looks like a couple of weeks ago Jon posted that we were down here and having a great time."

He held the computer so Vivian, who was still sitting next to him, could see but the other girls had to gather around behind him to see the screen. Jon's picture was a professional head shot, and Vivian thought he looked damn good in it.

"Not much activity, no threatening posts," Wendy said.

"Can you get into his e-mail?" Lucy asked.

"I don't know his password."

"What about the soap opera, do they have a website?" Kate asked.

"Yes, but I've never been to it." Pierre went to Google and typed in "obsessions soap opera."

Wendy rolled her eyes. "Soap opera names are so dumb."

Pierre clicked on the link to the soap opera and up popped a picture of the cast, sans Jon. "They sure didn't waste any time getting him out of the picture."

A headline announced the demise of their beloved soap star, Jon Tournay. The article had several pictures of Jon looking dapper on the set, and also a picture of him on a beach.

"News travels fast," Kate said.

"I wonder how they found out so fast?" Vivian said.

"I had to call Jon's agent with the news this morning," Pierre said. "The worst phone call of my life."

"I'm so sorry Pierre," Adrienne's foot no longer shook back and forth. She just looked down right forlorn.

"I wonder if we're going to see any paparazzi down here?" Lucy said. "Because that seriously looks like the Playa del Carmen beach in that picture."

"Dear god, I hope not," Vivian said. "That won't be good for my divorce."

Pierre looked at her. "If they're not here yet, you can bet they're coming."

27

The paparazzi will be here in force," Pierre said. "Jon's momentum was building. He was recently voted one of Canada's most eligible bachelors."

"Wow. Who knew?" Vivian said, but thought *he was pretty damn hot!*

"He was on the cover of a recent issue of *SoapStuds* magazine."

"*SoapStuds*? That sounds more like porn."

"Not in Canada, though he was half-naked in a few of the pictures. After the magazine his popularity skyrocketed. In fact, he wouldn't renew his soap contract because of the interest in him for a movie."

"How ticked were the soap people when Jon didn't renew his contract?" Vivian asked. "In America, when you're written off a soap it's usually in some way where one day they can write you back in. Sounds like Jon's character was blown to bits."

"Yeah, they weren't happy with his agent and gave him some shit. They didn't think he tried hard enough to get Jon to renew, but he was ready to move on to bigger and better things."

"That piss his agent off?" Al leaned on the back of Adrienne's chair. "Make it hard for him to place other actors with the network and hurt his income?"

"I don't know."

"You know, the timing of this is weird on many levels," Vivian said. "Maybe the soap people were mad enough to *really* off him."

"Surely not. It's just a soap opera," Kate said, who was not a watcher of soaps.

"To us it's just a soap opera, but to the TV execs it was business, and he apparently pissed some of them off." Vivian clicked on that thought and said, "Did you mention any of this to Detective Vega? The agent or the TV execs?"

"No. At the time I didn't think it was relevant, but now, it seems more important. Especially since I remember hearing him talk to his agent about

116

him not liking the direction they were taking his character."

"That could have chapped some hides," Lucy said. "What were they going to do that he didn't like?"

"He had always been the good guy, you know, married to Celeste and they had a baby. They were going to have his character have several affairs and Jon didn't like it. He felt like there was enough shit with the other characters and they should leave one good guy. He was pretty adamant about it."

"I definitely think you should bring it up." Arturo said.

Pierre clicked on the headline announcing Jon's death. A new blog page popped up with pictures of him from the show, a guest book where people could post their sympathies, and a snippet of the details surrounding his death.

Obsessions is sad to announce that Jon Tournay, who played Dominik Gagnon, was found dead in Playa Del Carmen, Mexico, early this morning. Circumstances surrounding his death indicate foul play.

Authorities gave few details but did say there is at least one suspect in the case.

Obsessions will provide additional information as it becomes available.

"Oh shit, Viv. I bet they are talking about you there," Pierre said.

Arturo turned his head and looked like he was trying to be uninterested, but it came off as uncomfortable.

"Nah, the cops probably told them that just to put a positive spin on it. Right, Arturo?"

An awkward silence followed Vivian's question. Arturo shrugged and stammered, "Uh…yeah, yeah, sure."

Yeah, sure, my ass.

"Fuck," Vivian said.

"Scroll down some," Kate said.

They stood over Pierre's shoulder and read the latest guest book entries with condolences and people saying how much they loved Jon and will miss him.

"Look how young he looks in that one!" Lucy pointed at a picture.

"Yeah, that's from five years ago when he first joined the show," Pierre told them.

They all sighed a sad sigh.

"I want to see more of the blog entries," Kate said.

Pierre got up from the lounge chair and handed the computer to Kate. "Here, you take over, I don't know if I can read any more sympathies."

Kate clicked on the next most recent post, Jon's farewell from the show. He had an outpouring of fans supporting him on his next adventure, but one entry caught their attention.

BW

I saw you tonight dancing with that woman. I saw you kiss her. HOW COULD YOU? How could you deceive Celeste, and that sweet little baby? I'm horrified. You should have died in the explosion, you don't deserve to breathe.

The post was made at 1:45 that morning.

Vivian was too stunned to speak, and so was everyone else except Lucy. "Oh...my...god...Viv."

"It has to be Stella," Vivian finally managed to get out. "That woman is nutso."

Snapping to, Kate turned to Arturo. "Come here and look at this. Does Detective Vega know about this?"

He gave a head shake and a noncommittal shrug. "I don't know. I don't know all of the details in the investigation."

Wendy asked Arturo, "Can the police find out the IP address from where this comment was posted?"

Arturo gave another shrug. *He's full of those today.*

Adrienne got up and whispered in Vivian's ear. "I'll call my brother and see if he can look into this. He's a cop in New Orleans, he may be able to help."

She then winked at Al. "Sweetie, let's walk down the street and grab a bite." Turning back to Vivian, she said, "Give Al your cell number, and we'll call you when we hear something."

28

Detective Vega walked across the sand toward the girls, Pierre and Arturo who were still poolside at the hotel. He looked odd wearing a suit on the beach. He also looked peeved.

"Have you found the murder weapon?" Wendy asked as soon as he was within hearing distance.

"What did you need to talk to me about?" He ignored her question.

Fucker's not going to tell us anything, Vivian thought. She pointed to the computer, "We found something on the *Obsessions* website that you need to see. Look at the comment that was posted last night. We think we know who posted it, and you need to find her. She may have been the one who killed Jon."

"How do you know who the BW is?" Detective Vega asked in his Mexican accent, but seemed uninterested.

How can he be so calm at a time like this?

Vivian gave him Stella's description, black spider tattoo and all. She also told him about the weird run-in with her at the Purple Peacock and the martini at Club Caliente. Vivian finished with, "She doesn't understand reality. She keeps calling him Dominik, his soap opera name. She's delusional."

Pierre explained that Jon's character, Dominik, was written off the show by being killed in an explosion. "The you-don't-deserve-to-breathe comment is sinister."

"Yep, sounds like premeditation to me," Vivian said.

Detective Vega looked skeptical.

"His agent got some shit from TV execs because he couldn't get Jon to renew his contract. They had to change the entire direction of the show because of it. That could have pissed off his co-stars since it affected them, too."

Pierre sat down on Adrienne's vacated lounger. "I gave Vega the agent's number this morning."

"Have you talked to the agent yet?" Vivian asked. "Jon was on the phone last night when I walked into the lobby. Maybe the agent heard something?"

Vega didn't answer, and he didn't seem to like Vivian questioning him.

Kate flipped Wendy's ponytail. "And don't forget about Ponytail."

"Oh yeah, there is also this creepy ponytail scar guy who has been following Jon around. He could be the killer," Lucy informed Detective Vega.

"And why do you think that, Ms. McGuire?" He bristled at the mention of this particular suspect.

"He has been everywhere that we were with Jon," Vivian said, "and he's scary looking."

"And?"

"And I think you need to find out who he is."

"Where all have you seen this ponytail guy exactly?"

"He was at the Purple Peacock two nights ago." Kate powered off the laptop. "He was watching people."

"There is no crime in that."

"And he was at the marina yesterday morning in the parking lot, taking pictures of boats," Wendy interjected. "We also saw him last night at Club Caliente, out on the balcony."

"Don't forget, Shorty and The Ladies were also out there." Lucy wobbled along the edge of the pool. Vivian was a little afraid she'd fall in.

Pierre stood. "Wait. Wait. Are you talking about Julio?"

"Yes, that's right," Vivian snapped her fingers. "I forgot that Jon said his name last night. We've been calling him Shorty."

Pierre explained to Detective Vega, "Jon went out on the balcony to say hello to Julio but only The Ladies were at the table. When Julio walked up he thought Jon was hitting on his women and shoved Jon."

Vega shook his head. "Julio may not be the most honest businessman here in Playa, but I do not see him committing murder."

"What kind of business is he in?" Kate said, putting the laptop back in Wendy's case.

"Tequila."

"What does he do dishonestly?" Vivian's interest in Shorty was piquing.

Vega gave no response.

"Will you look into these suspects?" Wendy eyed Vega, then watched Lucy as she continued to walk along the pool's edge.

The detective turned away, then paused for a moment and turned back. "You are suggesting that I need to look into a guy with a ponytail, Julio, spider woman, Mr. Tournay's agent, TV execs, co-stars and basically half of Canada."

Sarcastically, he added, "Anyone else?"

Irritated at his small-mindedness, Vivian got as close to Vega as she dared, put her hands on her hips and said, "Well I didn't kill him, and you need to find out who did."

Vega looked like he wanted to slap handcuffs on Vivian for making that comment. He turned and stalked off down the beach instead.

Vivian called after him, "Any chance we can get our passports back?"

He just kept walking.

This is craptacular.

Detective Vega disappeared down the beach and they all sat back down, Lucy included, much to Vivian's relief. No rescue needed.

"Think he's still pissed off about the Battle of San Jacinto?" Wendy, the history buff, asked.

"What was that?" Pierre asked.

"It was when Texas won their independence from Mexico in 1836 and became a republic."

"Remember the Alamo!" Kate shouted.

"Big loss for Mexico, huh?" Pierre said.

"Yep."

Vivian touched Pierre's arm. "I'm out of people. Is there anyone else y'all met down here you could have pissed off?"

"I told the police everything and anything I could think of," Pierre said. "Nobody stuck out to me. I never even noticed the ponytail guy or thought to check online." He rested his head in his hands, then continued, "I suck. I'm going upstairs."

He got up and walked away. Vivian felt bad for him and by the looks on the other girls faces, it was evident they all did.

"Now what?" Wendy asked.

"I say we just try to relax and take our mind off of things for a while." Vivian reclined her lounger. "I don't know what else to do and besides, I think we've done all we can for now."

"Let's do a shot," Lucy said. "I need a stress reliever." She signaled Manuel and ordered five shots of Tiempo Loco.

It'll help with my anxiety at least.

"What's with the five?" Kate asked. "You doin' two?"

"Nope, we gotta pour one for the homie."

"Huh?"

"Jon!"

"Oh, our homie, Jon."

Manuel handed Vivian her shot. "Sorry about *tu amigo*. I hear something, I tell you. *Tenga cuidado*."

"Gotcha."

The girls raised glasses and toasted to the recently departed, was gonna be in a movie, ex-soap star.

Lucy grabbed the SPF 75 and reapplied. She passed them the 15 knowing they wanted tans but also saving them from themselves.

"You girls are going to thank me one day. Trust me," she said as she scooted closer to the umbrella and put a towel over her face.

Kate and Wendy talked about the situation between themselves for a while and Vivian was glad they spoke so she couldn't hear them. She was overwhelmed between Jon's death and being questioned about his murder.

She needed something to take her mind off reality for a while and noticed two Hispanic kids playing "Baywatch" in the pool, taking turns saving one another and heaving each other up on the side of the pool. This was not easy for the girl, whose brother outweighed her by at least 30 pounds. The brother hauled his sister out and pumped on her stomach a few times until she spouted a stream of water. Then it was sister's turn to be rescuer. It was the distraction she needed as they did it over and over again, but it made her miss her kids.

"Wait a minute," Kate sat up suddenly with a fire in her eyes Vivian had never seen before. "Screw this waiting on Vega bullshit. We need to take matters into our own hands. We are going to find out more about our three suspects."

29

What do you mean 'our suspects' and 'find out more'?" Vivian sat up.

"We need to know more about Ponytail, Shorty and Crazy Stella." Kate said. "Find out who they really are and what they have been up to."

"Okay."

"It's better than just lying here all depressed because Jon's 86'd," Kate reasoned. "I hate to sound insensitive, but I'm afraid if we don't figure this out we may not be leaving in a few days."

Wendy looked at Vivian. "I agree with Kate. I don't trust Detective Vega to solve this, and I want my passport back."

Lucy, who apparently drank Jon's shot, removed the towel from her face and said, "Ditto," then dropped the towel back.

"But where are we going to start?" Vivian asked.

"We already have Al checking on Ponytail for us, so let's start with the marina and then go by the Purple Peacock and Club Caliente," Kate said. "We need to ask around, see if anyone knows anything about these people."

"If Shorty's not on his boat, maybe we can sneak on board, perhaps find something incriminating," Vivian said.

Lucy tossed her towel on the ground. "No way I'm stepping foot on his boat, much less sneaking around. If he caught us he'd kill us, too."

Wendy reminded them, "Seriously, be careful who you're accusing of murder. We don't want to give him a reason to come after us."

"I think he's into more than the tequila business," Kate said.

"Is it the boat or the two girlfriends?" Lucy asked.

"Both."

"Moving on," Wendy said. "We need to find out where Stella used the computer to post the blog comment."

Vivian sighed. "I hope Adrienne's brother can get that for us. Spider lady could have been on the computer anywhere, hotels, internet cafes, coffee shops. That's a lot of ground for us to cover."

"She could have also made the post from her cell phone." Kate held up her iPhone as an example.

"If we can get the phone number, then maybe Detective Vega could trace her whereabouts through that," Vivian said. "GPS or something."

"If she still has the phone and didn't ditch it," Wendy added, flashing on another book moment.

Lucy picked her towel back up. "I'm in. When should we start this? Tonight?"

"No need to wait," Kate said. "Let's get going."

"I could use another tequila shot right now," Lucy said.

"Lucy! You drank Jon's shot and yours!" Vivian said. "I can't believe you want more alcohol right now."

"Yep. I'm on vacation and I could use some courage for our mission. One more shot and I'll be good to go."

Lucy ordered another tequila shot and the girls decided that friends don't let friends drink alone, so they all toasted to the Definitely Defunct Soap Star.

No writing him back into the script.

Once in the room, Lucy went on a bit of a tangent about her stuff being handled by "nasty, germy space invaders who probably didn't wear gloves, certainly didn't wash their hands and could have contaminated her delicates," or something like that.

As Lucy jumped in the shower, Kate, Wendy and Vivian searched the room for listening devices. They looked through the nightstand and the dresser. No luck. They went through their luggage and purses. Kate bent down and peered under the bed. No bugs there, either. They couldn't talk about what they were doing, as they didn't want anyone who may have been listening to know what they were up to. Just as Vivian was about to deem the room bug free, Wendy looked under a lampshade and pulled off a small black device.

"Do you think this is one?" Wendy asked Vivian, holding it in her palm.

"I don't know. Maybe."

She held it out to Vivian. "Would you like to do the honors?"

"Are you sure that's it?"

"Well, I'm not totally certain, but I don't know what else it could be."

Vivian tossed it on the floor and stomped it into little pieces.

Kate walked over and looked down. "Is that what your phone looked like after you smashed it into Rick's head?"

"Yeah, pretty much."

After Lucy finished in the bathroom they all gathered 'round as Vivian flushed what was left of the bug down the toilet.

The rest of the girls got cleaned up quickly and as they left the hotel Vivian noticed the lady reporter was out front, joined by a news van which had its antenna thingy raised, and a male reporter looked like he was about to do a live broadcast.

"Let's go behind him and wave!" four-shot Lucy said, and before anyone could stop her did just that.

"Dear god, no! Avoid that area like the plague." Vivian, trying to stay out of the shot, grabbed her wrist and pulled Lucy behind her.

"Let's go around the far side of the hotel to get to the car." Wendy veered off to the left. "We don't want to be on TV. We need to stay incognito."

"Okay," Lucy agreed, defeated, and they were able to make their way to the car undetected.

It only took a few minutes to reach the marina, but they arrived only to find Shorty's boat not in its slip.

"Great. Now what?" Vivian asked.

"Let's go talk to Captain Juan, see if he knows anything," Kate suggested.

"Good idea."

The girls stood on the dock by the *Mucho Grande*. Captain Juan had his back to them, spraying the deck with a water hose. He turned their way and a fishy smell washed over them.

Vivian called out, "*Hola*, Captain Juan!"

He walked to the port side of the boat, next to the dock, and replied, "*Hola, señoritas*, you want to go on another fishing adventure?"

"We'd better not," Lucy said. "We don't want Detective Vega to think we're trying to leave the country and come after us."

Captain Juan looked bewildered. "*Que pasó?* You in trouble?"

"No, no. No trouble," Vivian smiled and said quickly. "We are looking for Julio who owns the boat *Belize It!* Have you seen him today?"

"What you want with him?"

"We need to ask him a question about a friend of his from Canada who was killed this morning."

"Ah, yes. I hear it some American lady." He cut his finger across his neck.

"Holy *caca*," Wendy muttered.

Vivian's face got hot. This was almost more than she could take.

Captain Juan wagged his finger at them. "One of you?"

Vivian laughed. "Nahhhh. We hardly knew the guy. We saw him hanging out with Julio a couple of times and just want to talk to him."

"Could you call us when you see his boat come back?" Kate politely asked.

Captain Juan thought about it for a second. Vivian stepped toward him and passed him a twenty. Money talks.

He took a step back and put it in his pocket. *"No problemo."*

Vivian wrote her cell number on a slip of paper and handed it to him. "Thanks. Please call us as soon as you see him come back."

"Adiós!" they called as they walked down the dock to the parking lot.

As Kate drove out of the lot, she glanced to her left and said, "Oh, my gosh, I think Ponytail's in that SUV."

Vivian turned to look. Yep, definitely Ponytail. "What's he doing here?"

"Maybe he's waiting for Shorty too?" Lucy suggested. "Or, maybe he's watching us? I don't know, but whatever the reason I need some food. I'm feeling a little queasy."

Wendy seconded the motion.

Kate glanced into the rearview mirror and watched him fade into the distance. "I don't like that guy one bit."

"We can grab a bite at the Purple Peacock." Vivian said as her phone rang. She didn't recognize the number, but answered in case it was Captain Juan.

"Yo, Viv, it's Al. I heard from my contact and have some news. Where are you girls?"

"Hey, Al. We were just heading back to the hotel. Are you there?"

"By the pool."

"We'll be there in a few." Vivian disconnected.

Kate looked again into the rearview. "Oh my gosh he's right behind us."

"What?" Wendy said.

"Ponytail. He's following us."

Wendy turned and glanced back. "Oh, shit."

Kate held the steering wheel in a white-knuckled grip. She glanced back in the mirror again.

"Hold on, girls, we're gonna lose him!"

30

Kate gripped the wheel tight, made a quick left turn and shot onto a one-way street, but going the wrong way. She dodged one car but the next one coming at them wasn't moving out of the way. Ponytail was in hot pursuit.

"Holy crap, Kate!" Lucy gripped the seat in front of her. "Don't play chicken with this guy, swerve out of the way!"

"There's nowhere to go!" Kate shouted.

As soon as the words were out of her mouth she saw an alley off to the right and made the turn, practically on two wheels, and almost hit a scraggly dog.

Wendy looked behind them. "He didn't turn down here. Maybe we lost him. "

But at the end of the alley Kate saw Ponytail pull out of a side street a few yards down. She turned right, going the correct way this time down another one-way street.

The SUV followed suit.

Kate had the gas pedal floored, but he was gaining on them.

"Kate, there's no way we can outrun him in this crappy car. You've got to out-maneuver him." Wendy grabbed on to her "oh-shit" handle. "Make some more turns or something."

"Hold on, everyone!" Kate said and took an abrupt left turn.

"He's still with us." Vivian glanced back.

The P.O.S. bounced along a narrow potholed street in a residential area. They zoomed past a couple of churches and a school. Then behind some houses. None had fences in the back. All had clotheslines.

Ponytail's bumper almost touched theirs.

I've got to lose him. They're counting on me, Kate thought.

"I've got an idea." She yanked the car off the pavement and onto sand and grass, driving directly towards the clotheslines.

"Kate, get out of the grass!" Lucy covered her eyes. "What are you doing? We're going to die!"

Sheets from the first clothesline flew over them. Muumuus in the next yard proved to be no problem. But a pair of big momma panties got caught on the antenna and looked like a surrender flag.

Kate had no intention of surrendering. She swerved around the last clothesline, through the field and back onto the road. Chickens ran for their lives.

Ponytail off-roaded it with them. Sheets plastered his windshield but he kept going. Muumuus and panties added a layer. He blindly plowed through the last clothesline, dragging it with him, poles and all. Then wrecked into a palm tree, coming to a dead stop.

Kate slowed down to the speed limit. Her hands shook. "I can't believe that just happened."

"You are a maniac! I never knew you could drive like that," Lucy said.

"I guess all those years of playing Pole Position with my brother paid off."

"Do you want to pull over and let me drive?" Wendy asked. "You must be coming down from a serious adrenaline high."

"Yeah, I think I will."

"Good job Kate!" Vivian pumped her fist in the air. "Way to save us."

Kate drove a few more blocks, then pulled into a gas station.

She stopped the car, jumped out, ran around to the other side, grabbing the panties off the antenna. She held them high in the air and ran in place singing "Maniac," doing a kick-ass impersonation of Jennifer Beals in *Flashdance*. The pent-up fear turned into laughter and tears of relief streamed down their faces.

They calmed down enough to continue on their way, but after all the turns in the chase, they were a bit lost. It took a while, but they finally recognized landmarks and found their way to the hotel.

The girls met Adrienne and Al at a table by the poolside bar. Vivian sat down and told them about the car chase and couldn't help but laugh again in the retelling of Kate's "Maniac" dance. Al, however, did not laugh. The look on his face scared her.

He leaned in close and spoke in a low voice. "Listen, my contact isn't sure who Ponytail is but suspects he's involved with some very tough people. It would be best to leave him alone, although you've probably just made him even more eager to come after you."

"Oh my god!" Vivian said.

"Shhh, Vivian, keep it down. My guy thinks he is affiliated with a certain organization that you don't want to mess with."

"Like the mob?" Lucy just couldn't help herself, the *Sopranos* influence kicked in again. "Is he a gangster?"

Al just shrugged at her questions. "I wish I had more info, but my guy couldn't tell me more. Just stay clear of Ponytail."

"Any word on the blog and IP address?" Kate asked Adrienne.

"My brother did have some luck with that." Adrienne pulled out a piece of paper and handed it to Vivian. She recognized the address on it.

"Your girl made the post from the vicinity of the hotel this morning at 1:45," Al said. "I already talked to the hotel manager. The security camera would have caught her if she walked into the lobby, but that's the only one they have. Detective Vega should request the video from last night, if he hasn't already."

"Holy shit!" Lucy shouted. "She was right here last night when you came back from Club Caliente."

Vivian's stomach soured as reality sank in. "Maybe she saw us walking on the beach." Tears clouded her eyes and rolled down her cheeks. "I shouldn't have left him out there by himself."

"Nonsense, Viv. He was a grown man." Kate patted her hand. "You didn't know Stella was watching you or what she would do."

Adrienne stood up from the table. "I wonder where she was watching you from?"

"I didn't see anyone here last night." Vivian wiped her eyes with a tissue. "We were a little drunk and not paying attention to anything but each other. She could have been anywhere."

Adrienne walked around the pool area. "How far down the beach did you walk? Show me."

Vivian's knees wobbled as she stood up but she willed herself to walk. She stood at the edge of the pool deck and glanced down the beach to the right. "See that last beach chair and umbrella? That's about how far we went." It was maybe 50 yards, not all that far.

"She wouldn't have been out in the open or you would have seen her," Adrienne said. She then glanced at a large potted plant, covered in red blooms, in the far right corner of the pool deck.

Vivian reached the same conclusion as Wendy and at the same time. She walked slowly around the plant and inspected it. "This is a pretty big and bushy hibiscus," Wendy pulled on a branch, "She could easily have hid back here. You couldn't see her but she could see you."

Lucy walked over to get a feel for the vantage point. "The pot alone is big enough to hide behind." She leaned closer and pointed to a branch. "Wait a sec, what's this?"

Adrienne, curious, walked over to the hibiscus and peered at the spot. "You need to call Detective Vega back."

"What is it? What did you find?" Vivian asked.

"Strands of long black hair."

31

The tunnel sensation kicked in and Vivian thought she'd better sit down before she fell down. Lucy and Kate rushed to the parking lot to tell Arturo about the evidence in the hibiscus and to call Detective Vega again. They quickly returned.

Vivian took a deep breath and let it out. "I just can't believe she was here spying on us and neither one of us noticed. How could we have been so blind?"

Al gently touched her arm. "Viv, Stella didn't want to be seen." His phone rang but he silenced it. "You can't blame yourself."

Wendy spoke up. "The hair Adrienne found in the plant is proof Stella was here and she could be on the video from the lobby. But neither proves she killed Jon. How do we know she didn't see someone else kill him? Maybe Ponytail or Shorty were also hanging around here in the shadows, and they killed him?"

"But on the blog she said he didn't deserve to breathe," Vivian argued.

"She was upset when she made that comment, but did she really mean Jon should be dead, or was that just crazy talk?" Adrienne played devil's advocate. "From where she was hiding, she could have witnessed his murder."

"Either way, she needs to be found and questioned," Lucy said and turned to stare out at the ocean.

"We need to fill Pierre in on this," Kate said. "I'll run up to his room and bring him down here."

"I'll go with you," Wendy said. "Buddy system."

Vivian tried to calm down while they were gone. Deep breaths and staring at the ocean with Lucy helped. She calmed down just as Detective Vega showed up, Kate, Wendy and Pierre arrived at the same time.

"What now?" was Vega's greeting.

Adrienne explained that she had family in law enforcement in the U.S. and they were able to trace the blog post to the I.P. address of La Vida de

131

Playa's wireless modem. "Sorry if I overstepped my bounds, but I want to help Vivian."

"And take a look at this," Lucy said as she wafted a long black strand of hair for inspection. "There's more in that plant." She indicated said plant.

Vega grunted and walked over to the hibiscus. "This could have been here for days." Nonetheless, he put a few strands of hair into a little plastic bag.

"It places someone with long black hair near the scene of the crime, and the security camera video from the hotel lobby may back that up," Wendy said in an even tone, trying not to yell at him for being an imbecile.

"Ah, yes, the video. We already have a copy of that. It is being reviewed."

With that, the he turned to leave.

Vivian ran after him and spoke up. "We were chased this afternoon by that scary Ponytail guy."

This stopped Vega in his tracks. Vivian almost ran smack dab into him. He slowly turned back to face her and narrowed his eyes. "I heard about an accident earlier this afternoon involving two cars careening through private property. I hope that's not what you're referring to. If it is, you could have killed someone else and we'd be having this conversation in jail." He stalked off, leaving Vivian flabbergasted, and everyone else, too by the looks on their faces.

"What? Kill someone else?" Lucy sputtered. "The nerve of that man! We were fleeing for our lives, afraid we were being chased by a killer!"

"Did you see Vega's face? He was pissed we got in that chase," Vivian said. "What is with him? What's the deal with Ponytail?"

Al shook his head. "It looks like he thinks you're it, Viv. It will be a miracle if he finds the actual murderer."

Vivian let out a big sigh.

"It's going to work out," Pierre said. "I know it will."

Vivian shook her head, not so sure how this would work out at all.

"Listen, I've got a headache. I'm going back upstairs."

After Pierre left, Vivian said, "Well this is just freakin' fabulous. Vega still acts like I'm the one who killed Jon. What a fuckwit."

"He must not have enough evidence or you'd already be in jail." Al stood up. "About that chase, have you searched your car for bugs or a tracking device?"

Vivian shielded her eyes from the sun as she looked up at him. "We think we found a bug in our room but none of us thought to check the car."

"Let's go out there and check it now. I know where to look."

They trekked out to the parking lot and waved to Arturo on the way. Al gave their car the once-over.

"Here's a bug." He removed a small device from underneath the dashboard. "I only found one, but then this car is pretty small."

He kept searching and pulled a blinky thing out from under the back fender and showed it to Vivian. "This is a tracking device." He tossed it across the parking lot and his phone rang again. This time he answered it, "I'll call you back," and hung up.

"Do you think Ponytail planted that?" Vivian asked Al.

"I'd put money on it," he said.

"No wonder I couldn't lose him this afternoon," Kate said. "He knew right where we were the whole time!"

Arturo walked up. "Car trouble?"

Vivian didn't want to tell him about Ponytail, the bugs or the tracking device, so she said, "We thought the car was making funny noises this afternoon. Al offered to take a look."

Vivian said to Al. "Thanks for checking it out."

"Yeah, thanks," Wendy said.

"Anytime," Al said and then offered Adrienne his arm, "Honey, let's go get a cocktail."

"I sure am hungry," Kate played along. "How about some dinner?" she asked the girls.

"Amen to that," Lucy said.

The diners in the hotel restaurant craned their necks to get a look at them.

As they sat down Wendy said, "I feel like such a hottie."

"Damn straight!" Lucy said.

Vivian knew they were just trying to make her feel better. She also knew, though, that the word was out. She had become the Deadly Dominik Destroyer.

Vivian switched places with Kate, putting her back to the rest of the dining room.

The waitress came over right away to take their order. Very un-Playa-like.

As soon as the waitress walked off, Lucy leaned forward and whispered, "So do you think Ponytail is in the mob? No wonder he's so scary looking. I wonder how many people he's killed?"

Wendy took a sip of her bottled water. "Al didn't come right out and say he was in the mob. He said 'organization.' That could mean lots of things."

"I think the mob is the most likely organization," Kate reasoned.

"It could be a drug cartel. We are in Mexico after all."

"Oooh, maybe," Lucy said.

"If he were with a drug cartel then why did he chase after us and why would he put a tracking device on our car?" Vivian pointed with her fork. She didn't know what to think about Ponytail, other than she didn't like him. Not one bit.

"Who knows?" Wendy said. "Regardless, we should follow Al's advice and stay clear of him."

"*No problemo* on my part," Lucy said.

"Mine either," Kate said.

The food arrived in record time. Yummy quesadillas and nachos. Vivian figured they put a rush on their food.

Vivian stabbed at a nacho. *Guess it's bad for business to have a murder suspect as a patron.*

32

Just as they finished their senior-hour dinner, Vivian's phone rang. She didn't recognize the number, and it didn't look like it was from the States.

She answered and Captain Juan said, "Julio *esta aqui*."

Click.

The girls decided to go talk to Shorty, see what they could find out about one of their "suspects." They paid the bill and headed for the car.

"The paparazzi count is increasing," Lucy noted.

Another news station had shown up, ready to report the scoop, whatever scoop there was.

On the way over to the marina Kate said, "So what the heck are we going to say to Shorty exactly?"

"Good question." Wendy looked at Vivian.

"I don't really know. He obviously likes women. Let's just go flirt with him and see where it gets us. What do y'all think?"

"Okay, but I think we need a code word or phrase," Wendy said. "Something any one of us can say that wouldn't sound too weird but lets the rest of us know we need to get out of there."

"That's a good idea. Okay, what's going to be our code word?" Lucy asked.

"How about 'ice cream'?" Kate suggested. "If any of us feels like it's time to scram, say something like, 'I'm hot, let's go get some ice cream' or something."

"Yeah, that sounds good," Vivian agreed.

"Okay, I can remember that," Wendy said.

"Damn, ice cream sounds good right about now," Lucy said.

"Do you want it to be tequila flavored?" Vivian chided.

"Ha ha, funny girl," Lucy replied.

Once at the marina, Vivian saw Shorty tiding up his boat. He was shirtless and wore a black knee-length swimsuit.

"Thank goodness he's not wearing a Speedo," Wendy muttered under her breath.

They ambled the length of the dock toward his boat, trying to be nonchalant.

"Hey, there," Vivian called. "Nice boat."

"*Gracias,*" he called back. "Just get her." He sounded like Speedy Gonzales, gangster-style.

"Well she's a beauty."

The deep V hull was painted a soft, buttery yellow. Stripes in a darker yellow, tannish-orange and black intermingled, crisscrossed and raced down the sides, then onto the deck. The stripes swirled together to make an enormous jaguar that looked like it was about to come to life and leap off the deck. Its mouth was open, fangs bared, ready to rip someone's throat out. The huge green eyes were striking, and Vivian had the sense that this cat sees all.

"I'm Vivian, this is Wendy, Kate and Lucy. We're visiting from Texas." She felt wired and fried at the same time and a trickle of sweat ran down her spine. *Just flirt, you can do it.*

"*Bueño.* Julio." He stepped over toward them and held out his hand to Vivian in invitation. "I making margaritas."

Vivian looked at the girls. Lucy nodded yes.

"Okay," Vivian said, and took his hand. *Oh Lord, here we go.*

Shorty helped the other girls on the boat and they gathered close to Vivian.

"Business must be good," Lucy muttered under her breath. Kate gave her a warning glance. Didn't want Shorty to hear that comment.

"A Baja 40 Outlaw. The fastest boat in marina." Shorty opened his arms and gestured at the surrounding, inferior boats.

"The paint job alone on this thing makes it look fast," Wendy said. "My dad lived on a sailboat for a while when I was a kid. I love being on the water. I wish I would have learned to sail." She paused, then added, "Hey, can you show me how to handle this?"

"*Es* too much for you to handle."

"You'd be surprised at what I can handle," Wendy said. Though she was smiling, Vivian knew that look in her eyes. He had ticked her off.

"I get margaritas. *Uno momento.*"

He disappeared down the narrow stairs.

Vivian sat down in the captain's chair and looked at the gauges. *Wonder what would happen if I...*

Kate interrupted her train of thought, "Ask him about Club Caliente." She went to stretch out on a vinyl bench at the back of the boat.

"Yeah, and then find out if he knows about Jon." Wendy sat down next to Kate.

"How am I supposed to do that?" Vivian asked.

"I'll help." Lucy said.

Shorty's head popped out of the stairway. "Salt?"

Kate and Lucy raised their hands.

"Be right back."

"You don't think he's poisoning those, do you?" Lucy asked.

"No! Come on!" Vivian said, though the thought did briefly cross her mind. In all honesty, she didn't really believe that he would.

A few moments later he came back up skillfully holding five plastic cups filled with margaritas and handed them out.

He proposed a toast. "To my new Baja babes."

Arriba! Arriba! Vivian thought to herself. *Geez.*

After taking a sip of margarita, Lucy asked, "Did we see you at Club Caliente last night?"

"*Si*, I go sometimes. I no remember seeing you." He gave them his best sly smile and said, "You like to party?"

Vivian thought back to her college days and remembered that "like to party," generally meant drugs.

"Excuse me?"

"I having a party Friday night. My house. You come."

Before Vivian could respond, Kate said, "At your house? Sure, we'll be there."

Hey, is that a good idea?

"Maybe I take you out on boat. We can have good time," Shorty said as he lifted his chin and gave them a look like "you know you want me."

Gross. Vivian didn't even want to think about what he was insinuating.

Just then his phone rang. It was conveniently in the cockpit so Vivian glanced at the number. It looked familiar.

Shorty walked over, picked up the phone and set it face-down.

Vivian figured she had nothing to lose, so she asked, "Didn't we also see you a couple of nights ago at the Purple Peacock hanging out with Jon and Pierre, the Canadians?"

His eyes narrowed a little as he responded, "*Si*, like me for my babes and my boat."

Egomaniac.

The phone rang again, Shorty glanced at the incoming number and silenced the ringer.

"*Matarlo. Pinche bendejo.*" He muttered under his breath.

The girls exchanged nervous looks with Wendy who put her hand to her neck and tried to nonchalantly draw her finger across it. She then pointed to the phone.

Vivian wanted to get his mind off his phone so she got to the purpose of the visit. "Did you hear about what happened to Jon?"

Shorty had a blank look on his face. "No, whaz up with *hombre*?"

She glanced at the girls, then looked back at Shorty. "He's dead. Murdered."

"Aye yo Santo!" Shorty exclaimed. "What happen?" He seemed genuinely shocked.

"We don't know," Lucy said, "but there's the man doing the investigating right over there."

She pointed to an adjacent dock, and sure enough, there was Detective Vega and he was talking with Ponytail.

Vivian's throat went dry and Shorty seemed to have turned pale, or at least as pale as possible for a Mexican.

Vivian coughed and looked at the girls with wide eyes. She turned to Shorty. "It was nice to meet you. We really don't know anything about what happened to Jon. But we're meeting with his friend, Pierre, later. Right now, I think I need some ice cream."

Lucy, such the bad actress, said, "Ice cream? Oh yeah, ice cream. Sounds delish. Let's go."

They thanked him for the margaritas and said goodbye as they climbed off the boat. It was all Vivian could do not to run like hell back to the rent car.

33

The girls walked quickly through the marina parking lot and jumped into the rent car with Kate behind the wheel.

As soon as the doors were shut, Vivian broke down in tears. "I'm officially freaked out now and what's with Detective Vega and Ponytail talking? Lucy, did they see us on Shorty's boat?"

"I'm sure they did," Lucy replied. "How could they not? I'm a little freaked out, too."

"Maybe he was checking up the lead we gave him. You know, talking with a viable murder suspect," Kate said.

"True, maybe that was it." Vivian wiped her tears and looked up the call history on her phone, though her hands were shaking. "Al called me from his cell phone earlier, remember? I think he just called Shorty. I think this was the same number on Shorty's phone when it rang a few minutes ago."

"Why would Al be calling Shorty?" Kate asked.

"Are you sure that was Al's number, Viv?" Wendy asked. "How good a look did you get?"

"I dunno. Good enough I think."

"Maybe they can't act like they know each other in public," Lucy suggested. "You know, like maybe they're involved in some illegal mob activity? Drug trafficking? Money laundering? Sex trade?"

"Oh god," Kate said.

"Why did you tell Shorty we were meeting up with Pierre?" Wendy asked. "We don't have any plans with him."

"I said it just in case he was thinking of taking off with us still on the boat," Vivian said. "I wanted him to know someone would be looking for us in a little while if we didn't show up."

"Good thinking," Kate commented.

Vivian put her head in her hands and took a deep breath. "Oh my god, y'all. This whole thing is starting to spin out of control. What if they don't let me out of Mexico in a few days? I've got to get home to my kids. Wendy, you're the only one of us who knows anything about boats. Do you think you could hijack Shorty's boat and get us to Galveston? My parents would pick us up."

Wendy tried to be the voice of reason. "Whoa, Viv. No, I couldn't get us to Galveston. The cockpit and gauges on his boat are complicated, and I don't know if I could figure it all out in time for us to make a clean getaway. We would have to stop and refuel, and besides, we need keys, and how could we get our hands on those?"

"We can search his house for them at the party Friday night," Vivian said. "If they haven't arrested me by then."

"Viv, you don't want to run," Kate said. "It will look like you're guilty and only make matters worse. We'd probably be picked up by the Coast Guard anyways, and you don't want to bring this mess home with you."

Lucy backed Kate up. "She's right, Viv. You didn't kill Jon and have nothing to hide."

Vivian let out a big sigh. "I know I didn't do this, but between Al, Shorty and Ponytail, my head is spinning. Our passports are with the cops, and I'm getting nervous."

Wendy reached over the seat and squeezed her shoulders. "Calm down, Viv. This is going to work out okay. Let's see what we can learn about Stella. Let's do what we talked about earlier and go by to the Purple Peacock and Club Caliente and ask around. Maybe the bartenders or the waitresses know something."

Wendy. Always level-headed.

"It's not like me to freak out like this but I am overwhelmed with the facts," Vivian said. "Fact one: Someone besides me killed Jon. Fact two: Ponytail is somehow connected to Detective Vega and he chased after us today — what was that about? Fact three: Shorty and Al are somehow connected. Al seems like a nice guy, but he may be connected with the mob and now he's calling Shorty. It's a lot to take in."

Wendy let go of her shoulders. "Hang in there, Viv. You'll get cleared of this, and we're going to help with that, starting now. Hang on to your 'oh-shit' handles ladies. Kate, get us over to the Purple Peacock pronto!"

Kate, a.k.a. Mario Andretti, got to the Purple Peacock in no time flat. The chase earlier must have given her a new lease on driving.

The girls grabbed four swings at the bar and Vivian ordered a round of beers from the same bartender that waited on them two nights ago. Hunkalicious recognized them and called Vivian "birthday girl."

Lucy took on the role of Detective Vega, asking him a slew of questions.

"Do you remember the crazy girl in here the other night? She had a black spider tattoo on her back."

The bartender stopped cleaning glasses and put down his towel. "Ah, the lady who cry. She drinking Sangria margaritas, many many." He held his arms wide for emphasis. *"Muchas."*

Hunk thought she paid cash but couldn't remember, didn't know what hotel she was staying in, and thought she came in alone. The only time he remembered her talking to anyone was when she made the big production with Jon. "That girl *es loco*," he concluded.

No help.

"What about the short guy with the two ladies?" Kate piped up. "Do you know anything about him?"

"Julio? He party animal. He get mad real fast, easy. He have two girlfriends," he raised his eyes on "girlfriends" then continued, "That all I know."

"Why do you say he gets mad easily?" Wendy asked.

The bartender leaned forward and lowered his voice. "He get in bar fight. *Cinco en dos meses.*"

Some customers grabbed a swing across the bar and Hunk walked off to serve them.

"That's five in two months," Wendy translated.

"Damn," Lucy said. "That's a lot of fights."

Vivian hoped Stella would walk in. They needed to find this girl.

They swung for about an hour waiting to see if Stella would show and had two more rounds. Loco lady did not come in. They decided it was time to high tail it over to Club Caliente. Though they never actually saw Stella there, she had sent Jon/Dominik a drink, so they knew she was there somewhere.

They drove back to the hotel to leave the car and Arturo let them park in "special parking" again. They walked to the club from there and Vivian felt like everyone they passed on the street was looking at her funny. Locals and tourist alike had heard about the Canadian who was killed and the blonde, female, American suspect. One couple even purposefully crossed to the other side of the street as Vivian approached.

Kate kept turning around to see if they were being followed. "All clear," she reported every so often. At least it was only a five-minute walk.

The same bartender from the night before was working and they ordered a round of Tiempo Loco margaritas. Vivian tried to recreate what Lucy had done at the Peacock.

He spoke good English, thank goodness, but didn't have much information. He remembered the woman who ordered a gin martini straight up, then had it delivered somewhere, but he didn't know where or to whom.

"Not the typical drink around here, but she paid cash and tipped well."

"Is the waitress here?"

"Si, aya." He pointed toward the balcony.

They made their way outside and picked a table. *Cooler air!*

They already had margaritas, but the waitress came over anyway. It was still early for a night club, and she must have been bored.

"Hola. Mas margaritas?"

"Habla Ingles?" Vivian asked.

"Yes, some."

"We were here last night with a group inside and you brought a drink to our friend."

"He was very fair skinned, *blanco*," Wendy threw out.

"Anyway, you brought him a martini that someone bought for him. A *señorita.*"

"Si."

"Do you remember what she looked like?"

"Black hair, green eyes, not from Playa."

"Did you notice if she had a tattoo."

"Si, la araña aqui," she said and pointed to her back.

"That means spider," Wendy said. *"Muchas gracias."*

She nodded and walked off, leaving Vivian in a somber mood.

"So there," she said. "We officially know that it was crazy Stella who ordered the drink. We have got to find this lady."

Wendy took a sip of her margarita. "It does help a little to confirm she's the one who sent the drink, but we pretty much already knew that. The question is, what was she doing in the hibiscus by the pool last night?"

"She had to have been spying on Jon and me," Vivian said. "Did she kill Jon, or did she see who did?"

Lucy swirled her straw around. "The lady's crazy. She must not understand that Dominik is a fictional character on TV. I bet she thought he was cheating on his soap opera wife and it pissed her off. She was crying at the Purple Peacock when she talked to Jon, remember?"

"That's jacked up," Wendy said. "She kills Jon because she thinks he's really Dominik, returned from the dead, and cheating on his soap opera wife. It's a stretch. I couldn't even make up a story like that."

Kate shrugged. "She clearly isn't the brightest bulb in the pack."

Vivian sucked on her straw, getting the last bit of margarita. "I'd say she's a three-watt."

34

After not seeing loony toons, a.k.a. Stella, at Club Caliente, they headed back to the hotel. Vivian felt a bit dejected in general and especially about not finding Stella and that nobody seemed to know anything more about this woman. Apparently she had no friends, paid cash and kept to herself. She could be long gone.

The girls had to walk around to the far side of the hotel to avoid the ever-growing crowd of paparazzi. Evidently word had traveled fast about the previously semi-famous, now infamous, soap star.

They ran into Adrienne and Al in the lobby, who were going to the poolside bar. Though Vivian wasn't really feeling up to it, Al convinced her she needed to pretend it was happy hour, on him! She did love happy hour.

Al ordered them a round of margaritas and Adrienne asked for an update.

Vivian gave her and Al the lowdown on going back to the Purple Peacock and Club Caliente. She conveniently didn't tell them they spoke with Shorty. Vivian didn't know what the connection was with Al, if it was his phone number she saw, so she figured it was best to not bring it up.

"Nobody seemed to know anything," Vivian said.

"When that's the case, you can bet someone knows something," Al said.

"What do you mean?" Wendy asked.

"Someone *always* notices something, whether they realize it or not," Al said. "You've got to find the right person and ask the right questions."

Al's shirt buzzed and he excused himself.

He was only six feet from the bar when the vultures, (three horny men), descended on the girls and Adrienne.

"Hey, ladies, can we buy you a drink?" This from a guy in a tangerine orange see-through shirt. *Cheesy!*

Lucy felt game and was apparently in need of another drink. "Margaritas are always welcome. Or tequila shots."

"Done. And what's your name?" He turned his full attention to Lucy. The other two guys flanked him and turned toward Vivian, Kate and Wendy.

Vivian rolled her eyes. She was in no mood, so she threw out their bar names, secretly signaling her dis-interest to the girls.

"I'm Roxy, this is Rita (pointing to Wendy), Consuela (pointing to Lucy), and Maria," (pointing to Kate).

"And I'm Portia." Adrienne stuck out her left hand and flashed her ginormous rock. She gave Vivian a wink.

"And what are you lovely ladies up to tonight?" Cheese-a-rama flashed a car salesman-y grin, showing off his crooked teeth. *He should have saved the money from these margaritas and put it towards braces.*

Nobody got to answer because Al walked up at that point and used his girth to move the cheese balls out of the way.

"You fellas got a lot of *conojas* talking to these ladies. Trust me — if you know what's good for ya, you'll steer clear of them. They tend to have a deadly effect on shmucks. Especially ol' blondie."

With that, the girls and Adrienne smiled innocently at them.

"Oh, you're *those* ladies," the head cheese said and took a step back. "Margaritas are on their way. Have a good night."

Their reputation preceded them. Came in handy this time!

Vivian turned to Al. "Thanks for that. Those guys were dorks." She wanted to ask if he was talking to Shorty but she clearly couldn't just throw that out there.

Suddenly they were interrupted by the female reporter who had been out front when they returned from the police station earlier. Guess they'd been spotted on their return from Club Caliente despite efforts to lay low.

"Are you Vivian Taylor?" the woman asked, holding a steno notebook and pen.

Vivian didn't answer.

"My name is Lupe Mendoza with *Escándalos.* I'd like to ask you a few questions about your involvement in Jon Tournay's death."

"Absolutely not!" Wendy yelled and jumped between them.

Vivian peeked around Wendy's shoulder. "No comment." She gave a little smile.

"She has nothing to say. Are you even allowed in here?" Wendy said to Lupe then turned to the bartender. He gave a shrug.

Al stepped up. "You need to get the hell outta here. She's got nothing to say."

The reporter looked around, for what, who knows.

"Beat it, bitch," Adrienne yelled.

The woman turned and walked out.

"Thanks y'all, for running her off," Kate said.

Al shook his head. "She's gone for now, but you can bet she'll be back, and there will be ten more just like her."

Vivian sucked down her 'rita. She was pooped, not to mention buzzed.

"I've had all I can take tonight," Vivian said and stood up. "Al, thanks so much for the help and the margarita. I'm going to bed."

The girls all agreed and finished up their drinks and headed to the room.

On their way up the stairs Kate said, "Viv, I think we ought to talk to Pierre about what we saw at the marina today. Let him know there's something going on between Detective Vega and Ponytail."

"Good idea," Wendy and Lucy said in unison.

Vivian thought about it for a minute. "Yeah, you're right. We should keep him informed."

"And let's check his room for bugs," Wendy added.

Always thinking, that one.

"We should invite him to Shorty's party," Kate said.

"He can rescue us when Shorty tries to either seduce us or kill us," Lucy smirked. "With Shorty's comment today on the boat and then his reaction to Detective Vega seeing us with him, I'm not sure which he'd want to do."

Vivian nodded in agreement. She knocked several times on Pierre's door but no answer. She dug in her purse and pulled out a scrap of paper and a pen. She wrote a short note asking him to call them or come by their room in the morning.

It was officially time to end the very long day, so they went to their room, did a quick bug sweep, their usual bedtime rituals and slipped into bed.

35

Day 4

Vivian woke with a start the next morning. She had a bad dream about being on vacation and suspected of murder. Then her memory clicked. That was no dream, it was a nightmare. Unfortunately it was also reality.

She got out of bed quietly and tiptoed to the balcony. The sun was just coming up on a beautiful morning. She melted into a chair, closed her eyes and took a deep breath, letting the sun shine on her face. She stayed like that for a few minutes, listening to the waves crash on the beach, then opened her eyes and looked at the sparking water.

The scene reminded her of a cruise she and Rick had taken a few years ago. They went to the Caribbean and hit all the great islands, St. Lucia, St. Croix, St. Maarten, Barbados.

They woke early one morning, made love and went to the upper deck to watch the sun come up. Rick kept his arm around Vivian's shoulders because she was cool. The air was a little damp and it was breezy as they sailed along. They sat there for a long time, not talking, just watching the way the sun slowly lifted up off the water and hid itself behind the clouds. One big, bright ray poured out of the bottom of the clouds and seemed to reflect off the water straight to them and only them. She thought it was magical.

Vivian heard the sliding glass door open and Lucy stuck her head out.

"Hey lady," she said emerging from the door. "You're up awfully early. You okay?"

"No, not really, but I'm trying to distract myself with this beautiful sunrise. It brings back a wonderful memory of a cruise Rick and I went on."

"Oh, you mean the cruise where you wanted to throw him overboard because he was such a dud?"

Lucy brought Vivian back to reality. She had ended up hating that cruise.

"God, how could I forget? I wanted to maim him before it was all over! He wouldn't dance with me, had to be practically dragged from the cabin for dinner, and we couldn't agree on any of the excursions."

Lucy sat down next to Vivian and put her feet up on the railing. She stretched her toes, inspecting her Bogota Berry painted toenails for chips.

"Yeah, he sucked as a cruise companion," she said.

"But we had some good times too."

"I know ya did, Viv. Otherwise you wouldn't have married the guy."

"But I did vow after that experience to never go on a cruise without a large group. That's the one good thing that came out of our cruise!" She paused for a moment. "Well, that and the twins!"

Lucy nodded her head.

"So what's up with Steve?" Vivian asked. "Do you miss him?"

"Not really. I mean, I guess I do sometimes, and I still see him pretty often. We go to dinner a few times a week, and I talk to him pretty much every day. I just don't live in the same apartment as him right now."

"Do you think this will be permanent?"

"I don't know yet. He's so unemotional. It drives me crazy. The man never gets excited about anything. I tell him I want a separation and I'm moving out, and you think he'd react in some kind of way. I got nothing. Even when we're in counseling he's so freakin' rational about everything. I just want to shake him to get him angry or something."

"Lucy, he's always been that way," Vivian said. "He's a rational guy. He takes time to make his decisions and doesn't jump feet first into anything without knowing the consequences. If you remember, that's one of the things that drew you to him. You, like me, are a non-planner. He kinda balances you that way."

"I know, but I'm just not sure it's something I can be around for the rest of my life. We're going to counseling and haven't given up yet. At this point, though, I don't know how things are going to end up."

Vivian looked her in the eyes. "You know we support any decision you make. We just want you to be okay."

"I know. Thanks, Viv."

They both leaned back in their chairs, enjoying the morning sun.

Lucy reached out and put her hand on Vivian's arm. "You're going to be okay, you know. We're going to help the police find out who killed Jon so you can go home."

Tears welled up in Vivian's eyes, she was trying really hard not to ruin the sunrise with thoughts of Jon's death.

"I just can't believe that he's gone," she said, trying to hold back the sobs that were threatening to let loose.

"I know, Viv. None of us can."

"He was so sweet and caring," Vivian said, as her voice broke. She doubled over, her head in her hands, and sobbed.

Lucy started crying too, emotions overwhelming her. She wrapped her arms around Vivian's shoulders. They stayed like that for a few minutes, letting the torrent of tears out.

Vivian felt drained and let out a ragged breath. "I guess I needed to get that out."

"Yeah, me too."

"Morning, ladies," Kate said sounding chipper, and joined them on the balcony. She had made herself a cup of coffee from the one-cup coffee maker. She could not get going without a cup of joe.

She slid the door closed and looked at the two girls. It was obvious they had been crying. She gave them a half-hearted smile and tried to sound upbeat. "The sunrise is bringing tears to your eyes, I see."

They give her half-hearted smiles in return.

Kate gave Vivian a comforting shoulder squeeze, then sat down and balanced her cup on the railing. "Wow, it's beautiful out here."

"Umm hmm," Vivian said, sucking in the salty air.

Kate got serious. "Okay, this may sound weird, but I was thinking we should try to find out more about Al." She blew on her coffee, took a sip and continued, "Who is he and what is he into?"

Lucy turned toward her. "You think so?"

"I do. I had one of my dreams."

Lucy and Vivian looked at one another and grinned.

Kate continued. "I was standing on the steps of a courthouse. Al was there and he introduced me to Slinky Sal. It freaked me out," she said with a shiver. "As I was standing there my dad walked up the steps. He told me to find out more about Al."

Kate was occasionally visited by dead relatives in her sleep. Didn't happen very often, so when it did she took it very seriously.

"So where do we start with that?" Lucy asked.

"Where else? The internet," Vivian said.

"But we need to make sure no one knows about it but us," Lucy said.

"Let's go down and get breakfast, then we can come back up to the room and Google Al on Wendy's laptop," Kate said.

Wendy shuffled out to the balcony and grunted her greeting. "The smell of coffee and ocean air woke me up, but at least the police aren't banging down our door."

Wendy was not a morning person and could be a little grouchy when she first got up.

Sensing an undercurrent of tension, Wendy asked, "Is everyone all right?"

"We are now," Vivian said. "We had a good cry and now we're ready to kick butt and take names. Since we're all up we might as well get to it."

"Need coffee first," Wendy muttered. "Smell it, don't see it."

Kate took a long sip of her cuppa joe. "Mmmmm."

Wendy watched her longingly.

Vivian stood up. "Let's grab breakfast and then Google Al and see what we come up with."

"Google Al?" Wendy asked.

"Yep. Kate had a dream," Lucy said.

"Well, by all means then, if Kate had a dream," Wendy said sarcastically.

Kate smiled, handed Wendy her half cup of coffee and they went in to get ready for a new day.

36

Vivian and the girls stepped into the hotel restaurant for breakfast and the few early morning diners stopped all action – forks piled with eggs, frozen in delivery, lips poised on coffee cups, interrupting a caffeine fix, page of the morning paper mid-turn, flipping to the rest of the riveting front page story - and stared at them, but primarily at her.

Vivian caught a glimpse of the headline "American Woman Questioned in Murder Case" along with a picture of their hotel's sign beneath it, prominently displayed above the fold on the front page.

Just what I need.

The diners refocused on their breakfast as the girls followed the hostess to a table on the far side of the dining room.

Vivian purposefully took a seat facing away from the restaurant and shook her head. She wanted to turn around and yell, "I didn't do it!"

Service was quick so they were out of there in no time, much to Vivian's delight. "My migas were fan-tab," she said, getting up from the table.

Lucy had a traditional breakfast with eggs, bacon and even pancakes, which she boasted were also fantastic. Wendy and Kate both had *huevos rancheros* and cleaned their plates.

"Quick and delicious," Wendy said. "My kind of breakfast."

Vivian swiped a discarded newspaper on the way out. She threw it onto the bed as soon as they entered their room. "Look at this shit! I'm the headline of today's paper." She flopped down beside it. "This can't be happening to me."

Lucy, after completing a room sweep for bugs, just in case, sat down next to Viv and read the article.

Kate wanted to prevent Vivian from having another meltdown. "Viv, like I said earlier, you are going to be okay. The true murderer will be caught and you'll be cleared of this nonsense."

"I don't know," Vivian moaned. "I'm not sure how much confidence I have in Detective Vega."

"That's where we come in," Wendy piped up, also trying to keep Vivian's spirits up. "We're going to look at all the angles and find out what we can about our suspects, just like we talked about doing yesterday."

Lucy, who had been quiet for most of breakfast, said, "Actually, Vivian, this article doesn't mention your name. Evidently the cops haven't released it to the press yet."

She thumped the paper. "All it says is an American woman is suspected of being involved in Jon's death. That she is staying in the same hotel where he was. It doesn't go into a lot of detail on the murder. The article talks mainly about Jon's fame in Canada."

"See, that's not so bad," Kate sat down on the other side of Vivian and slapped her knee. "No one at home will have heard anything about this."

Vivian took the time to read the full article and felt a little better, but only a little. Jon was dead, after all.

"You're right, the article isn't as bad as I thought," she said and tossed the paper into the trash.

Needing to refocus, she walked over to the desk and turned the computer on. Once online, she went to Google and typed in "Al Russo, Chicago." Several hits came up.

The first was a review of his restaurant, CinCin. Voted Chicago's best cannoli three years in a row. *Adrienne wasn't kidding.* The article referred to Al Russo III and showed his picture holding the award. *Yep, that's the Al we know.*

Next was an article from the *Chicago Tribune*. Al and Adrienne donated $10,000 to the area food bank and served an Italian-style Thanksgiving dinner to the homeless last year. The article included a picture of them dishing out the food.

The next few articles detailed good deeds Al and Adrienne had done in the Chicago area.

"Looks like they're very philanthropic," Vivian said and gave the girls a summary. "Animal shelters, firefighters, kid's charities like the Ronald McDonald House. They even donated to the local county hospital a few years ago."

Kate hovered over Vivian's shoulder. "So if they're such nice people, why is Al calling Shorty? I mean, I realize we've got nothing on Shorty, but something seems off there."

"It is a bit suspicious." Wendy peered at the computer screen.

Lucy joined them at the desk. "It can't be good."

They watched as Vivian pulled up a few more articles about the restaurant but nothing of any significance. She was about to call it quits when they saw a blurb saying "Al Russo, Jr. suspected in disappearance of Franco Gaspare in July, 1972."

"I knew it!" Lucy pointed to the screen. "I knew Al was in the mob!"

Vivian clicked on the link and read the article out loud.

> **Local restaurateur Al Russo, Jr. was arrested yesterday in connection with the disappearance of Franco Gaspare. Gaspare was last seen Friday evening leaving Russo's restaurant with Tony Mancuso, who was recently released from prison after serving three years for racketeering.**
>
> **Mancuso has refused to cooperate with police and would not return calls for comment. However, an anonymous source tells the Tribune that an argument took place behind the restaurant and that Mancuso left hurriedly.**

"It said Al Junior, Lucy" Wendy turned away from the computer and sat on the bed. "The Al Russo we know is the III. The article must be about his dad."

"Racketeering," Lucy said. "That seriously implies the mob."

"Ugh, I know," Wendy admitted.

"This is disturbing," Kate said. "But maybe we're on to something here."

"Let's see what else we can find on Al's father and grandfather," Wendy said.

Vivian continued scrolling through the headlines but with no luck. There was no follow-up on the story they had read and they couldn't find anything else about Al Junior. "I guess Al Sr. lived too long ago to make it to the Internet," she said.

"I think we've seen enough to confirm that Al's father must be, or was, semi-shady," Wendy said, getting up and pacing the room. "I don't really care if the Al we know is a little shady, but I don't want to get caught up in any of it. To his credit though, he has been nothing but nice to us and he has tried to help Viv."

"Just in case, maybe we should keep our distance from them." Kate said. "You know the old saying about 'the fruit doesn't fall far from the tree.' Al III is probably involved in the same kinds of stuff his dad was. Especially since he now runs the restaurant."

"I don't think we should affiliate with any mobsters," Lucy agreed. "But Adrienne said her brother is a cop, so maybe they're not totally bad."

"Uh…a cop in *New Orleans*," Wendy said. "The mob is big-time there."

"Really?" Lucy asked. "I didn't know that."

"Yep," Wendy said, nodding her head. "Started there, in fact. Sicilian immigrants."

Vivian closed the laptop and turned towards them. "I want to trust Al. He has tried to help me, but it makes me nervous that everything about him sounds suspicious."

Wendy stopped pacing. "We haven't heard from Pierre this morning. Why don't we go see if he's in his room? We need to tell him about seeing Detective Vega with Ponytail, and see if he will go to Shorty's party with us."

"We should also tell him what we know about Al now, and how he called Shorty," Kate said.

"Oh, and don't forget we need to search his room for bugs before we start talking to him," Lucy added.

Vivian stood up from the desk. "Good god. I can't live like this."

37

Vivian knocked on Pierre's door and waited for him to answer. No sounds came from the room.

"Try again, knock louder," Wendy said, "just in case."

Vivian rapped again, hoping to wake him if he was in there.

A thud sounded through the door. "Did he just fall out of bed?" Vivian asked.

"Was that a groan?" Kate said. They look at each other anxiously.

The girls heard footsteps. A shadow moved in front of the peep hole and there was a definite groan.

"Hey Pierre," Vivian gave a little wave and tried to smile.

The chain slid back and the deadbolt clicked open. Pierre answered the door looking pretty rough, and wearing nothing but wrinkled shorts.

Must have drunk himself into oblivion last night, Vivian thought.

"What's up?" he grumbled.

Vivian put her finger to her mouth and the four of them walked in, uninvited, and started searching his room.

"What are you doing?" he asked. "Quit going through my stuff!"

He did not look happy that Vivian just went through his suitcase and rifled his boxers.

"I found it!" Lucy turned away from a lamp similar to the one in their room and held the bug out for Pierre to see. "You want to smash it or should I?"

Pierre looked in a quandary at the tiny device in Lucy's hand. Since he didn't reply, Lucy put the bug on the floor and stomped it as if it were a giant, flying Pasadena cockroach.

Kate picked up the pieces and flushed them down the toilet. "I almost feel like we should have a ceremony, say a few words."

"It's not a pet goldfish, Kate," Wendy said.

"What the hell?" Pierre said.

"It was a bug you know, spy stuff. We had one in our room, too," Lucy explained.

They caught Pierre up on everything that had happened since he left them at the pool the day before. He didn't say a word during the entire spiel.

Wrapping things up, Vivian said, "When we were leaving Julio's boat, he invited us to his party Friday night at his house. Want to go with us?"

Between the information overload and his obvious hangover, Pierre looked sick.

"Are you okay?" Lucy called after him as he rushed into the bathroom and slammed the door.

The sound of water running started a few seconds later. They decided he needed more privacy and went out to the balcony.

About ten minutes later he emerged freshly showered and wearing a robe. He looked better but unshaven and still a little glassy eyed.

He slid the door closed to the balcony and leaned against the railing, facing the four of them. "Okay, let me make sure I have this straight. You went to the marina to talk to Julio, whom you also call Shorty, but he wasn't there. As you leave, the guy with the Ponytail chases you through town. Kate loses him so you come back to the hotel to talk with Al. Al tells you to steer clear of Ponytail, but he doesn't actually know who Ponytail is. Al's contact was able to trace the blog to the hotel and then you find Stella's hair, presumably, in a bush. You tell Detective Vega all of this. Then you go back to the marina, talk with Julio, and while you're there, you think Al calls Julio. You go to leave and see Detective Vega and Ponytail talking and shake hands. Is that about right?"

"Yes," Vivian answered. "It's like everyone is somehow connected. Al has tried to help me but I'm not sure I can trust him one hundred percent. I think it is best not to talk to him about Shorty though."

"Don't forget about the party," Lucy interjected. "We want you to go with us."

"Ok, yes. I will go with you but, wow," Pierre said. "What do we do from here?"

Everyone mulled this over for a minute.

"We need to search for Stella some more," Wendy said. "I don't want to get near Ponytail, Detective Vega or Shorty at the moment. We had enough run-ins with them yesterday."

"That lady is like water vapor. She's around but we can't see her," Pierre said. "Where should we look?"

"There's La Quinta Avenida in central Playa," Kate said. "I drove past it yesterday as Ponytail was chasing us."

"I'm surprised you were able to see anything but blurs on that chase," Vivian said.

"I looked down that street as an avenue for escape but saw the shops and restaurants and knew it would be too dangerous," Kate said. "It did look like a good area to buy souvenirs and I want to get something for Shaun."

"We have seen Stella at touristy nightspots, so 5th Avenue is worth a shot," Vivian said. "Anyone have any other ideas?"

Shrugs and head shakes all around. Nope.

"Well, then, meet me in the lobby in five minutes," Pierre said. "I need to get dressed."

From the lobby, the girls saw that the number of reporters outside seemed to have quadrupled.

"Great," Vivian muttered.

Lupe Mendoza saw them looking out the windows and shouted to her photographer. Whatever she said got everyone's attention, and the media frenzy suddenly rushed inside.

The front desk clerk flapped around trying to shoo the journalists out of the lobby to no avail. They descended on Vivian, shouting questions. She couldn't hear or even understand all of them thanks to the language barrier, but what she could make out appalled her.

"How did you do it?" "Why did you kill Jon Tournay?" "Was he a good lover?"

"Pull a Michael Jackson!" Lucy shouted at Vivian.

She gave Lucy a bewildered look. "What?"

"Cover your face!"

She heeded Lucy's advice and ducked her head. Pierre showed up moments later and took control, shoving reporters and photographers aside, making room through the crowd. Kate, Lucy and Wendy grabbed on and propelled Vivian out the door and to the parking lot.

They jumped in the rent car and slammed and locked the doors. Pierre took the hump seat in back.

Lucy just about ran over half a dozen journalists in her haste to get out of there.

"Holy shit," Wendy said. "What a fiasco."

"Al was right," Kate said with a sigh. "There are definitely a lot more reporters here than last night."

"I don't think I can take this crap every time we come and go from the hotel," Vivian said. "That was kind of traumatic. We need a secret entrance."

Pierre shook his head. "Jon was just getting popular in Canada, but I never expected this kind of turnout. This is insane."

"You need to buy a hat and a scarf at the market, Viv," Lucy said.

"I certainly don't want my picture plastered all over the newspapers and on TV down here, but it will become a real problem if this news gets to the states," Vivian said, stifling a cry.

Pierre turned and glanced behind them. "I think one of the reporters is following us."

Kate turned to look. "Yep, it's that Lupe woman from last night and her photographer. What news media are they with again?"

"*Escándalos*," Wendy replied with disdain. "I think it's the Mexican version of *National Enquirer*."

Lucy parked on one end of 5th street and they piled out. Lupe and the photographer parked close by, got out of their car and leaned against the bug-splattered front.

Vultures. Vivian shot them the bird.

38

Shops and restaurants lined La Quinta Avenida, stretching for blocks and ending at the Cozumel ferry dock. Most of the shops had completely open store fronts, in an attempt to invite tourists inside. Carts full of knick-knacks and racks of clothing littered the sidewalks up and down the street.

The girls and Pierre walked into the first shop they came to.

Kate stepped back onto the sidewalk and peeked around a rack of dresses toward Lupe and the photographer. "They're not following us."

"For now." Wendy swatted at a piñata hanging from the ceiling.

"Screw those assholes," Vivian said from the back of the store. "I'm diggin' this hammock. I've got two great trees in the backyard this would be perfect for."

"This is like the Sam's of Mexican touristy goods," Lucy remarked. "They've got just about everything in here. And in bulk." She held up a ten pack of spray-on sunscreen. "If it wouldn't put me over the baggage weight limit I'd be all over this!"

"It is way too crowded in here," Pierre said. "There's definitely nowhere for Stella to hide. Let's move on."

They crossed the street and went into another store selling mostly clothing. Dresses, lace tops that looked like doilies, colorful ponchos, guayaberas.

Lucy looked at the price tag on a frilly dress. "Oh! This is not the Sam's of Mexican touristy goods."

As they left the shop, Pierre reported, "Still journalist free at the moment."

"Excelente!" Vivian said.

They passed a shop under construction with a ladder leaning against the front wall. Lucy, not paying attention, was on course to walk directly underneath it.

Kate reached out and grabbed her arm. "Watch out, Lucy!"

"What?" Lucy asked.

"You almost walked underneath that ladder," Kate pointed out.

"Oh."

"What's the superstition with that?" Vivian asked Kate, thinking about the mirror she broke and threw away at the airport.

"It's bad luck," Kate said.

"We're having enough of that for now, don't need to add to it," Lucy said.

"No kidding," Wendy said. "Watch out for black cats, don't step on any cracks, and for goodness sakes, don't walk under any ladders! Don't go near a ladder, don't climb a ladder, just stay away from ladders."

"Any other superstitions we need to be wary of, Kate?" Pierre asked.

She gave him a smirk. "I'll let ya know if a situation arises."

They stopped at the next shop which was full of ceramics — turtles, iguanas, suns, and an entire section of ancient Indian-looking figurines. Kate was drawn to the phallic artifacts.

Memories of Kate's bachelorette party flashed before Vivian's eyes.

The girls had met at one of Kate's co-worker's house. Her neighbor across the street had several topiaries in the landscaping. One was supposed to resemble a horse maybe or a dog, they couldn't figure it out. What it most closely resembled was a penis on four legs. Vivian and Kate pretended to lick it while Wendy snapped a picture.

"Finding any four-legged topiaries?" Vivian joined Kate.

"Nope. Everything but."

Vivian picked up a coffee cup called over to Pierre, "Do you think this is proportionally accurate?" The cup handle was a weirdo guy with his wanger reaching to the sky. His thing was taller than his noggin.

Pierre gave her a look, made a "pffft" sound and shook his head.

Vivian had no intentions of buying anything at the jewelry store they stopped in next, but the over-eager sales people wore her down. She gave in and purchased a pair of silver hoop earrings. Kate bought a beautiful silver necklace studded with turquoise stones, Wendy a silver and jade ring, and germ-a-phobe Lucy wouldn't consider touching anything, much less purchasing it.

"Anyone hungry for lunch?" Pierre asked. "I didn't have breakfast this morning, and I drank my dinner last night."

Poor guy, drinking away his sorrows, Vivian thought.

"I smell something good," Wendy said. "It looks like the food market is just ahead. Let's go see what's cooking."

A crowd of people, tourist and locals alike, gathered in a courtyard where vendors sold all kinds of food out of carts — churros (Mexico's version of a doughnut), tacos, tortas, carne asada, menudo. You name it.

A mariachi band made its way through the crowd. Trolling for tips, no doubt.

Six or seven children, no more than age 5, trailed behind them, dancing. It reminded Vivian of her kids and made her miss them.

They had gone to a traditional Mexican wedding recently, complete with mariachis. Audrey and Lauren followed them around all night, dancing and clapping to the music. The twins slept through all the excitement. It never ceased to amaze her how babies could do that.

"You girls go find a spot to sit, I'll buy lunch." Pierre said. "Who wants what?"

They gave Pierre their order and thanked him for buying. The few small tables were occupied, but a bench surrounding one of several palm trees was open. They staked their claim.

Wendy spied a shop across the street selling kitchen and food items. "I need to buy some Mexican vanilla. It tastes so much better in my dad's sugar cookie recipe than the regular ass crap from home."

"Those must be some really good cookies if they're worth hauling vanilla all the way back," Kate said. "Give me that recipe, will ya?"

"They're the best," Wendy said. "Very moist, not the usual brick-hard, break-your-teeth sugar cookies."

As Wendy walked off, Vivian turned to Lucy and Kate. "I, personally, am all about the pre-made cookie dough. Why try to create your own when someone else has done such a tasty job for you? Slice and bake, baby. That's where it's at."

Lucy tisked. "Yeah, but you don't get the satisfaction of it being homemade."

"Screw that. I'm in my home. It counts. Plus, I get the satisfaction of no mess and 30 cookies done up in 30 minutes. That's the kind of satisfaction I need. At least when it comes to baking cookies, if you know what I mean."

"We know what you mean." Kate winked at Vivian.

"Y'all are so trashy." Lucy chided.

"Sex is important," Vivian said. "But I like for it to last more than 30 minutes!"

"Only you could turn a perfectly innocent baking conversation into a sex one. Though, you do seem to get a little bun in the oven, or two, any time you have it. I've never seen someone pop out four kids in less than four years. Your oven is workin' overtime."

"Yeah, well, this oven is off. Stick a fork in me, I'm done."

Wendy rushed up to them. "I just saw Stella!"

"Where?" Kate asked, hopping off the bench.

"I was in the store paying for my vanilla, and I just felt like someone was watching me. I turned around and there she was, just outside the shop window, glaring at me."

"Dammit." Vivian said. "We didn't see her."

"We were too busy with the baking and sex conversation to notice," Lucy said.

"Where did she go?" Kate asked.

"I grabbed my change, ran out of the store and down the street and tried to find where she went but didn't see her." Wendy pointed back toward the way they came. "She must have run off. There aren't too many people in the shops or on the sidewalk down there, so if she was still around, I would have found her."

"Shit!" Vivian yelled. "She was so close, then poof! She's gone."

"How does she keep doing that?" Kate asked rhetorically.

"I think she's stalking you," Lucy said pointing at Vivian. "So just wait a while. She'll turn up."

"Guess there's not much else we can do at this point since she disappeared – again," Vivian concluded.

Pierre returned with arms full of food, followed by three kids carrying two glass Coke bottles each. Food and drink were distributed with Pierre taking two Cokes and tipping the kids a few pesos. They ran away happy, eager to help the next tourist.

Wendy told Pierre about seeing Stella as they ate their hodgepodge of Mexican treats. Vivian got two soft beef tacos. Lucy and Kate shared a big dish of nachos, and Wendy took bites of a torta in between telling her story.

"Maybe she didn't go too far and will turn up again," Pierre said, then shoved the last bite of burrito in his mouth. "Let's hit a few more shops," came out muffled, and almost with beans. He grabbed a napkin. "Sorry."

Kate stood and gathered her trash. "I need to make a pit stop first. Anybody see a restroom?"

"You are really going to use the restroom here?" Lucy said. "Geeerrrms."

"You just ate nachos out of a roach coach. You realize that, right? Besides, I'm a good hoverer. I promise you no part of my body will come in contact with the toilet."

Lucy looked skeptical.

"I'll meet you in the next shop," Pierre said. "This is not a manly mission."

The girls found the restroom, which had a "front desk" feature. A young lady sat behind it, apparently, to sell toilet paper.

"There's no paper in there?" Kate asked.

"No, buy here," the lady said.

"How much?"

"Five pesos."

"Good grief."

Kate dug out some change and handed it over. In turn, she received a small wad of toilet paper.

She looked back at the girls, raised her toilet paper proudly in the air and headed in.

"I'll wait for her, buddy system, y'all go ahead with Pierre and we'll catch up," Wendy said. "Stay outta trouble and keep an eye out for Stella!"

39

Lucy, Pierre and Vivian worked their way through a very eccentric, very crowded shop that sold everything from clothing to cough drops. Vivian checked out the wind chimes and considered adding to her backyard collection. She loved listening to the chimes as the breeze blew through the live oaks.

Lucy started in on a rack of t-shirts labeled three for $10. Bargain!

She laughed and held up a t-shirt that said, "Mexican't – A person who wants to be Mexican but isn't."

She held up another t-shirt and called out, "Hey, I should have been wearing this the other day on the beach."

The shirt had a cartoon drawing of a worm drinking a shot of tequila. The caption read "One tequila, two tequila, three tequila, floor."

Vivian called out, "Gotta love trashy t-shirts," but thought, *Kate had actually said that very thing.*

Done with the rack of shirts, Lucy asked Pierre to try on a *serape* she might buy Steve. He held his arms out and twirled around in the bright blue with black and white striped garment.

Lucy, hand on chin, gave him a good look. "Not sure about that one."

Kate and Wendy returned from the restroom adventure in time to give their opinions. Neither liked the blue *serape* so Kate picked a bright, rainbow of fruit flavors one, complete with fringe. Pierre put it on, proudly sporting it for all to see, and threw on a giant straw *sombrero* that said, "Mexico" across the two-foot Speedy Gonzales point. The monstrous low and wide brim stuck out three feet all around.

He handed Lucy a purple, crushed velvet, silver-sequined mariachi hat. Then he spied a sequined fruit-covered hat, loaded with grapes, apples, a pineapple and a bright yellow banana topping it off, and popped it on Kate's head.

"Oh, yeah. That's sexy," he said. "You look fruitylicious."

"No, I don't," Kate said. "I look like Charo."

"Who?"

"Oh, you know, big lips, hips and boobs. Says 'cuchi cuchi' a lot."

Pierre didn't get it.

The shopkeeper, who had been up on a ladder dusting a shelf, came down and gave them the "stink eye."

Undaunted by his glare, Wendy moved on to the musical instruments and called for them to join her. Pierre passed Wendy a turquoise mariachi hat and handed Vivian a giant straw hat like his. Playing along, they put them on.

Vivian thought they all looked pretty ridiculous but was having such a good time that she didn't care. She had even momentarily forgotten her troubles and started humming to the sound of the wind chimes she was still holding.

This brought out the band dork in Wendy, who handed Lucy some *maracas*, Kate a guitar "to keep up the Charo image," she said, and Pierre a tambourine. She slipped a pair of castanets on her fingers.

Wendy started singing "La Bamba" and clicking her fingers to the beat of the tune only she could hear.

They all joined in, shaking their butts and playing their instruments.

Vivian started to sing but forgot most of the words so she did her best to fake it. "Blah blah blah blah, blah blah blah blah."

Mid-way through turn two, the sound of her wind chimes turned into a clank. She stopped to undo the two that had twisted around each other and was about to get back to butt shaking when she glanced up and froze.

Vivian locked eyes with Stella, who was right outside the store, staring at her.

Vivian tried to nonchalantly keep singing and chiming while completing her butt-shake circle. Time felt like it was in very slow motion. When she got all the way around she attempted to interrupt the song. No easy task.

"Guys! Stella's outside!"

For a second she got no response, then Wendy saw the look on her face and the words registered.

"Where?" she asked, turning toward the store front.

Lucy, still singing loudly and caught up in the musical moment, didn't hear what Vivian said.

Vivian was already moving out of the shop, trying to see which way Stella had gone.

Everyone followed her except Lucy, who was still La Bamba-ing with her eyes closed.

Kate stopped in the middle of the street to look around. "There she is," she yelled, pointing with her guitar.

Stella ran down the sidewalk between racks of clothing and other wares, past the shops they had visited before lunch.

"Let's get her!" Wendy yelled.

"Where are you going? Wait for me!" Lucy called after them, her *maracas* and other parts shimmying and shaking as she tried to catch up.

The *maracas*, tambourine, wind chime and castanets made for a musical chase. Vivian's wind chimes tangled up again and the pleasant tinkle became a muffled clank. Pierre held his *sombrero* in place with his tambourine so he jangled with every stride. Only Kate's guitar was silent.

The storekeeper ran out after them. Wendy, not breaking stride, turned around and yelled, "We'll be right back! *Uno momento! Lo Siento!*"

Vivian turned around and gave him a thumbs up. He didn't look happy and pulled his phone out of his pocket.

Lucy caught up to the crew and was at Wendy's side.

"What's going on?"

"It's the crazy lady!" Wendy pointed her castanets in the direction of the fleeing woman.

"Stellllllllllllllllllllllllllllllllllllaaaa!" Lucy yelled, Streetcar style.

The silver sequins of the mariachi hats winked in the sunlight as the "band" sprinted past the food carts. The strap of Vivian's *sombrero* was choking her, and the hat itself flailed in the wind like a loose sail. Kate's fruit hat was still in place, but her grapes flopped around and her pineapple whirled in the wind.

A group of tourists emerged from a shop, blocking the way and the view of Stella. Vivian pushed through them as quickly as she could, but couldn't see Stella anymore. Lucy ducked through the crowd, too and caught up.

"Where'd she go?" Lucy asked.

"I don't know," Vivian gasped, looking around.

The group continued down the length of the street, ending up by their car after not seeing any further signs of Stella. Vivian put her hands on the hood, doubling over from a raging stitch in her side. In fact, they were all gulping air, except for Lucy.

"What the heck?" Lucy said. "One minute I'm channeling Ritchie Valens, and the next I'm Marlon Brando! Where did Stella run off to?"

Sweat poured off Vivian's head and Pierre, wearing the *serape*, looked like he was about to pass out. Wendy helped him out of it and he sat down on the curb.

"She was right outside the store," Vivian replied, fanning herself with her *sombrero*. Her blonde hair stuck to her head, tight spiraly curls clung to her face. "She saw me doing the 'La Bamba' and took off. I was hoping to talk to her, but I guess she doesn't want to talk to me."

Vivian groaned at the sound of a siren drawing near. "Great, just what we need."

Lupe and her photographer did a double take when they saw the authentically-clad crew, but recovered quickly and scrambled out of their car. As they reached the girls and Pierre, notebook and camera ready, a police car pulled up.

Arturo walked over to them, shaking his head the whole time. *"Aye yai yai."*

A small crowd started to gather and stared at the quintet, a few took pictures with their phones.

Lupe and the photographer stood close by, taking notes and also snapping pictures. Vivian had a bad feeling about this.

Arturo said several calls came through about a disruption on La Quinta Avenida and some people stole merchandise from one of the shops.

His brown eyes sparkled. "I knew you would be here," he said to Vivian with a wink.

"Arturo, we saw Stella!" she said. "We had to try to talk to her, which then resulted in a chase and possibly some accidental shoplifting. We'll go back and pay for the stuff."

"Let's go take care of that first. Then we will deal with the other."

"Who is Stella?" Lupe butted in. "Did you steal that stuff?" she asked, pointing to their garb.

"Beat it lady," Wendy said, then turned to the group. "Give me some moolah. I'll go back pay for our unexpected souvenirs."

"No story here," Arturo told Lupe. The look on her face said she didn't believe him.

"Let me deal with the shopkeeper," Arturo said to Wendy as they walked off.

"You got it."

They arrived back at the shop and Wendy listened to Arturo tell the guy something to the effect of, "Stupid Americans, they got excited over seeing one of their friends and ran out of your store." *Thank goodness he's covering for us*, she thought.

The shopkeeper looked at Wendy. She smiled and waved her wad of cash.

She paid for the *sombreros*, musical instruments, *serape* and the wind chime.

Wendy gave him an extra $5 and said, "Sorry."

He slammed the cash register drawer closed with a "hump," but still didn't look too thrilled.

Back at the cars, Arturo handed Vivian a piece of paper. "Call me if you need help again. No chasing."

"Thanks." Vivian tucked his phone number in her purse. "I'll try to remember that."

"You girls are too much for me," Pierre said. "I'm going back to the hotel. Thanks for my *sombrero* and *serape*."

"Oh, a little something to remember us by," Kate said.

Arturo's job was done so he offered Pierre a ride to the hotel. Before getting in his car, he opened the trunk.

"No *sombrero* in the car. *Aqui.*"

Pierre, mixing cultures of Canada, Mexico and Texas (which does have its own culture) in honor of Jon tipped his enormous *sombrero* to the girls and said, "Eh," and turned to Arturo said, "No problemo-ola."

40

Vivian, Lucy, Wendy and Kate stood beside their rental P.O.S. on La Quinta Avenida, still wearing their *sombreros* and tutti-frutti hat.

Vivian contemplated what to do next. "Now what? Where do we go from here?" she asked the girls.

"We've lost Stella for now." Kate tried to set the pineapple on her hat back in place. "She certainly freaked out when she saw you, Viv. I wonder why."

"She looked horrified but it doesn't explain why she ran."

"She sure can run fast." Lucy took her *sombrero* off and fanned herself with it.

"She is one weird chick, and I agree with Kate, she's high-tailed it outta here," Wendy said, tapping her nails on the roof of the car in frustration. "What other touristy places could we look for her?"

"Let's check out the map. It's in the glove box." Vivian remembered seeing it when Al searched the car for bugs.

Kate spread the map on the hood and everyone gathered 'round.

"The ruins of Tulum don't look too far." Vivian said, pointing to a spot a little ways South. "Why don't we go there?"

"Do you think that's too far away from Playa? I mean, Detective Vega did tell us to stick around," Kate said.

Vivian felt the never-one-to-respect-authority side of herself rearing up. "Nahhhh. It looks like maybe 30 miles or so. That's not far."

"It doesn't look like there's anything else around besides Xel Ha, the aquarium," Lucy said.

"If I'm going to look at fish I better be wearing a swim mask and snorkel," Wendy said.

They all agreed. Of the two, Tulum sounded more interesting.

Vivian went to get into the passenger's seat and was practically strangled by the chinstrap of her *sombrero,* which was still hanging around her neck. She twirled around and yanked it off.

"Hey, it's not every day we wear these things," she said while the girls chuckled at her.

"We look absolutely ridiculous," Wendy said.

"You're right, let's put everything in the trunk." Vivian was ready to be free of her souvenirs, wind chimes included.

"I don't think they'll all fit in the trunk," Lucy said. "It's not the biggest I've ever seen."

"I can't have my new tutti-frutti hat gettin' smashed," Kate said, patting it gently. "It's stayin' with me."

They packed themselves into the car and headed towards Tulum, followed by the pesky reporter, Lupe Mendoza.

Five minutes into the drive, Lucy started digging around in her purse. "Does anyone have any cash?"

Kate, who sported her tutti-frutti hat while she drove, said, "After my very festive purchase I only have one dollar left."

"I spent the last of my cash paying the shop for my stuff and Pierre's." Wendy double checked her purse.

"That did it for my stash. I don't even have any change," Vivian said.

"I don't have any cash either." Lucy put her wallet back into her bag. "What if we get pulled over by the police? Aren't you supposed to have money to pay them off or something?"

"Why would we need to pay a bribe for a traffic stop?" Kate asked. "What would we get stopped for anyway? I'm not speeding."

Lucy leaned forward and gripped Vivian's seat. "I've heard that the police down here will pull over Americans for no reason and threaten to take them to jail. They have to bribe the police to let them go. The cops do it knowing people will pay them off, but we have no bribe money. They'll take us to jail! Haven't y'all seen those episodes of *Locked Up Abroad*?"

She really has watched too much of that show, Vivian thought.

"We've been through one round of bribes, we can handle another," Wendy said with sarcasm. "Anybody have a nice watch?"

Lucy inspected everyone's jewelry. She wasn't wearing any and neither was Vivian. Wendy had on small silver hoop earrings, and Kate, concerned about losing her wedding band and engagement ring on vacation, had left them at home and only worn a thin silver band in their place.

"We don't have on anything nice enough to pay them off," she paused for breath and continued, "Don't you remember what happened to those college students in Matamoros a few years ago? They were on South Padre Island on spring break and got into some trouble when they went across the border into Matamoros. They were taken to jail and the U.S. ambassador to Mexico could not get them extradited."

"Lucy, those kids picked a fight with a cop in a bar." Vivian tried to reassure her. "Besides, it was Matamoros, not Playa del Carmen, where they depend on the tourists. They wouldn't have any tourists if they were locking them all up."

Lucy, unswayed by the argument, continued, "Let's not forget that you're under suspicion of a murder, Viv. And they've taken all of our passports."

Point made.

"Kate, how about you pull into the next ATM you can find?" Vivian suggested.

It wasn't hard to keep an eye out for the next ATM, gas station or bank, because there was nothing on the road. This only got Lucy more agitated.

"Let me see the map," she demanded. "Maybe it will have a legend as to where gas stations, etc. are." She researched for a moment. "Nope, no legend, only the touristy highlights and roads."

Kate attempted to sound hopeful. "Maybe they will have a shop or something at Tulum. You know they've got to sell souvenirs, so maybe there is a way for us to get some cash."

"Yeah," Lucy mumbled. "If we make it."

Thought of more trouble with the police was unsettling and the rest of the drive was subdued.

Lupe Mendoza must have figured out where they were going and lost interest. She turned around halfway into the drive. Probably needed to get crackin' on writing the La Quinta Avenida story anyway.

The girls reached Tulum without incident and pulled up to the guard in the parking lot. "Fifty pesos," he said and held out his hand.

Kate reached into her purse and pulled out her lone dollar. "This is all we have. We are all out of cash."

The guard shook his head, still holding out his hand. "Fifty pesos," he repeated.

Wendy leaned into the front seat. *"No tenemos mas dinero, señor. Solamente uno dolares. Necesitamos un banco."*

The guard shook his head again, thrust his hand out farther, and said in a more demanding tone, "fifty pesos!"

Lucy was back in panic mode. She leaned out her back window. *"Señor,* we don't have any more money on us but we can get some if there is a bank. Is there one inside the gate? We'll go get some money and come back and pay you? I promise."

He only stood there, shaking his head.

Lucy continued to plea with him in earnest. Occasionally, Wendy yelled out *"Necesitamos un banco!"*

Lucy must have worn him down because he eventually barked at Kate, "GO!" and manually lifted the gate.

They entered Tulum a bit rattled, but feeling like champs after winning that round.

41

Tulum had a small shopping area with an ATM tucked into a corner by the restrooms. The girls took turns withdrawing 2500 pesos, around $200 U.S., per Lucy's instructions. Vivian checked her account balance while she was at it. It wasn't looking the happiest. *Damn!*

True to her word, Lucy ran to the parking lot and gave the guard 50 pesos. "I think he was surprised I paid him," Lucy said when she met up with the girls in the souvenir shop. "He had a bewildered look on his face but he gave me a map and this pamphlet on Tulum," she paused to look around, "this shop reminds me an awful lot of the last shop we were in on La Quinta Avenida. Did y'all do a Stella check?"

"All clear." Wendy opened up the map. "Self-guided tour. Y'all ready?"

They followed her out onto the ruin grounds, where it was unbearably hot.

"Holy crap," Kate said. "This is hot, like Africa-hot."

"I'd say it's more like hot-tamale hot since we're in Mexico." Wendy fanned herself with the pamphlet.

They ventured toward the Great Palace, Frescos Temple and El Castillo beyond that. Wendy stopped fanning herself long enough to read off a few tidbits of history. "Pre-Columbian Mayan city, one of the last cities inhabited after the Spanish arrived, built between the 13th and 15th centuries."

"Didn't they make the human sacrifices?" Lucy asked.

"How morbid, Lucy" Kate said, peering up at the many steps on El Castillo.

"Doesn't say in the pamphlet," Wendy responded.

Vivian was more interested in the big iguanas lying here and there, basking in the sun and soaking up the rays. She'd never seen a reptile that large, well at least one that wasn't behind glass, so she was intrigued. She stopped and looked at one as he rested on a rock. He was at eye level with her and wasn't the least bit frightened. In fact, he may have been bored, he opened and closed his mouth a few times and stretched his front leg out, then looked elsewhere.

At least something is enjoying the heat.

"I'm melting," Wendy said in her best Wicked Witch of the East voice and wiped a trickle of sweat off the side of her neck.

"I'm in need of some serious shade," Lucy said. "I'm going to suffer third-degree burns on my beautiful pasty-pasty white skin."

Kate stepped in front of them, hands on hips. "I didn't drive all the way out here a nervous wreck for us to not tour these ruins. I'm hot, too, but we can do this. We're sweating out toxins or something, right Lucy?"

Lucy groaned.

"Hell, I'm not *that* toxic," Vivian said. "We should have brought our *sombreros*. They would have at least offered some shade."

To appease Kate, the girls reluctantly continued their jaunt through the ruins. They even learned a few things, thanks to Wendy reading the brochure.

Lucy lagged a bit, so Vivian stopped to wait for her.

"I should have worn my tennis shoes," Lucy said. "These flip-flops weren't made for all these rocks."

Wendy, who was a good 15 yards up ahead of them, yelled, "Y'all need to come see this. This must be why the Mayans built their city here."

Kate reached her first and gasped. Lucy and Vivian trudged up to the column she stood next to and looked out at one of the most beautiful scenes Vivian had ever laid eyes on.

Tulum sat on a cliff about 40 feet above the sea. The beach below was completely deserted and the clear-water waves splashed invitingly against the white sand.

"Now that's where we need to be." Vivian pointed to the beach. "How the heck do we get down there?"

"I don't think we do, unfortunately." Wendy studied the map. "The brochure doesn't show a way down."

"How is it there is almost no breeze, yet Tulum sits high on a cliff overlooking the ocean?" Lucy took the brochure from Wendy and used it as a fan.

"I can't believe people ever survived without air conditioning." Wendy snapped a few pictures of the view and of them.

"I'm a modern girl, I need myself some modern a/c," Vivian said. "Let's get outta here. I either need some of those waves or some fabulous Freon blowing in my face."

Kate threw her hands up in surrender. "Okay, okay. I'm happy. I can go home and say I did something educational between killing sprees." She suddenly realized what she said and froze, covering her mouth.

They all turned and looked at Kate, shocked at her choice of words.

"Did you say 'killings sprees?'" Vivian asked.

"I meant the killing of my brain cells on vacation. Seriously! I didn't mean...you know!"

"Crap, Kate! Not even funny." Wendy slapped her arm with the map.

They all started cracking up. One of those crazed, I-need-a-stress-relief kind of laughs.

"Whew," Vivian said when she was able to speak again. *The heat must be getting to us.*

They stopped in the visitors center on the way out and bought some bottled water. Kate cranked up the car and they all hoped for cool air. Nope, non-existent so they drove out of the dirt parking lot windows down and waved at the guard. He didn't smile or wave back.

"How do you say 'Mr. Nice Guy' in Spanish?" Lucy asked.

Wendy gave a bark of laughter. "Ha, I don't know, *Señor Hombre Bueno?* Probably not. My Spanish education only goes so far."

"So that concludes the educational portion of our vacation," Kate said, getting back on the highway. "What's next on our agenda, ladies?"

"Let's get out of Playa for the evening." Vivian sat in front with Kate and was quick to answer. "Isn't there a ferry going to Cozumel? Let's catch it and go see what trouble we can get into over there."

"I'm not sure about the trouble part, but it sounds like fun." Lucy poured a little bottled water between her boobs.

"Well, that's one way to cool off," Wendy said. "It's not like the hot breeze is going to cool us off." She trickled some water down her shirt. "Ah, that feels good."

"Oh, I'm in," Vivian said as she unbuttoned her shirt and splashed water between her boobs.

Then she grinned and held the bottle out towards Kate. "Need some breastabule splashage?"

"Uh, no Viv. I appreciate the offer and all, but that's okay. I wore my cotton breastabule holder. It breathes."

Wendy and Lucy roared with laughter from the back seat.

The drive back to their hotel was uneventful. They periodically splashed more water on themselves trying to stay cool and kept an eye out for cops.

Once back at La Vida de Playa, Arturo let them into "special" parking and told them the fastest way to walk to the ferry. The girls left their impromptu souvenirs in the trunk, hurried to the docking area and hopped on just in time. The paparazzi hadn't seen them. They could enjoy Cozumel tonight and not worry about winding up on the evening news.

As the ferry pulled away from shore, Ponytail's wrecked SUV pulled into the parking lot. He got out and slammed the door, which popped back open. *Guess that stop sign did some damage.*

"He looks ticked," Wendy said.

"Guess he missed the boat!" Lucy joked.

42

Vivian didn't want to feel confined by the crowded, though air-conditioned, interior of the ferry, so the girls opted for the breezy and less crowded upper deck. She also wanted to smell the ocean and feel sunshine on her face.

A three-piece band roamed amongst the passengers, singing to ladies and hitting people up for tips.

"Reminds me of the taqueria on Richmond," Wendy said. "Great place for 2 a.m. breakfast. I'm going to have to request a song."

She wandered over and spoke to the guitar player, passing him a few pesos. She joined the girls at the railing as the band began a new song.

"This is our song!" she said.

After a few beats Kate asked, "What are they saying? One ton tomato?"

Wendy laughed and responded, "No, it's 'Guantanamera.' You've never heard this?"

Kate shook her head, as did Lucy.

"I consider the late night taqueria experience part of my college education."

Vivian had heard the song on her own taqueria adventures, and said, "Amen to that, sista! I'd cheers you, but we don't have any cheersing materials."

Lucy stopped the drink girl walking by who was carrying a small cooler filled with an assortment of beverage choices. "Round of tequila shots!"

"Oh no no no, not for me," Vivian said. "I'm tequila'd out at the moment, but I'll take a Dos Equis. With lime."

The drink girl nodded.

Wendy and Kate also vetoed the tequila but ordered *cervezas*.

"I'm drinking this for medicinal purposes," Lucy declared, holding up her shot. "It will help me relax and liven up all at the same time. Down the hatch."

We'll see about that, Vivian thought.

Vivian started to relax a little from the beer and being on the water. It also helped being on a vessel where no one suspected her of murder, was chasing after her, or was shoving a camera in her face.

The ferry was about to dock in Cozumel, when Vivian felt her stomach growl.

"Wendy, go ask the guitar player where's the best spot to eat over here." Vivian rubbed her stomach. "I'm starving."

Wendy waited for him to finish their last song before interrupting. She came back in a minute shrugging her shoulders. "He didn't suggest any restaurants but said we have to go to a place called the No Name bar."

"The what?" Kate asked.

"It's seriously called No Name," Wendy said. "He gave me directions and said it's not far off the main drag. There's no sign, just a blue door next to a gold exchange place. Said it's more of a hangout for locals."

"Ok, I'm in," Vivian said, feeling her stomach growl again. "Where should we eat?"

"We'll pass plenty of places along the way," Lucy said. "Let's just go see what looks good."

The ferry docked and they followed the crowd toward the main area of town. A line of taxis waited to take people to destinations farther away and a pushy guy offered scooters for rent. To Vivian, this part of town looked a lot like Playa del Carmen. Tons of shops with souvenirs, jewelry, pottery, etc. They walked past Señor Frogs, Carlos and Charlie's and waved off the merchants trying to get them into their stores. "My turn, my turn," they called.

The girls wandered up to a restaurant called the French Quarter.

"Anybody up for some Cajun and Creole food?" Wendy asked.

"Cajun in Mexico?" Kate looked skeptical.

"Let's go in and see what it's like. I'm starved!" Vivian said.

They walked in and felt like they'd been transported to Bourbon Street. Emerald green, gold and purple was the color scheme, accented by Mardi Gras beads and masks, along with gator heads, inflatable crawfish, and fleur de lis everywhere.

"This is cool," Wendy said. "New Orleans without the crowd."

"Or the smell," Lucy added.

They were seated at a table by a waitress who then took their order for standard Louisiana fare. Lucy ordered a "yard-long" hurricane, Vivian a Jax beer and Wendy and Kate both ordered a regular-sized hurricane.

The waitress arrived with their drinks and they laughed at the hurricanes. The little paper umbrellas were torn to shreds.

"Guess they've been through a hurricane," Lucy said, then sucked on her yard-and-a-half-long straw. "Maybe our next trip should be to New Orleans. This thing is yum!"

Lucy posed with her prize and Vivian snapped her picture.

"I love New Orleans," Wendy said. "It will have to go on the Getaway Girlz destination list for sure."

They stuffed themselves family style with red beans and rice, etouffee, jambalaya and gumbo, all of which tasted like a top tier New Orleans chef had made it. *Bam that, Emeril.*

They paid the bill and slowly stood up to leave.

"I feel like Jabba the Hut," Vivian laughed, then made some "Jabba noises."

Lucy belted out growling roars like Chewie and Kate beeped like R2-D2.

"I don't know y'all," Wendy laughed and walked away from them a little bit.

Mid growl, Lucy tripped over the curb. She had finished off her yard about three-quarters of the way through dinner and hadn't said much since.

"You okay, Lucy?" Kate asked. "We don't need any face-plants."

She gave a thumbs up, which was bright red from the hurricane, as were her lips. *How did she get hurricane on her thumb?* Vivian thought.

Once outside, they wandered toward the main square and worked their way through the crowd to see Mariachis playing in front of a large fountain and dancers performing what resembled a square dance. They looked like something out of the movies, the women in colorful embroidered dresses, their hair pulled off to the side in a bun and accented with flowers, and the men in black mariachi suits adorned in silver, hats, too. Children danced, also dressed in the traditional outfits. The little girls even had frilly fans.

Vivian had enough after a while and said, "Let's see if we can find the No Name place."

They walked away from the square, toward some shops and were beckoned in by the storekeeper. "Free gift," he promised. The lady behind the counter gave them each a small silver charm. Vivian got a starfish and Kate gave her the seashell charm she had been given.

"Awe, thanks. I'll have to put these on necklaces for Audrey and Lauren," Vivian said.

The ploy worked and they each spent a little bit in the shop. Vivian bought a small jewelry box, Lucy some earrings, Kate a charm bracelet and Wendy some magnets.

They left the store, planning to window shop their way to the bar, when another shopkeeper offered free beer.

"Can't pass up free beer," Vivian said, taking the bait. She then proceeded to pick out funny onesies, "My mom rocks" and "It wasn't me," for the twins. Both advertised Cozumel, Mexico.

"I need to sit down," Lucy said after several shops and a few more complimentary beers. "We getting close to the No Name, yet?"

Kate glanced around, then pointed down the street. "Look, there's a gold exchange place."

"And there's a blue door," Wendy said.

43

Vivian felt a bit apprehensive as they approached the blue door. What kind of a place doesn't have a sign?

Wendy pulled the door handle, cigarette smoke and the sound of thumping bass traveled down a short, dark hallway. "Tejano music. Great, I feel right at home."

Wendy lived in her grandparents' house which was built in the '50s. The neighborhood had morphed over the years and lovers of Buddy Holly's "Peggy Sue" had been replaced by lovers of La Mafia's "Como Me Duele Amor." The German and Czech-influenced Tejano music was often heard blaring from cars parked in the streets, driveways and yards, front and back.

"I don't know about this place." Kate crossed her arms, reluctant to go in. "The smoke, the music…and it looks kinda seedy."

Guns and Roses "Sweet Child of Mine" blasted out the door. "We're here so we might as well check it out" Vivian said and did the goofy sway dance made famous by Axel. "If it sucks, we'll move on."

Lucy nudged Kate forward, who sighed and walked through the door Wendy still held open.

The short hallway opened up to a decent sized bar lit mainly by neon beer signs, giving the small dance floor a greenish glow. It took a few seconds for Vivian's eyes to adjust, but she decided the place looked okay. The few locals in the place stared at them as they walked across the room and took a seat.

A waitress approached their table and threw down beverage napkins. *"Que quieres?"*

Wendy glanced over to the bar, looking for taps or any other indicators of what was available. "Have any specials?" she asked.

"Especial 'No Name' drink. *Tequila, jugo de naranja, es rojo y…"* she shrugged.

"Is it fruity?" Lucy asked.

"Si. Es fuerte."

"Oh, it's strong. Cuatro por favor." Wendy gave the girls a thumbs up, then ordered four.

"Love Lockdown" by Kanye West kicked on.

"I love this song," Lucy said. "Let's dance."

"Y'all go ahead. I haven't had enough to drink yet." Kate put her feet up in Lucy's vacated chair.

"I think I'll wait for my frosty beverage," Wendy said.

Vivian and Lucy had the floor to themselves. Vivian's white tank-top glowed green, and Lucy pointed out her floral bra showing through.

Vivian shrugged. "Didn't seem so noticeable at the hotel when I put it on this morning. These green lights show it off. Oh well!"

Two older guys sat down at a table right next to the dance floor.

"They're leering." Lucy turned so that her rump wasn't shaking in their faces.

"Just ignore them," Vivian replied.

One of the guys moved behind Lucy and started dancing. Vivian grabbed Lucy's hand and twirled her away from him. Didn't deter him though. Lucy had no idea he'd moved back behind her until he grabbed her waist and started to grind.

She turned around and wagged her finger at him. "No no no," she chided.

He gave her an innocent shrug and kept on dancing, but without touching her.

Lucy and Vivian finished the song and headed back to the table.

"This is freakin' good." Kate took a sip of her no-name drink. "I wish I knew what was in it."

Vivian tried it, too. "Damn. This is tasty. Wendy, you were a bartender. What do you think is in it besides tequila and orange juice?"

She took a sip and pondered for a moment. "Coconut rum, crème de cassis and pineapple juice maybe? Grenadine is what turned it red. It's hard to say. There's something else I just can't put my finger on."

"Well, I'm putting my lips on it. Yum!" Kate was almost done with hers.

The waitress appeared with four more. "From the man over there." She pointed to the wanna-be grinder.

They raised their glasses to him. *"Salud!"*

After a while of enjoying their drinks and shootin' the shit, Kate said, "We should probably head back to the ferry pretty soon. We don't want detective Vega lookin' for us and unable to find us."

A ray of sunshine shot down the hallway, illuminating the entrance just enough for Vivian to see the outline of three short shadows in the doorway. The door closed behind them, and her eyes adjusted back to the green glow. There stood Shorty and The Ladies.

"Holy crap!" Lucy had a panicked look on her face. "They followed us."

"No, no way," Vivian tried to reassure her. "We weren't followed. We've been here for a while already. If they followed us they would have come in right after us."

Shorty's eyes flashed with recognition and he and The Ladies sauntered over. "*Aye*, look who's here." Speedy Gonzales gangster-talk in the house.

Vivian glanced at the girls and then at Shorty. "Well look what the cat dragged in. What are y'all up to tonight?"

"Having good time," he said, then gestured to their table.

"Oh, yeah, join us." Vivian immediately regretted saying that as Kate's eyes got wide and she sucked in her breath. Thankfully, she regained her composure quickly.

The waitress scurried over and pushed a second table to theirs, and added three more chairs. Another arrived with three tequila shots and sat them on the added table. She then set down a full bottle of tequila and four empty shot glasses.

"So just out in Cozumel for the heck of it, huh?" Lucy asked.

Shorty sat down and his entourage followed suit. He introduced The Ladies as Eva and Josephina then said, "My family owns bar," he tapped an index finger on the table, then continued, "and two, three more. I like check, you know?"

He shot his tequila without flinching, it might as well have been water. From the corner of her eye, Vivian saw Kate cringe. One of his ladies refilled his glass.

"Besides," he continued, "I take boat out."

"So you own this bar?" Wendy asked.

"Mi familia." He gestured toward the bartender who held up a tequila shot in *salut*, then sucked it down.

"Oh," Vivian said. "I heard you were in the tequila business."

"We make best tequila in world." He picked up the bottle and turned the label toward them. "Tiempo Loco."

He unscrewed the top and poured four shots. "I vice president marketing *y* distribution."

"Every bartender or waitress we order margaritas or tequila shots from has recommended it. It's good." Kate picked up her no-name drink. "This is good, too."

"Glad you like," Shorty passed each of them a glass. "I have persuasive power." He gave them his best shit-eating grin.

What is his marketing pitch? Vivian thought. *"Sell only my tequila, or else?"* but said "Yeah, it's good stuff."

Lucy nodded in agreement.

"What about salt and lime?" Kate asked.

One of The Ladies scoffed.

"No need." Shorty held up his shot to toast, everyone followed suit. "To *de Loco*."

They clinked glasses and drank.

"Woooooo!" Lucy yelled. "Now that's what I'm talking about."

Vivian, needing the lime, coughed a little and patted her chest.

"Smooth stuff," Wendy managed.

His smile widened. "So why you in Cozumel?"

Vivian took a sip of her no-name drink and answered, "We just wanted to get out of Playa for a while. Needed some fresh air, so to speak."

"*Yo comprendo. Es* tense in Playa right now." Shorty poured Vivian another drink. His arm grazed hers as he poured. "I am sorry Jon *es* dead. He *es* cool guy."

Vivian was unnerved at his touch "Yes, he was," was all she could think of for a response.

"So when did you meet Jon and Pierre?" Kate asked.

"Few weeks ago, at the Purple Peacock," Shorty said. "We talk boats. I mention mine and he get excited. Said he going buy one like it," he put his thumb and index finger close together to relate smaller, "*pero más pequeñas*. I take them out and we hang out some. Sometimes we go to Peacock, sometimes other places."

Vivian's head felt a little swimmy from the tequila. "I only really got to know him that one night. I hate this has happened. I hope they catch whoever did it."

Everyone was quiet for a moment. Shorty broke the silence.

"The last time I saw Jon I get angry. I have too much drink. I feel bad, you know?"

The four girls looked at each other.

Shorty held his glass so Eva, or was it Josephina, could pour him another. "So what happen to Jon? Last time I see him was Club Caliente." Shorty picked up the tequila shot and pointed at Vivian with it. "He *es* with you."

Vivian's face got hot. "Well yeah, a bunch of us hung out at the club. Then he and I walked back to the hotel, and I went up to my room, leaving him on the beach," she said and took another sip of her drink, her mouth suddenly dry. "Next thing I knew, the cops were banging on our door to take us down to the police station."

"They took our passports," Lucy said. "Which totally sucks."

Shorty laughed and snorted, spilling some of his tequila shot. "They think you kill him?"

"Yeah," Vivian sniffled. "I think they think I did it."

"What about his *amigo*, Pierre?"

"He went with us to the market today." Wendy blew out a big puff of air, like she'd been holding her breath during the entire conversation with Shorty. "That was a fiasco."

"I hear some gringos run through the market in *ponchos y sombreros*. You?" Shorty asked, using his glass to gesture towards the four of them.

"Yeah," Wendy said. "We were running after this crazy girl, Stella."

"We thought we saw someone we knew from high school," Vivian interrupted, not wanting to tell him the Stella details.

"Long way from home see someone you know."

"We know a lot of people. I think we graduated with something like 600 people."

The girls all knew Vivian was covering. Their graduating class had closer to 400.

Kate, trying to get off the Stella topic, asked him, "So what about you, have you talked to Pierre or seen him since Jon…you know," she hesitated, "was killed?"

"I don't get close to police investigation. I don't go to hotel, see Pierre." He changed topics. "How you get here?"

"We took the ferry over, and, actually, we should probably be heading back," Wendy said.

"Stay. Hang out with me." Shorty leaned back in his chair and put his arms around The Ladies. "I take you back on Outlaw. Drop you on the beach at hotel."

Lucy gasped. She couldn't help herself. "That's okay, Julio. We appreciate the offer, but we don't want to impose. We'll just catch the ferry back."

"No no. You no want to leave. *Es* early. Party just get started." He looked around the No Name which had started to fill up.

"Besides," he smirked, looking at Vivian. "You no look like a killer to me."

44

Kate popped off her chair at the No Name Bar in Cozumel. "I need to use the restroom. Anyone else need to go?" She gave Vivian a look. "Buddy system."

"Yeah, I need to go." Vivian took the hint and got up.

Kate hurried Vivian into the tiny restroom. Shutting the door firmly, she whispered, "Viv, I don't feel comfortable going back to Playa on Shorty's boat. He's still on our list of suspects."

"Yeah, but he's not at the top of the list. Since he's still a suspect, though, that is exactly why we need to ride back with him. It'll give us a chance to go inside the cabin and look around. See if there's anything unusual. You know, a clue."

Vivian could practically see the wheels turning in Kate's head so she decided to press further.

"Plus, there is some kind of a connection with Al. I think for once Detective Vega is right, Shorty might not be a legitimate businessman, but I don't think he's a killer. I can't explain it exactly, just my gut instinct from talking with him tonight."

Kate wrung her hands, the internal debate still raging. "So you want me to risk my life, the life of my future unborn children with Shaun, on your gut instinct?"

"Boy you're laying it on thick, but yeah, I do. You know I'm usually right about my gut instincts."

"True, your gut has never steered us wrong before," she paused, then finally agreed. "Okay, we'll give it a shot. But you'd better be right!" She poked Vivian's gut on her way out the door.

The mood at the table was a bit awkward after Vivian and Kate's return. To break the tension, Kate asked The Ladies politely, "So, are y'all from Playa?"

Josephina, or was it Eva, answered, "Yes."

Not the long-winded types, Vivian thought.

Lucy laughed nervously. "It must be nice being by the beach all the time."

"Playa has much to offer," Shorty said. "Me, beaches, tourists." He rubbed his thumb and first two fingers together, "*Y* tourists drink tequila, no? *Es* good for me."

Shorty gave Wendy a sideways glance. "How about you. How much of my tequila you drink since you here?"

"We've all had our fair share." Wendy didn't miss a beat. She looked down at her depleted No Name drink. "In fact, I'm due for more right about now."

Shorty snapped at the waitress. "Another round for my ladies."

Lucy giggled.

"Cheers!" Vivian said. "*Gracias*, Julio."

"You dance?" Shorty asked as Daddy Yankee's "Gasolina" came on.

Vivian felt like moving, not sitting and said, "I'm in."

The seven of them almost took up the entire dance floor, it was so small. Vivian thought Shorty and The Ladies looked like they danced together frequently, as they had a rhythm all their own. They face one direction, with Shorty sandwiched in the middle, and looked like they were spooning.

"Do you think they sleep in the same position?" Wendy said in a low voice in Vivian's ear.

"Don't make me hurl."

"If we're going to catch the ferry we need to leave right now," Lucy reminded them. "It leaves in 10 minutes. We could make a run for it."

Kate positioned herself in front of Lucy and Wendy. "Viv's gut instinct tells her Shorty is not the killer, that Detective Vega may be right about that. She also thinks we need to look around the boat for anything suspicious, though, just in case."

Vivian danced around the girls and glanced over at the spooning trio, who were too occupied with groping and grooving to notice their discussion. "I don't think he's the one. Shorty may be a shady businessman, but I don't think he's our murderer."

"Okay, but if he turns out to be a murderer and kills us, I'm going to be pissed!" Lucy said.

"He's not going to kill us." Vivian raised her hands in the air as she danced, acting like they were having a casual conversation. "He just wants to have fun and impress us with his boat. Not bloody it up."

Wendy smiled at Shorty and turned away from him as she danced. "Let's let our waitress know he's taking us back to Playa. She can come forward if our bodies are found."

"Yeah, right, she works for his family," Lucy said. "She's not going to give him up."

"You never know," Wendy replied. "Her conscience might get the best of her."

"Y'all are acting like we're goners already. Shorty doesn't have any reason to harm us," Vivian said. "He just said he doesn't like to get involved in police investigations. If the four of us turned up dead, the police would be swarming all over him and Playa. We did tell Detective Vega our suspicions, remember?"

She danced for a few beats, then continued, "And we told Pierre and Al and Adrienne. They'd get justice for us, and maybe even a little revenge." She smiled on "revenge."

"Ok, let's make the best of our last night on Earth," Lucy said, and went back to the table to take a long sip of her drink.

Shorty left The Ladies on the dance floor, and disappeared through a door behind the bar.

The Ladies, Kate, Wendy and Vivian went back to the table and joined Lucy.

"So how long have you known Julio?" Lucy asked them.

One of them answered, "Long time." Then they both got up and went to the restroom.

"Guess they're on the buddy system, too," Lucy said.

"Yeah, even with their men," Kate said.

Wendy looked around to see if Shorty was close by. "We need to have another code word tonight. Any ideas?"

"How about 'pizza'?" Lucy offered. "We can say, 'I sure would like a slice of pizza,' and it won't sound suspicious."

"That works," Vivian agreed. "Hell, a big pepperoni slice sounds good right now. I'm tipsy."

Shorty came out of the door and walked back to the table. "You have good time?"

"That we are!" Vivian held up her No Name drink in emphasis.

Lucy finished off her drink, slammed it down and looked around at all of them. "I want to get a tattoo."

Shorty didn't look phased by her announcement, but Vivian was shocked. Kate and Wendy looked it too.

"Excuse me?" Vivian did a mock cough. "Did you just say you want to get a tattoo?"

"I did. I've been thinking about it for a while. Why not get it now?"

"*Es* place down street," Shorty said. "I know guy. *Es bueño.*"

"Well, there you have it. If Mr. Tiempo Loco Tequila Man said it's good, it's gotta be. Let's go." Lucy pushed back her chair abruptly, causing it to fall backward. She stood up, wobbling a bit. "And I'm doin' it!"

"We can't let her permanently mark herself under the influence." Kate waved around Lucy's empty glass and looked at Vivian and Wendy.

"You sure you want a tattoo and want to it get now, *in Mexico*?" Wendy asked.

Lucy nodded, then poured herself a tequila shot, spilling some in the process. Liquid courage.

"Let's just go." Vivian stood up. "Maybe she'll change her mind once she gets there and sees the needle."

Since when does Lucy trust Shorty? Vivian thought. *I guess somewhere in the middle of that last drink.*

"*Es* that way." Shorty pointed to the left. "Maya Tattoo. Ask for Dragón."

Dragón. Oh Lordy.

45

The Maya Tattoo's big neon sign flashed erratically and Vivian heard the buzz of electricity as she passed by it. The girls looked at the dozens of pictures boasting satisfied customers in the front window.

They went inside and were greeted with a silent stare from a hefty guy behind the counter. "I want a tattoo. Are you Dragón?" Lucy said.

"Si." He was covered in tattoos, at least the skin they could see. The silver looped nose ring was not sexy, nor were his giant, disgusting earlobe expanders. Vivian couldn't believe Lucy was about to let this guy touch her.

"Wonder how he got his name," Kate asked just loud enough for Vivian and Wendy to hear. "Do you think he breathes fire?"

"Shh!" Wendy looked at Dragón to see if he had overheard Kate. He had not, so Wendy said, "Let's not find out."

Dragón pointed to a notebook filled with pages and pages of artwork. Lucy began flipping.

"I can't believe we are letting her do this," Kate said a little louder and with more urgency.

"We aren't 'letting' her do anything," Vivian took up for their tipsy friend. "She's an adult. She can make up her own mind."

Lucy looked at them. "Hello! I can hear you. And besides, it's no crazier than riding back to Playa on a boat, by ourselves, with someone who *might* have murdered Jon."

Maybe she's more sober than I thought, Vivian thought.

After looking for a while, Lucy picked out an ancient Mayan symbol that meant "survivor."

"I want this." She held up the book for Dragón to see.

Vivian looked over Lucy's shoulder. "Interesting choice."

"¿Dónde lo desea usted?" Dragón asked.

Lucy looked to Wendy for help.

"I think he wants to know where you want it," Wendy translated.

"Oh, okay." Lucy turned and pointed to her lower back. "Here."

189

"Oh my god, no." Kate yelled. "You are *not* getting a tramp stamp."

Lucy started laughing. "I'm kidding. I was just testing y'all."

"Thank goodness." Kate said, breathing a sigh of relief. "I thought we were going to have to drag you outta here."

"Yes, there was about to be a tattoo intervention," Wendy said.

"Put it here." Lucy pointed to the outside of her left ankle.

"That's much better," Kate said. "At least you can wear socks and cover it up."

Dragón pointed Lucy into a reclining chair. He got out his equipment, needles and all, and carefully wiped down her ankle with alcohol.

"Have you sterilized those needles?" Lucy asked. "My life's at stake here."

Dragón just nodded and got to work.

Vivian, Kate and Wendy took a seat over by the windows as Dragón got to work.

Lucy was pretty calm and didn't seem to be bothered by the pain. Of course she was probably numb from the yard-long hurricane, the tequila and the no-name drinks. She was chatty, talking to Dragón about anything and everything. It was mostly a one-way conversation.

About halfway through her survivor symbol, Lucy got quiet. Vivian walked over to check on her. "How you doin' there?"

Lucy's face had turned pale. "It's starting to hurt a little now. Maybe I could use another drink?"

Dragón gave a slight shake of his head and grunted.

Guess that means no drinks.

Vivian thought a distraction was in order. "Try to think of something funny, Lucy. Remember the time I was going to color my hair and we decided you needed dramatic blonde highlights, like me?"

"How could I ever forget? That was one of the worst nights of my life! I ended up with orange hair."

Kate looked up from the tattoo artist magazine she had been skimming through. "I don't know the orange hair story. Do tell!"

"I know it but I never get tired of hearing it," Wendy said. "Tell it again!"

Lucy let out a sigh and adjusted herself in the chair. "Before Viv and I moved to Austin, I lived at her parents' house for a few weeks. One day, as we were running errands, she remembered she needed to get stuff to highlight her hair."

"I'm convinced that's why I'm going gray already," Vivian said. "I think I started coloring my hair when I was 14."

Lucy continued, "I'm not sure what possessed me, but I decided that I should highlight my hair, which I had never done before. In fact, I had never colored my hair at all. I grabbed the same box as Vivian, labeled 'Dramatic Blonde Highlights,' and we went back to her house to get things developing."

"This is where it started going bad." Vivian held back her laughter for the moment, but knew it was going to bubble forth shortly.

"Viv put on the shower cap looking thing and began pulling her hair through the holes. Now I had *a lot* of long, curly hair, so her mom offered to help me. She pulled and pulled and pulled, Vivian warned her along the way that she had pulled through too much hair. I wasn't worried; I was excited to have 'dramatic blonde highlights.'"

"I told you, though! I knew it was too much." Vivian let a giggle escape.

"We put on the chemical gloves, whipped up the formulated bottles and applied away. A few minutes into our waiting time, I told her that my scalp was burning."

"You did not! Not until the second time!"

"Yes I did! Let me finish." Lucy gave her a look.

"Oh no," Kate said. "Burning. Not good."

"Not good at all," Wendy agreed, though she had never colored her hair.

Dragón glanced up and shook his head. He put his hand on Lucy's leg, indicating she needed to hold still.

"Viv didn't seem too worried about the burning, so I dismissed it as normal," Lucy continued. "Ding! Off we went to wash our hair and of course use the conditioning treatment that came with the kit."

Vivian let out a sigh and another little giggle. Lucy ignored her.

"Finally, the time had come. I took the towel off of my head and looked in the mirror. All I could think was 'they weren't kidding around when they wrote "dramatic" on that box.' Being an eternal optimist, I was confident that once I dried my hair it would look better. Those bright yellow, chunky streaks all over would blend to create a perfect highlighted hairdo. Right?"

Vivian shook her head and mouthed, "no" to Kate and Wendy.

"I frantically started hair drying in order to accomplish this, but it wasn't working. In fact, the more I dried it the worse it got. Vivian was chomping at the bit to see what I looked like. She knew something was wrong from the tone of my voice through the bathroom door."

"She wouldn't come out for, like, an hour," Vivian said, covering her mouth to hold in the howls of laughter about to explode.

"There was no way around it, so I opened the door."

"Oh my gosh, it was horrific." Vivian couldn't contain herself any longer and started cracking up.

Lucy held her hands out, Vanna White style, toward Vivian. "Much like she is right now, she burst into laughter, and I don't mean a little supportive 'it'll be all right' chuckle, I mean a doubled over in tears guttural laugh."

"I fell on the floor actually, rolling around laughing. The picture of that orange hair will forever be burned into my brain."

"This, of course, brought me to tears, which I had held off up to this point. I tried to laugh, too, but I was not happy. It was almost 1 a.m., but Viv woke up her mom to get a second opinion. She inspected my hair and tried to tell me 'it's not that bad,' which made Vivian laugh even harder. She told her mom that she 'wouldn't walk down the street with me looking like that.'"

"Bad friend, Vivian." Kate wagged her finger at Vivian like she would a dog. "Bad friend."

"Wait," Vivian said. "It gets worse."

Dragón glanced up at Vivian. His cheeks were flushed, from holding back laughter she presumed.

"Oh no," Wendy said.

"Oh yes," Vivian said. "We came up with a new plan to try to return her hair to its normal color. We went back to the store to get more hair dye."

"We were about to leave the house when Viv's boyfriend called," Lucy continued. "She gave him the short version of the situation, and he and his friend decided to meet us at the store. I was in no mood to socialize and wore a scarf to cover up the monstrosity that was my head. Viv told me just to have a seat on a bench close to the door and that they would stand in line to buy the hair dye. They paid and headed toward me and Vivian, once again, burst into laughter and pointed at me. I was not amused. She explained that I was sitting on a bench next to Ronald McDonald and that his bright red hair and my brightly colored headscarf were just hilarious. I did not laugh; however, they could not stop."

Tears were now rolling down Vivian's face, and she was again doubled over in laughter. "You just have to understand, Lucy, you with your floral scarf and orange hair sitting next to Ronald McDonald. It was hilarious!"

Kate held the magazine up to her face so only her eyes showed. Wendy covered her mouth with her hand. Vivian knew they were cracking up, too and trying to hold it in for Lucy's sake.

"It was now after 2 in the morning, but I was desperate to remedy this hair situation," Lucy said. "We got back to Viv's house, I mixed the color and applied it to my hair. Vivian waited up with me while I processed, assuring me that everything would be fine. This time, though, my scalp really burned!

"I said something to Viv, but she told me that the stuff just stinks, it burns her a little, too, and it'll be over soon. I tried to ignore it — I wanted this to work so badly. Ding! I jumped in the shower and washed my hair. I really massaged the conditioner pack into my scalp this time, thinking that it may remedy the burning. I stepped out of the shower and looked in the mirror."

"How bad was it?" Kate asked.

"Well, the good news was that the color did cover the dramatic blonde highlights. Even though it was nowhere near my color, it appeared to be a normal color. I was exhausted and confident that this had worked so I went to bed with my hair wet. Oh, and did I mention my scalp still burned?"

"This does not sound good, Lucy," Wendy said.

Lucy continued, "The next morning I woke up, sat up in bed and looked in the mirror across the room. I was horrified! My hair was *not* a normal color. It was orange, and I mean tangerine orange. Also, I had red, burning blotches on my scalp. I scrambled out of bed and into Viv's room. She woke up, looked at me, and again, started laughing. I was frantic. I luckily had my hair lady's home phone number so I made an emergency appointment. She took one look and told me the burning sensation was an allergic reaction. If I had done anything else, my hair might have fallen out. She worked her magic for what seemed like forever—scalp treatment, conditioning treatments for my severely damaged hair, new color—and she cut off more than six inches."

"Is this when you had that burgundy hair color?" Wendy asked.

"Yep, that's how that color came into my life."

"I always wondered about that," Kate said. "And you straightened your hair then, too, right?"

"Not on purpose. It took my hair more than a year to recover the curl."

"That's a lesson, ladies," Vivian said, wiping the tears from her eyes. "Burning is bad."

Dragón put down his instruments and gave the new tattoo a final swipe with alcohol. "You like?"

Lucy looked at her new tattoo. "It's perfect. Thank you, Dragón!" She threw her arms around him and gave him a big hug.

Vivian could tell by the look on his face that he didn't like this show of affection. She got out her camera just in time to snap his picture. He didn't look too happy about that, either.

"We'd better head back to the bar." Vivian walked to the door. "We don't want Julio to leave us here tonight."

"Yeah." Lucy gave Dragón a final squeeze. "We might have to stay with Dragón tonight if we got left."

He grunted again, obviously not pleased at the prospect of house guests, even if they were four hot babes.

Maybe he only likes girl dragons?

46

Vivian had a feeling someone was watching her as she opened the door to the No Name. She glanced into the alley directly across the street as she held the door for the girls. Behind a five-foot stack of wooden pallets she could make out the orange glow of a cigarette butt. The moonlight gave off just enough light to reveal the person behind it. His hair was pulled back, and he had a jagged scar down his left cheek.

She hustled inside. "Oh my god! I just saw Ponytail across the street."

The girls stopped just inside the door and turned to face her.

"What?!" Lucy exclaimed.

"He's hiding in the alley."

"Who is he spying on, us or Shorty?" Kate asked.

"I have no idea, but he chased *us*."

Wendy opened the door a crack and peeked outside. "That's him all right. I can see why he'd spy on us, but why spy on Shorty?"

"Maybe he's spying on Shorty for the same reason we want to snoop around on his boat." Kate pulled the door closed. "To see what, if any, connection there is to Jon's death."

"We need to watch ourselves." Lucy made the sign of the cross. "I don't trust Shorty 100 percent, and I sure as heck don't trust Ponytail."

Shorty walked up, tequila bottle in hand. "*Hola, señoritas*. Everything okay?"

"We were just deciding what to do tomorrow," Vivian said and nervously tucked a stray strand of hair behind her ear. "Lie on the beach or go snorkeling."

"Beautiful beaches, beautiful water, *es* all good."

Shorty led them back to the table they had vacated earlier and grabbed for the shot glasses.

Vivian waved her hand to stop him. "Thanks, Julio. No tequila for me, but I'd definitely like another No Name drink."

"I'll take some tequila and a No Name. I need to numb the tattoo pain," Lucy said.

Julio looked her up and down. "Where?"

She held her leg up and proudly showed him her new tattoo. "What do ya think?"

"*Es bueño*. Dragón do good job."

Vivian could tell he wasn't all that excited about the symbol, probably not his style. He seemed more like a snake-and-fangs-tattoo kind of guy.

Vivian was unsettled at seeing Ponytail across the street and wondered what he was up to. Would he barge in there and demand something or attack them? Would he just watch in the shadows all night? She didn't know what to expect because she didn't know what "organization" he was involved with.

The girls managed to chit chat with Shorty while they finished their drinks, then Vivian asked, "Do you mind if we head back to Playa?" She pointed to Lucy, who had started yawning. "I think some of us are done for the night."

"*No problemo*," Shorty said, then pushed back his chair.

Vivian reached in her purse to pull out some money but he waved her off.

"You no pay."

"But what about a tip for the waitress?"

"I her customer, *es* her lucky day."

On their way out Vivian looked in the alley for Ponytail but saw no one. She noticed the full moon which would offer plenty of light on the boat ride back, but in her book it also meant the crazies were out. *Can't win for losing.*

As they made their way to the marina, they walked by street vendors selling tacos and other meats on a stick. The smells were intoxicating, but the girls were leery. It could be dog or cat tacos for all they knew. They ignored the offers of food and moved on, Kate checking behind them periodically and Vivian looking down every alley.

Everyone they passed recognized Shorty. They would look at him and nod. Almost like a respect thing.

Shorty, hand in pocket, approached four guys. He said something to a guy in a black t-shirt with red and orange flames on it. Flames slipped his hand in and out of his pocket and they shook. From Vivian's vantage point it looked like some sort of exchange took place.

"What was that about?" Lucy whispered.

"Just chill out," Wendy said. "Let's not speculate."

"We don't want to piss him off. We'll be fish food." Kate said.

"It'll be fine," Vivian said, though she was a bit nervous after the exchange. "At least we haven't seen creepy-Ponytail-stalker-guy."

Deal done, Shorty grabbed each of his women by the waist and said, "Let's move."

The marina was just down the street and the girls shuffled along behind, glancing at each other nervously.

Shorty grabbed the line and pulled his boat close to the pier, then helped The Ladies aboard. They disappeared below, into the cabin. He looked up expectantly at Vivian and crew, who still stood on solid ground.

"Guess I'll be first to walk the plank," Vivian joked and walked slowly down the pier. Behind her Lucy hummed a funeral dirge.

"Stop that! I'm about to push you in the water," Wendy muttered from behind her.

Kate choked back a laugh.

Vivian reached the boat and Shorty held his hand out.

She took a deep breath, grabbed his hand and climbed aboard.

47

Shorty helped Lucy, Wendy and Kate aboard *Belize It!*, and got busy readying the boat for departure. While he scrambled around untying lines, he told them they could find snacks and drinks in the galley.

Lucy wasted no time. She went down below and The Ladies came up carrying plastic cups. Vivian, Wendy and Kate took turns on the ladder leading into the cabin.

"Wow. This is pretty freakin' awesome." Wendy glanced around the galley which was at the foot of the stairs. It was complete with little fridge and microwave.

The head was just opposite the kitchen and had the necessary amenities, but no shower. A seating area and table were between the kitchen and an oval opening that contained the V-berth. The bed didn't reach all the way into the V of the bow, but almost. Shorty's boat was pimped out. He even had a flat-screen TV above the galley, visible from the bed.

The engines roared to life and the boat started moving. The girls exchanged nervous glances.

"Saint Michael, protect us on this journey with a could-be killer," Lucy prayed.

"It's fine." Vivian tried to reassure them. "We'll be fine."

"Just in case it's not, I'm helping myself to a rum and Coke."

Kate unscrewed the lid to a bottle of rum sitting on the counter and glanced up, into the berth. "Holy crap, that's some of the tackiest bedding I've ever seen."

They all looked over at the bed. Lucy gasped.

The bedding was satiny black with little white Playboy bunnies. The bunnies were extra illuminated due to the red mood lighting. Shorty must have had 10 pillows on the bed, each with white bunny tails as fringe. The crème de la crème was the huge, life size bunny, right smack dab in the middle of the bed. Bunny was on her side, looking like she was ready for, well… snuggling, spooning and Vivian didn't want to imagine what else.

"Holy shit. That's bad," Wendy said, shaking her head.

"I'll tell you one thing," Kate said reaching for a rum and Coke in a pink cup freshly stirred by Lucy. "I won't be searching for anything in there."

"Awww, it's their little love nest," Vivian said. "I can just picture the four of them spooning."

Kate made a gagging noise.

"We should look for clues while we have the chance." Wendy opened the door to the head and glanced inside. "Not much to search in here."

Lucy handed Vivian a pink cup. "I'll take the kitchen."

"Kate, you check over there in that storage cabinet," Wendy said, pointing to a small cabinet just aft of the galley. "I'll help Viv with the berth."

"What exactly are we looking for?" Kate asked.

Vivian walked over to the love nest. "I don't know. Anything suspicious. Anything that could have to do with Jon," she paused, "or even Al."

"I hate to think Al has anything to do with Shorty." Lucy rifled through a cabinet under the sink.

"I'm pretty sure it was his phone number I saw on Shorty's phone." Vivian said, pulling back a corner of the bedding, revealing a storage locker. "It's just too coincidental."

Kate's cabinet was full of boat stuff. Life jackets, bathing suits, liquor bottles. Nothing incriminating. Lucy didn't find anything more suspect than a couple of very sharp kitchen knives.

From the pilot's chair, Shorty could see Kate search through the cabinet. "Need something?" he called down to her.

"Oh, I was just looking for a jacket or something. I feel a little chilled."

"*El bano es* towels."

"That's okay. I'll just stay down here a few minutes. I'll warm up."

Vivian tugged on the handle to the port side storage locker but it wouldn't budge. She got a weird feeling about what she would find in there.

Wendy, however, was able to pop open the starboard storage locker without any trouble. Shirts, shorts, bras and G-strings. Wendy slammed the lid shut. "Gross. I need to wash my hands."

"Help me with this side, it's stuck," Vivian said and tugged on the handle one more time. The lid popped free and she gasped.

"What? Did you find something?" Wendy looked over her shoulder.

"Boy, did I. I think Shorty is kinda kinky!" She held up a pair of red feathered handcuffs.

"Oh, my!" Kate said. "Guess he likes to play cops and robbers! I got some similar ones at my bachelorette party." She took them from Vivian and swung them around on one finger, then handed them back. "Those feel much heavier. Maybe they're real?"

"Someone's coming!" Lucy whispered, taking a seat. Wendy sat down next to her.

A hot pink pump landed on the top step. Vivian closed the lid on the storage locker and scrambled to smooth the covers. With no time left to hide the handcuffs, she quickly dropped them into her purse and kicked it closed.

Kate sat down opposite Lucy with her pink cup and took a sip as Josephina/Eva emerged.

The Lady went to the refrigerator and grabbed a beer. She stopped to look at them, then clicked back up the stairs.

"Holy crap, we almost got caught!" Lucy said.

"Yeah, that was a little too close." Vivian blew out a big sigh of relief.

"I don't think there's anything here to find," Kate said, looking over to Vivian.

"Wishful thinking, I guess."

"There are a couple of hatches on deck we could go through, but that's not gonna happen with them up there," Wendy said.

"No way. Un uh." Lucy propped her leg up and took a gander at her ankle. "I think it brought us good luck tonight, though. So far, we've survived."

Eva and Josephina came back down together. One sat on the bed and the other stretched out beside the bunny.

"Let's go up." Wendy shot her eyes toward them.

They grabbed their cups and purses and carefully made their way up the steps.

Vivian sat in the co-pilot's chair, adjacent to Shorty, while Lucy, Kate and Wendy sat on the bench behind them.

"Almost back, maybe 15 *mas minutos*," Shorty informed them. "I drop you at pier next to La Vida de Playa."

"That'd be great, Julio, thanks." Vivian said, wondering how he knew where they were staying.

He took a swig of beer and put his cigarette back in his mouth. *"No problema."*

Wendy stood on steady sea-legs behind Shorty and looked over his shoulder at the gauges. "How fast are we going?" She paused for a moment while she looked at the complex gauges, then froze. "Holy shit, is that a gun?"

"What, gun?!" Lucy shouted. "Are you going to kill us? I'm too young to die!"

Shorty blew out a puff of smoke and laughed. "I no kill you. Gun *es mi amigo*." He looked back at Lucy and gestured with his cigarette. "Beside, if I want kill you *anoche*, would have two miles back. Better current."

"Well, thanks, Julio. That makes us feel better," Vivian said.

He looked over at her and winked. "I not murder suspect."

Touché.

Wendy cleared her throat and pointed to the gauges. "So how do all these work?"

He gave her a quick rundown in broken English, unsuspecting of Wendy's ulterior motive. He may not have told her if he knew she was contemplating stealing his boat in an act of desperation for Vivian's freedom.

Vivian didn't pay attention to his instruction, instead she looked out across the water and the moonlight reflecting off it, twinkling at her as they raced along. The effect was calming and she tried to enjoy it. There was no telling the next time she'd be able to lose herself in this kind of serenity. She wanted to sear it into her memory.

Shorty pulled up at the hotel next to theirs and tethered the boat to the pier, then helped them debark.

"Thanks, Julio. Appreciate the ride." Vivian waved goodbye and the other girls waved and said thanks, too.

"You stay out trouble," he smirked, wagging a finger at Vivian.

"Aye, aye, Capt'n," she said and saluted.

They set off down the beach, toward their hotel, and came upon the spot where Jon was killed. A piece of crime scene tape still stuck out of the sand, blowing in the sea breeze.

"Okay, this is kinda creepy," Lucy said.

Vivian slowed down and almost stopped.

"Do you think Shorty knew and dropped us at this pier on purpose?" Kate asked. "He could have dropped us off at the pier on the other side of our hotel and we wouldn't have had to walk by here."

"I don't know." Vivian was shaken up and propelled herself forward. She didn't want to think about dead bodies, murder, Jon, anyone of short stature, cousins that so closely resembled each other they could pass as twins, people with ponytails, asshole detectives, crazy bitches, or as Vega had put it, "basically half of Canada."

They made it to their room and did another bug sweep, just in case. Finding nothing, they got ready for bed.

After brushing her teeth, washing her face and putting on her jammies, Vivian plopped into bed. She was almost to a much-needed REM cycle when she sat up with a start.

"Oh, my god!"

Wendy clicked on the light. "What is it Viv, what's wrong?"

She jumped out of bed and ran to her purse, yanking it open to her horror.

"I still have Shorty's kinky handcuffs!"

48

Day 5

The next morning promised to be another bright and sunny day in paradise. A beam of sunlight slipped through a crack in the drapes and aimed directly at Vivian's left eye.

Lucy was already out of bed, doing her morning routine.

"Close the curtains," Vivian groaned, pulling the covers over her head.

Lucy yanked off her covers and started in. "Up and at 'em. It's detox day. Rise and shine, sista! No alcohol today, only H2O," she continued. "We're going to do yoga on the beach right now and water aerobics this afternoon."

Vivian reached for the covers at the foot of the bed.

"What time is it?" Kate asked, then rolled over, taking most of the covers with her.

Wendy didn't look too happy. "It's too damn early, that's what time it is."

"It's 7:30. Let's get a move on. Chop chop," Lucy replied, clapping with the chops.

"Lucy is torturing us today. Yoga." Vivian grabbed a pillow, throwing it over her face. Then thought better of it and threw it at Lucy. "And if I'm going, y'all are going."

"Whatever. She's making *you* do yoga," Wendy grumbled.

Lucy ripped the sheets off Kate and Wendy's bed.

"What the — " Kate started.

"Told ya," Vivian said.

After confiscating the sheets from both beds, Lucy threw the drapes open dramatically.

"Come on, ladies. Up, up! It's time to get up!"

"I don't want to exercise." Kate plopped her pillow on her head.

"Today is a new day and we are going to make it a good one, starting with something semi-healthy." Lucy tickled the bottom of Kate's foot.

"Sleep is healthy." Wendy moaned.

"Not as healthy as sunshiny yoga. Get up, lazy asses."

They gave in to Lucy's demands and crawled out of bed, still moaning and groaning about it. They threw on yoga-appropriate shorts, t-shirt, flip-flops and sunglasses and headed out.

Outside, Vivian looked around for the media. Only a few reporters were hanging around this early in the morning. They didn't appear too interested in the girls, *thank goodness*, she thought.

Lucy stood just out of reach of the water, her back to the ocean. The other three girls lined up facing her.

"All right, ladies, let's start with some deep breathing." She led by example, sucking in deeply through her nose, then breathing out through her mouth.

A nice breeze came off the waves and Vivian breathed deep with vigor. *Now this is some clean air*, she thought, *a far cry from the Get Down's orange-brown funkified air.*

Vivian was lost in her clean air moment. Lucy cleared her throat loudly to get her attention as she had already moved on to the first pose, the mountain. Arms held slightly outward from hips, feet together, chin high.

Now this is my kind of exercise. Standing.

Lucy led them through a few other poses: the chair, the warrior, the half-moon.

Vivian felt pretty good about her yoga experience so far. Seven years of ballet had given her and Wendy good balance, and Kate seem to be doing fine, too.

She was shocked by Lucy's extremely professional attitude though. She counted out loud, called out all the poses, and walked around to make sure they were perfectly positioned. It was like a whole new Lucy. A drill instructor disguised as a yoga instructor disguised as Lucy.

"Are you secretly teaching yoga classes or something?" Kate asked.

"Shhhh. No talking," the drill instructor responded.

Lucy pulled Vivian's leg up higher on the half moon.

"Let's move on to the next pose," she then said, walking back in front of the girls. She spread her legs wide and bent forward. "This is the wide-legged forward bend."

"What genius came up with this name?" Wendy was apparently still grouchy from her early morning wake-up call.

Lucy's butt was way up in the air. Vivian couldn't help herself and started giggling.

"Shhhh." Shushed by the yoga instructor.

Vivian could barely touch the sand with her hands, much less bend over like Lucy was. She could feel herself losing control, about to bust out laughing. "You know, Lucy, I'm thinking yoga may not be my thing."

"You aren't even trying!" She was still upside down and glared at Vivian from between her legs.

"I am, but I just feel so silly!"

Vivian stood up and saw stars as the blood rushed back to her head. "In other news, I'm hungry."

"We need a Paula Deen kind of breakfast," Wendy said, still in pose. "I'm needin' some biscuits slathered in butter. Let's go."

"That sounds fantastic." Vivian slipped on her flip-flops. "I could definitely use some cheesy grits and bacon. I heart bacon."

"I need some coffee." Kate was a good 30 minutes past due by her normal standards.

"Do they have grits in Mexico?" Wendy stood up.

"They better!" Vivian said, heading towards the hotel. "Let's go see if they do." She was determined to be done with yoga.

"Hell, no!" Lucy said. "Granola for breakfast today! Y'all have got to start living a healthier lifestyle. We aren't getting any younger. Viv is 30!"

Vivian stopped in her tracks and gave her a dirty look. She wasn't real excited about turning 30. She had loved her twenties. Well, at least most of them.

Kate and Wendy snickered as they pushed their sandy feet into flip-flops. Vivian, a September birthday, had always been the oldest in their class. Kate, Lucy and Wendy all had a few months to go before the big three-o.

"I remember a time when y'all were happy I was the oldest," Vivian said, pointing to them. "First to drive, first to be able to *legally* buy alcohol."

Wendy rubbed in her summer birthday. "Yes, but all those firsts are long gone, Viv. Now you're just the oldest."

"Yep," Kate said. "First to get gray hair, first to get wrinkles."

"Hey!" Vivian yelled, touching her face. She was a little paranoid about wrinkles.

"You look fine. Don't listen to them." Lucy reassured her. "But you need to remember to wear your sunscreen."

"Yeah, yeah, now about that breakfast." Vivian resumed her journey to the hotel. Wendy and Kate followed her.

"Granola!" Lucy shouted, fist raised in the air.

They kept walking, propelled by visions of cheesy, buttery, artery-clogging goodness.

Inside the restaurant, Vivian had the sensation of being under a spotlight. The patrons stared at her as she walked by, employees too. And again, the service was quicker than the typical Playa-time.

"What do y'all want to do with the rest of the day?" she asked after the waitress delivered their drinks. "I feel like we need to search for Ponytail."

"NO!" The other three shouted in unison and disturbed the other diners.

"That guy is trouble," Wendy said. "He may be involved with Detective Vega or he may be a killer," she pointed to Vivian with her coffee cup, "but either way, I feel like we'd be killed trying to hunt him down."

Vivian didn't really want to look for Ponytail. She knew Wendy was right.

"What about Stella?" she asked. "Should we try to look for her today?"

"She's a hard one to find," Lucy said as she squeezed lemon in her water.

Kate poured creamer in her coffee before responding. "I bet she shows up at the party tonight. She'll know you'll be there Viv, and she'll want to check on you."

Vivian groaned. She didn't like the thought of being checked on by Crazy Stella. She wanted to search her out instead.

"Let's take a walk down the beach, see if we spot her," Vivian said. "I'd feel more confident of my chances in getting out of Mexico if we found her, knew her story."

"We might never know her story," Kate said.

"If we take a walk down the beach, I'm vetoing water aerobics," Wendy said. " And I'll keep my eyes peeled for Ms. *Loco* in the *Cabeza*."

"Okay, no water aerobics." Lucy gave up that notion easier than Vivian expected. "But we're speed walking."

That's why.

"How about after the search?" Wendy asked. "I haven't had enough beach time. And that's important."

"There'll be time," Vivian said.

Only got two days left, might as well make the most of it. I'm either goin' home or goin' to the slammer.

49

The girls headed down the beach on their search for Stella, in the opposite direction from where Jon was killed. Vivian didn't want to get near that spot. In fact, she wanted to avoid it for the rest of their vacation.

Lucy walked fast, pumping her arms and leaving the others behind. She looped around the pool at the next hotel then marched in place, keeping her heart rate up, while she waited for the girls.

"Keep movin'," she said to them and resumed her pace down the beach.

Lucy went on ahead of the pack and by the time they arrived at the next hotel, she was nowhere to be seen. Vivian started to panic and her mind raced. They had broken their buddy system rule and this was the result. Had Ponytail kidnapped Lucy? Or maybe she had found Crazy Stella?

Just as she was about to start screaming Lucy's name, she walked out of the hotel shaking her hands.

"No paper towels in their restroom. What a dive."

"Lucy!" Vivian used her 'Mom' voice. "You scared me to death! Don't run off like that. I thought you had been snatched."

"Excuse me, but I had to use the restroom and if y'all could have kept up it would have been no big deal."

"Look," Wendy said. "We realize you've come from an anti-oxygen climate and feel invigorated by this shit, but we're huffin'. If you don't slow down my eggs and *frioles* are going to make another appearance."

"If you hadn't eaten that huge breakfast—"

"Maybe I'd be okay if they'd had grits!"

Vivian interrupted. "Ladies ladies. Let's chillax and stay focused." She turned to Lucy. "Lucy, please slow down. I'm not able to look for Stella walking this fast."

Kate wagged a finger at Lucy as they resumed their search. "Buddy system. No more rule breaking."

They found a happy medium between speed walking and ambling and continued the hunt. The next several beach front hotels had small pools and the guests could easily been seen as they passed. No one resembled Stella, though one woman caught Vivian's eye.

"Is she wearing a scarf? Seriously? In 80 degrees?"

"Looks like," Kate said. "Maybe she's got hickies to hide."

They looped the pools of several other hotels with no success. About a mile down the beach, bars took the place of hotels so they decided to turn around.

On the walk back, Lucy pointed out a woman lying on a towel in the sand. "That right there, is why y'all need to wear SPF 75 at all times."

Vivian glanced at her out of the corner of her sunglasses. She was horrified. The woman resembled a raisin and it was difficult to determine if she was in her twenties or fifties. Her skin looked like dry, crusty leather.

"People need to know when to say when to tanning," she said. "That's just down right ridiculous."

"She's off the pale scale," Wendy said.

The man sitting beside her stood up, revealing his banana hammock. However, no banana filled the hammock.

Kate shook her head. "That's awful."

Wendy gasped. "Horrible."

"Dear god," Vivian said.

"He's wearin' it loud and proud, though," Lucy laughed.

This got a round of laughs and the couple looked their way. Vivian waved and continued on.

The beach at their hotel was more populated when they got back so Vivian stopped to ask a few folks if they had seen Stella, describing her in detail. No one had, so the four headed up to the room to freshen up. Lucy started searching for bugs.

"Lucy, I think we've pretty much covered everything," Vivian said.

She didn't look convinced and kept at it. "You never know. They can be sneaky."

The search turned up nothing, as Vivian expected.

They left the room and Lucy put the "do not disturb" sign on the door.

"We don't need the room cleaned," she said nonchalantly.

"Lucy, I'm not sure that would deter anyone from breaking in and putting bugs in our room, but if it makes you feel better, okay," Kate said as she walked down the stairs.

Lupe Mendoza, the reporter from *Escándalos*, waited just outside the hotel lobby. She shoved a tape recorder in Vivian's face and started in. "Who was the mysterious woman you chased at the market yesterday? Where did you go after you left the ruins? When did you get back to the hotel last night?

What did you have to do with Jon Tournay's murder?"

This drew the attention of a few more reporters who had gathered at the hotel, and they rushed over.

Lucy pushed Lupe's recorder away from Vivian. "Get the hell outta our way. She didn't have anything to do with Jon's murder."

Wendy and Kate shoved other reporters aside, saying, "No comment" several times. The reporters followed them to the edge of the pool deck but no further. Vivian heard shouting, which drew the reporters attention back to the hotel. Vivian didn't turn around to see what the commotion was about.

Manuel greeted them warmly and settled them into four chairs. Of course, he got Lucy an umbrella, too.

"I no let them bother you," he said, nodding toward the reporters as he pushed the umbrella open.

"Thank you so much, Manuel. We appreciate that," Lucy said, adjusting her sunglasses. "Can we have four waters, too, please."

She then pulled out a plethora of sunscreen from her bag and passed it out to the girls. They obediently applied, helping each other out when necessary. Then they leaned their chairs back and enjoyed the sun. Well, except for Lucy, who had maneuvered her lounger to encapsulate herself in shade.

"Lucy, you just covered yourself in sunscreen!" Vivian said.

"Yeah, but I won't ever look like the California raisin lady we saw a little bit ago."

"Can we drink yet?" Wendy said, holding up her bottled water. "Something besides this?"

Kate looked up at the sky, as if she were telling time *Crockadile Dundee*-style. "It's not 5 o'clock yet."

"Oh behave, just until the party. You'll thank me later!" Lucy retorted.

Vivian leaned over to Wendy and told her they'd sneak shots when Lucy wasn't looking.

"I heard that," Lucy said.

Kate ran doomsday-esque scenarios for a while. The girls arrived back at the same decisions about suspects and where and how to look for them: Beach for now, Ponytail no-way, Stella will find them and Shorty at his party later.

After the strategy session, Vivian needed to relieve the stress and had noticed the hotel masseurs set up shop behind them on the beach. Four tables, long, flowy drapes surrounding them and a sign that said $25 USD for an hour was too inviting to pass up.

"I'm going to get a massage," Vivian said peeling herself out of her chair. "You can't beat $25 bucks and who knows, it could be my last one.

Anyone else want to go?"

"I'll go with you," Lucy said. "I learned my lesson, buddy system."

They returned a few minutes later, big grins on their faces.

"What's up?" Wendy asked, removing her sunglasses.

"We have lined up massages right now, for all four of us," Vivian said to Wendy and Kate. "Manuel is saving our spots so come on."

"I don't know…a massage right here in front of everyone?" Kate asked.

"Yes," Vivian knew Kate was worried about removing her swimsuit and added, "you don't have to get totally naked if you don't want to. Plus, they put you under the sheet."

Wendy, enthusiastically, and Kate, semi-reluctantly, followed Vivian and Lucy to meet their masseurs — three Hispanic women and one thirty-something white guy.

The man was of slim build with neatly trimmed brown hair and goatee. He delicately shook hands with Lucy.

"I'm Rodney, and this is Gloria, Maria and Isabella. Go ahead and get on a table, face down. Keep everything on." He patted the table he was standing beside and Lucy hopped up. "Once on the table, you can remove your top, or not, whatever you're comfortable with."

Everyone got half-naked, except Kate. The masseurs got to work, asking each of them if there was a particular spot they needed worked on.

"My lower back," Vivian said. "You can go to town." Since carrying the mongo-twins to full term, her back had never been the same.

Isabella rubbed something fabulous smelling in her hair. Then moved down and worked on her feet. Vivian sighed as the tension started draining away.

Lucy's masseur was chatty, telling them he had been in Playa del Carmen for a year. He was from Colorado and used to work at The Ritz Carlton in Bachelor Gulch, which he highly recommended.

"That place is fan-f-ing-fantastic," he said. "You girls should totally go there."

"Mmmm, good idea," Lucy said, enjoying feeling his hands on her back.

"Did you hear a guy was killed on the beach here the other night?" he asked.

Wendy lifted her head. "Yeah, we've definitely heard about it," she said in a tone indicating she didn't want to talk about it.

"Jon was hot. I had given him a massage," Rodney said and sighed. "His friend Pierre is cute, too. I heard they were hanging out with a local bad boy. I don't understand it."

"You mean Julio?" Lucy asked.

"Yes, honey. He and his two girlfriends come into our spa, the Tropical

Paradise Spa just down the way, on 5th. Actually, today is their usual day but they cancelled."

"I bet he's getting ready for his party tonight." Kate's words were muffled coming through the round face thingy. She sounded very relaxed already.

"Party?" Rodney asked.

"Julio's having a big blowout tonight at his *casa*," Lucy said. "He invited us."

"Oh, I want to go!" Rodney said in his best scandalous voice.

"I bet it's the more the merrier. Wanna come?" Lucy responded.

He did a little jump and clap. "I'd love to!"

Vivian glanced over to Kate's masseuse. She was giving Wendy's masseuse a "look."

Lucy saw it, too. "Is it a bad idea for us to go? Will we be in danger?"

Wendy's masseuse muttered under her breath, *"Tenga cuidado."*

Wendy translated. "She just told us to be careful."

Uh oh...

50

The girls returned to their loungers on the beach, and between the massage and the warmth of the sun, Vivian dozed off pretty quickly into a happy nappy. She had been out for a while when a shadow cast over her face. She opened her eyes reluctantly and saw Al's broad smile.

"Hey cupcake, kill anyone today?"

Vivian was speechless.

"I'm just kiddin', sugar." He winked.

He tossed a newspaper into her lap. "You gals made headlines. Have you seen the *Escándalos* today?"

"What?" She sat up and grabbed the paper. Sure enough, a picture of them in *panchos* and *sombreros* graced the front page.

The girls gathered around to get a look. Wendy translated the headline. "American Murder Suspect Chases Woman down La Quinta Avenida."

"At least we aren't as recognizable in our get-ups," Lucy pointed out.

"And my tutti-frutti hat," Kate added.

"Yes, and your tutti-frutti hat," Lucy concurred.

"You looked fruitylicious in your hat, Kate," Vivian told her.

"You gals look like you were attacked by the fleas from a Mexican flea market," Al commented.

"Actually, we did this to ourselves in a musical moment," Kate admitted and then added, "with Pierre's help."

Al slowly shook his head. The corners of his mouth turned up and his face was a little red. He was clearly trying not to bust out laughing.

Vivian cleared her throat to get their attention. "Wendy, can you read the rest of the article?"

"Okay, but the translation might be a little sketchy."

She grabbed the paper. "The police. La Quinta Avenida yesterday. Information from shop owners. Testimonies. Group of women and a man in merchandise of tourists and to take – that's not the right translation, carrying musical instruments. *Persiguió* – I don't know that word, pursued, maybe,

211

another woman down the street. Something about spectators.

"We might have knocked a few of them out of the way in our chase," Vivian said.

"Yeah, that must be it. Okay, one of the women is a participant, no suspect, in assassination of Jon Tournay. A Canadian celebrity. Police haven't released her name."

"Assassination. Oh god," Kate said.

"Store owner, Pedro Montoya, said the women were in his shop, playing with the merchandise when they commenced the persecution."

"We didn't persecute anybody yesterday," Lucy said.

"It's the translation. I think it really means chase. Only high school Spanish, okay? Cut me some slack. It goes on to say they paid for the merchandise but only at insistence of the police. It finishes saying no one involved in the chase would comment."

Vivian was speechless.

Lucy wasn't. "The nerve of that reporter! She makes us sound like horrible people."

"We should go talk to her right now and set her straight. That bitch!" Kate was evidently pissed off, too.

"Calm down, ladies, you don't want to go talk to Lupe." Al bit the tip of his cigar and spit it out. "You won't be able to set her straight. You keep refusing to talk to her so she's getting back at you. She wants you to approach her and make a scene. That would make more news and be another great headline."

"I just can't believe how she slanted this article to make it sound like we're the bad guys!" Kate said. "And she didn't even mention my hat."

"Al is right, we don't need to talk to Lupe, at all, ever." Vivian snatched the paper and threw it under her chair. "She will only make us, mainly me, sound like murderers or 'assassins' as she put it. So far we've only been in the local Playa paper. I can't have news of this getting back home and to Rick. Let's just lay low. If we make a scene, you can bet Geraldo or somebody will be down here in a flash trying to interview me."

Lucy, Wendy and Kate nodded in consent.

"I have more news." Al pointed at Vivian with his unlit stogie. "I saw that Ponytail fella here at the hotel yesterday. I think he was here looking for you."

"That S.O.B. won't leave us alone." She was pissed off Ponytail snooped around their hotel. *Maybe he's the bug planter?*

"I just wanted you to know he was at the hotel." Al got out his butane lighter. "I'm serious when I say you need to steer clear of that guy. He's no good."

"We saw him in Cozumel last night." Kate sat back down on her lounger.

"He saw us take the ferry over so I guess he followed us."

"You girls need to stay away from him. I'm outta here. You got my number if you need me."

"Where's Adrienne?" Lucy asked.

"She went shopping, grabbing some gifts for the cousins back home. We have dozens of them, you know."

"Dozens of cousins. That's funny," Vivian joked, even though she was still pissed about Ponytail being there yesterday.

"You ladies have a nice afternoon. Don't kill anything but brain cells." Al lit his cigar as he walked off and blew out a big puff of smoke.

"Let's think about this for a sec," Kate said. "Al is trying to say Ponytail was here looking for you, or us, yesterday. But just three days ago, the night Jon died, he was sitting at the poolside bar watching us eat dinner with Al and Adrienne."

"We hadn't done anything more incriminating than kill brain cells at that point," Wendy noted. "Not that we've done anything incriminating since," she finished with.

"So was Ponytail here for us, or for Al? And why would Al intentionally try to place the blame on us?" Kate asked.

"We need to search our room again for bugs," Lucy said, getting back under her umbrella.

Good point all around. Son. Of. A. Bitch.

Vivian closed her eyes, hoping to block out the current conversation and resume her nap since there was nothing they could do about Ponytail, the paparazzi, or anything else for the time being. She figured she might as well try to lower her blood pressure, catch some rays and some zzz's.

51

V ivian awoke from her nap on the beach to the sound of some definite selling.

"Two for one. Two for one," a guy said. "I sell you good time."

Holy crap, what's this guy sellin'? she thought.

Her eyes adjusted to the sunlight and she saw a guy in a ratty, straw cowboy hat talking to Kate.

"You have fun." He waved his arms toward the ocean.

"What exactly is he selling?" she asked groggily.

"He wants us to go parasailing," Kate responded.

Not what she was expecting.

"Oh, that sounds like fun," Wendy said and sat up in her lounger.

"I don't know," Lucy said reluctantly. "What sort of safety standards do they impose in Mexico?"

"How much?" Vivian asked, ignoring Lucy.

"Seventy-five dollars each," he responded.

"What? That's crazy!" she exclaimed. *"Loco!"*

"I'll give you $75 for all of us," Wendy offered.

He countered with a hundred.

"How long?" Vivian asked.

"Forty minutes," he said. "Twenty minutes each two. Plus boat ride."

"Ok, sold. $100," Wendy agreed. "But I need to run up and grab some cash."

The man looked pleased and signaled a guy out in a boat.

"I'll go get the fundage," Vivian offered and hauled herself from her chair and hoofed it up to the room. She used the keycard and checked out the room for any sign of disturbance or bugs. Lucy would be pleased to hear the results.

She got into her secret stash, counted out $120, including a bit more for tip, and headed back to the beach.

The deal-maker, who said his name was Paco, greeted her at the water's edge, took the $100 then waded with her out to the boat. Lucy, Kate and Wendy had already loaded up, strapped on life vests and were sitting in the back. Paco helped her up the little ladder, gave a wave and said *"Hasta la vista."*

"Guess he's strictly the beachcomber sucker-seeker," Lucy said and laughed.

A stick of a man handed Vivian a life vest and introduced himself as Raul, then introduced Santiago, the captain.

Vivian got situated and Santiago gunned the boat, taking them out to deeper water.

The captain stopped the boat and waited for Raul to give Kate and Wendy instructions then strapped them into their harnesses and put them into place on the back of the boat. They looked nervous sitting on their butts, holding onto their harness for dear life.

Santiago gunned it and Kate and Wendy shrieked as they flew off the back, a rainbow colored parachute pulled them up, up, up and away. After about 40 feet of line had zoomed out, Wendy waved but Kate still looked petrified.

Raul watched the giant reel pump out the line attached to Kate and Wendy. Vivian saw a little blue flag go out. Then a red one.

"Uh, Raul. I saw a red flag. *Rojo.* Is that bad?" Vivian said.

"Oh no. Is okay. Is okay. Wait for yellow."

"If you say so," Vivian said, still hesitant. *Red usually means stop, doesn't it?*

Kate and Wendy looked like little ants in the air at this point. *Have I paid $100 to see them face their doom?* she wondered.

The reel produced a yellow flag and Raul hit a button. The line quit unwinding and Vivian breathed a sigh of relief. She and Lucy waved at the girls, who waved back.

Wendy and Kate floated for a while as they cruised along the coast. Eventually, Santiago signaled to Raul and he hit another button which began to reel Kate and Wendy back in. He periodically watched them and checked the line as it rewound.

When they got to the blue flag, Santiago killed the engine. They watched Kate and Wendy float down, slowly but surely, until they were right above the water.

"Should they go for a little swim?" Santiago asked Lucy and Vivian.

"Oh yeah, definitely!" Vivian said.

They yelled as he dipped them into the water. Santiago started the engine back up, and the boat moved forward slowly. Wendy and Kate were totally barraged with water and they worked to keep themselves in the trapeze-type contraptions. He eventually got them back into the air and he and Raul laughed at the accomplishment.

Lucy got up and crossed the boat to Santiago. "Do *not* do that to us or no tip."

"Si, señora."

He brought Wendy and Kate in successfully.

"How was it?" Vivian asked as they got out of their harnesses.

"I wasn't expecting the little dip in the water. It was awesome though," Wendy answered. "The water is so clear, the beach so beautiful. You can see forever."

"Kate, what did you think?" Lucy asked. "You looked scared to death."

"I was a little nervous, I'll admit. But once we got up there I was able to enjoy the view. I didn't mind being dipped in the water too much. It was refreshing."

It was Vivian and Lucy's turn. Lucy repeated her warning, giving Santiago her I'll-kick-your-butt-all-over-Mexico look. He gave them the thumbs up and away they went.

Vivian screamed as they were swept up into the air off the back of the boat. Lucy was silenced by fear. As they floated higher and higher, Vivian loved the quietness and feeling of flying. She looked at Lucy, who had her eyes closed.

"Lucy, open your eyes."

"That's okay. I'll pass!"

"You've got to see this, it's beautiful. Come on!"

She reluctantly opened one eye, then the other. "Wow. It's pretty up here."

"I know! Look, there's the Purple Peacock." Vivian motioned to the club. "And there's our hotel. Holy crap! Look at all the paparazzi down there! They're all over our hotel. And from here you can see news vans on 5th. *No bueno*!"

"They're multiplying like rabbits. It's going to make it harder to avoid them."

Santiago took them down the beach a ways, past the ferry, nightclub area and other hotels.

"This is so cool," Lucy said. "I'm glad I opened my eyes."

Santiago turned the boat around, back in the direction they came, and Raul started reeling them in. They were back in the area of the ferry dock, close to their hotel. Vivian saw a bright red dress that immediately caught her eye.

"Lucy, look at our hotel, outside the bar by the pool. See that woman in a red dress and with the long hair? Is that Stella?"

"I can't tell it's so far, and I'm 20-20. Do you think it is her? Why would she be at our hotel?"

"I can't be positive it's her from here. Maybe she's looking for us."

Vivian tried to signal the boat to pull them in faster, but Santiago and Raul couldn't tell what she was doing. Instead, they dipped them.

"Dammit!" Lucy sputtered, wiping the water out of her eyes. "No tip for them!"

"Wendy and Kate probably offered them double," Vivian said as they got closer to the boat. Santiago and Raul both sported giant grins as they landed.

Raul shrugged and pointed to Wendy. "Big money."

"I knew it!" Vivian yelled.

Wendy slipped Santiago a twenty and gave him a wink. *"Gracias, musto gusto."*

Lucy watched this exchange as she got out of her harness and gave Wendy the stink eye.

Wendy blew her a kiss and said, "Payback's a bitch!"

Vivian was in a hurry to get back to the hotel to see if the woman in the red dress was, in fact, Stella.

"Take us in, Santiago," Vivian requested. *"Andale!"*

She turned to Wendy and Kate and filled them in on what she saw.

"What is Stella doing at our hotel?" Kate asked. "Who was she talking to, did you see?"

"I didn't see her talking with anyone, and honestly, we were too far away. It might not have been her."

Santiago got them back to the beach quickly. They hopped off the boat and made their way through the surf straight to the poolside bar. There was no one in a red dress that remotely looked like Stella, either from up in the air or two feet away.

Vivian leaned in close and asked the bartender if he had seen anyone fitting Stella's description. She gave him every detail, tattoo included. He said he did see that lady, but she left. He pointed south.

Discouraged and disgruntled, they started back to the beach.

"Excuse me, Mrs. Taylor. I need to see you." Vivian heard from behind her and turned around.

Detective Vega.

52

S hit. What does he want? Vivian thought.
"Mrs. Taylor, I need a word," Detective Vega spoke up again as he approached her at the hotel pool.

"You need a word with me? I need a word with you!" she retorted. "We might have just seen Stella here at the hotel. I can't be certain because I was parasailing, but it looked like her."

He ignored her ranting. "We need a DNA sample from you." He looked at the tech guy with him and motioned for him to go ahead.

The tech pulled out a long cotton swab and came toward her.

The paparazzi caught wind of what was happening. Armed with pocket recorders, notebooks and cameras, they started to swarm. One look from Detective Vega stopped them before they got too close.

Just what I need, she thought, but said to him instead, "Those cameras could zoom in on the chicken pox scar on my cheek from a mile away. Not sure stopping them ten feet away is going to help anything."

"Hold the fuck on!" Wendy said, ignoring the distant crowd and snap of pictures. She stepped between Vivian and the tech guy. "Don't you need a warrant for something like that?"

Detective Vega's gaze could have cut Wendy in two. "Welcome to Mexico."

Vivian scooted Wendy to the side. "It's fine. I've got nothing to hide. We danced and we kissed, but I sure as hell didn't kill him. Go ahead," she told him. "You need to swab inside my mouth, right?"

"Viv, they could try to frame you," Wendy said. "I don't think you should do this until you speak with an attorney."

Yeah, my jackass husband or Slinky Sal. Neither would be much help in Mexico.

Vivian opened wide and Enrique, the tech guy, swabbed her mouth. It only took a second. He stuck the swab into a vial and put a stopper in it.

Satisfied, Vega reminded them, "Don't venture too far from Playa," and stalked off.

"Damn! I really do not like that man," Vivian said, turning away from the crowd of journalists and nosy tourists. "He must have found something to compare my DNA to, right?"

"They probably just needed to sort out what they found," Kate said. "Match things up."

Her stomach did a little flip. "Can I have a drink now?" She didn't want to think about possibly being framed by Detective Vega.

"Okay, but just one," Lucy said. "And only because you had to give a DNA sample." She wagged a warning finger at Wendy and Kate. "None for y'all though." She linked arms with Vivian as they walked back toward their lounge chairs.

"I'm surprised you agreed to the DNA test so easily." Kate said as she ran up on the other side of Vivian and linked arms.

"I'm not sure I had a choice in the matter, actually."

"You three look like The Monkees," Wendy teased from behind them.

Vivian started singing "The Monkees" theme song, swinging her right foot out and then her left.

Kate and Lucy chimed in and followed her lead on the feet.

"It's official. Y'all are dorks," Wendy said and laughed. "I'm pretending not to know you."

The three musically maneuvered themselves to the loungers Manuel had saved for them from earlier, laughing and singing the whole way. Wendy sat down and did as she said, pretending not to know them.

"You know, for band dorks, we sing a lot," Lucy announced as she plopped down.

"Wow, I'm impressed you call that singing." Vivian leaned forward, reaching behind her lounger, trying to adjust the doohickey and let herself lie completely flat. "I've almost got it," she panted, searching, searching for the thing. Dang! I should have adjusted before I sat down.

"You look like a pretzel," Lucy said, shaking her head. "Let me help you."

"Guess I don't have monkey arms."

Before Lucy could help, Manuel appeared and helped her.

"Thank you!" Vivian called after him.

"Y'all should reapply," Lucy said as she got back under her umbrella. "We're close to the equator here."

"That would mess up my sunbathing, and I can't have that," Vivian said. "Plus, I put some on earlier. And, I have darker pigmentation than you."

"Yeah, yeah. But don't say I didn't warn you."

219

"Pass the sunscreen, please," Kate said.

"I'll take the 15," Wendy said. "I sunbathe semi-responsibly. My olive skin can take it."

"Wrinkles," Kate said in a sing-song voice.

Wendy ignored her.

Vivian reached down under her seat, dug around in the sand and found her sunglasses. "That's what these are for." She gave them a good shake and slid them onto her face. A few granules dug in. Back home, I cherish a peaceful moment like this. As if I'd let a little sand bother me now.

Next thing she knew she was in the middle of an earthquake dream. Her body shook but not the ground, she realized.

"Up! Up! Up!"

Do they have earthquakes in Playa? she thought.

"Viv, you are sunburned," Wendy said. "Your pale scale has shot up dramatically. Unfortunately, I'm afraid it will probably peel off in about five days."

Groggy, Vivian pulled off her sunglasses. "Huh?"

"I'm not going in public with her like that," she heard someone say.

"What? Like what? What happened?" she demanded, still half asleep.

Lucy sat down on the end of her lounger. "Viv, you should've reapplied."

"I fell asleep. How bad is it?" She looked at the three of them. They stared back at her, trying not to laugh.

"Oh my god, I must look ridiculous."

"The raccoon eyes are not that bad," Kate responded, covering her smile.

"Oh crap. Let's get up to our room so I can assess the damage."

They gathered their stuff and traipsed up to the room. Vivian went directly to the bathroom and closed the door.

"Holy crap," she said, staring at the crimson glow reflecting off the mirror.

"Viv, your face is not so bad," Kate comforted through the door. "You can probably cover it up with make-up."

"Make-up, my ass," Wendy commented. "It would take the entire town of Cover Girl to blend her eyes in with her face."

"I can hear you!" Vivian yelled. What am I going to do? she thought desperately. She looked at herself and all she could see was red (95 percent) and a bit of white (eyeballs included). Apparently, thinking she had a good base tan was a misconception.

Lucy stood outside the door. "Viv, there's not a lot you can do. You've damaged your skin. You need to just let it breathe. It'll heal faster."

"But we've got this party tonight," Vivian called. "I can't go like this."

"It'll be dark. No one will notice," Kate tried to reassure her.

You'd have to be blind not to.

"You need aloe lotion," Wendy said. "Use mine, it's on the counter."

"Viv, lots of tourists come down here and get raccoon eyes. No worries," Lucy said, then continued her thought, "I'm going to call Pierre's room and make sure he's getting ready to go with us."

"Okay." Vivian glanced at herself in the mirror again. It wasn't often she wished for the wet-bar mirrors from home with their two-tone, tacky squiggles, but right now they'd offer a distraction.

She took a cool shower with super light water pressure and slathered on the aloe. She was hot, so she wrapped herself loosely in a towel and lay down on the bed while the other girls got cleaned up. After a second application of aloe, she dressed delicately, being wary of the redness all over, especially between her boobs and near her armpits. Those areas were an even more unnatural shade of red. Her softest dress barely touched the tip of her nose as it slipped over her head. "Oooouch!"

Not a good sign.

She returned to the bathroom and fixed her hair and put on make-up as best she could. "Well?" she asked the girls.

"You did better than I coulda done with those eyes," Wendy said, nodding approval.

"That has got to hurt," Kate said.

"I have to admit, you will stand out," Lucy said. "No way around it."

Great.

Vivian looked at herself one last time in the mirror, resigned. "Let's go kick some ass!"

53

Wendy and Kate looked cute in their sundresses and sandals and Lucy in her sundress and FMPs. Vivian felt self-conscience in her redness.

Pierre waited for them in the lobby. He hugged everyone but stopped short when he got to Vivian. "Forget to reapply?"

"I had myself a little *siesta*."

"I told her to reapply," Lucy chided.

Vivian growled, which was not something she usually did unless she was reading a book to her kids, but this called for it. She thought she sounded a little like her dog, Cooper.

Pierre put his hands up. "Sunburned or not, you still look great."

On their way out, they asked the guy at the front desk how to find Julio's house. He gave them directions on a sticky note.

"Apparently everyone does know where Shorty lives." Wendy slid her sunglasses on.

Pierre helped them muscle through the paparazzi and the girls surrounded Vivian, helping to protect her sunburn and keep the vultures from getting to her. None of them responded to the questions thrown at them.

They made it to the car without incident and Vivian got in the passenger seat, cringing at the thought of fastening her seatbelt. Pierre took the back seat with Wendy and Kate, humpin' it again.

Wendy saw the seatbelt hesitation and said, "Buckle up for safety, Viv!"

No sympathy.

She grabbed it and gently pulled it across her lap.

Designated Driver, Lucy, barreled toward the exit of the parking lot, eager to run over any paparazzi who got in the way. Several blocked the exit, but then jumped aside at the last moment. "Jackasses," she muttered under her breath.

Lucy had the directions stuck to the console above the useless air conditioning vent. Vivian concentrated on holding the lap belt up off her thighs. Kate pointed out what she considered architectural marvels, which Vivian thought looked like they were about to fall down. Wendy shook her head to the beat of music that only she could hear. Pierre looked like he was trying to minimize the impact from the bumps in the road.

They stopped at a light and some kids ran up to their car selling gum. Lucy rolled down her window and bought some to be nice. "Gotta support the local economy," she said.

I would have bought some if I could move, Vivian thought. She saw one turn and whisper to the other. Then they both turned and looked at her, laughing. *Never mind, I'm not that sorry anymore.*

Lucy pulled through the intersection and Wendy informed her, "I think we're being followed again by that Lupe woman. You going to try and lose her?"

"I can't drive like Dale Earnhardt back there." She hooked a thumb toward Kate.

Pierre reached forward and touched Lucy's arm. "If I have to, I'll take care of her once we get to the party."

I think he likes Lucy just a little. Vivian thought and smiled to herself.

They wound their way around Playa and came to a sandy road leading to a monstrosity of a house, situated on a long stretch of beach. There were no neighbors within sight. Julio must like his privacy.

The narrow road was already lined with cars half a mile from the house. Lucy mercifully dropped Vivian, Wendy and Kate off at the circular driveway in front, as Vivian's long distance walking abilities were questionable considering her skin tone. Pierre volunteered to stay with her.

Kate just stood there staring in awe at the house. By the look on her face, Vivian thought she might drool.

"Damn, he must be doin' pretty well selling tequila," Wendy said.

"I'd say so," Kate stammered. "Do you know how much that cost?" She pointed to the entrance. "That's what you call a structural glass wall. See those plates of glass behind the window? Those are glass columns. Nice."

She was right, it kicked ass. The all-glass entrance was two stories high and flanked by two walls clad in white marble, not the tiled crap they had at home. Just above the door hung a slender glass canopy suspended by thin, stainless steel rods. The rest of the house was white stucco, not crusty but troweled to a smooth finish.

"That kinda reminds me of the white fondant on my wedding cake," Vivian said and laughed. "Makes me want to lick the walls."

On both sides of the entrance, two pair of tropical wood trellises nestled into the garden. Cast concrete columns that Kate described as "very Japanese modern" supported the trellises and provided a spot to tie back the white drapes. A loveseat under each pod completed the resort-style cabanas.

They found a nice bench near the front door made of matching marble. Vivian's butt melted into it like butter.

"Ahhh…nice and cool," Vivian said. "My butt is happy. The rest of me, not so much."

A steady 'thump thump thump' came from the house, and Vivian saw some skinny, tan (not sunburned), scantily clad girls through the window behind them.

Great, Vivian thought. *Hoochie mommas.*

Vivian heard giggling and made out Lucy and Pierre coming down the road. She watched Lucy push off Pierre in a playful manner.

"Looks like they enjoyed the walk," Kate said, watching them too.

Lucy was all smiles as she walked up the grandiose entrance. "Wow! This is some house."

Vivian pointed to Kate. "She's in architecture loooooove."

"It's true," Kate said. "I admit, I'm fantasizing."

Pierre cocked an eyebrow at her.

"All fantasies include my husband, not Shorty!"

"Where's Lupe?" Wendy asked, changing the subject.

"She turned down the sandy road with us and parked way back," Lucy said.

"We had to park all the way back there, too and I gave her my best intimidating glare as we walked past her car," Pierre said.

"So she was just sitting in her car?" Vivian asked.

"Yep, and on the phone."

"Calling for reinforcements, no doubt," Kate said.

"Great," Wendy said and turned toward the door. "Shall we?"

"How's my make-up?" Vivian asked, feeling her cherry red face turn even cherrier at the question.

"I think it may have melted off," Kate said reluctantly.

"No, it didn't," Lucy responded. "You look fine. Let's go in."

Two guys walked up to the porch while they were discussing Vivian's make-up and walked in the door.

"Looks like this is a house-is-a-rockin'-don't-bother-knockin' kinda party." Vivian stood up and clapped. "Let's get to it."

Pierre reached for the door handle and pushed it open.

"Ladies first."

54

According to Kate, Shorty had left no architectural detail unturned. The solid aluminum door handle floated out from the glass and was cast in the shape of a long piece of driftwood, a nod to nature in the slick modern façade, she pointed out. The interior was a complete 180 from the cheesiness of his boat.

Crisp white abstract furniture hovered above a sand-colored terrazzo floor dotted with chips of sea green marble. Above their heads, the white coved ceiling softly changed to a pale blue as it stretched out to the ocean into a wide cantilevered canopy. The transition to the exterior was seamless as the 15-foot sliding folding doors tucked away into a pocketed stack on one side.

"This place is fancccccyyy." Vivian was shocked by, first, the sheer number of people who were there, and second, the house itself. She figured Shorty would have a place straight out of gaudy land. Not so. This place was sleek and modern and totally fabulous.

Kate stopped and stared at what she said appeared to be a Chihuly original suspended from the 30 foot foyer. It was triple-tiered and a tangle of greens and blues like a knotted-up giant jellyfish.

"Holy crap. I could pay off all my student loans for what that cost," she said.

They made their way through the living room dotted with delicate glass tables on spindly chrome legs. Lucy couldn't resist and stopped at the sofa.

"Ooohhh la la...B&B Italia!" She sank gracefully onto a long white sofa.

"I think I will join ya, Lucy." Kate sat down gently and ran her fingers along the curved arm of the sofa.

"You ladies look right at home." Pierre grinned, watching their delight.

Glass screens etched with a kelp pattern divided the room into several seating areas. The panels were transparent and spotless and had changing LED lighting at the top and bottom, creating a sort of tasteful-disco atmosphere.

"Thank god for those lights," Vivian said and laughed. "I'd totally be one of those shmucks who runs right into 'em because they're so clean."

"What about the pattern?" Wendy asked.

"Oh, that wouldn't stop me," Vivian admitted. "I've run into more obvious."

Wendy turned to Lucy and Kate, who were still caressing the couch. "No drooling on the furniture," she said and offered Lucy, then Kate, a helping hand out of their lounging positions. She about-faced to the kitchen-turned-bar. "It's time to get a drink!"

The kitchen was space age with sleek, seamless appliances and large integral sinks with the smooth white countertop. Standing at the island was a young Hispanic knockout of a girl, playing bartender.

"Can I get you something?" she asked.

She was surrounded by all sorts of liquor, but lots and lots of Tiempo Loco tequila.

They conferred and Wendy listed off what everyone wanted. "Cosmo for Kate, piña colada for Lucy, margarita for me and a beer for Viv, *por favor*."

"Where's Pierre?" Lucy asked.

"Dunno," Kate said. "Guess he wandered off. I'm sure he can fend for himself."

The bartender mixed up the cocktails and placed them on the counter.

"*Gracias*," Vivian said, grabbing the beer. She squeezed in a lime, then threw it back for medicinal purposes.

Yummmmmmmmy! She thought as the cool liquid went down her throat.

"That is quite possibly the best beer I've had all year."

Lucy had a bottle of water in one hand and her piña colada in the other. Kate took a sip of cosmo and gave a nod of approval.

Vivian looked around for Shorty or one of his ladies, not seeing any of them.

"Check out Mr. Macheezmo over there," Kate said, pointing with her drink to a short, greasy-haired guy with his shirt unbuttoned almost to his belly button. He had zero chest hair. None. Smooth as a baby's butt.

"He has *got* to be related to Shorty," Lucy said, referring to his lack of height.

"That guy is pretty hot." Vivian nodded toward a tall, slim-built guy wearing a white loose-fitting button down shirt and dark pants. He was also wearing his sunglasses. She could tell he was one of those guys who would never take off his sunglasses, no matter how dark it got. His clothes screamed "I'm sexy and I know it."

"Maybe he's blind," Kate joked.

"This crowd definitely feels like the who's who of Mexico," Wendy said.

Trendy haircuts, pinky rings, slinky dresses, designer duds, overpowering cologne, etc.

Vivian tilted her beer back and finished it. Wendy went to grab her another. Upon her return, she said, "I just saw Shorty outside. Let's go say 'howdy.'"

They followed Wendy back to the living room and through the sliding door that opened to the backyard. An infinity-edge pool blended into the ocean horizon and was fed by a waterfall from under a long, low stone bench. The backyard was lush, covered in tropical plants, some with leaves the size of small umbrellas. Just off to the side of the pool, was a large square fire pit surrounded with plush white patio furniture and more plants past that, forming the edge of the garden. A solid wood gate led down to the beach from the rear corner of the garden.

"Heyzoos Kristo," Vivian said. "I feel like I'm on some sort of outdoor living show. And shit, the people in the pool all look like they stepped out of a magazine, and I'm not talkin' *Good Housekeeping*."

Several girls were in the hot tub and twice as many guys hovered around. They had the classic signs of men who were considering making a move but hadn't worked up the courage yet.

"Are we at the Playboy mansion?" Kate giggled.

"Well, he did have the sheets," Wendy said and laughed. "And the bunny."

They laughed and wandered through girls in bikinis and guys in Speedos, a few with bananas, to reach Shorty, who was talking with two other guys on the far side of the pool.

"Howdy," Vivian called as they walked up.

"*Hola.* Glad you here," he said in his best Spanglish. "You need drink?" He snapped at a waitress walking by.

"No, no, we're good, thank you."

He gave Vivian a head-to-toe look. "You have *mucho* sun."

"Yeah, we had a bit of a disagreement today. I lost."

"Aloe vera. You need." He started to flag down another waitress.

"Not necessary. I'm all stocked up. Thank you, though."

She stuck her hand out and shook with one of the two guys standing next to him. "Hi, I'm the sunburn victim, Vivian Taylor."

"*Es* Victor *y* Joel," Shorty said, but looked like he would rather have not introduced them.

Vivian turned to Joel. "So how do you know Julio?"

Shorty cleared his throat. "They work *para mi.*"

Doing what? Vivian wondered.

"You must be sellin' the hell outta his tequila," Lucy said. "This place is freakin' incredible!"

Victor and Joel didn't respond. It was Joel's hand she shook and he looked down right awkward.

Vivian didn't think they were going to get any more info out of Shorty on what Victor and Joel did for him. She said, "Thanks again for the invite, Julio. As Lucy said, rockin' house!"

"Thanks, *es* new. Maybe nine months."

"It is spectacular, thanks again for inviting us. I guess we're gonna go mosey around. Hang out with all the pretty people."

"Mosey. I like," Shorty said with a head nod, then stretched his arm out invitingly, "*Mi casa es su casa.*"

"Thanks," she said.

They all waved, then walked around the pool terrace and fire pit. The lush vegetation brushed against their arms and shoulders as they settled into a private cabana, draped in bougainvillea. They sat in a u-shaped sectional under a white tent with white drapes whipping around in the breeze. The ocean was only yards behind them, beyond Shorty's own tropical paradise.

Vivian heard rustling in the bushes and saw the flash of a bulb. Paparazzi town had sprung up just outside Shorty's dense natural barrier. "Crap, Lupe's troops are here," she said. It looked like most of the press from their hotel had relocated to this strip of beach.

She started to call out to Shorty, but he had evidently already seen them. He said something to Victor and Joel, who sprang into action. They rushed down to the beach, yelling in Spanish at the paparazzi. The reporters and photographers scurried off, like crabs on the sand.

Vivian was getting a clearer picture now of what Victor and Joel do. Shorty said "jump" and they said "how high."

"Whoa! Remind me not to piss off Shorty!" Lucy exclaimed.

Vivian was horrified and looked at Shorty to see if he had heard her.

Shorty just gave them a wink and walked away.

Vivian gave him a half-hearted smile. *That could have ended badly.*

55

The girls sat on couches in the private cabana. Wendy leaned close to the girls and said in a hushed tone, "I realize we don't really take Shorty for killin' Jon, but he's into something. Maybe we should take a little looky-loo around. See what we can find."

"Looky-loo?" Vivian looked at her dumbfounded. "I'm sorry, but did you just say 'looky-loo'? Because I'm not sure I can hang out with anyone who uses the term 'looky-loo.'"

Wendy laughed. "Yes, I did say looky-loo, but only because you said mosey. Who uses mosey?"

"I was trying to be Texan-y."

"Well I am Texan-y," she said, then continued in a drawl as thick as molasses, "and I'm gonna mosey myself around and take a looky-loo. Y'all should join me."

"Yes'm," Vivian said and turned up her beer, sucking it down for its pain-killing qualities.

The girls moseyed through Shorty's house and the growing crowd and made their way to the back corner where a staircase twisted through a couple of suspended landings 20 feet up to the second floor. The stairs were practically a work of art, constructed of thick planks of wood treads cut into wedges and placed at odd angles to each other. Kate was mesmerized and in love.

Vivian, however, was about to hurl at the thought of climbing those stairs with her sundress rustling over her sunburned thighs. She went back into the kitchen and grabbed another beer before moving forward.

"Maybe there's an elevator?" Vivian said upon returning to the girls.

"We're here already," Kate said. "Let's just go on up."

Vivian looked up at the stairs and had a physical reaction, a double whammy of chills and a stomach flip. Her dress, even though it was soft, wasn't going to feel good on her legs. She took the first few steps, gripping the handrail with one hand and her dress and beer with the other, trying to pull it away from her legs.

"It's not so bad, huh, Viv?" Kate tried to encourage her.

"It hurts like a mo-fo."

Lucy darted past, smacking her butt.

"That was not motivating."

"Come on, Viv. You can do it," she called, almost from the top of the stairs.

Vivian pushed herself more quickly to the top, released her dress and took a big swig.

"I hope you have learned a lesson to always reapply your sunscreen." Lucy wagged a finger at her.

"Yeah, yeah," Vivian grumbled.

At the landing they found themselves at every guy's man-cave wet dream — pool table, giant flat screen, overstuffed yet stylish sofas, modern nudes framed in glass panels and, of course, a solid white, backlit marble bar. There was nobody up there, as all the action was downstairs and outside, making Vivian think maybe all those people knew something she didn't.

"Okay, which way?" Kate asked, doing a quick search of the bar.

"I vote left," Lucy said. "Most people, as righties, go right. Let's go left."

"Let's divide and conquer," Wendy suggested. "Viv, you and Kate go left. Lucy and I will go right. Meet back here in five."

Kate and Vivian walked through a couple of guest rooms, each with private bathrooms that could pass for luxury suites in a five-star resort. They looked through night stands and dressers but found nothing unusual. Nothing in the closets, no secret passages. In no time, they were back in the man-cave. Vivian tossed balls around on the billiards table while they waited for Lucy and Wendy to return.

They rounded the corner. "Nothing fun over there. Just a few rooms and a huge bathroom with a kick-ass four-head shower," Lucy said.

"Same here pretty much, but check that out," Vivian said, pointing toward the windows.

Wendy walked over and pulled back a royal blue velvet curtain in the back of the game room. It revealed a spiral stair with a thin bronze handrail and thick wood treads cordoned off by a braided gold rope.

Never one to respect boundaries, Vivian immediately felt the need to go up those stairs. They all looked at each other and smiled, knowing they're going.

Kate reached out to move the rope but Wendy stopped her. "Let's not touch it. Let's go under - just in case."

Kate looked nervous. "In case of what? It sets off an alarm?"

"You never know. This house looks pretty high-tech," Wendy said.

They slipped under the rope, some more gracefully than others (Vivian blamed the sunburn), and reached the top of the stairs, where they were confronted with two separate, ornate doors decorated with a Mayan-esque symbols. One had a serpent handle. The other a lizard.

"Oh my god," Lucy said. "I'm a nervous wreck!"

"It's gonna be fine," Vivian said. "We're just taking a look around the place if anyone asks. Kate's an architect and she's intrigued. Plus, Shorty did say his *casa* was our *casa*."

"Right. Okay."

Vivian reached for the door with a serpent carved around the iron knob. Click. It wasn't locked so she pushed it open.

She was surprised by what she found — a traditional dark wood study complete with a huge claw-footed desk, built-in shelving stuffed with antique books, a computer and a long, built-in file cabinet secured with decorative brass locks.

Wendy sank herself into the desk chair. "Damn, I'm gonna have to get me one of these. This is the Rolls Royce of office chairs," she said, swiveling around.

Then she started opening drawers, going through them carefully, trying to make sure everything was put back in its place.

"What are you looking for?" Kate asked.

"Beats me, but this is what they do in the books I read."

Vivian started pulling out books from the bookcase, waiting for a wall to open up and spin her around or something.

Kate tried to open the file cabinet. "Locked. Damn."

Lucy went around the room gently lifting the pictures a little to see what was behind them. No hidden safes in here.

"Hey, look, *The Joy of Sex*!" Vivian held up the book and laughed, then held up another, "Oh, and a Kama Sutra book! No wonder The Ladies like him. He studies."

"Let me see one of those." Kate grabbed the Kama book and started flipping through.

Vivian glanced over her shoulder. "Never done that before," she said, pointing at a page and giggling.

"I don't even think my body would bend that way!" Kate answered, closing the book and putting it back on the shelf.

Wendy pulled an envelope out of a drawer and opened it. "Y'all need to see this."

She was staring at a picture of Shorty with The Ladies in front of a fountain.

"Okay?" Kate said, bewildered. "He takes pictures in front of fountains? I don't get it, what's the big deal?"

"I know why it's a big deal," Vivian said. "That, my friends, is Buckingham Fountain."

"In England?" Kate asked.

Wendy and Vivian looked at each other.

"Chicago."

56

How do you know that's in Chicago?" Kate looked at the picture Wendy found in Shorty's desk.

"Vivian and I went there when we were in college, remember?" Wendy tapped the photo. "Jerry Springer."

"I don't remember that. Y'all were on Jerry Springer?" Kate asked.

"Well, yes and no. We were in the audience but Viv got a TV close up."

"Oh, yeah," Lucy said. "The show about Internet hookers right?"

"That's the one. My hair was maroon." Vivian looked down at the picture again, now resting on top of the desk. "I don't know why I did that."

"We all have hair regrets," Lucy said with a sigh.

"Remember that guy in the audience who asked the nasty hooker lady that if the money was as good a she claimed, why didn't she go see a doctor about all the sores on her legs?"

"Gross!" Lucy and Kate yelled at the same time.

"I thought it was a good question," Vivian shrugged. "Remember how the end of Jerry's nose would move when he talked?"

"You don't get to see that on TV," Wendy said, and turned her attention back to the photo. "Anyway, this is definitely Chicago. Viv and I have a picture in front of this same fountain." She paused, then asked, "So what does this mean? Is Al in cahoots with Shorty?"

Vivian gave her a look. "What is it with you and words tonight? Did you just say 'cahoots?'"

"Yes, and I like that word, so zip it."

Vivian threw her hand up and gave her a "whatever" look.

"This picture doesn't look very old," Lucy said, picking it up and looking at it closely.

"It's starting to look like Al and Shorty definitely know each other." Kate moved back to the file cabinet and gave the lock another pull to no avail. "I would assume it is a 'business' relationship."

"I don't want to believe it, but there are lots of coincidences," Vivian said.

"Al seems like such a nice guy," Lucy said.

"But if he's in cahoots with Shorty, it can't be a good thing." Wendy noted.

Silence.

"Let's keep looking around," she said. "Maybe we could find some other evidence."

"And look around for the keys to the boat, in case we have to make a break for it," Vivian reminded them.

Lucy shook her head. "There will be no break-making needed, Viv."

"Hey, I've got to get back to the States one way or the other."

"We are going to get the bottom of this, Viv. I can feel it," Kate reassured her.

They took a few more minutes going through the bookcase and the desk but didn't find anything of significance. Not even anything about the tequila business.

"Let's move on and see what's behind door number two," Lucy said in a bad game-show voice.

"Shorty must have another office at Tiempo Loco headquarters," Vivian said. "Be good to get in there."

The other three girls just stared at her as if she'd lost her mind. They all started to respond at once when they suddenly heard a door upstairs open and close. Lucy clapped her hands over her mouth and motioned for them to hide behind the desk.

They didn't need any convincing.

"Holy shit!" Lucy whispered frantically. "What if they come in here? We'll be dead meat!"

"Sonofabitch!" Wendy said as quietly as possible. "There's nowhere to hide really."

"How about we lock the door?" Kate asked, gesturing toward it.

"We *so* should have thought of that." Vivian delicately crawled out from behind the desk and quietly turned the lock. *Whew!*

They heard the door beside them open and close and stayed behind the desk, crouched down, for several minutes. Vivian's nerves were shot and she dealt with it by giggling. Pretty soon Lucy was too. Wendy had her finger on her mouth, telling them to be quiet but it was too late. Kate started in and it was over. No turning back. They held hands over mouths and giggled quietly, wiping tears from their eyes.

After a few minutes and a few deep breaths, Vivian spoke. "Why are we still crouching back here? My sunburn is kickin' my ass. Plus, the door is locked."

"Because," Wendy said, "Shorty doesn't have a deadbolt, only the lock on the doorknob. Anyone can pick that, right?"

They heard the door next door open and close and held their breaths.

The doorknob to the study jiggled a couple of times and someone shoved on the door, but it held in place. They heard footsteps going downstairs and waited behind the desk for a few more minutes. Just because.

Finally, Vivian stood up, her knees quivering and her brow wet with sweat. "I think the coast is clear. Let's go check out what's behind the other door, but let's hurry."

Wendy shook her head. "I don't know if my nerves can take much more."

"It'll be fine," Vivian said. "Let's just make it quick."

"Yeah, right. Famous last words," Kate moaned.

"I have to pee. Maybe there's a bathroom next door," Lucy said hopefully.

Vivian slowly unlocked the door and peeked out. Seeing no one, they left the study and entered the next room, which must have been Shorty's bedroom. It was huge and the décor reflected the rest of the house, very clean, modern.

"I didn't know people actually lived like this," Vivian said.

"Yeah, apparently Shorty's doin' well," Kate said, flipping a switch that turned on soft, cove lighting above the extra-wide platform bed.

Vivian walked over to the sleek wall of windows that opened out to a broad balcony. "Holy crap-ola. Look at this view."

"Stay away from the windows, Viv! And Kate, turn off those lights," Wendy said. "People are all over the backyard. They might see us."

"Oh my god! Look! There's my birthday kiss guy!" Vivian pointed out the window.

Lucy popped up beside her. "Ooh la la. Yep, there he is, Pasqual. He's hotty hot hot. Let's go get you a belated birthday kiss!"

"I'm in!"

"Door number four was definitely a damn good door," Wendy said. "But y'all need to back the hell up. We're gonna get busted in here for sure."

Kate hurried to the light switch and flipped it off. Lucy and Vivian reluctantly backed away from the windows.

"There aren't a whole lot of places to search other than the nightstands and under the bed," Kate noted.

"I'll check the bathroom," Lucy called out as she walked across the room, "and give it a whirl!"

Vivian headed over to the sleek nightstand on the left and Kate and Wendy went to the one on the right.

"Let's see what kind of music Shorty listens to." Kate reached for the iPod docking station sitting on the nightstand.

The room filled with the '80s hair band Poison, playing "Every Rose Has Its Thorn."

"Seriously?" Lucy called out from the bathroom. "That's what he listens to while he's Kama Sutra-ing?"

They couldn't help but bust out laughing.

"I figured him more as a porn techno-mix kind of guy," Vivian said, giggling.

Wendy, trying to keep a straight face, told Kate to shut it off in case someone walked up the stairs and heard it. "Besides, it's putting awful images in my head of the threesome."

Gross!

Still smiling, she told Vivian to check behind the picture hanging on that side of the bed. She then peeked behind the one on her side. Neither of them found anything behind their pictures.

Kate dropped down to her knees and pulled up the bed skirt. "Nothin' under here. Not even a lost sock."

Wendy and Vivian almost simultaneously opened the nightstand drawers, both shocked at what they found.

"Bingo!" Wendy shouted.

Kate stood up and looked in Wendy's drawer. "Holy shit!" she said, pointing into it.

"Don't touch it!" Wendy yelled. "We don't want your fingerprints on it!"

"I'm not going touching it," Kate said, all hint of laughter gone and obviously disturbed at what she saw.

"What is it?" Vivian asked, "because I'm not touchin' my discovery, either."

Lucy came running out of the bathroom, her hands dripping wet, and went over to Wendy and Kate. "What'd you find?"

She looked down and gasped.

"A gun," Wendy said.

"Fuckin' A. That is some gun," Lucy whispered.

"Is that a box of bullets?" Kate asked, peering further into the drawer, careful not to get too close.

"It is," Wendy said. "The box says they are for a Smith and Wesson 1911 .38 Super."

"Sounds like it would get the job done," Vivian said, shaking off a chill that had run up her spine.

Wendy closed the drawer with her knee and wiped off the handle with her dress. "What's in your drawer, Viv?"

"The mother lode of sex toys." Vivian closed the drawer, not wanting to picture Shorty and The Ladies playing with those. "This is one naughty dude."

Kate, apparently intrigued, went over and opened the drawer. "What on earth does this do?" she asked, pointing to a blue dolphin-shaped, battery-operated device.

Lucy suddenly shushed them. "I think I hear someone coming up the stairs again!"

They stood frozen, like deer in the headlights, listening.

Tap. Tap. Tap.

Lucy waved them over toward the bathroom. "Quick, follow me!"

57

They tiptoed as fast as they could after Lucy, following her into a man's closet which was dimly light by a small window.

Vivian, slowest to run and last to enter, pulled the door closed gently. They waited, listening.

They heard the distinctive click, click, click of women's heels on the marble floor.

"At least it's not Shorty," Kate said.

Lucy covered her mouth, holding back an "oh shit!" Her eyes relayed the message.

They heard some shuffling and then the obvious sound of tinkling.

Like earlier, Vivian's fear turned into giggles. She kept her hand over her mouth as Wendy pushed her into Shorty's pants. "Don't you dare make a peep!" she whispered threateningly.

Vivian contained herself enough to remove her hand.

Lucy spoke softly. "I saw a copy of *SoapStuds* next to the toilet. I had to pee, so I went ahead and used their bathroom. Anyway, Jon was on the cover. Guess Shorty and The Ladies have been doing their research on him."

Suddenly they heard a bit of an explosion.

"That's not very lady-like," Kate giggled.

"Shit happens," Wendy said.

"I'd like to read the magazine, but not that copy." Vivian said, and laughed quietly.

This brought on a new round of the giggles for all of them.

A few moments later they heard a flush, followed shortly by another flush.

"At least she did the courtesy flush," Wendy whispered. They all covered their mouths and stifled laughs.

Water ran in the sink, then the sound of heels on marble again.

"Let's give it a few minutes before we open the door," Kate said. "To let her leave and air things out!"

Vivian took the opportunity to look around. The closet was the size of a small bedroom and Shorty had more clothes than most men accumulate over a lifetime. An island with drawers on two sides sat in the middle. One wall was lined with shelving containing row after row of shoes, hats and sunglasses.

How many pairs of sunglasses does one person need?

"Look, he has a Bears hat, Bulls hat and a White Sox hat," Kate pointed out.

"Quite the Chicago sports fan," Vivian said sarcastically.

"No Cubs hat?" Wendy asked.

"Guess he's not a closet Cubs fan." Kate poked through his dirty clothes with a hangar.

Hahahaha. Good one, Kate.

Vivian went through the drawers in the island. Nothing exciting, just the usual men's undergarments and socks. "Shorty is a boxer guy, not briefs," she called out. "He also wears wife-beaters."

Lucy opened a cabinet in the corner, revealing a collection of long, gold, machismo chain necklaces. She donned the chain with a large J. She pointed a finger at them and said in a crappy Mr. T impersonation, "I pity the fool who wears this necklace."

Vivian couldn't hold back any longer and busted into a laughing fit. Kate handed Lucy the White Sox hat. "Put this on, a little cock-eyed."

"Hehehehehe…you said cock." Vivian could be so trashy.

"Here, put on Shorty's White Sox jersey," Wendy said, tossing it to her.

This completed the ensemble, and Vivian snapped a picture. *Classic.*

Kate opened the door a little and listened for any sounds. "I think we're in the clear. Put back the outfit, Lucy, and let's get outta here."

Lucy removed the hat and the jersey but paused with the necklace. "What do you think? Souvenir?"

"No!" they all whispered in unison.

"Check out the size of this Jacuzzi tub." Kate said stepping out of the closet then into the tub. She sat down and stretched out. "I think all four of us would fit in here."

"Let's see," Lucy said and climbed in. "Yeah, there's plenty of room for two more people."

Vivian gingerly climbed in, too. "I need me one of these."

Wendy was last in. "Wow, he is over the top on everything."

Vivian pulled out the camera and took a shot of all their feet joined together in the tub. Kate cracked open the bubble bath and took a sniff.

Lucy looked across the large expanse of bathroom and pointed. "I didn't have a chance to open that door. I bet it's The Ladies' closet. We gotta check it out."

"This Carrera marble is pretty nice stuff," Kate said as she stepped out of the tub.

Lucy opened the only remaining door they had not checked behind. She made her best Angelic sound, then said, "This is my dream closet. Look at the design, Kate. This is fabulous."

"I am going to have to take pictures so I can use this as a model for the house I'm going to build me and Shaun someday." Kate got her camera out of her bag.

"Okay, enough of this," Vivian said, knowing they'd pushed it about as far as they could. "Let's head back downstairs and mingle, maybe find out who some of these people are."

"Just a few more pictures," Kate mumbled.

Wendy looked in the cabinets under Shorty's sink. "Only the usual manscaping supplies." She then looked under The Ladies' cabinets, "Oh, yuck. Feminine products, including douche. I'd just rather not know these things about them."

Vivian opened the drawers in the bathroom vanities. Shorty had a year's supply of toothpaste in one drawer, six roll-on deodorants and about ten bars of soap. "Shorty buys in bulk," she announced.

The Ladies' vanity was about the same, except they also had tons of makeup.

"I think I found the town of Cover Girl," Vivian said and glanced in the mirror at her crimson face. *Nope, wouldn't do any good.*

Kate had hopped into the shower. "Girls, y'all gotta check this out," she said, snapping more pictures. "Shorty could have a party in here!"

"Uh, I think he does. How does this thing even work?" Vivian asked. "I don't see a shower head anywhere."

"You see the slits in the ceiling and along the sides? Those shoot out streams of water and they're motion activated." Kate waved her hand in front of a thin stainless panel, and sure enough, a perfect vertical jet of water appeared and splashed onto the iridescent mosaic floor, getting Vivian's feet wet.

"The water sprays in various ways, like rain, a cascade, a heavy downpour, whatever," Kate said. "Those pinholes are lights, too. I bet they change colors."

They got out of the shower and walked back into the bedroom, heading toward the door. Kate paused at the nightstand and picked up a remote control. "This has too many buttons on it to be for just the TV. Let's see what else it does."

Just as Wendy held up her hand in protest, a section of ceiling opened up and something lowered into the bedroom.

"What the hell is that?" Wendy stammered.

"Holy crap, is that what I think it is?" Vivian asked.

Kate walked over to the apparatus, inspecting it. "My my my...I do believe what we have here is a sex swing."

"And how do *you* know that?" Vivian asked, eyebrows raised.

"It's obvious!" Kate responded. "This is the seat, and these two straps hold up your feet, and these along the back hold up your shoulders and head. Here, I'll show you."

Lucy stepped between her and the swing. "Hold it right there. God knows what kind of germs are on that thing. Let me look for some Lysol in the bathroom."

"It's under Shorty's sink," Wendy informed her.

She reappeared with a spray can and took it over to the swing and doused it top to bottom.

"I can't believe you want to touch it, much less get in it," Lucy said as she went to put the Lysol up.

"You and Shaun must be kinky!" Wendy said.

"I'm workin' on him!" Kate said and laughed, then skillfully maneuvered herself into the swing.

"If I didn't know better, I'd say you've been in one of those before," Vivian said, watching her contort herself. "That would kill my sunburn."

Kate gave her a sly smile.

Wendy and Lucy just stood and stared. "Wow" was all they could manage.

"Voila!" she said. "Give me a push!"

"No push, but I am taking a picture," Vivian said.

"Damn girl, you look like a pro," Lucy commented.

"Okay, let's see you get yourself out of that contraption so we can head downstairs," Wendy said. "We need to find Pierre. He's probably wondering where the hell we went."

"Million bucks he wouldn't guess where Kate's at right now!" Vivian said.

Kate wiggled out of the swing and grabbed the remote. She pushed buttons trying to get it to retract back into the ceiling. Lights flickered, the flat screen turned on and off, the fan moved and the drapes started to close.

The swing remained.

"Crap! What are we going to do?" Vivian asked.

Wendy, already standing at the door, said, "We get the hell outta here. Leave the swing."

"Maybe it'll give them inspiration tonight!" Lucy said.

This got a round of "ewwwees" as they headed out the door.

58

The girls snuck out of Shorty's domain, through the man-cave and back downstairs. They found Rodney, the masseur, in the middle of the living room gleefully dancing, waving and making a fool of himself. "Hey, girls!" he called.

Lucy waved and made a drink sign. He gave the okay, then pointed toward the kitchen.

They made their way through the crowd to the bar. Rodney got there first and scooted the bartender out of the way. "I've got this one, honey," he said.

The bartender didn't look too happy about Rodney being in her bar.

"I'm making you girls a Rodney Special," he said excitedly, reaching for martini glasses. He grabbed several ingredients and started pouring and shaking.

"You're shakin' it better than Shakira," Lucy said and laughed.

He skillfully poured five lovely beige beverages, then dropped a little red kiss of grenadine in the middle of each glass. So lovely. So Rodney.

He delicately handed each of them a glass.

Vivian gave hers a sniff. "This smells pretty foofy-lala."

"Just wait till you taste it, honey, but first a toast." Rodney lifted his glass dramatically. "To life ended without permission," he looked directly at Vivian, shaking his head. "To love ended before fruition. To Jon."

Love? Fruition? What the????

Everyone clinked and started sipping except for Vivian. She was too busy staring at Rodney, who wasn't sipping but pouring his drink down his throat.

After a quick beat, he put his empty glass down and said cheerfully, "Who wants another?"

The girls had barely made a dent and Vivian hadn't even had a sip, being too shell-shocked, but he started grabbing for fresh glasses.

Vivian scooted over toward him. "Um, Rodney?"

"Yes, honey, drink up."

"What's this love and fruition crap? You looked at me."

"Did I?"

"Yes, you did. Looked right at me."

He started mixing fresh drinks. "I might have," he stopped to think. Then shrugged his shoulders and resumed. "Well, what the hell, everybody knows. No offense sweetie."

"Knows what?"

He started the ass shaking again. "Well, that you're the…" He paused, leaned in close, whispering, "Suspect."

It was hard for her to hear the word spoken out loud, and she almost dropped her glass.

"Excuse me, but I am *not* the only one. There are several," she hesitated and lowered her voice "suspects."

He poured out the drinks, handed another to Vivian and lifted his own.

"Well you're the only one I've heard about," he said, picking up a drink. "Plus, I saw you that night at Club Caliente. The two of you made that place really sizzle, and it was already hot."

She took a ginormous first gulp of the Rodney Special. *Damn, that's tasty.* Everyone else had already grabbed their second pour. Two-fistin' it. Apparently the Texas girls liked the Rodney Special, too.

"We were just dancing! He taught me how to salsa!"

He held his drink out to the side with his pinky stickin' out. "I've seen a lot of salsa, and let me tell ya, the heat between you two was scorching. The ignition of fruition was beyond comprehension for those of us who've seen love before. And honey, that was love."

More like lust.

"Just how many Rodney Specials have you had tonight?" Vivian asked. "Because yes, that was some sexual tension that *could have* led to fruition had my inhibitions not been hindered by my intuition. Instead, there was some masturba…"

"*Whoaaaa*…y'all sound like U2's "Let It Go" gone *way* wrong," Wendy said loudly, waving her Rodney Special in the air.

"What?" Rodney questioned.

"You know," she said, then sang a few lines. Every word ended in "ion."

"That was lovely, but shhhhhhhhhh. I've heard enough!" Rodney slurred and put his finger to his lips.

Dammit. Suppression.

Lucy pointed at Rodney, "You need to get away from the bar," she pointed to Vivian, "and I'm guessing you could use some fresh air."

Rodney started to protest but Vivian pushed him outside with the girls. He didn't protest.

Kate took a swig of her drink as she stepped onto the patio and almost spit it back out. Managing not to choke, she said, "There's Shorty over there on that lounger, with The Ladies. And there's Al and Adrienne. Right next to him!"

"Interesting," Vivian said, then turned her back to them and finished off her first Rodney special and half of the other.

Adrienne saw them almost immediately and walked over. "Hi, girlfriends! Can you believe this house? It's amazing!"

"Oh my gosh, we know. And the pool! Wow," Vivian said glancing over at it, then introduced Adrienne to Rodney.

He put down his drink and grabbed both of Adrienne's hands, pulling them out to either side of her. "Let me get a good look at you, honey. You are bedazzling from head to toe." He twirled her around.

She wore a sexy, scarlet, clingy dress with rhinestones around the low-cut V-neck. It showed every curve, leaving nothing to the imagination. She had on enough bracelets to be heard from miles away, and her sky-high silver strappy heels provided just the perfect accent.

Rodney whistled. "Yes, ma'am, you are quite the diva."

"Aren't you cute," Adrienne said with a big smile on her face, obviously lovin' the attention. "And how do you know these girls?"

"I had my hands all over that one," he said, pointing to Lucy. "I'm just kidding. I'm a massage therapist. These ladies were privy to my services earlier today and invited me to the party. Said it was 'the more the merrier.'"

"What are y'all doin' here?" Vivian asked her.

"Beats me. This isn't generally Al's scene, though you never know with him. He's full of surprises," she paused looking Vivian over. "I see you had a bout with the sun today."

Vivian groaned. "Yeah, and the sun won."

Rodney took Adrienne's hand again. "It was so nice meeting you. There's a guy over there I know from my gym. He's a trainer, actually, and let me tell you, I'd like him to teach me a few things. I've had enough Rodney Specials, I think, to work up the courage to go talk to him."

"Go get 'em, Tiger!" Lucy waved her fist in the air, Rocky Balboa-style.

"See you later, I'm sure. Unless I get lucky!" Rodney said with a grin and a clap, then flitted off toward the trainer.

Vivian watched his approach and saw the trainer smile at him. "He just might get what he wished for."

The girls were laughing at Vivian's comment when Pierre appeared suddenly at Kate's side. His face was flushed and he looked freaked out.

"You are *not* going to believe who I just spoke to."

"Who?" They all asked in unison.

"Crazy Stella."

59

I was over by the fire pit, sitting down," Pierre motioned in that direction, then continued telling the girls about his encounter with Stella. "She came up and sat next to me. Like, right here." He indicated how close.

"What did she want?" Vivian interrupted.

"She asked me where Dominik was."

Vivian shook her head, frustrated at Stella's inability to grasp reality.

"I didn't even bother to try to explain the character thing to her. I just told her he was murdered on the beach a few nights ago."

"Did she seem shocked? Or surprised?"

"She was definitely shocked," he replied, wiping his brow. "She put her head in her hands and just started sobbing. I sort of felt bad for her, she seemed so distraught, but then again, I'm not sure what to think."

"She didn't ask anything about the police, or if they knew who killed him or anything like that?" Kate asked.

"No, but I did try to ask her a few questions. She got even more upset, then just jumped up and ran inside the house. I ran after her but lost her in this crowd. She is quick."

"Let's split up and see if we can find her," Vivian suggested. "Maybe she's still around."

"I'll help, too," Adrienne said. "Upstairs isn't as crowded. I can run through the game room and bedrooms quickly."

Vivian's brain was in overdrive at Pierre's tale but it did register that Adrienne must have gone upstairs snooping around. *Was that who went into the master bedroom while we were searching the study?*

"Great!" Wendy said and came up with a game plan on the fly. "Pierre, why don't you go check the front of the house and down the road, just in case she's leaving. Kate, Lucy, y'all hit the kitchen, dining room and part of the living room. Viv and I will check the far side of the living area and the media room. Meet back here on the patio when you're finished."

Vivian felt like they should all throw their hands together and yell "break" but there was no time and they all took off.

The house was packed, and it wasn't easy to make their way through the crowd.

Vivian and Wendy took their time weaving through the living room, checking every face. The DJ was set up in the far corner with a "dance floor" in front of him. They boogied their way across to get to the media room where couples lounged about on oversized chairs. A huge flat-screen TV played music videos without sound.

Vivian tried to get a good look at the girls' faces, which wasn't always easy. There seemed to be some tonsil inspections going on, a lot of groping, and apparently clothing was optional in this area of the house. *Didn't need to see that.*

"You won't find me sitting on any of this furniture!" Wendy shook as if she had the heebie-jeebies. "No Stella, though I tried not to look too closely at the girls in here."

"Oh, I don't think they care," Vivian told her. "I got a good look. A little too much of a good look."

Wendy shook again at that and they went back out to the patio. Lucy and Kate were already there.

"We didn't see her," Lucy said, hands on hips.

"There must be half a gazillion people in this house," Wendy said. "I think a fire code is being broken, if they have fire codes down here."

"How can this chick keep vanishing into thin air?" Kate asked with exasperation.

Vivian scanned the backyard in vain. She didn't see Stella, but instead, Al. "Look, Al's over there talking with Victor and Joel."

"Who?" Lucy asked.

"The guys who work for Shorty."

"What's up with that?" Kate said. "Al's always in places or talking to people that seem a bit odd for a guy who just owns a restaurant in Chicago."

Vivian couldn't hear their conversation, but saw them all laugh at something Al said. He shook both of their hands and then wandered off.

Pierre came back after a minute, looking sweaty and frustrated. "I didn't see Stella anywhere, and I ran up and down the road a little."

"Maybe somebody should check the study and the 'love nest,'" Kate said with a grin.

Just then Adrienne came barreling out of the house, which was not an easy feat for someone of her small stature.

"I found her!" she exclaimed, sounding winded. "And I think she's the killer."

"What?" Vivian exclaimed. "Where is she?"

"Upstairs, on the couch in the game room. I'm supposed to be getting her a glass of water. Y'all go stay with her."

Pierre led the way as the group rushed as quickly as they could through the crowded house.

As soon as Pierre stepped on the landing, Vivian knew. She knew Stella would be gone and there'd likely be no finding her.

The couch was empty.

Kate unhooked the rope blocking off access to Shorty's study and bedroom and flew up the stairs.

Lucy, hot on her heels.

Pierre ran towards the bedrooms to the right of the man-cave.

Vivian and Wendy ran through the ones on the left.

Everyone returned to the man-cave within seconds of each other and ran back down the stairs, passing a surprised Adrienne on her way up with the water, who turned and followed them down.

Pierre ran out the front door.

The girls split up and ran through the house again, shoving people carelessly out of the way.

Adrienne, still holding the glass of water, waited on the patio for the girls when they returned to the designated spot.

Pierre joined them seconds afterwards, short of breath.

"She's nowhere," Pierre gasped. "Gone."

"What happened when you talked to Stella?" Vivian asked Adrienne.

"I went upstairs into the game room and saw a woman with long black hair hunched over, crying on the couch," Adrienne explained excitedly. "I was able to see the tattoo you talked about on the small of her back, the spider, so I knew it had to be her.

"I went over and asked if she was okay. She was sobbing, very upset. She said she's been looking for Dominik for two days, wanting to apologize. Said she saw his friend here and he told her Dominik is dead. That he was murdered on the beach two nights ago."

"And?" Vivian prompted.

"I asked her why she needed to apologize, and she said – get this - that she had *lost control*."

"No way!"

"I asked her if she argued with him on the beach and she said YES!"

"Did she say how she hurt him?" Kate asked.

"No, but she did say he was cheating on his wife, that's why she was so upset. She said, 'I was so mad, then he fell down. I don't know what happened.'"

"Then what?" Lucy asked.

"I tried to console her. She just kept saying she needed to confess. And she was grasping a cross necklace she was wearing. I asked her if she wanted a glass of water, and she said yes, so I ran down here to tell you girls. You know the rest."

"This totally means Stella is the killer!" Vivian exclaimed.

"We've got to call Detective Vega," Wendy said.

Vivian dug Vega's card out of her purse. Her fingers shook as she tried to dial. It took three attempts.

"It's ringing!" she whispered.

"Dammit! Voicemail."

"Hey Detective Vega, this is Vivian Taylor, you know, from the murder. I'm here at Julio's party, and Crazy Stella, remember, we told you about her, was here and just confessed to my friend, Adrienne, that she accidentally killed Jon, whom she thought was Dominik, the soap opera star, cheating on his wife. She was here just a minute ago but seems to have disappeared again. She can't have gone far so we're going to search for her, and you know, make a citizen's arrest or something when we find her. Can we do that in Mexico? Anyway, come as soon—"

BEEP!

"It cut me off!"

"I think he probably will get the gist of it." Kate tried to reassure her.

"And it's true, she can't have gone far," Wendy said. "Y'all want to split up again and search for her?"

"I'll search the beach," Lucy said. "I can run fast if I take off these shoes."

Vivian considered what to do for a moment and looked over to the fire pit, where Stella had been seen. She hoped to see her again, but spotted Al instead, talking with Shorty, Victor and Joel. They looked serious.

Shorty glanced up and caught her looking at him.

Adrienne followed her line of sight and called, "Al, honey. Come here, we need your help."

Al excused himself and walked over to them. Shorty and company went inside.

Just as Al asked what they needed help with, they heard, *"Policia! Nadia Mueve!"*

60

*P*olicia! *Nadia Mueve!"* Detective Vega shouted again, louder this time.

Vivian spun around to see that Vega had burst through the front door, followed by, of all people, Ponytail. Guns drawn.

Police in bullet proof vests ran in behind them and through the gate in the garden. Party guests threw their hands up, looking at each other confused. Several looked a little nervous and some tried to run off but couldn't get out.

"Ponytail is a cop!" she gasped in shock, throwing her hands up like the rest of the crowd, hurting her sunburned shoulders. She turned back around to face the girls and Pierre, whose arms were sky high. Al and Adrienne weren't standing beside them anymore.

"Where? Where?" Vivian stammered, pointing a finger to the space that had just been occupied by them.

Pierre kept his arms in the air and nodded toward the beach. "They took off that way."

Al must have ducked through all those plants.

"What do we do now?" Kate asked.

"Whatever they tell us to do," Pierre said, watching the police break people into groups, frisk them and sit them down.

"We haven't done anything wrong," Vivian said. "We need to talk to Detective Vega."

Lucy's right foot tapped uncontrollably. "I've never been in a raid before and I do *not* want to be put into a paddy wagon. Plus, I can't do another trip to the police station. If you recall, the first one didn't go so well for me."

A cop came over to them, yelling something in Spanish.

"I think he wants to see our IDs," Wendy said.

Wendy told him they didn't have their passports, and that they needed to talk to Detective Vega. That it was about the murder of Jon Tournay.

The officer squinted his eyes at her, then walked back to the house. He talked to two other cops, pointing in their direction, before he went inside.

250

"At least there wasn't any shooting or anything," Kate said.

"This is crazy." Lucy said. "And I need to pee!"

"You're gonna have to hold it." Vivian used her 'Mom' voice again.

They all took a seat around the fire pit as the two *policia* took a stance on either side of them.

Vivian whispered over to Wendy, "Are we being guarded or held?"

"I'm pretty sure the latter."

Detective Vega walked out the back patio doors about five minutes later.

"Thank goodness you're here!" Vivian yelled and stood up.

The *policia* standing around them took a few steps toward her and reached for their weapons.

"Está bien. Yo las conozco," Vega said to them.

They backed off.

"Did you get my message? We found the killer! It's that lady, the crazy fan. She's a total whack-job!"

"What message?" he asked, sounding uninterested.

"I just called you, right before the raid. We found out who killed Jon! She practically confessed!"

"Of course, she's vanished now," Lucy said.

"Slow down, Mrs. Taylor. Who killed Jon?"

"Crazy Stella, his fan! We told you about her, remember? She's the one with the tattoo who thinks he's actually his soap opera character."

"Ah, yes. I remember," Vega said, nodding his head.

"She was here, went up to Pierre, and asked him where Dominik had been for the past two days."

"I told her he was found murdered on the beach," Pierre interjected. "She freaked out and ran into the house. That's when Adrienne found her and she confessed."

"Who is Adrienne?"

"She's staying at our hotel. Adrienne Russo," Vivian informed him.

"And where is Adrienne now?"

"I don't know. She was standing right here with us before you came in guns-a-blazin'."

"I will have to talk to her, see if her story is the same as yours. Where is Stella?"

"Oh, that lady has a tendency to vanish like invisible ink. She took off before you got here. I bet she's long gone," Lucy said, shaking her head.

"We need to search the house for her."

They followed Vega inside, but Vivian knew they wouldn't find Stella.

As they walked through the living room they saw Shorty, Victor and Joel handcuffed, and sitting apart from each other on a couch.

"Are they under arrest?" Vivian asked Detective Vega.

"*Si.*"

"What'd they do?" Lucy asked, trying to sound nonchalant.

Vega ignored her.

He took them through the house and past various groups of party-goers but they could not find Stella. They did see Rodney; however, zip-tied and sitting in a kitchen chair next to the trainer.

He turned his rear their way and waved one of his zip-tied hands at them, and called over his shoulder, "Yoooouuu whooooo! This is an exciting night, huh! You girls sure know how to pick 'em!"

"Hey Rodney!" Vivian said, then shrugged. "Who the hell knew?"

Detective Vega looked over at her. "He is with you?"

"Yep. He's one of ours."

Vega pulled a knife out of his pocket and indicated Rodney stand up and turn around.

He gave them an "oh" look, and did as he was told.

Free of restraints, Rodney put himself between Vivian and Lucy. "I'm definitely one of them, and so is he." He pointed to the trainer, then said quietly to the girls, "I generally only use handcuffs , of any sort, in combination with lubrication."

More than I wanted to know.

Detective Vega cut the trainer loose as well, then put the knife back into his pocket. "Mrs. Taylor, looks like Adrienne and your so-called murderer are nonexistent."

She hung her head.

Frustration.

61

The party was definitely over and most of the guests had been allowed to leave. Rodney and trainer guy hit the high road after giving a round of hugs.

"Well what now?" Kate asked, exasperated. "Where do we begin to look for the phantom black widow woman?"

Vivian's phone buzzed with an incoming text message. She flipped it open and saw it was a message from Adrienne.

Hope this helps you out. Al said we r outta here. Good luck!

She scrolled down and saw a picture of Stella on Shorty's couch in the man-cave.

"It was definitely her, then," Vivian said, as she passed her phone around to everyone.

"Let's take this picture to some hotels tonight and see if they know her, if she's staying there," Kate suggested.

Lucy took the phone and looked at the picture. "Yeah, ok, but you know, my mom's stories of Catholic school are coming back to me. Remember Adrienne telling us what Stella said about confessing? I think it means something. Maybe if we see churches while we're hotel hopping we should check them out too. Maybe she's Catholic and will be looking to confess?"

"Good call, Lucy. Great idea," Vivian said.

They hiked out to the car and squished in. Kate got behind the wheel, Vivian called shotgun and Pierre was humpin' it again, flanked on either side by Lucy and Wendy.

They scanned the streets, looking for any sign of Stella, as Kate drove them through the main area of town. Lucy thought she saw Stella once and jumped out of the car as Kate brought it to a screeching halt. Lucy scared some poor girl half to death as she ran up to her and grabbed her arm. Close resemblance from behind, but definitely not the crazy lady from the front.

They took turns (with the exception of Vivian) running into hotels with the phone, showing the picture of Stella and had just hit their seventh when they passed a church. Lucy hopped out and checked the door. Locked. She went around to the side, but still no luck. They moved on.

They tried a few more hotels with still no luck. They also tried two other churches that were locked up tight as the Mona Lisa in the Louvre.

"I'm tired," Lucy groaned.

"I know. Me too," Kate said. "It's almost 5 a.m. and I think we're coming to the end of our options. We've covered almost every hotel and church we've seen."

"Where in the hell does this girl disappear to?" Wendy asked the rhetorical question that had been on Vivian's mind.

Nobody spoke for a moment.

Vivian took a deep breath. "I think there's something I need to tell y'all."

Sensing the seriousness in Vivian's tone, Kate pulled over, turned off the car then twisted around to face Vivian. Pierre and the girls in back looked worried.

"When I was, uhhmmm," Vivian paused, not wanting Kate to freak out. She started again. "When I got off the plane I went to powder my dent."

"Your dent?" Pierre asked.

Vivian pointed to the indention in her forehead. "When I pulled out my compact it was broken."

She held her breath.

"So what," Lucy said. "We'll buy you another one."

"Uh, okay," Wendy said, not understanding why Vivian had just told them that.

But Kate knew. She gasped, mouth agape and hand on her chest. "You broke the mirror, didn't you?"

"Well, the mirror was broken, but I don't know that I really broke it. I just found it like that."

"Oh my god Viv, that's why this is happening. This is the beginning of seven years of bad luck!"

"Now hold on a second," Wendy said holding up both hands. "I'm not really a believer in all that mumbo jumbo."

"Look what has happened," Kate said. "Jon is dead and Vivian is suspected. It has to be because of the mirror."

"Seriously," Wendy said, still not buying it. "All because of a three-inch mirror?"

Pierre squeezed Vivian's hand. "I don't really think you breaking a mirror had anything to do with Jon getting killed."

"Well, whether it did or didn't, I felt like I needed to tell y'all," Vivian said.

"Maybe it did have something to do with you being suspected, though," Lucy said, then changed the subject. "I think we should call Arturo and see if there are any other Catholic churches we missed."

"Worth a shot." Vivian dialed Arturo.

A groggy voice answered. *"Bueño."*

"Hey, Arturo, it's Vivian. I'm super sorry to be calling you so late, or early. We were at Julio's party tonight and Stella basically confessed to Adrienne that she killed Jon. In the chaos of a police bust, compliments of Detective Vega, she disappeared. We told him but we're not sure how hard he's looking for her, so we are, but we're running out of options. We've searched almost every hotel but think she may be at a church in town. We've hit the church on 15th and *Iglesia De Presbyteria* on 20th. Are there any others we might have missed?"

"There's the House of Hope on Avenue 25, then *Companerismo de la Comunidad de la Riveria*." He paused then said, "Stella confessed?"

"Yes, pretty much. We think she might be at a Catholic church. Are any of these Catholic churches?"

"If you're looking specifically for Catholic you need to search *Señora del Carmen, de Fatima*, and *de Guadalupe*. It doesn't sound like you've been to those."

"Arturo, if we had time to search only one, which do you think would be the most likely?"

He paused for a moment. *"Del Carmen.* It's downtown and closest to the hotels."

"Ok, what's the address? We'll head there next."

He gave her the address and she repeated it while Wendy wrote it down.

"Thanks so much Arturo. Sorry if we woke you."

"It's okay. I'll be in touch if I hear anything."

They wound their way through the streets of Playa and came to *Iglesias Señora del Carmen* church, where a car was parked out front.

"That car looks like a piece of crap rental like ours if you ask me," Lucy said with disdain.

"This could be it!" Vivian was excited, hoping they could take Stella into custody. "Citizens arrests or not, I'm not leaving this church without Stella."

"Amen to that," Kate said as they got out of the car.

"Yeah, we're takin' this hussy down!" Wendy whispered.

"I'll show her floozy!" Vivian responded.

The church looked relatively small with a flat stucco façade and peeling white paint, a few small openings and a typical bell in a small arch centered above the entry. The shaped parapet leading up to the bell was outlined in a band of blue paint. As they pushed open the ornate iron gates, the hinges creaked with age.

Kate whispered, "I feel like we're going to Taco Hell!"

"I think the offering plate must be falling short here," Pierre muttered.

Lucy shushed him as he grabbed at the decorative giant wooden door and pulled.

Unlike the other churches, this one opened.

62

The girls and Pierre tip-toed into *Iglesias Señora* del *Carmen* and paused, letting their eyes adjust to the darkness. The church was lit only by a few prayer candles and what little moonlight shown through the windows.

Vivian saw a dark lump of something in front of the altar. That something suddenly sat up, facing the back wall.

"Are you here, God?"

They all stopped dead in their tracks.

Silence.

"Can you hear me?" This time the voice was a little louder.

Everyone looked at Vivian, eyebrows raised. She nudged Pierre to respond. He got it.

Please, God, don't strike us with lightning for this!

"Yes, I can here you, my child. I am here," Pierre answered calmly, making his voice extra low. "I want to help you."

"Oh thank you, thank you," the woman's voice responded with relief. Suddenly the dark form was upright, reaching skyward to the crucified Jesus on the cross. "I knew you would hear me."

Just then the door opened behind them, and Arturo nudged his way in.

"What are you doing here?" Vivian whispered.

"I felt like you needed me." He put a finger to his lips, indicating they needed to be quiet.

Pierre had gone up a few pews and was crouched down. "Tell me, child, why are you here?"

"I've done something," she stammered. "Something terrible."

"Confess your sins."

Damn, he's good!

The girls crouched down low behind the last pew. Arturo got next to Vivian and they both peeked over.

257

Stella was looking up at the Jesus. "I think there was an accident, and I didn't mean to do it. I just got so mad."

"Tell me more."

"Dominik was dancing with this woman. A woman not his wife! He was kissing her!"

"And that upset you?"

"Yes."

"Did you do something?"

She choked back a sob. "I followed them to the beach. They kissed again, and I knew I had to take up for Celeste. She beat breast cancer, even after the hospital almost killed her by administering three times the dose of morphine. She's been nothing but faithful to Dominik and was right by his side while he recuperated from the car crash off a cliff where he lost his memory and was almost eaten alive while awaiting rescue. How could he do this to her? And that sweet, little premature baby?"

Stella paused to take a raggedy breath. "The other woman finally left and I confronted him. I told him he was wrong for cheating on Celeste. He kept saying he wasn't Dominik. That his name was Jon and that he wasn't married. Why would he lie?"

The church was very still. Vivian held her breath.

Pierre responded. "And then what happened?"

Her voice shifted from despair to anger. "I, I," she stammered. "I grabbed a shell from the sand and swung at him. I didn't mean to hurt him but he made me so angry!"

Stella put her head in her hands, sobbing. "He fell down and I ran, but I just wanted him to leave that floozy alone and go back home to Celeste. She needs him!"

She paused for a breath, then said in a weak voice, "I didn't know. I didn't know."

"What didn't you know?"

"I didn't know he was dead. That I killed him." Stella drew in a breath and wailed, "God, help me!"

Arturo looked at Vivian, eyebrows raised.

"I must arrest her," he said, touching around his waist. He looked down, then shook his head. "*Aye, ya yai.* I arrested someone today and didn't get my cuffs back."

A 100-watt went off in Vivian's head. "Hold on a sec!"

She reached into her purse, dug around and pulled out Shorty's red, fuzzy handcuffs. She dangled them in front of Arturo's face. "Will these help?"

He rolled his eyes but took them anyway. "I'll never live this down."

He quietly tip-toed up the aisle to Stella, who was still kneeling at the foot of the giant cross, crying. He popped a fuzzy handcuff on her left wrist.

"You are under arrest for the murder of Jon Tournay."

63

Day 6

Vivian watched as Arturo walked Stella up the aisle of *Del Carmen* Catholic Church toward the heavy wooden doors.

Wendy leaned over to Vivian and said solemnly, "Probably not the walk down the aisle she envisioned for herself, huh?"

"I'd say not. Poor delusional woman."

As she passed them she looked at Vivian. "This is all your fault, you…you…marriage-wrecker."

The girls all said in unison, "He wasn't married!"

Rays of sun peeked through the doors as Arturo opened them up to the break of a glorious day. He led Stella outside just as several police cars pulled up.

As they followed them out the door of the church, Vivian asked Arturo, "How did the police know to show up here?"

Arturo grinned and answered, "Oh, Detective Vega just has a way of knowing where you'll be."

What is that supposed to mean? Did we miss a tracking device on the car? Did he plant something in my purse?

Speaking of Detective Vega, he walked up looking worn out. And pissed. "So I see we have found Stella. You still can't leave the country. No charges have been filed yet."

"But she confessed. Arturo heard her." Vivian protested.

"She had not been read her rights, so the confession will not hold up, if it happened."

If it happened, asshole.

"What about the DNA? Did you run it?" Wendy asked.

He turned and walked away. Obviously not a morning person.

Vega shouted orders to the *policia* and techs who spread out over the grounds and inside the church. One guy snapped pictures while the rest searched in and around everything. A pair of cops went through the other crappy car out front, that was then hooked to a tow truck. The techs dusted the altar and cross for prints.

Another detective briefly interviewed the girls and Pierre individually. Their stories matched and there was no cause for concern. Just needed statements, the detective told Vivian.

Arturo spoke with Vega, then led Stella to a patrol car, getting jabs from his counterparts over the red fuzzy handcuffs, and sat her in the back seat. He slammed the door and patted the top of the car.

As the patrol car pulled away Stella looked out the window at them, tears streaming down her face. Vivian couldn't help but feel sorry for her. She needed meds.

"That lady is bonkers." Kate shook her head.

"Yep," Wendy said, watching the car turn the corner. "But I have a feeling Mexico isn't a plead insanity kinda place."

The group stayed and watched as the crime scene investigation winded down. The priest showed up and blessed everyone within sight, including the girls and Pierre. Vega seemed irritated at the priest's presence and wrapped things up quick.

"The donger needs food," Lucy said as the police took off, including Vega. "And right now, I'm the donger."

"I'm a donger too," Vivian said and laughed.

Wendy and Kate both said they were dongers.

"Back in the day, Jon was in love with Molly Ringwald," Pierre said.

"Let's have breakfast in his honor," Kate suggested.

"Celebrate him," Vivian said.

"I think he would like that."

Arturo was just getting in his car and Vivian asked him where to go since his suggestions had proved to be good so far. He recommended a Mexican version of Denny's. They were all a little riled up after leaving the church and ate a monster breakfast. It kicked ass. Vivian didn't know if it was the resolution with Stella or real hunger, but the south of the border version of "moons over my hammy" was the best egg, ham and cheese toasted sandwich she had ever had.

Pierre talked a little about Jon, remembering some good times. The blow-out of a party they'd had in high school where people jumped off the roof into the pool and Pierre lost his virginity; the Mardi Gras trip they'd taken in college where they'd handed out tons of beads to all the 'worthy' women on Bourbon Street; the spur of the moment trip they'd taken to London that almost caused Jon to miss a red carpet event for the soap. He showed up in jeans and a t-shirt, but still made all the best dressed lists.

Wendy got out her camera and pulled up the picture of Jon and Vivian with the sandcastle, on the day they met. Seeing his picture saddened the group but this was a breakfast of celebration so, eyes just a little watery, they did a cheers to Jon with their orange juice and coffee.

"To the best friend a guy could have," Pierre said.

"To the best kisser in all of Mexico," Vivian said.

"To his interesting choice in shirts," Wendy said.

"To the shots he bought us," Lucy said.

"To our friend, who we will remember in our hearts always, Jon," Kate said.

To lighten the mood, Lucy and Pierre re-created the church scene for their waitress. Lucy knelt in front of their table, using the carafe of coffee as the cross. The group had a good laugh at Lucy's impersonation of Stella, but the waitress didn't seem to get it.

"Lost in translation, maybe?" Pierre said and laughed.

Vivian had wanted to take a nap in the shade, out by the pool, but by the time they got back to the hotel, sleeping by the pool no longer sounded like the best idea. Her adrenaline was long gone and breakfast filled her to the rim. All she wanted was a comfy bed to crash in. On their way up to the room, Pierre asked Lucy if she'd like to join him in his room. She politely declined, but Vivian thought a teeny weeny, itsy bitsy super miniscule part of her was tempted.

Trashy.

They sleep for about five hours, got on their suits and zombie-walked to the beach, wanting to enjoy it on their last day of vacation. Manuel had loungers ready and double umbrella'd them since Vivian was so sunburned. He also brought them a round of complimentary Tiempo Loco tequila shots, including one for himself. He toasted to freedom and clinked glasses with each of them. Apparently he'd heard about Stella's arrest. He gathered up the empties, stepped in front of them, shook his hips a little and gave them his version of "Jailhouse Rock."

It was a doozy, and definitely woke Vivian up.

Wendy had ordered them a bucket-o-beer so they sat back and relaxed a bit after Manuel dropped it off, still humming.

"What are we going to do about our passports?" Vivian asked after a while, digging her feet into the sand.

"We may be headin' over to the reporters and giving them a story of

American hostages being held in Playa if we don't hear somethin' soon," Wendy said.

"Hey look, there's Arturo!" Lucy said, poppin' out of her lounger. She ran over to greet him and walked back, her arm looped through his, looking pleased.

"He has our passports!" she announced.

"Yes, I do." He reached into his pocket and handed the passports to Lucy. He then turned to Vivian, "I also brought these." He held up and shook the red, fuzzy handcuffs Vivian had swiped from Shorty's boat.

"Thought you might want them back."

64

Vivian sat up in her beach lounger and snatched the red, feathered, fuzzy handcuffs out of Arturo's hand with a mischievous grin. "Oh yeah, these are my new lucky cuffs."

"Never know when you'll need to make a late-night arrest," he joked, sitting down on the end of Lucy's lounger and gave Vivian a wink.

Now that I'm about to be single, never know, indeed.

"I thought I'd pass on that Stella is being arraigned on Friday," Arturo said. "She gave another confession to Detective Vega, same story as the one in the church, and we found the murder weapon in her motel room."

"How did she kill Jon exactly?" Vivian questioned.

"She sliced his jugular with a large, broken piece of shell. He didn't stand a chance."

Everyone was solemn and quiet for a moment.

Vivian looked out at the ocean for a moment, remembering how Jon had picked up a conch shell the night of their walk and given it to her. Little did either of them know he would be mortally wounded by such a thing only moments later.

"So she just happened to find a murderous shell handy, at night, on the beach?" Wendy asked. "That's hard to believe."

"Not really," Arturo said. "The inside of the shells gleam in the moonlight when they're wet and some are very sharp. Here, I'll show you."

He walked down to the surf and came back holding several pieces of conch shell about the size of his hand. "See how jagged? And this one is almost like a razor."

Kate grabbed it and lightly scratched her arm with it. "Ouch!" The broken piece of shell did more than leave a scratch, it drew blood.

"They can be very dangerous. People cut themselves accidentally with these all the time."

"You sure this wasn't premeditated?" Wendy asked.

"The evidence backs up her story. We have matched her fingerprint to

264

the shell found in her motel room and though it was cleaned off, the DNA from the trace amounts of skin and blood still on it will match Jon's. It's a solid case."

"So, she just randomly did this? She was only provoked because she saw Jon kissing Vivian?" Kate asked.

"We've been working on her background and Vega has spoken to law enforcement in Toronto, where she resides. A month ago she was arrested for stalking another celebrity, who had a restraining order against her. The police required psychiatric evaluation as she was violent and showed signs of delusion when they tried to apprehend her. The doctor diagnosed her as being schizophrenic and prescribed anti-psychotic medication. Being her first arrest, she was just given probation and released after time served. Judging by the full medication bottles in her motel room and her behavior down here, she most likely hasn't been taking her meds."

"Wow," was all Vivian could say.

"Who was the other celebrity she stalked?" Lucy asked.

"A Canadian reality TV star. She was obsessed with the show and it was taken off the air. She decided to continue watching it in person, I guess."

"Did Stella just happen to be in Playa del Carmen, or was she stalking Jon, too?" Wendy asked.

"She claims she just happened to be down here, that she never stalked him. But we may never truly know."

How sad. Jon was killed on accident by a fanatic who's off her rocker, Vivian thought.

"Guess you have it wrapped up pretty tight," Kate said.

"It appears so, which is why Detective Vega allowed me to bring your documents. We know how to reach you, should the need arise," he said with a sly smile.

"Good Lord, I hope the need never arises!" Lucy exclaimed.

"Hey, what happened to Shorty?" Kate brought the back of her lounger up and asked.

"Yeah," Vivian said. "Why was he arrested? What did he do?"

Arturo shook his head. "I can't really talk about it but it involves a lot of money and smuggling. We don't have evidence yet on his US counterpart, but Julio was trying to, uh, smuggle, uh, stuff out of Mexico and into the US."

"See! I knew it! I knew he was up to no good!" Lucy said, pointing to Vivian with her beer.

"Stuff, huh?" Wendy interjected.

"We didn't find any 'stuff,' large sums of money or anything else illegal on his boat," Lucy said. "Darn! And we looked good, too!"

Arturo gave Lucy a stare, then slowly shook his head. "I don't want to hear anymore."

"We all knew he was into something but he was still nice to us," Vivian told him. "I wasn't too worried about hanging out with him."

"He was new to the trade and therefore, not as corrupt as others," Arturo said, then finished with "yet."

"Also not as competent, hence the arrest," Wendy joked.

"What's with Ponytail? He's a cop right?" Vivian asked. "He was right behind Detective Vega in the raid at Shorty's house."

"If he's a cop, then why did he chase us?" Kate asked matter-of-factly.

"Ahh, that's another subject I can't really talk about," Arturo answered and looked at Vivian. "But don't forget that you were the last person to see Jon alive. They needed to keep tabs on you. I volunteered for that assignment but was turned down," he said with a grin.

He reached over to Kate and gave her a high-five. "Good driving, by the way."

"Watch out NASCAR, here I come," she said and laughed.

Vivian hesitated, but then asked anyway, "So what about Al and Adrienne Russo? Did anything happen to them last night?"

"Not that I heard. Why do you ask?"

"Oh, no reason," she replied a little too quickly.

Guess they made it back to Chicago.

"I have to get back, the media have descended upon the police station and I need to keep them in line," Arturo informed them and stood up.

"If you're ever in Dallas or Fort Worth, look me up," Vivian said.

"Of course, and I hope you come back to our beautiful town again soon."

Not sure how I feel about the "soon" part of that statement, she thought but said, "It is a gorgeous place, but I think I've seen enough of Playa del Carmen for a while."

"Yeah, I'll say," Lucy said. "A dozen churches, countless hotels, the police station…"

"A nasty tattoo parlor," Kate teased.

"Hey! That was in Cozumel, not Playa." Lucy replied and then added, "And besides, I don't have an infection."

"Yet!" Wendy threw in.

Arturo laughed and took Vivian's hand. He kissed it lightly and said, "*Mucho gusto.*" He kissed Kate, Lucy and Wendy's hands, too and walked off with a wave.

"That first day of cleavage and flirting has certainly paid off," Vivian said, watching him walk away.

"No kidding," Wendy responded. "It has certainly been a good thing we had him on our side."

The girls ordered another bucket-of-beer and relaxed in their loungers, shades on, and were quiet for a while. The sound of the surf and the seagulls had everyone veggin' out.

Vivian dozed off and awoke a bit later to Pierre sitting on Lucy's lounger, rubbing sunscreen on her back.

"My my," she joked. "I see you have heeded your own advice and are reapplying."

Lucy gave Vivian a smile. "It was time and the three of you were looking at the back of your eyelids."

"Yeah, yeah."

"I still can't believe how good you were last night at the church, I mean, this morning," Lucy said to Pierre.

"It was Vivian's idea, and once I caught on, it just seemed like the thing to do. I knew we had to get her to confess," he answered.

"Have you talked to Arturo yet today?" Wendy asked drowsily, still reclined in her lounger.

"Yeah, he came to see me a little while ago."

"Look what I got back!" Vivian laughed and held up the red fuzzy handcuffs. "Do you guys need to borrow them?" She looked back and forth between Lucy and Pierre.

Lucy stood up and kicked sand at her, "No!" and ran off to the clear blue water.

Pierre watched her the whole way. "She's something else."

"That she is!"

"So what's next for you? How long are you staying down here?" Kate asked.

"Jon's parents are flying in tomorrow afternoon. There is a lot of paperwork and what-not they have to deal with to get Jon home."

Vivian sighed. "Yeah, that's going to be rough for them. It's good you are here to help." She paused for a moment, then continued, "We got our passports back and are leaving tomorrow. I do wish we could be here to help you with all of that."

"Thanks Vivian, but I understand you have to leave. In fact, I'm surprised you weren't on the first flight out today that you could catch."

"We all needed this one last day at the beach to relax. A vacation, so to speak, from our crazy vacation," she smiled at him.

"So what are you guys doing for your last night?" he asked.

"You're lookin' at it," Wendy said and clinked beer bottles with Kate.

"Want to join us?" Kate asked. "We don't even plan to leave the hotel."

"Funny, now that you have the freedom to leave, you don't want to," he said.

"That's the important thing about freedom — choices," Vivian said and took the last swig. "And right now, I choose to sit here and drink another beer."

Lucy bounded back up the beach, shaking her wet hands at them. "You guys look like you need some cheering up. Let's do a shot!"

The Lucy answer to everything on this vacation. She really wasn't like this in her typical, everyday life.

She flagged Manuel and he turned the shots around quickly.

The five of them raised their glasses.

This time Vivian offered a short, sweet toast.

"To Jon."

65

Day 7- Adiós

Vivian watched the conveyor belt as the baggage handlers rhythmically loaded it. From her window seat she thought she saw her mega bag at the bottom of the pile. She leaned her forehead on the glass and kept watching. Yep, that was it. The baggage handler had to use both hands to lug it across, and looked pretty pissed doing it.

Sorry.

Now that it was on its way up, she dug around her seatback pocket for the barf bag. She didn't think she was going to lose it, but it did double nicely as a fan. The lady next to her gave an apprehensive look.

Vivian leaned her head back and started thinking about what awaited her at home.

Four beautiful kiddos.

A decent house.

A mom-mobile.

A meaningful job.

A 92 page document entitled "divorce decree."

Damn.

Her phone chirped, signaling she had a text message.

Just checkin on u girls. We r home. Heard on news that Stella wuz it. Knew it! Keep in touch. Love ya, A.

Vivian smiled and turned off her phone. Good to hear for sure that Al and Adrienne made it home okay. She liked them both though she wondered

269

what Al was up to and how much Adrienne knew. She didn't care enough to let it get in the way of their friendship.

She looked up to see a familiar face. Birthday-kiss Pasqual. He saw her immediately and flashed his pearly white smile.

Wow, he's tan.

She gave him a wave.

She thought he was about to pass up her aisle when he stopped and looked at the lady next to her. He asked if she minded switching spots with him. She looked at Vivian holding the barf bag, then jumped at the opportunity, throwing her seatbelt into Vivian's lap.

He reached up to put his bag in the overhead compartment which made his shirt lift up and his shorts go down…just enough to see a nice little bit of tummy and a beautiful tan line. At least an eight on the pale scale.

Mmmmmmmmm. He's "Bringin' Sexy Back."

Vivian stuffed her barf bag back into the seat pocket, hoping he hadn't seen her fanning herself with it. If he did, he didn't show it. He smiled as he sat down next to her and reached for the stray half of his seatbelt.

She tingled all over as his hand grazed her thigh. *Oh yeah, it's time to move on.*

He looked at her with his deep blue eyes. "I've always wanted to see Texas."

She gave him a smile.

I'll show him the very best of Texas.

Yeeeeehhhhhhaaaaaaw!

Acknowledgments

We want to thank Angela Wenk and Lea Rogers for their friendship and inspiring book fodder. Cheers to the original Getaway Girlz, clink!

Thank you to our other Getaway Girlz...y'all know who you are! We wouldn't have shi-tah-tay, choot 'em, backseat bars or many, many other hilarious things without you. "It is our pleasure" to thank you for traveling with us so we can be inspired by the crazy adventures. We heart you all.

Special thanks to Janet Neff not only for her friendship, but also for her enthusiasm and never-ending support. Now go write YOUR book!

Thanks to Josh Weathers for the use of his sweet serenades. We know you'll go far!

We want to thank Dana Isaacson with Random House for his insight and commentary, John Dycus for making us better writers, the DFW Writer's Workshop for listening to us read every week and offering constructive feedback, Susan Breen with the Algonkian NYC Pitch and Shop conference for guiding us and always answering our questions, Cherry Weiner for her advice, and the Writer's Unboxed Facebook community – what a great bunch of writers.

We would also like to thank the following people who helped make this happen with their skills and services:

Lea Rogers, cover design – Angela Wenk, logo design and photo editing – Reid Hobdy, promoter extraordinaire – Bill Preston, photography – Studios by the Ferry, videography – Marni Getchell, web design – Naresh Rambaran, initial web design and hosting – Erin Cox, photo editing – Lauren Mahoney, the Playa del Carmen "dead guy" model, Steve Frechette, another "dead guy" model – Paula LaRocque, for the initial read and commentary – Jackie Meeks for final book edits – Kelli Fitch, beta reader – John Howard, FW Promotions – Luis Estrada, video ideas – Frankie's Sports Bar and Grill wait staff for the keeping us well served in drinks and munchies. Y'all rock!

We've been working on this for a while and so many people have cheered us along our way. We know we're forgetting people. We'll get you in *Rocky Mountain Mayhem*.

Thank y'all!

Johnell would like to thank…

Thanks to my kiddos for being wonderful, smart, funny, creative and respectful (usually!). And for understanding when mom has to go on her "girl" trips! Or sing and dance in the car. Or embarrass you in the school cafeteria. I hate to tell you, but it never ends. Love ya! Thanks to my parental units. I'll only write about you when necessary. Promise. Thanks to my "real job" for letting me be loud and supporting me through the chaos. I know we already said thank you to our friends, but I can't express enough gratitude for all of you who helped me in my time of "transition." It was ugly, but y'all helped make my world pretty again.

Robbyn would like to thank…

Thank you, David, for five wonderful years and your love and support with this project. Thanks Mom for your unconditional love and friendship. Thanks Dad for being the best Dad a girl could have. I don't know how you and Donna endured 8 years in a row of high school football games, but thanks (from Steven too) to the both of you for being there to watch us march. Thanks Steven for being a great brother and for your nautical knowledge. Sorry I shot you in the butt with a BB gun, but at least you'll always have something to remember me by! I'd like to thank my bosses Con Browne and Jason Pitarra with Envoy Mortgage for their understanding with my writing passion. You guys are the best.

Watch for the next book in the Getaway Girlz series:

Rocky Mountain *MAYHEM*

Available December 2012

www.getawaygirlz.com

facebook.com/getawaygirlz

twitter.com/joanrylen

youtube.com/getawaygirlz